ISBN: 978-1-7347551-2-1

Any similarities to historical events, real people, or real places are purely coincidental. Names, characters, places, and events are works of fiction.

WARNING: This book contains interior art of an adult nature that some may find disturbing.

Cover and Interior Art by: Jon Hammond

Book design by P.J. Smith

First printing edition 2020.

Publisher Mailing Address:
Coalition Books
P.O. Box 74
Saco, ME 04072

www.aworldgonewrong.com

Special Thanks

During the creation of this book, many people offered their insight and help along the way. My family and friends always lifted me up and kept me motivated. While I could write an entire book just thanking all of those who have been there for me, I want to take a moment to address my beta readers who had the dubious honor of reading an unedited manuscript.

Chanaia Curry: Your help was invaluable, and you kept me honest more often than not. You weren't afraid to throw punches and I needed that. I would be so lucky to have your knowledge in the future.

Martin Cheung: For providing great feedback and powering through the manuscript. Your knowledge of different fandoms helped me shape a tale many will enjoy.

Casey Nickles: For providing the ultimate compliment in the form of your emotions. The confidence it gave me cannot be overstated and it helped me see this work through to the end.

Finally, a huge special thanks to my illustrator Jon Hammond who provided far more than just some pictures. Our collaborative meetings helped shape certain parts during the editing process and I cannot thank you enough for the care and time you gave my work.

To My Beautiful Children,

Irene and John,

My Guiding Lights In The Mist.

A World Gone Wrong

By: P. J. Smith

Published by Coalition Books

Part One:

To The Surface

Chapter One: The Undercities

There were voices all around, echoing in the blurred chamber of my mind. Numbers, dates, names; none of them were familiar. The gray haze that enveloped my vision betrayed no shapes or details to what little sight I had left. Panic welled up inside me, and I attempted to scream, yet no sound came from my throat. My body had become numb, and I lost the sensation of movement. The weight of my body was absent.

"What's happening? How did I get here?" My panic rose to a fever pitch...

In a cold sweat, I sat up in my bed, the thin blanket flying to the floor beside me. I stared blankly at the blue-lit wall just above my gray metal dresser. My breath came in heavy gasps before I began to calm. The lights gently rose to a more natural white while my mind came to grips with reality.

"Holy shit." I ran my hand through my short dark hair and patted my body, looking around to get my bearings. I was home by the look of it. Still recovering from the freakish nightmare, I sat up over the side of the bed, rubbing my face and looking at a clock. It rested in the center of a display projected onto the back wall from the ceiling. At the moment, it was just a clock, a clock telling me I was probably going to be late.

"Skippin' breakfast, I guess." I stood and moved over to the flat, silver door on the right side of the room, which dutifully slid open. Shuffling down the hall to the washroom, I couldn't help but think of the ridiculous day ahead of me. It was one of those times in a person's life where they really had to ask, "how the fuck did I get here?". Honestly, I couldn't answer that question. When the mutaphorm attacks began a year before, no one really knew how or where life was going to end up. We spent our whole lives being taught that the surface was a blasted wasteland that nothing could inhabit, and yet those

2

monsters that obviously needed food to survive long enough to terrorize us, had randomly shown up; it was a blow to our reality.

The washroom was my closet of privacy and freedom. Even if my apartment was usually a population of one, I still felt an extra sense of freedom on the throne, a sort of naive part of me that silently hoped the CORPS didn't want to watch me shit and shower. Hot showers were nice. A true marvel of technology, the CORPS were pretty smart when they built their behemoth underground. Water could be recycled almost indefinitely, which made the little luxuries easier to obtain. Obviously, we had to use existing groundwater sources to supplement, but the end result was a nice hot shower, moderately clean dishes, and the beer could flow. That last one was pretty important when you've never seen the sky.

The CORPS is better known as the Coalition of Organic Research and Planetary Science. A mouthful, though, some snooty people might prefer the name "Coalition" to "CORPS." Suffice to say, they do a little more than their name let on. They ran the joint because they built it, and that fact wasn't changing anytime soon.

What's a man to do when your family's gone, and all that's left is an endless grind? My answer was simple enough: see the sky. Find the surface, make a life, or die trying. It would beat keeping grain secure all day.

After the zen-like contemplation of shower time had run its course, I finished getting prepared. I donned my usual outfit of loose-fitting, fatigue style pants with enough pockets to make authority figures uncomfortable. I slipped on a gray, snug shirt and, of course, *the shoulder-pad*. A gift from the old man a couple of years ago and another marvel of gears and lightning. Magnetic shields were all the rage those days among security forces. While not considered contraband, it wasn't easy to get. It took the form of a black, armored shoulder-pad that stuck out like some kind of steam-punk pauldron.

The shield wasn't my only stylish accessory. I learned my lesson after a fall and a broken leg as a kid to keep a impact harness on you whenever things might got hairy. A simple set of brown, leather-like straps that crossed in an X pattern across my chest and back. It all hooked into a belt, which, along with some other technological magic, prevented injury from falls. It created a sort of cushion by absorbing the energy of a fall and redirecting it outward. I remembered history classes back in the day that talked about those bad boys being used as weapons.

I grabbed my duffel bag and moved off to my living area. It was a simple place, meant for one person. The room was small, my attached kitchen was no bigger than a walk-in closet. The refrigeration unit had been built into the wall, which provided some counter space that was occupied with the usual appliances a bachelor needed to feed himself.

A simple dark-blue couch adorned the back wall across from the kitchen area, connected to the hall that led back to the bedroom, facing what appeared to be an empty wall. I walked up to it, dropping the duffel bag beside me. I waved my hand a few centimeters in front of the wall in a quick, yet intricate gesture. The wall faded, being only another projection, hiding my safe, keeper of the actual contraband.

The safe was biometric and opened as soon as I turned the handle; inside were a few essential goodies. I packed the various gadgets away and grabbed my trusty sidekick. The sidekick, of course, was a weapon that not many were allowed to have, but luckily for my ragtag group of cohorts, I happened to work security for Tier A. Protecting the food afforded you decent equipment. It was a sleek and long handgun, magazine-fed from the bottom, and featured kinetic absorption technology. Like the harness, it could redirect energy as it was being released, thus minimizing the recoil. It was a high-caliber pistol that barely moved when you fired it and damn if it didn't make a guy more accurate. Being a bit large for a pistol, I stuffed it into the bag.

The why of it all came right back to the surface again. The mutaphorm attacks were quick and unexpected in a bad way. One day, through ventilation systems and other cunning entrances, ancient menaces came down on anything in their path. According to Coalition bureaucrats, they were holdovers from the War. The Republic of Tantil was known for its genetic and protein research; we got to see the fruits of their labor, several generations later.

The nastiest of the creatures, what the common folk called stalkers, were the meanest customers anyone could ask for. Stalkers were bred to see in near-total darkness, with a touch that was sensitive enough to hunt by sight or vibration, and the capacity to catch the scent of prey from obscene distances. They were massive, hulking creatures, resembling a big ape with canine legs and clawed hands at the end of their muscular arms. Their murder mitts weren't really the worst part about them: The bastards were smart and somehow could communicate through sound waves a person couldn't completely
 perceive.

My family and some of my friends were among the casualties of the first attacks. They were brutal, and even the Coalition Elites, similarly enhanced, had been unable to protect everyone or unwilling; I still hadn't decided on that. That was all a year before our little plan.

I stared a moment into the darkness of the now mostly empty safe.

5

The paranoid part of me imagined the faces of people watching just beyond the wall. Shaking my head, I shut the safe, which gave a strong clank, the lock finding purchase. I took a moment and grabbed some fruit and meat from the fridge, and a bit of bread, stuffing it all into the bag. The culture of those that started underground wanted to preserve pieces of their past. It might not be the most efficient food, but it did wonders for morale.

Packed and ready, I headed out. The door slid open, obeying my presence. Even after seeing it hundreds of times, the sight just outside any living quarters was an awe-inspiring scene to behold. I walked the short distance to the rail, attached to a long, winding walk-way with many apartment doors, numbered by level and number of quarters (mine was "30-15").

Beyond the solid safety-rail was a cylindrical chamber that went both up and down for oppressive distances. In the center was yet another colossal cylinder, only this one was a structure of sorts, connected by large struts that stretched out in a star pattern to the outer walls. Connecting all of this, in an impressive spiral of gleaming metal and gears, was the tram system. Many trams were connected to it, set up in such a way that there was always a free one not far off. They moved at break-neck speeds, whizzing and whirring throughout the chamber. They would bring you up or down to other living quarters or bring you to different modes of transportation to other tiers.

The Undercities themselves were made up of multiple tiers that, if looked at on a diagram, would resemble a buried pyramid structure. Each Tier served a different purpose and varied in both depth and overall size. The Living Section was on Tier B, the second-lowest section of the structure, but also the largest if depth was taken into account. It was where everyone lived when not working or studying. It included many amenities, such as libraries,

6

restaurants, and recreational centers.

Tier B was also where the term Undercities was coined. There were roughly two million inhabitants stretched out over several sections of Tier B, each viewed as a city in and of itself. There was room to grow, though it was my generation that saw the first people settle into the last remaining empty section. No one talked about it, but the Undercities couldn't support indefinite growth.

People walked by, all in a hurry, either to get to work, hit the books, or meet up with someone. I used to take a chair out there and just sit, admiring it all. It ticked people off sometimes, and I saw that as an added bonus.

"Not today," I muttered under my breath before moving over to a part of the rail that had a small, holographic control panel. With a gesture, I called my tram and waited while several full ones passed by. It wasn't a full minute before an empty one found its way to me.

Trams were cramped affairs, circular in shape, with enough sitting room for five people. I took a seat and spoke simply "Lower Tier Transport Station." A small, two-toned chime responded affirmatively. Silently, the tram zoomed down its track.

The tram-system didn't afford one too much time to think, but my mind couldn't help going back to the dream; it wasn't the first of them, and I was beginning to get a bit paranoid about everything. A few weeks before, a close friend, Micky, had stumbled upon a drunken revelation one night at a Section 6 pub. Section 6, being the least populated, had a lot more places for fun than living. In all honesty, it was a thought we all had but were afraid to say it.

"The CORPS lied to us." He said it simply, but surely. We all knew what he was talking about. They knew the surface was livable, and they knew it was dangerous. All of their technology and those beasts still made it into the lowest tier to kill hundreds of people. Even if they were allowed into the cities for whatever tinfoil hat reason one cared to have, it meant that there was a way out. It was simple logic really: If something can get in, then something can get out.

Everyone at the table that night had lost someone during the Week of Terror. We felt empty, going day-to-day in a hopeless grind, and so we made a decision: If we were going to die anyway, we wanted to die having seen the sky. What else was there to achieve in a place like the Undercities? Escape seemed like our only option.

The small chime came on again, and the tram door slid open, waiting for my departure, others already prepared to enter. I gave a polite nod and walked through into the high, almost circular area that made up the Tier Transport Station. These were bustling affairs, with artists showing off various performances, people rushing to work, and others shuffling home from a long day. It was split into two sections down the middle: The one I came from which led to the different areas of Tier B and then on the other side, identical tram doors, only these led to the much larger Tier Transport Pods. These held up to twenty people, all sat in a circle around the edge of the pod.

I was headed to Tier A, where the initial attacks had occurred. I walked across the station, a stern-look on my face as I tried to calm my racing heart. As always, there was no luck in getting a pod to myself. It filled as soon as I was able to sit, folks pushing by, chatting, talking, oblivious to the dystopia around them.

Tier A is where all of the food was produced. It contained truly huge hydroponic farms, as well as livestock areas that went deep underground, making up the bottom of the six-kilometer hole that was the Undercities. The CORPS always took practicality over anything else, and while they could and did grow protein in labs, livestock served several purposes. Besides the materials their flesh could provide, their emissions could be harvested and used for other purposes, providing a natural gas resource. It was a massive undertaking to feed our society, but a fruitful one to be sure. The CORPS forewent automation in favor of keeping people skilled and employed. This meant that Tier A is where most people worked. Not to say that many things weren't automated, most things were, but only enough to serve the Coalition's agenda.

The people within the full tram car were continuing to chat away. The car took longer than the others, not so much due to distance, but the volume of riders. The system was designed to run continuously, keeping travel efficient and predictable. Over the last few years, a five-minute ride turned into a six-minute one. That might not seem like a big deal, but it was just another quiet sign that the number of people would soon create serious problems.

It was one of the biggest reasons some of us believed that we were being lied to. As efficient as the place seemed to be, it really didn't feel like it was meant to be a permanent solution for the survivors of the War. In fact, given the sheer level of precision that Coalition scientists and engineers were capable of, it wasn't farfetched to believe that the Undercities were built with an expiration date, just another phase in one massive experiment.

The door of the tram opened, and we all piled out into an almost identical looking station, though there was less fanfare on Tier A. Everyone there tended to come and go as quickly as they could. This was also one of the few places one could find armed guards outside of the research labs of Tier D.

There wasn't exactly a lot of violent crime in the Undercities. The CORPS made sure that living requirements and medical care were met for all people, so no one was precisely *impoverished*, so to speak. There was only a small amount of civil unrest and no real issues with mental illness. This always seemed a bit odd to me, because I could never personally pinpoint a reason for it. Hell, most people were incredibly healthy in the Undercities. Disability was almost entirely the exclusive province of unintended injuries.

Given the setting, violence generally boiled down to the same things: passion and rebellion. While some people had been known to lash out from the mental toll living underground can cause, the reasons for violence tended to get a little over the top and were often politically motivated.

"I guess I really shouldn't be too judgmental about it." The thought crossed my mind when I stopped to think of the possibilities of what was to come.

That's the thing, the big one right there: rebellion. The CORPS didn't precisely come down on our civil liberties in any overt way, but it was there. There were things we weren't allowed to research, places we couldn't go, words that, if said, would lead to a lot of inquiries and possible reeducation, of which no one ever returned *normal* from. They also chose whether or not one could start a family, enforcing this with birth control. It always seemed odd they would care so much, considering that room still existed. It drove home the idea that things were a little too well planned in the underground.

It didn't help that our leaders weren't precisely elected. While true, the one known as the Arbiter was chosen by the people, the candidates were always pre-selected. Besides this infuriating practice, the actual decision-makers and paper-pushers were all brought on internally. While someone could join the CORPS proper as a scientist or soldier, it was just like reeducation; no one ever returned the same person from such endeavors. These thoughts continued to swarm my mind as I pondered the possibilities. I think something within me was trying to find an excuse to just turn around and go home, but that part was weak and his voice, but a whisper.

Tier A was more cavernous than the others, consisting of a grid-like system of halls lined by massive sliding bay doors. There were lift systems that would bring people from one end to the other, but there was a lot more walking area there than most other places. Each door led to hydroponic farms, livestock areas, and storage facilities. Many of the doors had security checkpoints set up in front of them to prevent theft and sabotage. Petty-theft was an occasional problem; some people just can't handle the rationing of anything, regardless of the reasons behind it. Being a have not, it turned out, was not the only motivation for larceny.

Chapter Two: The Escape

I made my way down the first large corridor, heading to a big, industrial lift. I pulled out my PCD (Personal Computing Device), a small, thin, rectangular screen that was voice, touch, and gesture controlled. Everyone had one, and they made lots of things convenient, such as checking the time. According to the clock, I had a few minutes to spare. A week ago, I had volunteered for transport guard-duty. Down in Tier A, that meant the very dull job of moving between shipments, but it meant I officially belonged there at that specific time.

From my duffel bag, I pulled out a necklace adorned with a security clearance ID. The ID was more for anyone who decided to hassle me; the frighteningly omniscient security system knew who belonged. A small blue series of lights washed over me, as they scanned the contents of my person. This took a minute or two longer, likely due to the weapon and equipment I had. Nothing illegal, though, I made sure of that. Bringing the good stuff was *my* job. With a chime of approval, the massive bay doors to the industrial lift slid open.

The chamber, like most things in the underground, was massive. It had a twenty-five-meter radius, with a set of bay doors on each side of the chamber. That bad boy was designed to move big items, with a tall ceiling and a built-in harness system to keep things held down. Usually, people didn't ride the lifts alone, and it wasn't long before I had company.

The first thing I noticed was the large hover lifts that carried big crates, likely filled with supplies for the lower levels. Everything was kept in Tier A that was needed in Tier A, with a few exceptions; efficiency as always. Looking around, I could see several freight workers chatting about the day-to-day. Two of them were mostly quiet, and I couldn't help but smirk looking at them. They felt it too. Things were going to become very different for us. I was just glad to see everyone decided to show up. Not everyone on the lift was in on our little plan, of course. The less that knew, the safer we were.

Standing with a hand on the controls of the hover lifts was a lanky, dark-skinned man. His hair was kept short and professional, and he wore traditional work overalls with even more pockets than my getup managed to supply. He had piercing blue eyes that gave away the nervousness he was feeling. Next to him was his brother, who got all the short genes in the family. He had a bit of a grin on his face, and his hair was a bit more unruly and poofy than his big brother's. He was the daredevil of the two, and somehow, I felt like he was going to enjoy the adventure. I envied him for it.

Then, next to me, a petite, yet obviously fit woman stood. She too had a worker's cap on and unfashionable overalls. She had a bit more style about her than our other friends. Her hair was medium-length, and dyed bright red, which didn't match-up with her brown eyes, but honestly, she had her own flair about her. There were only four of us among the rest. The lift had roughly ten other workers on it.

"Nervous?" The woman next to me asked, the grin shining through her voice. Another person happy to up-end their life over a maybe.

"What? About a boring escort shift?" I raised a brow looking to her, a little miffed she couldn't muster more subtlety.

"Right, of course." She kept her smirk and looked forward again. "Me too," she said almost in a whisper.

Our team wasn't the worst in the land, but we weren't precisely heroes either. I was the proverbial muscle, though I wasn't a meathead. Lys was our tech-head. She knew her way around most systems and was good at getting into places she didn't belong. She was always the curious one growing up. It was her that suggested we find a way out where the mutaphorms had initially entered the Undercities from.

The shorter fellow, Mick, was a theoretical engineer. He actually worked in the upper tiers and swears that the scientists up there are, quote, "the creepiest mother fuckers you ever laid eyes on." He was the one who had access to the juicy information about the tunnels at the bottom of Tier A. They were first used when the place was built and had served as access-ways for materials and workers. The tunnels were sealed off a long time ago, but it was the only way he reckoned that the beasts could have breached our home.

The bigger guy with him was nothing special, at least not to most of us. He was Mick's older brother Raylund. Ray, as we called him, was a simple man. He worked in Tier A and, like me, officially belonged there. Mick insisted we take him along. They only had each other left, which made Ray loyal. He was tough, not overly annoying, and could probably hold his own if need be, so I didn't object. Besides, strength in numbers was not a bad idea.

After a ride that took us down a few levels and through parts of the Tier, the massive bay doors slid open with a lot of noise and a couple of orange caution lights flashing. Everyone began piling out one by one. This wasn't any kind of significant shipment, and only one guard, me, was assigned to it. That was how we wanted it. As the last person piled out, we all waited just before exiting the lift. I stood next to a panel on the wall being projected outward in a small display. With a simple gesture, the door began to close. It was nearly shut before someone actually noticed we were still on the lift.

14

Lys quickly took my place at the panel and activated the emergency protocols, keeping the doors from opening temporarily. "We only have a few minutes," she said plainly.

Mick was already looking for a panel on one of the side walls. Finding the seam, he fetched a wedge-like tool from a bag his brother was holding and pried a 2-meter-wide section away from the wall. The metal plate fell with an unsubtle thud, revealing a cramped and dark, but accessible access shaft, barely wide enough for us to go single file.

"Color me impressed," I said simply, but fairly. "I honestly thought we weren't going to find it."

"Yeah, well," Mick started, "we did. Now let's get the fuck out of here before they get that door open." He ushered us into the dusty old shaft and kept himself last in line. When we were all through, he pulled out a suction cup looking device and used it to grab and pull the panel back into place. After this, he retrieved an industrial multi-tool, one of the functions being a quick-welder. Quickly, he sealed the entry behind us, buying some time.

Chapter Three: Monstrous Holdovers

I had gone in first and already retrieved my sidekick. In my other hand, I kept a small flashlight facing forward.

"Move down to the end, it should open up," I could hear Mick behind me.

"Should?" I didn't like how unsure he sounded.

"Yeah, should. Trust me."

"Famous last words," I muttered and pressed on. It honestly felt like an eternity moving through the tunnel. Everything was happening so fast, and my mind was having trouble processing it all. If we got caught, it was straight to reeducation, and who knows what sort of punishment on top of that. I don't think anyone had tried to escape before. After a while, I came to a four-way intersection, including the way we came.

"Hey bud, where are we going now?" My voice sounded frustrated. Mick said nothing of creepy labyrinths.

"Just keep going. Those shafts lead to the outer wall. There are other access ways like this one, though they're better sealed than the one we came through." I was sorry I asked. Lys was quiet, which was unusual for her.

"Penny for your thoughts?" I was trying to break my own anxiety.

"They don't make those anymore," she replied matter of fact-like. "Just pay attention to what's in front of you. I don't like the idea of leaving unchecked hallways behind us."

"Neither do I." Lys was right. This didn't feel good at all. While there hadn't been any mutaphorm attacks in months, that didn't mean there weren't any stragglers, and we were in prime straggler territory. The walk was excruciatingly long. Every turn, I swore I heard another sound, echo, or saw a shape in the distance. My mind was not being kind, and part of me wanted to panic. Having others with me made it all possible, and I wasn't too sure if I could've done it on my own. I just kept thinking about the possibility of seeing the sky while pressing on. Eventually, I heard a sound I knew wasn't my imagination.

"Wait a sec." I stopped.

"What now?" Lys asked impatiently.

"Do you hear that?"

"Yeah, that whooshing sound?" Lys whispered.

"Yeah, that one. Coming from in front of us." As we pressed forward again, the sound became louder the closer we got to its source. It wasn't long before an uneasy feeling dropped over me. I saw my light spill outward when the corridor finally opened to a new chamber. The chamber was absolutely colossal, and words couldn't adequately describe what I could see. It was dark, of course, given our location. The exit opened to a narrow walkway that jutted out from the side of the wall about three meters wide. It was enough to safely walk on, but didn't make a guy feel comfortable about it. The source of the whooshing noise became apparent as I flashed my light around.

"Shit, put it down!" I heard Ray yell behind me as the light settled on a cloud of largish, winged creatures, roughly the size of small children, each with leathery wings and clawed talons at the bottom of their torsos. They were swarming in an awe-inducing large cloud. Their flapping wings were making the sound, and they didn't seem to like the light. In unison, they let out an ear-piercing screech. The creatures spiraled up into the air, before swooping down towards us. Everyone, without hesitation, scrambled back the way we came.

The swooping noise was deafening as the cloud of horrors flew passed the access tunnel we took cover in. Luckily, it was enough to keep us safe as they flowed fast and flew back down the tunnel beyond.

"Yeah, that looks safe," I commented.

"What are we even doing here?" Demanded Ray in a rush of emotion.

"Not getting eaten by winged monsters," was my sarcastic reply, which didn't seem to help matters.

"Relax," Lys chimed in. "Here," she handed me what looked to be some sort of whistle. It was made of plastic and colored black, with grooves to aid in whatever sound it was designed for

"A whistle? Who exactly am I signaling for help?" I asked, giving her a questioning look.

"No one ya big dummy. You don't pay attention to the equipment unless it goes bang." Lys crossed her arms, giving me a look that said she was disappointed. "These were made shortly after the first attacks. A lot of these things were designed to communicate with each other using sounds we can't hear ourselves. The right pitch should drive the buggers off." I looked over the small device and gave it a quick blow. It came out as a high-pitched whine that didn't seem very loud.

"And I'm supposed to trust my life to a fucking whistle?" Mick asked, channeling his brother's fear.

"Yep." I pocketed the whistle. "You can always turn back, tell the CORPS you're really sorry and won't vandalize their stuff or try to break out again." I turned to meet his gaze, and his look told me he got the picture. "Let's get the hell out of here before something pops up from behind one of them hallways behind us."

18

Slowly I crept back out of the tunnel and into the gigantic chamber beyond. There was a faint blue glow coming from the walls, which gave off a strange sort of illumination to the place. Not enough to read by, but enough to allow a bit more sight. I wasn't about to rely on some mutated lichen, however. The flying creatures seemed to have flown off to another section of the cave, so when everyone exited the tunnel, I set my bag down, knelt, and began to rummage through it.

I produced four pairs of roundish, almost goofy looking goggles. They were used by engineers and maintenance workers and were basically miniaturized night vision/IR goggles. They adjusted based on the environment and the battery on them would last days of continuous use, so hopefully, we didn't have to wait that long.

"What's our plan with all this anyway?" Ray asked as I handed him his goggles.

"What do ya mean?" his brother asked. "We talked about this already."

"I know what our current plan is, what I mean is when it's finished. Y'know, how are we not gonna starve to death?" It was a fair question, to say the least, and one I hadn't given a lot of thought to. It wasn't about surviving, but just doing it, getting there. I think most of us had some sort of a death wish deep down, but one where we didn't rot and grow old in some underground city. I also had serious doubts about the state of the surface. Part of me expected to see vast and lush wilderness or even cities that still existed. Live or die, I had to know.

"I was a bit of a biology buff back in school," Lys offered, holding up her PCD. "I brought some old books from before the war, stuff about the flora and fauna we might find up there. I also remembered to bring a few battery packs, just in case."

"Glad to see we're prepared." I strapped the goggles to my face and switched them on. I looked up at the massive cave we were in. "Now, to get up there." We could see the walls and strut support systems that made up the exterior of the Undercities. Seeing from that perspective brought a sense of scale to the place, but I couldn't help noticing that most of the cave seemed natural as opposed to dug out. While it was easy to see where they did do some digging and carving, it looked like the original architects chose their worksite wisely. This cave or system of caves had always been massive.

"You know," Ray stated, "I'm beginning to think this place is less underground and more like a hollowed-out mountain." It was a surprising burst of insight, but it made sense.

"Path of least resistance." his brother replied.

"Can we cut the banter and move on? We're kind of moving blind here." I was nervous, and it showed.

"Not quite," Mick spoke with his cocky grin that seemed to convey *my turn*. He pulled out his own PCD and flipped through a few screens, before holding it up to the wall next to us, projecting a display. It showed his estimation of how the structure was built, based on maintenance blueprints.

"We don't want to stay on the outside like this forever. Besides being exceedingly dangerous, we may run into anything from deadly gas to ravenous monsters. Either way, we want to get up, approximately three kilometers."

I gave a whistle. "Geeze, that's a fuckin' climb and a half."

"Why three specifically?" Lys asked, giving my arm a punch.

"A friend of mine who's an actual member of the CORPS Engineering Section said that building materials were shipped here from somewhere else using an underground rail-system. It's too long to follow, but there would have to be maintenance access to the surface. We just need to cl-"

"Shhh!" Ray interrupted, grasping his brother's shoulder. "Listen." We were all silent for a moment. In the background came a low, fast clicking sound, organic in nature, it sounded like it was coming from something's throat.

"Stalkers," I declared under my breath. "Fuck, they must feed off of the other shit in here. We have to go now!" The clicking sound for a stalker's throat was part of the process of making the signals they use to communicate with each other. It was the only way to tell when they were nearby, but if they're close enough to hear their almost chitter like clicking, then they were just about on top of you.

In near panic, Ray and his brother ran to the wall behind us, looking for whatever footfalls they could find, such as conduits and gaps between panels. This part of the place wasn't designed to be pretty, and there was a lot of exposed scaffolding and framing. Lys quickly followed suit, but I knew that stalkers were faster and able to climb. We were on a somewhat narrow cliffside, with only one way we knew of close by to get to it; it wasn't about to pop out of any random hidey-hole. I widened my stance and readied my sidekick. I pulled the whistle from my pocket and placed it in my mouth, squaring my shoulders and aiming the weapon in the direction the sound had come from.

"What the hell are you doing?" Lys hollered behind me. I didn't answer, instead taking a long, deep breath through my nose to calm the panic welling up in my chest. The first thing I saw was the large clawed hands gripping the side corner of the wall where we came out. In the blink of an eye, it ripped itself from the shaft and landed on all fours facing me. Drool came from its hungry maw, its seemingly intelligent eyes focused on the weapon in my hand. There was no warning, no roar, or any kind of indication of its next move. With a mighty heave of its front arms and massive kick from its hind legs, it pounced towards me, closing the distance at a frightening pace. I gave the whistle a blow, causing the creature to grunt and somewhat lose balance, giving me an opening for a clean shot.

The loud bang echoed through the cave, disturbing some fliers off in the distance and causing a light ringing in my own ears. I fell back in a scrambling move, avoiding being crushed by the falling creature. It collapsed in front of me in a heap on the ground. Blood poured from two holes on either side of the stalker's head. The back of its head had been rendered into a grisly wreck from the exit wound. I wasted no time scrambling to my feet, knowing another one might be nearby. Hitting the gun's safety, I tucked the weapon into my pants, put the whistle back in my pocket, and quickly began to climb.

"That was fucking stupid!" Lys yelled in an exasperated huff.

"It's dead, I'm not, move along," I said between grunts from climbing. While I couldn't see Lys's face from where I was, I knew she had a scowl. Lys and I were like siblings that never lived together. In a way, we were the only family either had left. If one of us was going on this fool's errand, both of us were. People often joked about us hooking up, but really, it would've been like kissing my sister. She was attractive to be sure, but it was never about that.

After a few minutes of climbing, Mick called out, "I found a little alcove!" Looking up, I saw him disappear into an opening in the framing. It took a minute to catch up, but soon we all managed to climb into a small metal box, with what looked to be some kind of ventilation access, sealed off by a heavy-looking grate. There was only crawling and sitting room, but the rest

22

was welcomed.

Crawling in with everyone, I sat with my back against the wall, sitting next to the ledge. I closed my eyes and just breathed for a moment as the adrenaline faded and the reality of what just happened set in. I couldn't hear the chatter around me over my own heartbeat. I leaned over and looked back down from where we had come, almost out of instinct. I was treated to a heart-dropping sight. Perhaps one hundred meters below, I could see two more stalkers had come out to investigate their fallen comrade.

"Everyone shut the fuck up." My voice projected seriousness. No one was offended and obliged quickly. I pointed down to where we had come from and held up two fingers with wide eyes. Everyone understood immediately. All I could do was hope. Hope they didn't smell us, hear us or feel us somehow nearby. While I could probably shoot them while they climbed, I really wasn't interested in seeing how high they could jump, how quickly they could climb, or whether or not the whistle was just a minor irritation to them.

Lys scooted next to me and leaned her head towards me. We both looked at each other for a moment, the mutual fear evident, before looking back down again. They were gone, which was even more disconcerting. At least they weren't climbing the scaffolding.

I waited for what seemed like an eternity. Finally, I spoke. "Obviously, we can't stay here and going back sure as fuck ain't an option now."

"Well, like I said, we have to climb to get out of here," Mick explained.

"I gotcha," Lys replied, fumbling through the bag she had brought. From it, she produced a suction cup looking device with a thick steel ring attached to the top of it. It was clearly electronic, with a switch near part of the ring. "I have four of these things. I wanted to get more, but I'm lucky these didn't get noticed as it was."

"What are they?" I inquired.

"They're magtethers," Ray interjected. "We use these for a lot of different jobs. Maintenance guys use 'em a bunch too. They're electromagnetic and can stick to metal surfaces with enough strength to hold up to over four hundred kilos."

"What he said," Lys continued. "I figured if we were gonna be doing a lot of climbing, that it would be a good thing to have."

"We could attach some rope to those rings and maybe use them like grappling hooks on the wall." I pondered about the little devices she brought.

"That could work. Hope we're all in shape," Mick spoke with a grin, looking to his brother, who smirked.

"Don't worry about me, nerd. It's your spaghetti arms, I wonder about."

"Alright, kids, settle down," Lys interrupted. "We have to be smart using these things. The amount of force they'll create as soon as they come close to any kind of metal is obscene. The things will break your arms if you don't set it against the wall before turning it on."

"So much for the grappling hook idea. I'll climb up ahead." I put my thumbs between the harness straps across my chest. "I'll live if I fall. I'll set up ropes when I find a good checkpoint, and you guys can follow after."

"Alright, hero boy. Let's do this then," Lys said, pointing to the exit. I moved my head side-to-side, cracking my neck before looking down to check the situation. The corpse was no longer alone, now featuring a swarm of winged beasts, picking at the carcass. The good news was they wouldn't be hungry for us right away.

I looked up at the daunting task before me. It looked like the framing was more covered further up, which was going to make climbing tough. I grabbed the magtethers from Lys and moved to begin my ascent.

It's amazing the thoughts that can go through a person's mind when they're doing a strenuous task. The mind wanders in much the same way it does when relaxing in the shower. What we were doing was absolutely crazy. There was a good chance that our endeavor would leave us all lunch or worse, we emerge to a toxic wasteland and die up there instead. Was it really preferable to the alternative?

"Yes, it is," I assured myself. Of course, it was preferable. We all die one day, probably in pain, and likely not in any enjoyable fashion. Might as well go out with a bang than rot away in a stagnant prison. Eventually, I got up to a point featuring another narrow, man-made ledge, which was attached across the edge of the structure. It seemed that the Undercities became narrower as one went up. I didn't have enough rope to set up four climbing rigs, but I was able to get two set up and lower them down.

"Come and get it kiddos," I called down. I stood and inspected the area that I was in. By the look of the superstructure, it seemed like the lower level had a lot more support than the ones above it. Tier A was huge and likely needed more structural-support. There were lightly corroded metal panels lining the walls, which stretched up for a staggering height. From that distance, it actually looked like the structure went beyond the ceiling, stretching through it. It was a breathtaking image to behold.

I looked back down at my companions, who were slowly making their ascent. We already had gone a decent distance in a short amount of time, but my arms were on fire, and I knew this wasn't going to get any easier. As they

25

got close enough, I helped them climb over the ledge and onto the solid surface. Ray and Mick collapsed in heaps when they finally managed to make it up, huffing and puffing. Lys retrieved her devices, and I snagged my rope before taking a seat myself. We were exposed and exhausted.

"Hydrate up, boys," Lys said as she grabbed a bottle from her pack and took a swig.

"Just a fountain of good ideas," I gave her a nod. Everyone took a moment to hydrate and take in the scenery. The place made a person feel absolutely insignificant, yet in retrospect, it also made one feel powerful. It truly astonishes the marvels people are capable of when they get together for a common goal. Sometimes, it was almost supernatural in size and scope. Legends and myths don't compare to the reality of it all.

"Can you imagine what it must have been like building this place?" I asked between sips of water.

"I dunno," Ray answered. "You never really think about it livin' in there. Can't really imagine there bein' nothin' here at one point."

"And yet, there wasn't anything." Mick joined in. "Nothing at all. Took a bit of hubris if you ask me."

"Hubris isn't the half of it," Began Lys. "Think about it for a second. The amount of time and planning that went into this place is mind-boggling, right? It's the ultimate outcome of years of research and development. Probably whole generations of scientific study went into something like this."

"What's your point?" I pressed for her to continue.

"Well, isn't it obvious? This thing wasn't made in response to mounting tension between nations. This monster had to have been part of some master plan, one that's generations in the making. I mean come on, do you really think

26

for even a second that they made this place on a whim? Just got their heads together one day and *found a solution*?" She was making a lot of sense, but the puzzle didn't seem complete to me.

"Alright, so let's say your tinfoil hat theory is right," I started. "Let's say that this was some big goal of somebody's way back when. What for? Fuck man, look at Tier B. It's filling up and fast. One day, there won't be enough room. You gonna tell me that eggheads that can build a big bastard like this didn't have the foresight to know it'll eventually fill up? No way, they definitely knew, and that's why I think there's a livable surface up there."

"You know," Mick interjected "this place does seem somewhat maintained. I mean, yeah, there's some corrosion, but everything essential is damn near pristine. Then you have the records."

"Records?" Lys inquired, looking to Mick.

"Yeah. I mean, it wasn't a big surprise that the CORPS had records and blueprints for this place. They're meticulous scientists. What surprised me was how much of it was classified. It's not like escape attempts are common."

"We're the first ones I've ever heard of." Ray interrupted.

"Right." Mick continued. "So I don't see why hiding something like that would be important at all. It kind of dawned on me here."

"What if they were planning on using this stuff again?" I asked, and he pointed at me with a nod.

"Exactly. Why? What's the point unless those files include plans for moving back to the surface."

"I guess that does make me feel better about this shit," Ray muttered.

"Well," Lys said, putting her stuff away. "Let's get out of here, shall we? I think we were lucky enough to get the rest we did."

"Agreed." I stood up along with the others. "Where to now? I swear you better not say up." I gave Mick a look.

"Well, I mean, up is kind of the answer, but I got ya, buddy. We're just above the highest point of Tier A, where it meets Tier B. This section will be a bit easier. We need to find where the tier-to-tier tram system is."

"What's so important about that?" Lys wondered.

"It should have a ladder system for maintenance access that goes with it. The system goes up for more than half the distance we need to go."

"Well." I said, "Let's move on, then." I gestured to the walls. We picked a direction and began walking along it. While the ledge itself was barely three meters wide, it stretched for a staggering distance. We could hear the winged monsters flapping in the darkness, though it seemed like they avoided the structure itself. I was curious as to why that was.

In the distance, we could see a square section of the structure attached to the cave wall, moving up along it. It was large and looked like it could house the tier-to-tier tram system within. As we approached, we could actually hear the sounds of the machines running just beyond the walls in front of us. It was weird to think of all those people, unaware of our little expedition to the surface.

"There it is," Mick announced as we approached. "We need to find a panel like the one we found in the cargo lift." We all began searching, feeling the wall, banging our fists lightly against it for hollow spots. Finally, we found an area with a slight, rectangular seam along the surface.

"Lys, let me see one of those magtethers," Mick requested, holding out his hand. She rummaged through her pack and handed him one. He put it towards the center of the wall section and then activated the magnet. He gave

28

it a few quick tugs, the wall budging slightly, but remained closed.

"Get out of my way nerd," Ray demanded, eliciting a scowl from his brother, who obliged. He grasped the ring with both hands, bracing his legs, and gave it a quick tug. The wall section came off with a pop, sending Ray onto his ass with a grunt, squeezing a laugh out of Mick. He stood up and let the wall section fall to the ground by deactivating the electromagnet.

"Laugh it up, spaghetti arms."

"I will." Mick answered defiantly. Lys and I gave each other a smirk and shook our heads.

"Aw shit," Ray spoke while hopping between his feet.

"What now?" I asked.

"I gotta piss." I just gave him a look, closing my eyes for a moment before fixing my gaze back on him.

"So piss? I ain't gonna stop ya."

"Hurry it up, huh?" Lys demanded, putting her hands to her waist.

"Yeah, yeah." Ray walked to the ledge and just let it flow right there. "Little kid me is kinda jealous."

"Really?" Lys asked incredulously.

"I mean to be fair, I think every little boy wanted to take a tinkle off the rails in Tier B." Chimed in his brother.

"You're joking." She looked to me, and I sucked my lips in trying to hide my smile, turning away. "Men will forever be gross."

During the conversation, I could see Ray glance down, and a look of terror washed over his face, making his skin several shades lighter in the process.

"Oh, fuck!" He yelled. He pulled himself from the ledge and scrambled to put himself away, sprinting to the panel he had removed. "Stalkers!"

No one needed an explanation. Mick, Lys, myself, and finally, Ray all scrambled into the opening as fast as we could. It was only wide enough for us to enter one at a time and only extended two meters before ending at a ladder. We all began to scramble up as fast as we could. My pulse was pounding in my ears as I climbed.

When Ray made it in and up a few meters, I could hear the massive footfalls of the monsters beyond. A muscle-bound arm, murder claw wide, reached through the opening. Fortunately for us, stalkers were far too large to fit through the maintenance access we were in.

We climbed for what seemed like an eternity but was really only ten or so meters before everyone stopped on their respective rungs.

"Is everyone alright?" Lys asked, catching her breath.

"Yeah, all in one piece," I replied, hugging the ladder and getting what rest I could.

The next sound I heard was utterly unexpected and sort of shocking. Ray erupted into a hearty, long belly laugh. We asked him what was so funny, but I doubt he heard any of it as he laughed for a good solid minute before finally calming down.

"I did it. Hahaha, I did it. Oh geez, I can't fuckin' believe it."

"What the fuck did you do, Ray?" I demanded.

"I got 'em, I got the damn bastards. Right in the head. I got one in the eye!" He lost it yet again, nearly falling from the ladder, but catching himself and just continued to laugh. At this point, his brother got the picture and started losing it himself.

"You pissed on a stalker?" He bellowed out.

"Right in the eye!" We were all laughing at this point. I couldn't help it. Stressed or not, it was one of those once in a lifetime moments.

"Looks like we've got a world record for the most dangerous leak ever taken." Lys joked before we all started laughing and snorting again.

Ray wiped a tear from his eye. "Oh, hahaha, oh man, I needed that."

"Alright kiddies," Mick said. "We have a lot of climbing to do.

Chapter Four: A Bloody Menagerie

The way forward was going to be rougher than any of us had imagined. We always knew there was the possibility of dealing with various monstrosities, but the reality seemed a lot worse. All of the climbing wasn't helping the mood in any way.

"How far up is this ladder going for Mick?" I sounded a bit like an impatient kid.

"You don't want the number. The sooner we get up here, the sooner we can rest. There should be some kind of maintenance room coming up soonish."

"Soonish?" Lys asked, her own irritation showing.

"Yep, soonish." The shaft we were climbing was gruelingly hot. Our body heat probably wasn't helping matters. We must have climbed the ladder for what seemed like a solid half-hour.

"Here we are, rest for a sec." I heard Mick say as we all stopped and hugged the rungs in front of us. We had come up to what looked like a hatch, with a sliding door. There was a moment of frustrated cursing, and then with a loud creak of metal scraping metal, a red light began to flood the shaft, allowing us to remove the goggles.

We all climbed through the opening, which led into a medium-sized room, full of empty shelves and lockers. The room itself was disconcertingly clean and maintained. If someone had told me it had been cleaned out only a day or so before, I would have believed them. The only other exit seemed to be another hatch like the one we had come through. The ladder continued up the wall, stopping at the closed hatchway above. We all took a moment to collapse onto the floor and rest for a while. After a few minutes, Mick shut the hatch we had come through, using a manual lever that was on either side of the opening.

"We can rest here."

"Planned on it, bud," I replied and reached into my bag for food and water. I pulled out some meat and cheese and went to work, feeding my angry stomach.

"Sandwiches, really?" Lys asked.

"Yeah, fuckin' sandwiches. Cans are heavy, and if we don't find food in the first couple of days out there, it won't matter much anyway. Maybe if we had some vehicle to escape in."

"I guess that's fair." She cracked open a can of stew she had brought.

"We safe in here, lil bro?" Ray asked.

"Of course," Mick replied. "The only ways in or out are too small for those bastards." With that statement, we all went silent for a long while, just eating, hydrating, and relaxing.

I took a moment to reflect on everything that had transpired up to that point. As far as I could tell, we were beating the odds. We had barely been down there a few hours and already had survived a few hairy run-ins. Whether it was some kind of strange death wish or force of ideology, we were all moving forward.

"What do you hope is up there?" Mick broke the silence.

"Trees," I answered first in a matter of fact manner.

"Trees?" Ray asked.

"Yeah, trees. I read about 'em back in school and had a bit of interest here and there. They would be a sign of a livable surface, I think."

"I dunno." Answered Mick. "I'm not convinced we're going to like what we see."

"Actually, I think we will find trees," Lys spoke, setting the now empty can down. "Look around us for a second. I mean, if the radiation was so bad that the surface was unlivable, you would expect to see a lot of stuff down here affected by it too, but look around." She pointed in the direction we had come. "The glowing lichen is everywhere, thriving. Those big bat-things couldn't survive without a source of food and water. Same thing with the stalkers." She put her hands behind her head and leaned back. "I bet there are all sorts of life we haven't encountered yet, and I have a feeling the surface has some too." We all took a moment to reflect on this. In the end, she was probably right. There was no way any of the things we have seen could have survived without some kind of ecosystem. The lie was beginning to unravel before our eyes.

"So, what's our plan of attack anyway, Mick?" I inquired.

"Well. We'll be looking for a sort of tram station. Right now, we're just trying to get further up. There really weren't any areas in the higher tiers where we could have gotten out and not got caught."

"More damn climbin'," Ray gave an exhausted sigh.

"That's right, bro. Lots more climbing."

"What do you mean by tram station?" Lys queried.

"Well." Mick started, "The CORPS historical records talk about a processing hall where people came from the surface down to the Undercities. Unfortunately, we won't be able to use the tram that was attached to it. If it is still in operation, the car is somewhere on Tier E, and we aren't getting in there." Tier E was the tippy-top of the giant structure. There the CORPS administrative division oversaw just about everything. It's the smallest Tier and

34

restricted to anyone that doesn't work there or isn't on official business. Most people had never seen it, and thus most of Tier E was shrouded in mystery.

"So who cares about the tram if we can't use it?" I asked, crossing my arms over my chest.

"We can still use the shaft itself. The tram might not be running, but we could walk it. It has plenty of maintenance access there as well, so getting in shouldn't be too difficult."

"And once we get there?" Lys continued the interrogation.

"Once we get there, we take it all the way to the surface. The main processing hall is the final destination as it were. If we make it there, then we've *made it*." Having it put into perspective brought a little hope to the situation. It all seemed plausible, especially in comparison to what we had already been through.

"Well, we should probably get going soon." I stood, gathering my things. "The sooner we go, the sooner we get there."

"Fair enough," Ray answered and stood. Mick, with a bit of a groan, stood and moved for the ladder. Lys followed suit, and we waited for Mick to get the next hatch open before everyone got back onto the ladder.

The ladder climb was long, painful, and tedious. Taking frequent rests, we made our ascent. We were making considerable progress, as the ladder made its way up a large portion of the superstructure. However, the tier-to-tier transport system we were following only went as far as Tier D. Getting to Tier E and the somewhat fabled surface tram shaft would be a monumental amount of work. I feared being exhausted when some ridiculous event occurred, like getting chased or worse. When we finally made it to the top, Mick stopped short of opening the hatch we encountered.

"Alright, so this hatch leads to the old construction and maintenance access ways of Tier D."

"And?" I asked, a little frustrated. My legs needed a rest.

"Well, chances are, dangerous gasses are floating around up there."

"The industrial zones," Lys said as the light bulb in her mind switched on.

"Precisely. While there's a good chance it's all clean in there, the surface might be toxic, so we came somewhat prepared." As Mick explained this, Ray steadied himself on the ladder and pulled his own bag from his back, rummaging through it. He produced a mask that fits over both a person's nose and mouth. There were round cylinders on the sides of the mouthpiece, with tiny holes that looked like an exhaust system. He handed one to me.

"Pass 'em up." He ordered, producing three more. "These are filter masks. We use them whenever something nasty leaks and needs to be fixed."

"Cool as hell if you ask me," Mick explained. "They pull and filter out all of the molecules in the air that get near it, leaving only the oxygen. They also store oh-two inside the cylinders themselves. You get of couple hours of air when they're full."

"Smart idea." I mused. We all took a moment to fit our new fashion accessories over our faces. Finally, Mick found the manual release lever and opened the hatch. We ended up finding ourselves in a maintenance room that was identical to the one below us. The idea of rest was a welcomed sight. Everyone found a spot to sit and settle for a few precious moments.

"Oops." I heard Mick say, and Lys immediately shot him a glare.

"Listen, we don't do oops here." She declared.

"Well, I mean, it's not a big oops. Just jumped the gun on the masks."

"I swear, if you are about to fuckin' tell me that we have more ladders to climb, I might shoot you," I spoke matter of fact like.

"No, no ladder. Take a look behind you." I turned from where I had been sitting, and I could see a sliding door attached to the wall behind me. I laid back with a sigh of relief.

"You're lucky." I joked. Everyone took a moment to relax in silence as we caught our breath. We chilled there for probably a couple of hours. No one bothered to take the masks off. We really didn't know if the atmosphere in there was clean and honestly, we probably should have been wearing them beforehand.

"You still haven't explained the oops." Lys sounded irritated.

"Right. I thought that the hatch was going to open up to an area like the one we found when we first got out here." Mick shrugged.

"Wait," I interjected. "Didn't you basically have a map? Blueprints and shit?" I didn't like what dots my mind was connecting.

"Kind of. They're old. If the CORPS did any kind of top-secret construction, abandoned or otherwise, then it might not be on the records I was able to get a hold of." Ray shot me a sideways glance, the kind you give to the conspiracy nut who won't stop talking about brainwaves.

"So," I interjected, "what you're trying to tell us is, we have no idea what could be on the other side of that door. We could end up captured as soon as it's open." Lys gave me a look as if to say that her brain had suddenly made the same connections.

"Give me a break, man." Ray finally spoke up. "What kinda secret shit do you think the CORPS is doing all the way up here?"

"Any kind. It doesn't matter what. I just think we should be more careful. Maybe not assume we're alone out here."

"He's not wrong," Lys backed me up. "But we also can't just go back either." The paradox of the situation was unsettling.

"Look, guys, let's just go." Mick finally said, standing up. "If we're damned if we do or damned if we don't, I'd rather do." He made his way over to the door and found the panel beside it that contained the manual lever. The others stood up as well because the truth of the matter was he was right. Giving it a pull, the large door slid open, revealing the dark areas beyond. Luckily our goggles enabled our sight.

We followed a meter-wide metal hall for a short while before finding another doorway. This doorway, though, was ominous in that it had clearly been torn open at some point. Massive, gaping claw marks marred both sides of the center as if these claws had pierced the metal and pried the door open. We all stopped in stunned silence, staring at the door with rapt anxiety. We all knew what it meant, but we also knew that going back was never an option. I pulled out my weapon; I thought it better to have it ready. I moved myself to the head of the line and slowly walked forward. My heart was pounding. What I wouldn't have given for a recon drone or something that could let me see around the corner. These creatures were still somewhat mysterious, and I really had no clue just how intelligent they were. We very well could have been walking into a trap.

I put my back against the wall just before reaching the door and slowly, carefully peeked my head in to survey the area beyond. What I saw stunned me. The facility was large, probably twenty meters side-to-side and twice that again long. It appeared to be the remnants of an observation hall. On either side of the wall were windows looking into some sort of a menagerie. A few

38

of the windows were broken, and the room was a complete mess. Computers and various clerical equipment had been scattered throughout the room. What looked to be a security checkpoint on either side had been demolished in a variety of ways.

None of that was the strange part. The weird part was the absolute lack of bodies and how old the wreckage seemed to be. This wasn't a recent event by any means, and there was no sign of human casualties. Nary a bloodstain could be found, and it was evident that no cleaning team had touched the room since whatever incident had befallen it.

"What do you see?" Lys whispered behind me.

"A mess." I carefully stepped into the room, trying to see or hear any indication that we weren't alone. Cautiously, my companions followed suit.

We were all in a bit of shock over the room. Not the specifics of the mess, but the existence of it entirely. This place was obviously designed to observe creatures within controlled environments. By the looks of some of them, all manner of creature once inhabited this research station. Morbid curiosity took over, and I began to inspect the wreckage more closely. There were remains of animals I didn't recognize, including a somewhat mummified stalker corpse. Everything in here must have happened, months, if not a couple of years ago, and that's when it hit me.

"Those bastards," I whispered, standing in the middle of the room looking around. "Those murderous, pieces of shit!" I finally screamed and kicked a chunk of debris across the room.

"What?" Ray asked, confused.

"Don't you get it," Lys answered for me. "Look at it," she said, motioning towards the stalker corpse. "They released them. They brought them down and then released them."

"What? Come on, that's a bit paranoid." Mick replied. "I mean sure, they definitely brought them down here, but how do you know this wasn't an accident?"

"Look around you," I said. "No bodies in sight, yet no cleanup. They had the power to bring them down here, but not the power to contain them. I mean, what accident occurs in a sealed-off place like this where these monsters suddenly escape and wreak havoc, but don't leave any bodies?"

"Okay then, what the hell is the point? I don't see why it's to anyone's advantage to sick monsters on civilians." Part of me was having a hard time not seeing Mick's point. It did seem to make very little sense, but then again, so did the entire situation.

"I don't know, but I sure as hell know, none of this feels right."

"Maybe there's a log or something left behind." Lys posited, rummaging through some of the debris.

"That's a bit of a waste of time, don't you think?" Mick asked.

"He ain't wrong on that department. Unless we're suddenly planning a revolution we can't rightfully win, I don't think it matters at this point. Still, I think we need to be careful. Who knows how long ago this happened, but I ain't taking the chan-" at some point, Ray had gone exploring, looking through one of the broken windows of a holding cell. I was interrupted by his scream.

"Help!" was the one coherent word I heard. Upon turning, I saw a big, meaty claw come out from the broken part of the window and sink deeply into Ray's torso, before gripping and dragging him through. Glass shards tore him up as he nearly folded in half, being pulled through the opening.

As fast as I could, I moved in front of the glass and could see two stalkers inside, Ray being tossed about like a rag doll. Blood was everywhere, and I knew he wasn't going to make it. I'm not sure what came over me. A great calm settled over my panicking heart. I drew my weapon and began to fire until the magazine was empty. One of the monsters managed to get away, finding its way through an open access hatch inside of the enclosure. The other was dead on the floor, and next to him, so was Ray; besides the wounds he had sustained, a clean bullet hole was visible on his forehead. I had shot him.

"*Ray!*" Mick screamed in utter horror as he ran towards the enclosure. I put my weapon away and immediately grabbed him, trying to pull him back.

"We have to go, Mick!" He was screaming incoherently but was much weaker than me. I wasn't sure whether or not he had seen his brother, and I really didn't care either. Survival had taken over, and deep down, I knew I did Ray a favor. No part of me wanted to imagine being devoured alive.

"No, we can't leave my brother! He's my fucking brother, let me go!" Mick kept screaming, but Lys came over and helped me pull him away towards a door she had found on the opposite side we had entered from. Like the others, it needed to be manually opened. Once Lys got it opened, all three of us pushed through, and she immediately closed the door behind us.

Chapter Five: The Fall

We found ourselves in yet another maintenance shaft, this one much larger than the others, however, with sealed off exits lining the sides. It looked as though the seams in the doors had been adhered-shut somehow. As soon as the door was closed, I let Mick go who ran to the door, his fists pounding on it a few times before he defeatedly sunk to the floor.

"He's gone." Tears welled in his eyes. "Just like that. So fast. Damnit, we let those things devour him!" He screamed, turning and staring at me. I turned away from him.

"No, we didn't," I spoke softly, choking back my own tears.

"What do you mean?" Lys asked, looking over to me. I could already tell she knew what happened.

"Your brother was a goner. He was bleeding everywhere, nearly torn in half. I shot one of the bastards, another got away, but I, I shot Ray." I finally looked back to Mick.

"You what?" He demanded, getting up in a flash, looking at me face-to-face and grabbing my shirt. I just stared at him with guilt. "Why?"

"Because there was no way we could save him. Best case scenario, I got both monsters, and he bleeds out slow. Worst case, we all end up dead." I managed to meet Mick's gaze. "And I seriously expect you to do the same to me if I'm about to get eaten alive." He stared incredulously at me, before swinging his fist into my right cheek. He wasn't much of a fighter, it didn't exactly leave me injured.

"Mick!" Lys exclaimed, ready to jump between us.

"It's okay, Lys. I don't blame him." It was amazing to see how many emotions were going through Mick's face all at once. You could see the varying stages of grief, all hitting him at the same time. Finally, he embraced me in a hug, his eyes shut tight, tears falling from them.

"It wasn't supposed to be like this." He sobbed. I hugged him back.

"I know, man. We were all supposed to make it out together." That's when Mick pulled away, and his eyes met mine. I couldn't read what was there, but it almost seemed like there was something he wanted to say but chose not to.

"Come on, guys. I hate to be the jerk to say it, but we don't have time. We have to leave before the one you missed comes back." Lys was absolutely correct, of course. I gave her a nod before looking to Mick, who then nodded back.

"Lead the way navigator," I said to him. He took in a deep breath and tried to compose himself. Everything must've suddenly overwhelmed him again because he turned away and began to vomit. Lys moved over to him and gently rubbed his back. After a couple more retching sounds, Mick managed to compose himself.

"Yeah. Okay, yeah, the mission."

"Sure, we can call it that," Lys spoke softly. He gave another look before nodding again and brought out his PCD.

"These were the maintenance halls I was expecting, though I didn't expect most of these doors to be sealed. Probably has something to do with the menagerie, I imagine. We follow these down to the end. Hopefully, that door isn't sealed, but it should lead to an area just outside the superstructure itself, like the first one we found."

"Sounds good, boss. Lead on." I was absolutely impressed by how quickly Mick seemed to be recovering. He was obviously, deep down, more than some pencil-pushing nerd. A small part of me was even slightly disconcerted with his reaction. I honestly thought he would be more unforgiving.

We began to walk down the access way, Mick exchanging a glance back at the door we had come from. It was at this time that we heard the first bang emanate from it. Neither of us needed another motivator as we began to run for the exit. Having seen the previous doors, we knew it wouldn't hold it for very long. I could hear my own heart inside my chest again as the panic began to well up. If it weren't for all the adrenaline pumping through me, I probably would have had a breakdown right then and there. Somehow, I managed to hold it together.

By the time we reached the exit door, we had heard the smashing sound of the door behind us finally being ripped asunder, and the hulking grunts of the beast were growing closer. Mick wasted no time, prying the panel near the door open and going for the manual lever. Luckily for us, this door had not been sealed off like the others. The door opened, and as we rushed out, I nearly met my own demise, as the barely meter-wide ledge appeared before me. It went down for an incredible depth. Looking up, I could see we were very close to the ceiling of the cavern the Undercities had been built in. The plan that came to mind was quick and full of a stupid amount of risk, which was par for the course.

"Back against the wall!" I yelled to my companions, motioning to the wall on the side of the door. They did so without protest until they saw me stand in front of the open doorway, seemingly ready to face what was charging down it. Lys was afforded no time to protest. As soon as the hulking beast got

44

close and hunched down, ready to pounce, I immediately dove to the ground on the right side of the door. This caused the lumbering creature to leap passed the door frame and right off the cliff ledge. It flailed about as it fell, eventually fading from sight. I scrambled to my feet, clutching my chest and looking down at the massive drop before me. A cloud of winged-beasts swarmed from the walls and swooped down to earn a potential meal.

"You're fucking crazy," Lys growled in a huff. Mick went to the manual lever on our side of the door and shut it.

"Don't knock it, it worked," I replied, finally mustering a bit of a smirk. I couldn't lie, even to myself, that felt good. In a sort of protest, I spat down the gaping pit in front of me, in the direction of our fallen nemesis.

"Lovely," Lys commented before looking to Mick. "Mick? Where are we going now?" Mick was staring down at the black abyss below, with a thousand-yard stare in his eyes. I placed my hand on his shoulder, causing him to jump a little.

"We gotta go," I offered simply. Mick lifted his head and turned his face to mine. I couldn't read his emotions, and that somehow bothered me.

"Yeah. You're right." He walked passed me and down the narrow ledge. "The tram shaft should be this way." His voice was monotone, and it sounded like he was on some kind of auto-pilot. We followed Mick, single file down the narrow ledge, keeping a hand on the wall next to us to make sure we were steady. There was a powerful breeze coming from above, that occasionally gusted, suggesting one or more openings in the cave. Being this high up, I suddenly had an appreciation for the wonders of nature. This cavern or series of them had obviously been there before the CORPS developed it. It's incredible to imagine the different ways it could have formed. It also made me hate the CORPS a little bit more. I could only wonder what this place looked like before it was infested with people.

After a few minutes of walking, we finally came up to a narrow cave entrance that had been bored into the wall. It followed alongside a truly huge tube that connected from the superstructure to the far end of the cavern wall. I hadn't even noticed we had been walking across it because of its size. The entrance itself only had crawling space to speak of.

"That's a maintenance bot access way. I doubt it's in use anymore since the tram isn't needed." Mick explained. "We should be able to get in from here."

"We've been moving for hours. We have to be close." Lys almost sounded excited.

"Very close," Mick replied. "I mean, we have a hike still, but once in the tram tube, it's straight to the entrance hall."

"And then the surface," I finished the thought off, and the others nodded in agreement. "Well, lead on nerd." I gave Mick a smirk. He gave me one back, which was creepier than I imagine he intended.

"Well, I'll head in first." Mick moved to crouch down. I'm not exactly sure what happened, either part of the ledge gave out, or his foot slipped in the clumsiest of fashions, but I had nearly no time to react as he slipped and fell off the edge. My hand reached out as fast as it could and grabbed at his backpack. Somehow, I manage to snag it and brace myself enough not to be pulled right off the ledge with him.

"Mickey!" Lys yelled behind me, grabbing onto my waist to steady me and provide a bit of an anchor point. Mick nearly slipped out of his backpack, but it twisted around his arm. He looked up at me, and an odd expression

46

came over his face. He seemed annoyed somehow. I could feel his arm slipping, the lock that had been made by the strap failing.

"Grab on with your other hand!" I yelled out to him. It was too late. The strap let go, and he dropped silently down below. He didn't scream, he didn't flail. It was the most disconcerting thing I had ever seen, like he accepted his fate. I was still clutching his backpack in my hand, staring at it.

"John, we have to go!" I heard Lys cry out behind me. I must have been staring at the bag for a while, in sheer disbelief over what had happened. I looked at her finally. It had all happened so quickly that I wasn't really processing what was going on. Lys looked panicked, and I finally got to hear the whooshing sound from our flying friends down below.

"Yeah. Yeah, let's go." I turned to attempt to crawl into the maintenance shaft. As I knelt down, I swore for a moment I saw a blinking light coming from the pit below. When I tried to focus, it was gone. My imagination was beginning to get the best of me.

Chapter Six: Live Free or Die

We crawled through the small access shaft, and it wasn't long before we came to an opening. It looked like it had been forced open a long time ago. It opened up into a darkened tunnel that, as seemed to fit the theme of the place, was unnecessarily huge. We had made it. Luckily, our goggles still had days of juice left in them, and we were able to see the path ahead.

Once we climbed down from the access shaft, I sat down and opened up Mick's backpack. "Looking for his PCD?" Lys inquired.

"Yeah," I answered but didn't look up. "Mick showed us that map earlier. We need to know what direction to go."

"I mean, we only have two," she offered with a smirk, but it faded when I failed to look-up. I found the PCD and was able to get in.

"Huh. Weird."

"What?"

"Well, I just expected some sort of password or asinine security or something. No biggie. Here." I handed her the pad. She was better with technology than I was anyway.

She sat down with me and took a moment to pull out what few rations we had left. I could see she was deep in thought, and I couldn't help but admire her strength of will. After everything we had been through, we both would've been justified in having a nervous breakdown right then and there. The fact was, she was focused; that or she didn't expect to survive. An odd sense of calm can wash over you when you accept your inevitable fate.

"Found it." She declared at last, revealing the map to me. "Though, to be honest, I already knew we needed to go that way." She pointed down the tube. "You know because I pay attention and have a sense of direction." she grinned and punched my arm playfully.

"Yeah, fuck you, Lys," We both had a laugh. We stared at each other for a moment before I looked down at Mick's backpack. "We have to make it now."

"Yes, we do." She stood up once more. She offered her hand to me, and I took it, pulling myself up. We embraced in a long hug before we walked towards our destiny side-by-side. We walked for what seemed like an eternity. We were silent, reflecting on where we were, what we had lost, and the possibilities that lied ahead.

The scenery left me in awe in much the same way as the rest of the Undercities had. At one point, this system was used to transport hundreds of thousands of people to relative safety. It must have been a race against time, but just like everything else, the CORPS was prepared. The level of dedication it all took was the type to literally move mountains, and it left me feeling small and insignificant in the grand scheme of things. I always had to wonder: What was their ultimate goal? Why rescue all of those people, why build the place, just to lie about it? What was the point in keeping people in the dark concerning the state of the surface?

Once upon a time, those sorts of thoughts would be the subject of ridicule if I heard others entertain them. I can't really remember what it was that sent me into full-blown conspiracy theorist territory, but I also never imagined any of it would be validated. So far, those theories were valid, and I wasn't sure what scared me more. The fact that there was some larger plan at work that I was not privy to or the fact that I had somehow figured that out.

"What's on your mind?" Lys asked, looking over to me as we walked.

"A lot of things, I guess. You ever feel like, I don't know, like-"

"Like we're supposed to be here?" We stopped.

"So it ain't just me then." She shook her head. "Been thinking about it since we found that menagerie."

"Me too. It seemed like it was, I don't know, recent. Like someone made it look like it happened a while ago." I walked over to the wall to my right. There was a flat surface that ran along the edge, big enough for sitting. It looked like it was some sort of track for maintenance robots or something similar. Lys walked over and sat down next to me.

"You know, there has been a part of me thinking this since the stalker incident a few years ago." She pulled some water from her pack and took a long pull before offering me some. Gladly I took it. "It took me a little bit to realize how staged that seemed." She spoke in a matter of fact sort of way. "You don't think the war was fake, do you?"

"I mean, maybe? I guess I never really thought about it that far. How could they hide something like this, though, if the surface is all fine and dandy?" I took a long pull from the water and handed it back.

"I guess that's the only reason why that part is the hardest to believe, but I don't think it can be even close to what they fed us as kids. I mean, think about it. There's a whole pack of those things down here, all those bat-monsters, the fact that they were even able to build and keep this place, to begin with. I just feel like, if it was as bad as they say, then there's just no way all of this could be possible."

It wasn't like we hadn't had this conversation before. Truth be told, we had had the conversation dozens of times. That time felt different somehow. We suddenly had more evidence than we could have ever hoped for. Yet, I was still troubled. Some dark truth was dangling in front of us, and neither one of us could grasp what it was.

"Look, Johnny, no matter what happens." She took my hand in hers and met my eyes. "Promise me one of us makes it to the surface. I promise, too, even if I have to leave you behind." She had a hint of sadness in her voice. We both knew the ramifications either way.

"I promise." We embraced in a long hug. "Come on, time to go, Lys." she nodded her head, and we both hopped off the platform. Quietly, we began walking down the tube once more. Unexpectedly, the shaft started to curve and slant up. It looked like we had to be getting close to the end. Once we got closer, I began to feel uneasy. There were some old crates off to the side of the tube, and they looked like they hadn't been there very long. Like someone, months or even weeks ago had set up some sort of camp there; there were even abandoned bedrolls.

"Look at that," Lys exclaimed, almost breathlessly. "Do you think someone else made it out?"

"Maybe. I mean, I really doubt the CORPS would let news of an escapee out if it did happen." Lys got a look on her face that had a hint of horror to it.

"How do you suppose they explained our disappearance?"

"Honestly? Fuck 'em. We didn't break anything, so we probably *died* in some kind of work-related accident. Maybe the bastards will send in more monsters, and we'll be among the casualties or worse yet, blamed for it. At this point, nothing is beyond these fucks." I was angry and wasn't afraid to show it. Just the thought of there having been others was uplifting, but part of me knew better. This didn't look like the camp of escapees. It looked like a guard post of some kind. "I have another theory."

"What's that?"

"Whoever was here was trying to keep something in. If that surface is livable and those beasts escaped their cages, they have been defending their little secret."

"Gives me shivers just thinking about it," Lys admitted.

Finally, we rounded the bend and came across a humongous door. It appeared to open sideways from the center and looked like a gigantic security hatch of some sort. I felt absolutely tiny in its presence. I couldn't help a giddy feeling that began to well up inside of me at how close to our journey's end we finally were. It didn't take long, however, for those feelings to fade. The door had large barricades in front of it, with weapon emplacements that weren't in a state one would call abandoned. They were left there for future use. Mounted guns still rested on cylindrical pylons on either side and the center of the barricades. There were supply crates strategically placed to make advancing enemies maneuver less effectively, but still allowing access to their contents.

"Something's not right about this." I began to walk towards one of the barricades before Lys held her arm out to stop me.

"Do you hear that?" She asked, and I concentrated, trying to listen out, eventually hearing it too. Heavy clawed footfalls running from behind us, and it sounded like there were more than a couple of them.

"Get behind the barricades!" I yelled. Our enemies rounded the corner, and we could see them clear as day. There were four hulking beasts, stalkers like before, pounding their way towards us. Their clawed arms and feet propelling them forward in ape-like fashion. There really wasn't a lot of time to react to it all. Either they had managed to find a way through or had been

52

quietly following us from behind. Either way, they were earning their nickname in frightening form.

As soon as one of them became visible, a loud, piercing siren began to wail, like some sort of emergency system had been activated. It wasn't long before the siren was drowned out by gunfire. The turrets behind us came to life and began firing at the advancing predators. I felt rounds whiz right passed me, but Lys was not nearly as lucky. I didn't hear her reaction, but I saw the effect as a spray of blood burst forth from her torso, just below her left shoulder, forcing her to the ground.

My ears were ringing, and I had no time to watch the carnage. I ducked low and grabbed onto Lys's pack strap, frantically dragging her behind cover. After what seemed like forever, the gunfire stopped, leaving the area blanketed in smoke. Nothing was coming near us as far as I could tell. The automated system must have cut the creatures to pieces.

"No, no, no, Lys, no, oh, fuck no." I could barely hear myself speak, as my ears slowly and miraculously recovered from the deluge of fire.

"John," she spat up blood as she spoke. "Johnny, you promised."

"No, no, I'm not leaving you here!" I tossed my pack down and ripped her top at the wound site. It was horrific, her chest had been wrecked by the exit wound, and the logical side of me knew she didn't have much time. Reaching into my pack, I pulled out my first aid gear. At that point, I was patching her up with hopes and dreams, but I was in a panic, and I wasn't going to just do nothing.

"Johnny-"

"Shut up, Lys. Ain't the first time I lied to you, now save your strength. I'll carry your ass if I have to." Tears were streaming from my eyes, getting caught around my goggles. She was all I had left, and I wasn't about to let her go that easily. Using everything I had had barely any affect on her bleeding, but it might've given her a few more minutes anyway.

"Alright, I'll be right back." I almost said *stay here*, but thought better of it. I stood and looked around, the smoke slowly fading into the vents above. I felt like I was on the verge of a breakdown as I searched for some sort of way in. I noticed that the center of the massive bay doors had an indent that looked like it had an entrance of some kind built into it. When I approached it, there was a whirring sound that came from the wall. A small orb stuck out, bathing me in a blue light before retreating back inside once more. Then the indent opened-up.

I didn't spend any time actually looking at what lay beyond; I rushed over to Lys. Her eyes were closed, and I immediately thought the worst. "No, Lys, you can't go yet! We're so close, come on Lys!" Slowly she opened her eyes and gave two weak, pain-stricken coughs.

"Not yet, Johnny. Not done yet." As she deliriously spoke, I hunched down and, as gently as I could, picked her up in my arms.

"Nope, we ain't done yet, Lys." She weighed more than I thought, or exhaustion was finally taking its toll. I didn't care either way as I walked to the door, her labored breathing letting me know she was still alive.

The logical side of me was screaming. Lys had been shot, she was a goner. Who knows what kind of ridiculous rounds those things were spitting out. The building I was entering was most likely dumb huge, just like everything else, and she would be long dead before she got to see the sky. We could still be underground. Absolutely none of it mattered to me in the end. I wouldn't be able to live with myself if I didn't try, and at that point, I wasn't

54

sure I was going to be able to live with myself either way; no reason to add to it.

Eventually, my mind managed to come to some sort of arrangement. Passing through the door, we entered, as anyone could guess, a genuinely gargantuan chamber that resembled some kind of abandoned lobby or terminal. I carried Lys through a big queue area, with long since deactivated scanners and contraband detection devices. The large bay door behind us likely wasn't meant to open after it was sealed. Whatever tram was used would probably stop and connect to the wall on the other side, and the door we came through was how people boarded and disembarked.

There were long rows of chairs, desk areas, food court, and all. It was all covered in a significant layer of dust. The wall was lined with what looked like screens. They likely once sported information and entertainment for those who were waiting. The place wasn't threatening and looked like it had been designed to put people at ease. Considering its stated purpose of ushering people away from nuclear devastation, it seemed appropriate.

"Johnny. Look." Lys's hand pointed up to the ceiling. I don't know how I hadn't noticed it. Perhaps it was everything else or my dying friend in my arms, but I failed to realize that the ceiling was made of glass. Our goggles were still on, which adjusted to the light that shined from above. The blue expanse, with grayish, almost sickly colored, fluffy puffs floating about nearly overwhelmed me completely. With Lys still in my arms, I dropped to my knees, carefully enough not to drop her.

My chest was filled with an intense feeling I couldn't describe. The goggles were protecting our eyes but allowing us to see everything clearly. I could see the bright sun in our sky, the fabled watcher that kept us warm. Even during the day, it looked like the heavens expanded indefinitely in all directions. My heart raced, and I thought I was going to pass out. I was crying again but hadn't noticed.

I looked down at Lys and set her down on the floor. Her eyes were closed, and her breathing was slowing to a stop. I just stared at her, as a numb feeling washed over me. A feeling of utter happiness and despair at the same time. It was a feeling I had no conceivable words for. No way to adequately describe the intense sense of loss and success all at once.

"We did it, Lys. We made it." I took her hand in mine. "I told you I'd carry your ass if I had to. You did it. You got to see the sky." For a very long moment, I felt like I could see dust standing still in that timeless second. A moment where my sanity was brought to its breaking point. In all of the mental anguish and celebration, I had become unaware of my surroundings. At some point, I had been joined by others, others that encircled me.

Nearly all of them were dressed in black, military fatigue-style uniforms. Their heads were covered by black masks that showed only their strangely glowing eyes. On their left shoulders, they each bore a rank-insignia. On their right was the crossed swords behind a globe symbol of the CORPS military division. They each carried sleek and equally dark-colored rifles. Their sidearms were clearly visible at their sides and a knife was nestled in their boots.

"Target secured. You may enter, Doctor." One who was training their weapon on me, not a meter away, spoke. They likely had a headset that was concealed by their mask.

Yet another indescribable sensation washed over me, and I began to laugh. I laughed long, and I laughed hard. I looked up to the sky, hugging myself as laughter spewed forth from the darkest place I had ever known.

56

A man in a white coat entered from a door on the far end of the lobby. He had light skin and a bald head. It was hard to gauge his age, but he definitely appeared older than me. He had no facial hair to speak of. His pupils were almost entirely black, and he seemed disappointed somehow.

"I was hoping she would have made it. Thirty-three percent success is better than none, but she was the better candidate. Oh well. You know, that's my favorite part of research; unexpected results." He said this all so nonchalantly like he was talking to a mouse in a cage. I felt a rage the likes I had never experienced before well-up inside of me. It exploded outward almost immediately as I tried to lunge towards the man in front of me.

I heard two pops from behind me as my right arm, and left leg exploded in fiery pain. One of the soldiers behind me had shot me twice like I was a stationary target. I screamed out in pain, falling over Lys's body before quickly rolling off, writhing in agony.

"Still prepared to fight? Perhaps I was wrong in my initial observations. Sedate him and bring him to the transport. We have some history to make." Before I had any kind of chance to react, one of the soldiers, using a single arm and little effort, grabbed the back of my shirt and lifted me up. Another came up and jammed some kind of device into my neck. With a click, I could feel something injecting into me and causing the world to fade to black.

Part Two

A Never-Ending War

Chapter Seven: Awakening

The world was a swirling maelstrom of memories, dreams, and thoughts. I was falling, but I wasn't in danger. Everything rushed forth, abstract concepts coming as mere sensation and mere sensation were tangible places I could go. I could hear voices, mostly my own, everywhere around me. Some were accusing me, while others called out to me; my family, friends, and colleagues. My life was rushing all around me in a chaotic mess I could not discern.

Some voices were louder than others. I could hear Mick and Ray, arguing about something stupid again. I could listen to Lys goading me on to do something I probably shouldn't, all for a laugh. My mother was screaming, my sister was gone.

I couldn't move at all. I had no sensation of body. I didn't know if it was all just a dream or if this was someone's sick idea of an afterlife. Some voices became much louder than others. Mick was saying something about sub-conscious mumbo-jumbo while calling me a subject. Ray's screams echoed through my mind and all around me. Sometimes it was loud enough to drown everything out. Sometimes I had to strain myself to hear them.

"How long have I been here?" I couldn't speak, but my voice echoed out the question anyway. Somewhere I could hear Lys speaking my name. I couldn't see her, I couldn't tell where the sound was coming from. It's always out of reach. I can never answer the call.

Suddenly, everything started swirling back to a kind of reality. It happened fast, like a vacuum pulling everything back into focus. I could move again. I found myself sitting in a metal chair in a dark room. At least it seemed dark because there was blackness all around me, but I could see my hands with perfect clarity.

"Well, it would seem the initial test was successful." It was *his* voice. The one who had sprung the trap. I looked up, and I could see him standing there, in a gray, formal uniform, the kind typically worn by high ranking members of the CORPS science division. He was standing there with a simple, patient look on his face, perfectly illuminated by an unseen light.

"You son of a bitch!" I growled out and sprang from my chair, leaping towards him. I stumbled, passing through him like he wasn't physically there. I hit the ground with a groan.

"Immediate, complex response to stimuli and a clear indication of an intact memory. Very fascinating." The way he said it was cold and calculating. He was analyzing my every move like I was some animal to dissect. Slowly, I picked myself back up and stared at him, committing his face to memory.

"Where the hell are we?" I demanded through grit teeth.

"*I* am sitting in a VR suite, adjacent to your bed. You are currently connected to a Sub-Conscious VR system." I gave him a blank stare. His tone was if everything he said qualified as normal.

"Let me get this straight. We're in some simulation in my brain?"

"Put in grotesquely simple terms, yes. We are in some simulation in your brain."

"And what exactly do you want from me? Is this your new sick version of prison?"

"No.," he replied. "Not even close. This system is designed to test your cognitive abilities while keeping you asleep, which at this point, I assure you is a blessing." My look softened when I heard this. I couldn't help but feel fear. I could literally be being dissected as we spoke.

"Go on."

"This interface will be useful to you later. It will allow you to explore environments before actually entering them and interact with other operating systems more effectively." I got a dumbfounded look on my face.

"Wait, what? Useful to me? You're not going to punish or kill me?" He laughed at this as if I had asked him if up was down.

"Of course not. At the moment, we are making sure that your mind is intact. So far, everything seems to be going swimmingly."

"Who the hell are you?" My voiced carried a growl.

"I am Doctor Xavier Ronyn, head of the CORPS Cybernetics Division. And you, my friend, are history in the making. I'm finished here." When he uttered the last phrase, he faded from view. As soon as he disappeared, it was as if a hammer hit reality and shattered it like glass. Everything became total darkness.

I awoke, screaming, which I immediately stopped doing as soon as I realized I was in a bed. My racing heart calmed quickly, and I took stock of my surroundings. I was in a well-lit room, the walls themselves emitting light in a space that was some-what claustrophobic. The room was roughly a three-meter square box with a bed and a sink off to the side. There was also a small swivel chair in the corner across from the bed I laid on. The room was empty. The place itself wasn't what startled me; in fact, nothing did, which was a bit disconcerting in and of itself. I was calm, not exactly at peace, but I was in control of my faculties in a way I wasn't able to adequately describe.

The wall across from me seemed to slide open, and just beyond a woman of striking appearance stood. She was tall. In fact, I seemed to know she was precisely twenty centimeters shorter than me. She wore a white lab coat, with a rank insignia on the left that put her on a level similar to Ronyn. Her coat bore a symbol with swords crossing over a shield which had a red cross on it, the mark of the CORPS Medical Division. She held a PCD in her hand and walked into the room with an almost haughty confidence. She took a seat and gave me a warm smile.

"Very remarkable."

"That's what all the ladies say," my voice was monotone. I folded my arms over my bare chest. I did have a loose-fitting, light-blue pair of pants on that looked like some sort of patient getup.

"I'm sure." She looked down and, with a stylus, seemed to mark something on her PCD. "Your recovery rate is absolutely remarkable. The A.L. zero-four-seven actually worked." As she spoke, I silently studied her. Somehow, I knew a lot about her physical capabilities just by her posture, and I was sure I could guess her weight within a gram or two. It would've been shocking if I was capable of being shocked. At that moment, it didn't seem like I was.

"You wanna say that again, so I actually understand it, doc?" I quirked my left brow.

"Of course. This is one of the many sessions we will have. For now, I am here to answer your questions and, in so doing, answer some of my own." She crossed her legs and set the pad down on her lap. "So, in layman's terms, as part of the augmentation process you underwent-"

"Augmentation?" My good friends irrational emotions, came swimming back for a moment. Whatever they did to me, they couldn't prevent me from feeling violated.

"Yes, augmentation. The process was incredibly rough on your body, and under normal circumstances would have killed you." She had the same, infuriating nonchalance as Ronyn.

"What does this have to do with A.L. zero-four-seven?"

"Simple. That is the model of nanomachines that were finally successful. They healed you, among many other things. They are what makes your entire suite of abilities possible."

"Are you telling me I'm swarming with little robots?" The thought was incredibly creepy.

"Essentially, yes. They regulate your system, reconstitute base matter into any material your body needs, including self-replication of the machines themselves. They are integral to your survival."

"Y'know, ya say that like I was born with the little bastards or something. I was surviving just fine without 'em before." She gave me an almost sympathetic look.

"Well, unfortunately, that is no longer the case. If it helps our relationship along, I am not the creator of the project, nor am I its head. I am simply the inventor of the things that are keeping you alive."

"Among other things," I spoke mockingly.

"Yes. Among other things."

"So, is this my spiffy new home? Nice. Assholes didn't even leave me a bucket to shit in." She actually laughed at my comment.

"Well, it's good to see you have not lost your sense of humor. For the record, you don't need one anymore." Surprised, I stopped to think about it.

"You know, I ain't gonna lie, that's kind of awesome." I looked back into her brown eyes again. "Okay, so I have these tiny little builder bots inside me, making whatever a growin' boy needs, and I don't have to drop deuces anymore. What the hell is the point?"

"The point is to continue the evolution of our species, of course. Again, I am not responsible for the project, and therefore the why is out of my

66

grasp." She picked up her PCD and made a few notes.

"C'mon, you can give me a better answer than that. Why do I need the bots to live? How long have I been out?"

"Well, if by out you mean, how long before the completion of stage one, which started when you left the Undercities, roughly five years." She gave me a moment to digest this information. Five years. Lys, Mick, and Ray had been dead for five years. I had somehow survived and had basically been asleep for that same amount of time. Five long years.

"To answer your first question, it is because, to put it frankly, much of your body has been replaced with a suite of systems designed to enhance every bodily function while also imparting new abilities. Your digestive system has been replaced with a storage system, for instance."

"I'm sorry, did you just say storage system?" It all had to be some sort of sick joke.

"Yes, for food and anything else you manage to consume. The nanomachines in your system will break down and use everything you take in. Everything from healing wounds, to increasing oxygen flow to muscles, and keeping your hormone levels stable. Any leftover matter they cannot change into anything useful will be excreted through sweat as normal."

"Huh. Okay, what else?" I had been violated, that much was clear. Whatever it was they had done to me was allowing me to handle it like it was no big deal, but I was still analyzing everything about what she was telling me. It did me no service staying in the dark.

"A lot of things which we will go over as time goes on and testing begins. One thing we can discuss before finishing today you have probably already noticed. Your brain has been enhanced in several ways, and due to the nanomachine clusters inside of you, your emotional state can be nearly completely regulated. This will have many side-effects I hope to study and learn about." She was eyeballing me like I was some sort of prized specimen, and it made me exceedingly uncomfortable.

"Yeah, I noticed. So, I have to ask even though I might not like the answer. Where are we?" It was somewhat shocking it hadn't come to my mind sooner.

"Tantil, Sector 20-11. You're on the surface, John." As the words fell from her lips, I found myself at a complete emotional loss.

Despite whatever technological magic was coursing through my veins, the idea of it all still caused memories to flood back into my mind. I could feel Lys in my arms and see the mesmerizing sight of the sky through the glass panes of the long-forgotten entrance to the Undercities. The memories and sensations were real. I could see any memory I wanted to in that way, and little to no time seemed to pass around me. I saw the blank stare of Ray's dead eyes and the look of calm? Yes, a look of calm on Mick's face as he fell. So many memories were vivid in my mind. At that moment, it was a curse.

"What's your name?" I opened my eyes, meeting her gaze.

"I am Doctor Alonna Lyrul. Want me to skip the fancy titles?" She gave a playful smirk.

"Yeah, I'm good, thanks. Why me? What's the point?"

"Well, the point, of course, is to further the development of our species. Why you specifically, I am not sure. Again, I am not the head of this project, John, nor am I privy to the snatch-and-grab plot that led to you being here." Her tone was sober for a moment as if to stress that she and I were, in some respects, in similar positions. "What I can tell you is that I prepped for the possibility of three subjects, yourself being one of them."

"Wait, wait, time-out." I crossed my hands back and forth before looking up to her again. "Three? There were four of us."

"There were three of you." She corrected with confidence. "You were also accompanied by an escort for lack of better term." I looked away and thought about that for a moment. An escort. My mind skipped back to that calm look on Mick's face. Then it snapped back to several other memories. His knowledge of the superstructure, the PCD he left behind with all the conveniently available schematics we needed, and that blinking red light at the bottom of the cave.

My thoughts then reflected on Lys. Perhaps it was bias, but I couldn't suspect her. She was my kid sister in more ways than I could count; the only real family I had had left. She hadn't acted weird, and everything seemed right. I do remember she seemed suspicious, suspicious of Mick.

Then there was Ray, of course. Ray was Ray. He was handy, knowing his way around equipment and would have really shined on the surface. He hadn't acted weird either. In fact, he was downright terrified most of the time. He didn't deserve to go the way he did.

I finally met Alonna's gaze again. "Mick. That slimy little nerd. Y'know, it makes sense that he'd roll with you yahoos."

"Well," she quirked a brow, watching my reactions, "as I have said before, John, I have no knowledge of the actual operation. I don't know any Micks, and I would imagine any escort would have been using an alias anyway. What is interesting if I may turn this around, is I see that you are reacting very quickly to new information, forming working theories from memory."

"Yeah, I noticed that too. I remember specific details that I would have never thought to care about." I shook my head a moment, realizing she had skillfully redirected my line of thinking. "Let's get one thing straight, doc, I ain't impressed, and I am sure as shit not cooperating with these stupid lab rat games. You and your friends had no right!" I stood up quickly, my voice raised, and my finger pointed directly at her. I was in control in ways I had never thought possible. I wasn't experiencing anger, I was using it.

Alonna immediately scrambled to her feet and put her back to the wall, stopping when she realized I hadn't advanced. "Good. You and everyone else here should be scared. It ain't right what you or anyone else did. You should have just let me die." She began to speak, and I raised my palm up. "Just don't. Get the fuck out of my room." I sat down, running my hand through my hair. I disappointingly realized I had been given a crew cut. Eerily I felt no scars, but literally, nothing was making me any happier about my situation.

"Just one piece of advice." She said bravely. I looked up at her. "We *are* on the surface, John, and I can say with certainty that field testing inevitably lies in your future. You may want to play the lab rat games if you want to see it. That's not a threat." The wall next to her moved once more, revealing the door to a guarded hallway. "It's just a statement of fact." She turned and walked out of the room, the door sliding shut behind her.

I wanted to scream, to freak out and rip apart anything not nailed down in the room, but I couldn't or perhaps wouldn't. What Alonna had said at the end had a lot of merit. Play their games? I could do that. It could even be my ticket out of there. The more I thought about it, the more I realized it was also my ticket for a little payback. Apparently, they had augmented me a lot. So much so that they replaced organs with storage systems. They were probably fixing to train me, test me, and learn about how useful their little gizmos were.

Maybe I could somehow make them regret turning me into a cybernetic monster.

I laid back and got myself comfortable, figuring that I could be in the cell for a long time. As I laid there staring at the ceiling, which carried the same off-white color as the rest of the room, I suddenly began to laugh. It started as a little snort and ended in a chuckle.

"Don't need no bucket to shit in." I shook my head at my own childishness and let out a sigh. I was going with the flow at that point and wasn't sure what to make of my situation. Under normal circumstances, I probably would've had a nervous breakdown.

"Perhaps," I thought to myself, "that's what I want to believe." Truth be told, being calm under pressure, analyzing everything around me without effort, and apparently healing like some cheap comic book character all sounded pretty rad in my book. Whatever else they had in store wasn't my issue either. It was who wasn't there, enjoying it with me.

Chapter Eight: Deep Thought

They lied to everybody. I was in a facility on the surface. If the land wasn't wholly livable, it was still tamable. If our schooling also wasn't a lie, there would be enough land that no one would have to live in cramped quarters. That lie eventually cost lives, let alone potential. Obviously, the CORPS were in some kind of control on the surface.

Our history teachers used to tell us that the CORPS was formed some two-hundred years ago. They were scientists from all over the world, some even holding positions in various governments. Their goal, as they told us, was to continue the advancement of society and to study the world around them. At some point, a global war erupted among some of the world's greatest nations, the two most prominent being Tantil in the west and F'Rytal to the east, across the ocean. The conflict, according to the CORPS, started over ideological and economic shifts. Apparently, Tantil had made strides in gene and protein engineering. They had begun the practice of what had been known as "designer babies"; children that were genetically altered before birth to rid them of any defects and often to favor whatever traits the parents were hoping their children would have. This created a whole issue with their people due to their mostly capitalist society. The only people being born with genetic defects were the poor, and the religious elements within their culture didn't take kindly to upsetting Ma Nature's plans.

F'Rytal, on the other hand, was a technological powerhouse and had been for centuries. Many advances in rocketry and computer science came from that nation. They were also an interestingly religious people. They worshiped some sort of machine god and strove to be more like the things they built. One thing they shunned often was bio-sciences. That wasn't to say they didn't have medicine, they were against upsetting what they referred to as the *natural order* of things. If you lost a limb, it could be replaced with a prosthetic, no problem. That was the wonders of technology after-all, but to say, enhance a child's mind before they were even born by altering the very structure of their being? That was a sin. Couple this with their isolationist nature, yet enthusiastic tendency to take what they wanted, be it land, resources, or people, and the world was ripe for war. This was, of course, the CORPS's account, and thanks to them, I could finally remember the dullest parts of my schooling.

The CORPS claims, after everything was getting heated, they had already been funding projects such as the Undercities. Apparently, they had upper-class members from several nations, including Tantil and F'Rytal. They probably could have outright bought small governments if it had behooved them to do so. They claim they had been ushering people in for years, beginning the setup of the Undercities when it became clear that the war may go nuclear. That didn't make much sense to me anymore. When I saw the lobby entrance of the Undercities, it was absolutely gargantuan. It was clearly designed to house tens of thousands of people at a time. The only way it wouldn't have been visible for kilometers out is if it had been built into a mountain, which would make sense considering everything else. Geography wasn't really covered in any detail in our schooling. There was no need for it, so I wasn't entirely sure where it had been built.

After all of my rambling thoughts, I began to get a bit frustrated. I wasn't drowsy, nor did I think I could fall asleep if I tried. I was bored, recalling a bunch of memories and playing imagination detective with my situation.

73

After a long, long moment of ceiling staring, I decided to get up and start exercising. I had to do something to keep my mind clear. I dropped to the floor and began to do push-ups.

I was always decently fit. My profession alone, in my mind at least, demanded a modicum of physical ability. I could drop and do twenty real quick without much of a sweat. That was the first thing I noticed. I was pushing myself up and down quickly, with almost no effort. My body felt light as a feather. I blew through one hundred and wasn't even sweating, nor was I tired. I just kept going. My mind focused as I exercised. Instead of popping into every memory I wanted to forget, I began to think of the future, of escaping. My mind went for a recent memory.

Each time the door had opened, I saw that the hall had several guards in it, eight in fact. They all bore the same elite trooper get-up as the ones that had taken me in to begin with. None were standing by the door, I saw that much. They were smart, every soldier had clear sight of my cell. They were all heavily armed. As I exercised and thought about it, I knew, somehow knew, that they were all armed with three firearms. A rifle, SMG, and sidearm. Each was packing high caliber ammunition as well. I wasn't entirely sure how I knew that, but I did. It was a ton of firepower for one person, to say the least. What I was surprised about was that I also seemed to know they weren't packing any other ordinance. You would think smoke or even flashbangs would be carried by prison guards, especially prison guards, mostly ready for war. They were also sporting heavy-duty armor. It was light and maneuverable but made out of some robust materials.

"What am I a scanner or something?" I mused out loud in mid-push-up. There was no way I could tell all of that just by looking at them. I felt like

74

I could know more, too, if I got a better look. Either way, one thing was sure: I wouldn't be escaping out the front door.

I want to say I lost count, but I hadn't. I had reached two hundred push-ups before I decided to sit back down. I was getting slightly fatigued, but it faded almost immediately after taking a seat. To say I had been augmented at that point seemed like an understatement.

The CORPS wasn't known for employing cyborgs as soldiers, which they clearly intended on my future profession. Instead, they preferred gene and protein therapy; improved technology from what the Tantillan government had used. Their soldiers were often ridiculously strong, with an unmatched endurance. They healed quickly, and one was generally more than a match for a dozen regular soldiers. The fact that eight of those bastards was considered a reasonable number to guard little old me suggested I was an upgrade. A big one. Those freaks outside my door were the things of nightmares. What does it mean when monsters feel the need to gang up on you?

Chapter Nine: Training Day

I could feel the hairs on the back of my neck rise, and I was aware that someone was approaching my door. Somewhat tall, just below two meters, and small framed at only sixty-eight kilos. As the door opened, I felt my fist grip the sheet I was sitting on. It was him, head-shining, arrogant looking, lab coat wearing, future corpse mother fucker. It was Ronyn.

"You," I growled through grit teeth.

"Yes, me. Careful, I would keep your temper under control if I were you." His voice was filled with a calm, smooth grace. It was infuriating. I don't know what it was, but I must have overloaded whatever they put inside of me that was keeping me calm. I lunged with a power behind my fist, the likes of which I had never felt before. They wouldn't kill their pet project, and so I was going to get a good lick in. At least I thought I was until everything turned bright blue for a moment. A flash appeared where my fist was about to land, mere centimeters from his face. I felt electrical currents run through my body, and I dropped to the ground, convulsing before quickly recovering.

"I tried to warn you." Slowly, I began to pick myself up. "Absolutely remarkable. That shock would have nearly killed most people, and here you are, recovering in seconds." He didn't mockingly say this. Instead, he had a sick sort of pride in his voice that was a tad bit creepy.

"Can't blame a man for trying." I plopped back down on the bed. My head was pounding, but quickly clearing.

"I would have it no other way; data is data. Speaking of, come with me. It's time you learn a thing or two." The door remained open, and he motioned for me to exit.

"Ballsy, ain't ya?" I growled, walking past him and out into the hall.

"For now, sure. You aren't aware of what you are actually capable of, and I highly doubt you would get *that* creative." His remark was curious to be sure. Clearly, I had no idea what they had done to me. As I walked, I analyzed my surroundings. The walls were made of some incredibly dense material. I couldn't sense anything beyond it. The Elites in the hall began to walk as we passed each pair, following behind like some sort of overkill entourage. We walked to a circular door that slid open like a metal iris.

Stepping through, I found myself in a large, almost labyrinthine set of hallways, each the same width as the one I had entered. It branched off every few meters. There were at least two guards, one on each side, each time the hallway branched off. Under normal circumstances, it would have been a challenge keeping track of where I was going, but now I was committing the layout of the structure to memory, laying breadcrumbs only I could see.

After moving down a few of the hallways, I realized the structure was modular. Each wing was attached to an air-lock system, explaining the strange doors. It was also apparent to me that the structure could probably be taken apart and moved if necessary.

Finally, we came to a junction where another air-lock style door laid before me, and a typical door was just off to the side. Ronyn entered the side door, speaking before letting it close behind him. "Enter the room when the door opens." I glanced over to see the stairs he was going to ascend, I then looked back to the door in front of me. With a metallic sliding sound, it opened, revealing a black chamber. Boldly, I stepped inside.

The chamber reminded me of the one I saw in my dream when Ronyn had spoken to me, though I was beginning to have the sneaking suspicion it wasn't exactly a dream. I could see my body indicating the room was lit, but the walls were pure black. Once upon a time, it would have been impossible for me to tell the dimensions of the room because of the color scheme, however now I could see the grid pattern that adorned the floor and walls.

"Welcome to the training room." I heard Ronyn's voice come over an intercom. "Here, we will test your skills, from basic reflexes, combat prowess, and survival instinct. If I were you, I would take the test as seriously as possible. While you may have already guessed, we do not desire your termination at this time, however, observing how well you heal from otherwise mortal injury would be valuable data. Try not to get hurt if you do not want to undergo those sorts of tests." Even in my current state, I felt a twinge of fear. I had a feeling I would be undergoing those tests whether I liked it or not.

"Well, let's get this over with." Upon saying this, the room shifted in a nauseating manner. I was now in a warehouse of sorts, with metallic walls, catwalks above, and crates lining the floor around me. I was in some kind of holographic chamber. The CORPS had definitely upgraded in ways even I had never imagined.

"You have one external implant that is vital to your survival. If you grind the back of your teeth on the right side, you will feel a click." I looked up in a bit of shock at that.

"Excuse me?" but didn't get an answer. What I got instead was the immediate feeling of intense dread. Reflexively, my eyes focused on two of the crates in front of me. A CORPS Elite was standing between them with a sidearm aimed at me. I could feel as if the world slowed down for a moment, my eyes fixating on the barrel of his weapon. I immediately dove to the right, behind another crate, watching the sparks from the ricocheting round, mere

78

centimeters from where my head was. I scrambled, moving a few more containers down the line and put my back against it.

"Fine, okay, tooth." I did as I was instructed, finding it odd I hadn't noticed it before. I had to do a sort of underbite to get at it and apply a decent amount of pressure. It would be pretty hard to accidentally hit it while eating. With a click, a most disconcerting piercing feeling came from under my forehead just above my right eye. It didn't necessarily hurt, but it didn't feel pleasant either. A small rod protruded from my skull, before opening in front of my eye, revealing a circular screen. Immediately a heads-up display appeared, and I could see a map of the area I was in. From it, I spotted three enemies moving in, including the one that had fired uncomfortably close by. I could tell what direction they were looking, and their distance and speed. I now had a strange but assured understanding of the composition of the materials around me, how strong they were, what weights they could sustain. It was all coming in an instant.

Back up against the crate, I could see a soldier coming closer, right up to the edge of where I was. I had no weapon, no plan of attack, and my training never included hand-to-hand combat. I had to try, though. As he walked by, I reached out and grabbed his ankle, yanking as hard as I could. Apparently, as hard as I could was some next-level strength, because as I pulled, he came smashing to the ground, rag dolling against the crate in front of me. When he rolled to face me, I lost no time, making a fist and smashing it into his masked face with a bone-crunching sound. He went limp immediately.

There were two more still in the room, moving into flanking positions on either side of the warehous. I reached down and grabbed the gun off the corpse of the first bogey. They were closing in and closing in fast. It would only be a second before I was in their sight. I looked up at the crate in front of me and got that urge you get when you know you can make a jump. So, I leapt. I leapt hard up and forward, clearing four meters in a startling burst. I sailed over the crate in front of me, hearing gunshots as I landed. I dashed to the right, moving at breakneck speed. It was fast and furious, my heart not pounding though, instead beating steadily, moving to the rhythm of my body.

I was coming up alongside the soldier that was to my right. I didn't have to pay attention to the readout. Whatever it was they did to me, made me take in all the things I saw, including the HUD. Under normal circumstances, it would have been distracting.

I knew I was going to quickly come up to where the other soldier was. As I stepped by his cover, I decided to do something we only saw in the entertainment districts. I dove hard to the side. Everything was happening fast, but for me and my reflexes, I might as well have been slowly falling. I fired once, and my shot was accurate, popping him in the side of the head and slamming it into the container behind him, creating a spatter of blood. The grisly sight was shocking, but only somewhere deep down inside.

I had no time to celebrate any kind of victory. I saw it before I heard it, the third soldier had done what I did, but instead landed on top of a crate not far from me. I could see him there, a sub-machine gun in his hand. As my arm raised to aim, he fired. My shot got off, and I knew it would land, but so did his, two shots striking me in the gut. I could feel all the wind get knocked out of me as the force slammed me to the ground. My bullet found purchase in the soldier's forehead, however, spraying viscera behind him.

"Gah, fuck!" I cried out as blood spat from my mouth. I could feel the exit wounds behind me. The world wasn't getting dark, and I wasn't getting weaker, though. I slid, so my back was against a crate. The blood wasn't free-flowing and had already begun to slow.

"Very impressive." I heard Ronyn's voice above me. The environment slowly faded into the bleak blackness from before. My breathing was painful and labored, but the pain was fading. Whether from healing or some sort of painkiller from the nanobots, I had no idea. Knowing how things were going, it was probably both.

"Right now, the machines inside of you are keeping you up and active. The blood flow should be stopped, and the nanomachines are working overtime, sealing your wound. It will take a few hours for them to get you back into any working condition." The door that I had entered from slid open, and it was at this time I realized I didn't have the gun anymore. It was probably a hologram-like the rest of everything else that had appeared. My eight guards came piling in, and two of them picked me up by my arms. I shrugged them off as I stood, with a stubborn look. Slowly I began to walk on my own back down to my cell.

From the hallway, I heard Alonna's voice. "Move out of my way!" She appeared through the door before I could hobble towards it. She took one good look at me, and then she seemed to glare at the right wall a moment. She knew where to look to give Ronyn a death glare.

"I just wanna lay down, doc." My tone was frustrated, but also somewhat defeated.

She took a penlight from her pocket and shined it in my eyes a moment. "Yes, I'm sure you do. Well, considering it was a simulation, any bullet fragments have already been removed. Can you walk?" There was actual concern on her face. I half expected her to ask me a million inane questions about the pain I was in. Instead, she seemed to care about her patients.

"I'm walkin' now, ain't I?" Standing there wasn't getting any harder like it should have been.

"So you are." She looked to one of my guards. "Make sure he makes it back to bed." Her eyes made their way back to me. "Please don't be stubborn. The healing process works better when you are resting." I wanted to roll my eyes, but instead, I nodded almost sheepishly and, along with my crew of creepy bastards, left for my room.

Everything was absolutely surreal. There I was, gut-shot. I should've bled out back in that chamber. Instead, I was walking back to my bedroom on my own steam, somehow still able to function. I clicked my tooth and let the computer slide back into my forehead, leaving no mark of its presence behind. My walk was almost a limp as I held my right arm over my torso, where I had been shot. The guards didn't seem to be in any kind of rush.

My head was swimming, and absolutely nothing about this made sense. How did I end up in this situation? There was no way they could have orchestrated our desire to leave the Undercities. That was natural, right? I really couldn't tell. I was a puppet, but I couldn't let my spirits get crushed. I had to keep my goal in mind. One day, somehow, I was going to kill Xavier Ronyn and make him regret every augmentation he authorized. I really had nothing else left.

The walk of shame ended with me shuffling into my room and sitting, slouched on the bed. The pain was there, but tolerable and ever improving. I felt like crying but knew I wouldn't be able to bring myself to do it. I don't know how long I sat there in silence, at least I wasn't paying attention to the time anyway. Finally, the door slid open, and Alonna walked in once more.

"Good evening John." Her voice was soft and sympathetic. Somehow, I don't think her ethics mirrored those of Ronyn's. "How are you holding up?"

"Livin' the dream, doc," I gave a sarcastic chuckle. "Weird fuckin' question for the poor bastard shot in the gut." I looked up at her and could tell she was feeling guilt deep down. She hadn't pulled the trigger, but where does the moral line really lie?

"Well, your answers are very telling. Can you lay back, please?" She requested, moving the chair next to the bed and sitting down. I gave her a look, a hint of defiance before I eventually complied.

"Very fascinating." While she was good at playing a sympathetic game, she was horrible at making me not feel like a lab rat. "Take a look at this." She was pointing at the bullet holes in my stomach. I sat up on my elbows and looked down. There was scarring where a wound should've been.

"What the hell?" The bleeding having stopped was one thing, and the fact that they weren't quick to give me medical attention had rendered me unworried about the wounds themselves, but it was an accelerated healing that bordered the fantastical.

"I told you. The nanomachines can provide you any compound you need. Blood cells, skin, muscle, even bone, and marrow. Your skin will likely heal before anything else. Can you tell me how you feel physically?" I laid back down with a wince.

"I dunno. It hurts, but it feels like the pain is being dulled. I have less energy than I had before. My body wants to rest. Also, I'm hungry. It's a weird kind of hungry."

"Your digestive system is no longer what it once was, so that's not surprising. The nanomachines will need you to replace the matter they are using to repair your body. Food and anything else you consume will work. It works best if you try and go for nutrients and compounds that they need to only slightly convert, otherwise, certain processes, such as healing, will take longer."

"So still have a balanced diet for a growin' boy?"

"Basically. You can survive on sand if you had to, but it's not preferable." I sat up again and gave her a stupified look.

"Sand? Like, soil, dirt?"

"Indeed. There are many compounds in the soil that they would be able to utilize." I shook my head and laid back down.

"Beginning to think Lys was the lucky one."

"Dead is never lucky, John. We are here to survive, and soon enough, you will be surviving better than anyone walking on this world."

"Yeah, until you make more." I scoffed.

"Be that as it may. You *are* the lucky one. You just don't know it yet. Now hold still, please." She took a vital-pak out of her pocket. It was a small device, rounded on one side, flat on the other, and roughly twenty centimeters long. It attached to the forehead and provided a full set of vital readings to a PCD. She pulled her pad out and looked over the data. "Well, you are in extreme health and healing a bit more rapidly than we predicted. Can I level with you, John?" She placed the pad onto her lap, looking to me. I turned my head, making eye contact.

"Sure."

"You're lucky you decided to get shot today. Ronyn has absolutely no regard for medical ethics. He's not a medical doctor in the traditional sense. Do not test him." She was almost pleading. "He knows he has his life ahead

84

of him. You are not irreplaceable."

"Alright. I gotcha." I gave her my best attempt at a reassuring smile before looking back up at the ceiling. "Can I sleep anymore?" I asked truthfully.

"Yes, actually. Your systems can go into a power conservation mode, but your sensor suite will remain active. It will be a bit like sleeping with one eye open. Sleeping will also accelerate your healing process. Should your injuries be truly horrific, the nanomachines may even place you into a restorative coma, so try to be mindful of where you are when you decide to do questionable things." She gave me a warm smile, and I couldn't help but let my guard down. At that point, any kind of compassion was welcomed. She was definitely good at her job.

"Don't lose limbs in a war zone, got it- wait. What happens if I do lose a limb?"

"Honestly? I can tell you what should happen." She said gravely.

"Should?" I quirked a brow.

"Yes, should. You are somewhat of a prototype, John, we are learning from your experiences. Suffice to say, if the nanomachines function properly, you should, eventually, regenerate any lost body part, including the augmentations that went with them. Depending on what you lost would dictate how long it took. Some injuries could take days, others could take weeks or even longer. In fact, part of the time you spent asleep was the nanomachines repairing your body post-surgery." I let it all sink in. I had to learn everything I could about what they did, and what I could do. If I had any hope at all in freedom, somehow, someway, it'd be the machines the CORPS shoved into me.

"Alright, I think I gotcha. So, gut-shot with decently high caliber rounds doesn't count as bad enough?" She laughed at the question.

"No, John, not quite. I hate to burst your bubble, but there was not much vital where the bullets actually passed. Under normal circumstances, bleeding out would have been what killed you. Now, I have some questions if you don't mind."

"I guess I can give ya a chance, doc. I ain't got nothing better to do than piss and whine about my new piercings." She gave a bit of a giggle, and I waved my hand, finally meeting her eyes. "Ask away."

"Can you describe your perception. How did things look to you, and was there anything you would not consider normal that you perceived?" She had her PCD in hand again.

"Uh, well," I sat back a bit on my elbow, so I was lying on my side, facing her. "The same thing I notice now, really. Everything."

"Everything?"

"Yeah. A mote of dust can't fall without my knowing about it. I don't have to pay attention either, it all comes in and processes as easily as anything did. I guess that's weird." She seemed to be typing on her screen as I spoke. "I guess the weirdest thing is the soldiers seemed slow."

"Can you elaborate please." The scientist was coming back into her voice.

"Well, at first, I thought maybe it was some kinda glitch in the hologram, which considering everything about it would've been forgivable, but then I realized they weren't moving slow, I was moving fast. The effect seemed to get stronger during tense moments."

"Hmm, that's interesting. We were wondering how your brain would compensate for the heightened awareness. It seems your awareness voluntarily increases and decreases with the need. It takes a lot of energy to make your mind and body move at the speeds it is now capable of." She explained it all as if it was simple elementary, but it still hadn't been a day since I woke up a cyborg and ended up with new holes. New holes that were now scars, fading ones at that.

"Yeah well, it's fuckin' weird let me tell ya. It's hard to get used to, yet at the same time, it ain't. Not sure if I'm making any sense."

"Good, I am glad you segued into that line of thinking. Your emotional responses, can you describe them for me? We can always wait if any of this is too difficult." She got that warm look about her again.

"Nah, y'see, that's the problem. It isn't tough, but it should be. I should be in a ball crying in the corner, and yet here I am, nonchalantly describing it to you like it was no big thing. Yet-" I trailed off thinking about earlier.

"Yet?" She insisted, and I met her gaze once again, with a severe look in my eye.

"Yet if I wanted to, I could channel everything into a righteous rage." I left it at that. The look on her face told me everything I needed to know.

"Well, I think I will leave you to rest. That's enough questions for now."

"What, no more tests? You guys haven't bludgeoned my head in yet, the day is still young."

"Well, if I were you, I would keep ideas like that to yourself and away from Doctor Ronyn." I peered at her a moment before giving a scoff.

"That bald prick doesn't scare me." I caught the smirk that came across her face when I said this.

"We shall see. Food will be sent to you soon. It is absolutely imperative you eat as much as you can." The door to my room slid open, and she stood to leave.

"Sure thing, ma." I gave her a wink, and she shook her head, leaving me once again to my solitude. I laid back and put my hands behind my head, relaxing there a moment, letting all of the things I had learned sink in and process. Getting out of this place wasn't going to be easy, and I would be a fool to think they weren't using the machines inside of me for tracking. There had to be a way around it.

It wasn't long before my door opened again, and a short, wire-framed man entered the room. He was young, maybe twenty, with a crew cut and wide eyes. Hurriedly, he set my tray of food down and quickly rushed out of the room, like some sort of boogeyman was behind him. To be fair, I can't say I blamed the poor kid.

I walked over to the little table that was in the room, where the tray had been left and realized they had provided a personal feast. The plate consisted of some sort of meat that looked like poultry, with three different vegetables and even a fruit side. There was a strange, gray-colored drink that had a decidedly bland taste to it, as well as a glass of water.

"Well, damn. Happy holidays tonight." I was starving, absolutely ravenous. It was a type of hunger I hadn't felt before, and I also hadn't noticed until the food was right in front of me. I suppose it wouldn't be to my advantage suffering from hunger pains. I sat and began to eat. It was the first real meal I could remember since the night before leaving for the surface. If I was to believe what I had been told, it was my first meal in years. I ate heartily. I also ate quietly, not really thinking about anything in particular, instead, just enjoying the moment. It was what I had.

Finally, I had finished and shuffled back to my bed, plopping down. I could feel my eyes get heavy, and slowly, I drifted to sleep, sort of. It was a strange kind of sleep. I was aware of the room and what was going on. I was aware of when the same assistant showed up to take my tray. I could sense a mote of dust as it floated through the air system. Despite this, I dreamed.

Chapter Ten: Old Friends

I found myself drifting, watching a group of friends in a late-night pub, somewhere in an entertainment module. There was music, there was merriment, but the friends were dire, serious about the task ahead of them. They knew it would be their end, but is it better to die old and stale or young with glory?

I floated through the air and found myself staring down a long tube, an ancient tram system, left forgotten. The people on one side were forever sequestered away from the world beyond, and on the other, monsters lurked. I flew on, flying by the ravenous teeth and claws of the beasts, skimming through the gunfire, the blood. I flew to the sky, the endless expanse of the world beneath me. I flew up, beyond that lobby, the waiting room of servitude and let myself be free.

The testing, the fighting, the simulations, and the questions all continued. First for days and then days became weeks and weeks became months. If it weren't for the implants, I would have lost track of time and my sanity.

They had me fight a wide variety of enemies. Creatures from the surface, contingencies of CORPS troopers, rioting citizenry, anything they could think of to throw at me. I learned a lot about what I could do. My strength had increased and could be further enhanced to incredible heights, amounting to nearly a ton of lifting power. My wound healing was more robust than I thought, turning aside what would have been otherwise crippling injuries and allowing me to go on despite them.

My headset computer could analyze substances I held and touched, right down to the molecular level. It can do this in a limited fashion at a distance as well. All of it thanks to the nanomachines running through my

All in all, I was a guinea pig. I rarely got a day to myself, always being dragged off for some other inane combat test. It was beginning to feel like all they cared about, especially when they brought me to the simulator room. Everyone except for Alonna began referring to me as *XR001,* fully reducing me to the status of a number.

One day I had been taken out of my room earlier than usual. Normally, Ronyn would take some time to remind me of my place in things, update me on stuff I didn't care about, and a plethora of other painfully mundane stuff a scientist you hate can think of. Today though, seemed different somehow.

"Good morning XR001." Ronyn's spine disrupting voice came over the intercom. "I hope you rested well. Today we conclude in house combat testing of your augmentations and implants."

"You must be overjoyed." I rolled my eyes.

"Excited would be the term I use. We are going to test your skills, problem-solving, and combat efficiency in one test today. At the conclusion, we will begin the next phase of the project."

"Y'know, I have no fuckin' clue why you feel it's necessary to tell me all of this. It's not like I can say, hey, you know what, fuck this, I'm out. Just cut the chatter, and let's do this." By that point, I had run out of patience for Ronyn. Every day he gave me new reasons to want to strangle him with his own entrails.

"Very well." With that, I extracted the headset above my eye and stood ready. The room shifted, something I had finally grown used to. The ceiling formed into a sort of gray, overcast sky, the ground becoming asphalt beneath my feet. I was on a city street of some sort. I began to run as soon as everything came into focus and just in time too. The simulation had started with two Elites aiming sidearms at me from either side, not ten meters away. I quickly dove for cover in a nearby alley.

"Cute," I muttered under my breath. There were ten others, I could sense them closing in. Five were coming from up the street to my right and three from the other side. There were two others in buildings on either side of the street above us. As I came to this realization, I stepped back two steps as a bullet ricocheted off the ground from a sniper who could see me. I was already cornered like an animal, but that was their problem.

I looked up at the buildings I was between and saw that the one with the other sniper was right next to me. There was no fire escape or anything, but there were windowsills. I crouched and then jumped, clearing roughly ten meters before my hands found purchase on a sill. With a great heave, I pulled myself up. Realizing the soldiers below were closing in, I smashed my fist through the window I was looking at. My hand was cut deeply, the blood slowing almost as soon as it spilled.

I crawled through the window into the condemned building. Most of the walls already rotted or broken. I was moving fast, disrupting the dust with my movements, feeling everything around me. Eventually, I made it to a door, where just behind it was one of the snipers. I reached down at my feet and picked up a piece of concrete lying among the wreckage of the building. I gave it a quick toss, caught it, and then kicked open the door.

My eyes focused as the door swung open, my body crouching and twisting into a spin. In a blurred motion, the piece of concrete left my hand and smashed into the turning head of the sniper, who was only just beginning to realize he had company. His head slammed back against the wall behind him, but the sniper across the street was already taking aim. Dashing forward, I managed to grab the body as it impacted the floor and swung it around to the window he had been in front of, tossing the corpse while I dove to the ground. As quickly as I did this, the body exploded into a spray of blood from the other sniper, trying to get a good shot of his actual target.

I reached for the rifle left by the dead soldier. With one hand, I swung the weapon around, using the sensor suite and headset to hip fire it, turning the dome of the sniper across the street into confetti.

Below me, three other soldiers were attempting to aim at me as the other five had found a way into the building and were quickly moving up the stairs. I walked almost casually over to the body of the sniper and pulled a sidearm from his hip. Glancing out the window, just far enough to avoid getting hit by the hail of gunfire from below, I could see a metal lamp post across the way. I took a couple steps back, aimed, and fired three shots at the pole, using my superhuman perception and calculation to ricochet three headshots into the bogeys below.

The soldiers in the building with me were only two floors away when I decided to pick the rifle back up. It was high powered and more than adequate. I aimed at the floor and began to fire, picking off three more utterly out of sight as the others finally made it to the level I was on.

The last two began to fire, hoping the plaster wouldn't stop rounds. They were right to try, as the plaster did nothing to stop me from using the pistol and popping the remaining enemies from my hidey-hole of a room. I heard the slow clanking of the final shell hitting the ground. My focus centered on the headset and then to my own senses. I was alone again. Slowly the world faded from focus, and the blackness of the simulator room greeted me once more.

"Truly impressive. Mostly unscathed even." I never could stand Ronyn's praise, not because it wasn't genuine, but because it *was*. It was pure, egotistical praise of his own genius. It was enough to make me sick.

"How often are we gonna do this, Ronyn? How many pixels do I have to orphan before you decide I work?"

"As I said, this was the last in-house combat trial. You are ready to begin testing in other areas and to embark on phase three."

"What's phase three?" The door opened, and a familiar voice spoke. It was a voice that, despite everything, what I already knew, and what had been done to me, absolutely floored me.

"Come with me, XR001, and I'll show you." It was Mick. He was standing there, PCD in his hand, a mostly expressionless look on his face. He was wearing a lab coat and rank-insignia that put him below Ronyn.

"You son of a bitch." I walked over to him with a purpose. I could tell he was nervous but stood his ground.

"I think you already know why that is a mistake, John." I got as close as I knew I could get, staring directly in his eyes.

"Why? Why you piece of shit?"

"Why what?" He asked without betraying emotion.

"You know what!"

"Because it was my job."

"Was he even really your brother? Huh?" I wanted so badly to wring his scrawny little neck.

"Yes, he was, and I'll remind you who shot him."

"Yeah, well, never forget who put him in a position to get shot."

94

"You're right, and if it makes you feel any better, I don't think I'll ever forgive myself for it." He gave me a grave look, and somehow, I believed him. The dumb prick was probably hoping his big brother would be picked for the project. It didn't matter. If anyone was higher on my list than Ronyn, it was Mick. "Now, are we going to sit here and argue all day, or are you ready to get to it?" He cocked his head slightly to the side, almost arrogantly as he asked the question.

"Lead the way." My eyes never left him. He began to walk down the halls, leading me to another section of the facility, allowing me to learn more about its layout. The place would likely seem labyrinthine to the casual observer, but I could tell the structure was circular in shape. The modular design was probably a security precaution due to the nature of the project. Having it in one fixed location was an obvious liability, but to what I had to wonder. Did the CORPS have enemies on the surface? All the combat training wasn't for nothing, and I couldn't help but notice areas that looked similar to the one that led to my cell.

Eventually, we came to another nondescript door, which dutifully slid open for us. I could see down the hall before entering that many of the doors were spaced far apart, giving the impression that each was the gateway to a large room. The room we entered confirmed my suspicion through its size. It was about half the size of the training simulator, but its back wall was dominated by a massive set of screens and computer systems. With the level of technology the CORPS could bring to bear, any computer that size had to be an impressive piece of work. Mick walked to a leather swivel chair in front of the computer panels and spun it around to face me.

"Take a seat." I shrugged my shoulders and walked over to the chair.

It wasn't like I had any real choice in the matter. If I wanted to escape, I had to cooperate for as long as necessary. "Good. Ronyn said you would be defiant."

"If listening to your dead ass means Ronyn was wrong about something, that's fine with me."

"Charming. Okay." He grabbed a nearby chair on wheels and took a seat next to me "I'm sure you have questions. It will probably make this go faster if you ask those first instead of me giving you a big speech." He was a professional at work; it seemed his demeanor was one of business.

"You can start with why the hell I have to deal with you. Is this some sick joke?"

"No, but it seems like it doesn't it? You're dealing with me because I wrote the software used inside that once hollow skull of yours." I gave him a disapproving look at the comment.

"You're not helping your future chances for survival."

"Neither are your incessant threats for you. Look, we're stuck in this together, so you might as well deal." He donned a sincere look, trying to make peace with me.

"Not like I have much choice, do I? Fine, so what's next?" I crossed my arms over my chest and leaned back in my chair.

"We're going to test your recall and interface systems." I quirked a brow.

"I'm sorry, interface?"

"Yes. You have the capacity to interface with many different computer systems, as long as you can get an entry of some kind, such as through a port." He must've noticed the look on my face. "Don't worry, I'll walk you through
96

it."

"Thanks, dad." My voice dripped with sarcasm.

"Extend your CIHUD." He pronounced it as *sigh-hud*. I just looked at him like he was speaking a foreign language.

"The fuck is a CIHUD?"

"The device that comes out of your head, you simple ape." He shook his head in frustration. "It stands for Cybernetically Integrated Heads-Up Display."

"Man, you clowns really like your acronyms, huh?" I bit down, and the CIHUD extended out. "Whoa man, you guys are good. This thing says you're a dick. Uncanny accuracy."

"Are you done?" He rolled his eyes at me.

"Nope, but get on with it anyway." He reached down to one of the panels below the large screen and opened it. From it, he produced a cord attached to a BUD (Basic Universal Data) port. He handed it to me, "what do you expect me to do with that?"

"Put it up to the tip of the CIHUD, like you were going to hook up to it." I shook my head and did as he stated. While I could only feel the movement of it, I could tell that the tip that protruded from the CIHUD was somehow transforming. Eventually, I heard a click. As soon as it happened, my whole body jerked, and my senses were assailed with sensations, I couldn't quite describe. Everything was rushing in, and it almost felt like my head was beginning to swell. I had nearly moved to rip the cord out before it subsided, and I became keenly aware of the computer system in front of me. Its systems and processes were becoming part of my own mind.

"How do you feel?" I stared at him for a moment, and the screen next to us flashed to life. A small window opened up on the screen with a text cursor. It began to type "Like I want to strangle you." onto the screen.

"You just don't stop, do you? Fine, well, it seems that it is as intuitive as we initially thought. You have access to the system here, but the access is not total. You are hooked into the computer, but the computer is not hooked into you. There are redundant systems in place to ensure that you couldn't necessarily be hacked through your CIHUD."

"Necessarily?" I didn't speak the question, instead allowing the computer to do the talking.

"Anyone with access to your system's original architecture could probably find a backdoor. Always use caution." He spoke the last bit clinically, without an ounce of actual concern to be found. I was barely listening, truth be told. The sensations were hard to process, even with my augmentations. It was almost like accessing the computer system was akin to moving parts of my body, and the information I was reading was like pulling up memories. I could move to different areas and then remember the data there.

The system was blocked on all sides. I didn't have much knowledge of computers, and even while hooked up to one, I barely knew what to do with it. "So what's the point? I'm no hacker, whether it's a keyboard or my brain."

"Not yet, anyway. Unhook yourself, the CIHUD will know your intent and disconnect you safely."

"I hear and obey." My sarcasm didn't seem to phase him as I grasped the cord hanging in front of my forehead and pulled lightly. It virtually fell off the needle. "Hey, I can't help the curiosity, how the hell did that work?"

"You mean the port?" I nodded. "It's made of an alloy that has fibers all over its surface. The CIHUD uses your sensor suite and normal perceptions to figure out what sort of port it is and then attaches itself as needed. Here, you'll want to keep this." He grabbed the cable that was hooked into the computer, unhooking it and handing it to me. "It's an extension cord, basically." I took it and wrapped it up, keeping it in my hand for now. "Also, this." He reached into a large pocket at the side of his lab coat and handed me a thin black PCD.

"And what is this?"

"Some books for you to read. You aren't a hacker now, but you will be by tomorrow morning."

"What?" I gave him an incredulous look. "You expect me to read a book, let alone more than one by tomorrow? The fuck am I in school all of a sudden?"

"Pretty much." He gave out a laugh that made me want to grind his face into the tile floor below us. "Don't worry, I'm quite frankly jealous of how quickly you can read. You can read it the old-fashioned way or use your new toy. Your choice, but tomorrow there will be a test." His grin was almost sadistic. The door we had come through opened, and two fully loaded CORPS soldiers entered, waiting for me silently.

"Mick, I mean this with sincerity," I said, standing and meeting his gaze. "I will kill you and not just for your brother. He's the cherry. I hold you responsible for Lys and that, mother fucker, should keep you up at night." For once, Mick had nothing to say, turning his own gaze to the floor. Part of me couldn't help but think he was waiting for the day almost as eagerly as I was. I walked over to my chaperons. "Lead on, boss." One moved to walk ahead of me, the other staying behind me. They led me back to my room.

When I got back to my cell, I took a seat at my bed and soon realized there was a delicious smell coming from the small desk. I looked up and saw a tray full of food. There was some sort of meat, mashed potatoes, a few vegetables I didn't recognize but smelled delicious. It was another mountain of food. On the tray was a small piece of paper with delicate, almost beautiful handwriting.

"For your morale." I read aloud and couldn't help but smirk. There was only one person I had met so far that looked like she had any form of compassion. Maybe the good doctor had a crush on me? While the thought of a CORPS scientist liking me was utterly revolting, my mind was wandering to the more carnal side of my fantasies. It was surprising, really, the only bit of irrational thinking I had done since waking up. "Thanks, guys, the one thing you leave is a fuckin' libido. Great." I muttered to myself while grabbing the tray and taking a seat.

As I ate, I grabbed the PCD Mick had given me. As my finger tapped the screen, it came to life, showing some icons representing ten books. Computer theory, a guide to various languages, hacking and cracking, you name it, it was there. "So much for light reading." I took a large bite of meat, some sort of poultry, and clicked the book on computer theory and started with the basics.

Flipping through the pages, I noticed something astonishing. Just glancing at the book allowed me to read it and even comprehend it. I could just fly through, scrolling passed each page and then remembering everything about it. Character count, verbatim recitation, even the general concepts of the words themselves. It was as if just seeing it was enough. I had to admit, it was an awesome experience and could be beyond useful.

I got through about half of the books before I decided to play around a bit. Sure, I absolutely hated the CORPS and everything they had done to my family and me, but I wasn't a fool. Hell, I would've beat my ass as a little kid for the opportunity to have superpowers. I would never forgive Mick, Ronyn, or any of the bastards in this organization, but silently I thanked them for the means to exact vengeance. Patience would win out, and I would eventually make them regret their decisions.

Chapter Eleven: A Handle On Things

I never really sleapt well after my awakening. While I was capable of a sort of sleep that allowed me to pass the time more quickly, it wasn't the same thing. Sometimes I still had dreams, but why sleep if I didn't need to? Honestly, I never really liked sleeping. Imagine how many hours are wasted in life just lying motionless in a bed, getting nothing done. I spent my entire life sleeping, I would take the opportunity to be awake.

After an evening's worth of time, the door opened again, revealing Alonna. "Well, well, I was expecting good old Mick this morning." She quirked a brow, pausing a moment before entering the room. The door closed behind her before delicately sitting on the chair at my desk. She swiveled to face me and crossed her legs.

"Mick, you mean your escort?"

"Yeah, y' know I never thought to ask him his real name. Don't need to know a dead man's name." I spoke in a matter of fact manner like it was some sort of lost wisdom.

"A dead man?" Alonna tilted her head.

"Look, Ronyn is always on my list, always will be, but that son of a bitch pretended to be my friend. He let his own brother died. The one woman on this planet I actually understood, died in my arms because of his bullshit machinations. I don't care if I die in the process, Mick is a dead man walking." I met her gaze, and part of me was trying to freak her out again, hoping maybe she'd leave the room. Instead, her gaze made me uncomfortable. She was staring into my eyes, almost deeply, seemingly distracted. I could tell her heart rate was elevated like she was nervous, but not afraid.

"Well, I do not believe that will be happening any time soon, so shall we get on with our day?" Her voice carried a diplomatic tone to it.

"Sure, whatever. What strings are they pulling on this puppet today?"

"Oh John, no need to be so dark about it, soon you will be going outside." Even the implants couldn't prevent the rush of excitement that washed over me. I had only seen the sky once, briefly before it was cruelly ripped away from me. The prospect of seeing it again made me almost giddy like a child.

"Alright, you've got my attention, doc." I leaned forward, intently listening to her every word. Despite everything they had done to me, she was damn good at manipulating my behavior.

"We're going to have Doctor Rolley finish his computer training with you today."

"Wait, wait." I interrupted her. "His name is Rolley? What a fuckin' loser." She snorted in laughter at this sudden outburst. I couldn't help but grin before thinking better of it, donning my best sour puss.

"In more ways than you know. Once he has completed your training, you will be briefed on the first official field test they will be sending you on."

"Field test?"

"Yes. You will be sent on a mission of sorts. I don't know the specific details, but it will certainly involve travel." She was lying about not knowing, I could tell by the spike in her vitals and the nervousness that betrayed her voice. I decided not to press it.

"Can I ask you something?"

"Of course. That is why I am here." She smiled, and her nervousness began to fade. She clearly wasn't expecting me to be so cordial about the conversation.

"Why are you always the one coming in to tell me about stuff? What I'm going to do, what I'm supposed to eat, how my healing works. Like I get that you invented the nanobots, but it feels like it's more than that. Like you're my personal doctor or something." Oddly, the question made her blush.

"Well, because I am. I am your Handler, John. It is my job to watch over you, make sure everything is in working order, and to attend to you medically if need be. I am even meant to be your counselor and morale officer. I am, for all intents and purposes, your primary care physician, among other things."

"Huh, well, that's interesting. Hey, if it makes you feel better, your very presence isn't disgusting me right now. Guess they picked well." She rolled her eyes at my statement, but despite it, I could sense empathy from her and somehow a bit of sadness too. There was something personal about all of this for her, and I couldn't quite pinpoint what it was.

"Anyway, it is important that you understand the dangers you may encounter. I hope you ate your meal?" I smiled at the question.

"It was actually the best one I've had in a very long time. Even better than the first one. Y'know, lately, they just slap a bowl of unflavored slop on my table and call it good."

"That slop is a mix that contains everything a growing boy needs. Now, with your permission, I would like to examine you before they send you out tomorrow."

"Wait." I stopped her a little confused "I'm really leaving that soon?"

"Yes," she answered simply before pulling a small scanning device from her coat pocket. "However, you are not my only responsibility, and I may be unavailable." She was lying again. "I want to make sure I dot all my i's and cross all of my t's." Once more, I chose not to question it. My gut told me it was the right course of action.

"Fair enough." She walked over to me before waving the device across the vital areas of my torso. She looked over the small screen that was on its side and then pulled a needle from her other pocket.

"Blood sample?" She asked politely.

"I mean, am I even allowed to say no?"

"No, but I would prefer to have your permission." She really didn't share the ethics of the monsters around her. If she wasn't obviously brilliant, she wouldn't belong in that setting. With a shrug, I rolled up my sleeve and presented my arm to her. She tied a tunicate and then expertly retrieved a file of blood from my system. She detached the vial from the needle and then attached it to the head of her scanner. "Happy little nanobots. You're cleared to see the sky, John."

"I, uh. Thanks, I guess." I was a bit taken aback by the entire conversation. I wasn't sure how long I had been in that facility, let alone conscious while there, but it felt like years. In reality, it had only been six months, but now every minute was going to drag on in the worst kind of way.

"Anytime. Be careful out there, you're more precious than you know." Her hand rested on my shoulder for a bit, and she stared into my eyes again. I felt creeped out by it, like the look you expect a stalker to give you. Her tone was also disconcerting like she was saying goodbye for more than just a day. Eventually, she turned and exited my room. Immediately after, my ever-silent escorts showed up.

"Heya fellas, catch the big game last night?" They didn't even move.

"No? You guys are a fuckin' hoot, y'know that?" I got up and pushed passed them to exit the room. They quickly assumed their usual formation around me, walking me down the halls back towards the simulator rooms. I could feel the frustration growing inside of me as I had hoped this place was finally behind me. When we got to the door, I just angrily walked through it.

"Here, I am dickheads. Another day to screw with me, right?" I had my arms out and gave a little spin and strut as I walked into the room. Ronyn wasn't present this time; instead, Mick's voice came over the intercom.

"That's right big guy. My turn to have a little fun. Now, this simulation isn't like the combat ones you're used to. There are objectives, and if you fail them, you will be required to try again. I'll keep you up all night long if I have to."

"Oh, baby, don't get me excited now." I attacked with my usual blend of sarcasm and hatred. "So what are we doing today, Mickey? Blowing up an orphanage, stealing plans for a doomsday device? Can we make it a little interesting for once?"

"Oh, this will be very interesting. You will find yourself inside an enemy compound. Your mission will be to infiltrate. No one is to know you are there, and no one is to see you leave. I can't stress this enough, if they find a body before extraction, the simulation will end, and you will need to restart it. Inside the simulated compound, you are to find their mainframe, interface with it and obtain a list of locations of other bases. Once you have obtained this information, you leave the way you came." I rolled my eyes and prepared myself.

In all honesty, it wasn't even worth describing the test. I want to say it was tense, that there were narrow halls and cunning traps, but what fun is infiltrating when you don't even have to see everything? You duck under a box here, slide behind a wall there, knock a fucker out if it suits you. It feels like cheating.

The compound itself seemed like something someone who played too many cheesy stealth games as a kid would have cooked up. Dimly lit for some reason, guards walking in patterns. Frankly, it was almost insulting. It wasn't until I got to the mainframe room that I realized where the real challenge would lie. It was even less lit up than the rest of the place, containing row after row of large servers. The room was at an unholy high temperature from the heat of the machines. It wouldn't be a very comfortable data extraction, to say the least.

I moved through the room, bee-lining it for the terminal I could sense. It was a simple affair, a small keyboard and screen sticking out of the side of one of the server stacks. I reached into a side pocket my slacks had and produced the cable that Mick had given me. By this point, my CIHUD was already out, so I hooked myself in. The strange, almost shock-like sensation that ran through me would be something I'd never get used to, but it faded quickly. It was then that I had a moment of horror. My senses were dulled, and I was left only with the five feeble ones I was born with.

"Shit, shit, shit," I whispered and crouched low as I heard the door slide open. I would somehow have to concentrate on hacking the server while avoiding detection from enemies I couldn't sense. The little prick upstairs was probably laughing it up. "Okay, think, concentrate," I muttered to myself and closed my eyes for a moment.

I found myself standing in a blackened room, like the one I was in when Ronyn first introduced himself, inside of my head. I realized I had a modicum of control over the environment. Concentrating, I could suddenly see numbers and words floating about all around me. The system was encrypted, and I would need to break it. I took a quick peek at the real world for a minute. I could see one guard, moving up a different row. It seemed like time moved slower while I was using the system, buying me some time.

I closed my eyes again and looked at the encryption. A day before, it would have been utter gibberish to me, but even at the speeds the data was floating, I was able to pick out and discern patterns. There was an equation to it all, and it seemed kind of hilarious to me that I was even able to pick it out. Sure, the books that Mick had provided had some math in it, but I was also remembering all of the crap I never paid attention to in school. Having perfect recall had its perks. I worked out the encryption and found myself in the simulated file system. After that, finding the information was a piece of cake.

"Hey! Is someone there?" I heard emanating from reality. I opened my eyes and could barely see between the stacks. The guard had his weapon raised, clicking on a flashlight. He hadn't noticed me yet. I disconnected my CIHUD, which gave no resistance as promised. I scrambled off behind the adjacent stack and waited, my breathing completely stopping, though I wasn't precisely holding my breath. More perks of the cybernetic life.

"Okay," I thought to myself. "Just wait for the curious prick to move away, and you'll be fine."

"What's this?" I hear, finally able to sense my surroundings again. I realized that even in my augmented state, I was still capable of boneheaded moves. I left my cable attached to the terminal. Being able to sense my opponent now, it was time to take him down. Then I stopped and realized I couldn't get caught. Leaving a body behind wasn't conducive to a quiet exit.

Quietly I made my way to the door I came through and made sure it made plenty of noise when I opened it before ducking back into the shadows.

"What the hell?" I could sense him rushing for the door as it closed shut. He opened the door again and looked back and forth, of course seeing nothing unusual. He reached a hand to his ear. "We may have a possible intruder. Begin sweep and clear protocols." The confirmation came soon after, and he exited the server room, assuming whoever it was had left. The simulation didn't end, indicating they needed to actually catch me or find real proof of my presence. I used it to my advantage and quickly made my way out of the bunker after retrieving my cable.

Upon making it to the elevator, that the training mission had started in, everything faded back to the eerie black of the simulation chamber.

"Congratulation. With that simple test, this concludes the beginning of Phase Three." Mick's voice came over the intercom.

"You do realize I have no fuckin' clue what the difference between the phases are right? I swear you guys just like hearing yourselves talk."

"Charming as always. If you want to know, Phase Three is field testing. As you may have been made aware, tomorrow, you're going outside."

Chapter Twelve: Jailbreak

The night went uneventfully after the simulation. It's one thing to be excited about something that's on the way, it's quite another when you are aware of every second that passes. Finally, the moment came.

The door to my room slid open, and my least favorite person, Ronyn, stood there.

"Great. You here to send me off, dad?" If my sarcasm had venom, I would've used it to kill him.

"No, I am here to brief your handler."

"My handler? I thought that was Alonna, ain't she already privy?" I raised a brow, a little confused.

"Indeed, she is your handler. However, the Administrator has her on other duties for the moment." From behind him, a tall and wiry young scientist emerged. He had short blonde hair and baby blue eyes that looked like they didn't have the first clue what was going on in the world. His lab coat looked a little big on him, which gave him an even more green appearance. He approached me.

"Greetings! I uh, I'm-"

"I don't care who you are," I said and looked to Ronyn. "You can't be serious." I knew Alonna was busy that day, but I was insulted by her replacement.

"XR001, you will learn very quickly that I am always serious. Doctor Langstan, please pay attention." I noticed something about Ronyn I had never seen before. His cold, icy demeanor had been disturbed by something. I would have loved to know what it was, but something clearly had pissed him off.

"You will accompany XR001 on a data extraction mission. The details are in your PCD. You are not a medic to the unit you will be with, he is your only concern, even if it costs your life. Am I understood?"

"Y-yes, sir. Of course, sir. XR001 will come back in one piece." The kid was nervous, and I had a feeling he wasn't exactly ready for what we were about to get into. What the hell was Alonna doing, and why wasn't there an adequate backup? This was very, un-CORPS-like behavior.

"I don't care how many pieces he comes back in as long as they are living."

"Y'know Ronyn, I am going to enjoy watching you die one day," I didn't even look at him, instead, meeting the gaze of the kid, which did nothing for his nervousness.

"I'm sure you will." I didn't like his answer. Casually he walked out and left me alone with my guards and the greenest kid you'd ever meet.

"Alright, kid, brief me then." I put my hands on my hips.

"Uh, well XR0-"

"Call me, John."

"Uh, right, John, let's make our way to the garage, and we'll talk there." He was fiddling with his PCD like he was trying to find the answer to my question. After a moment, he looked back up.

"Well, lead the way then." I motioned for him to lead on and followed when he left the room. Despite the demeanor I was trying to give off, I was excited. If it wasn't for the implants, I would've been bouncing off the walls in glee. I was going outside. The only time in my life I got to see the sky was through dirty glass, while holding my dying friend. The second time I would be planning my escape.

While I doubt the effort was necessary, I made sure to pay attention to the layout of the areas of the compound I hadn't been in yet. Just in case I ended up back there, it would be a good idea to know my way around. I was mostly silent on my way through the halls, contemplating what we were about to do. My mind was full of questions; what sort of data was I extracting, and most of all, from who? Was a compound overrun, or was I about to meet an enemy of the CORPS?

First, we stopped at a smaller hallway that ended with a door on either side. We entered the door on the right, and I saw what looked like a locker room. There were three rows with benches between them and a shower area nearby. On a bench closer to the door, there was a duffel bag.

"Please, get dressed. Everything you have been requisitioned is in that bag." He motioned to the bag and then waited patiently.

"A little privacy?"

"Oh, right. Of course." He moved to exit the room, and one of the guards just shook his head. "Oh, right, no, you'll be fine. Just get dressed."

"Should I do a little dance too?" He stumbled as if I expected him to answer the question. I just shook my head and went to the bag. What I noticed inside brought back a flood of memories from escaping the Undercities. It was *my* clothing, cleaned and pressed. It also contained most of the equipment I had brought, sans the gun because, of course, they took it. Shamelessly, I got dressed. When I was finished, I felt better than I had in a while. It's hard to feel confident when you're always shirtless.

"All done. I hope you enjoyed the view." He began to stammer again. "Let's just go."

"Right, of course." We exited the room and began to walk down the

112

halls again.

We made it to a broad set of double doors that looked reinforced, unlike the others. There were two guards there, dutifully waiting for those with the authorization to enter. Having it, they let us pass when the doors slid open. Beyond was a large garage. There were various vehicles inside with designs I had never seen before. Some had wheels and open tops with gunner seats. Others had metal treads wrapped around a complex set of wheels and cogs, complete with heavy armor and sporting a wicked-looking long barrel at the front. It looked like some sort of panic room on wheels, with guns.

At each area that a vehicle was parked, there was a station full of maintenance equipment such as lifts, powered wrenches, and welding machines. At the back, the entire wall appeared like it could lift-up, allowing some or all of the vehicles to exit at the same time. Workers and soldiers were buzzing all over the place, confirming manifests, climbing into various machines, and loading weapons. Obviously, I was going to have company.

I was led to one of the tanks without a turret. It was almost cylindrical in shape, with a spinning radar dish on top, and no windows to speak of. Clearly, this was operated through cameras and sensors. The back opened, the door sliding up and into the ceiling of the interior with a quiet whir. Almost simultaneously, a platform extended from the floor of the interior, resting on the ground, and inviting us to enter.

"This is our ride XR, er, John. Get in, please." He motioned for me to enter, and I obliged without protest. I was reasonably sure I could give him a hard time in other ways. The interior was lit with red lights, giving off a tense ambiance. Six other soldiers piled in with us, making the space more cramped than it already was. They were uncomfortably silent, not enjoying the banter you would expect from comrades at arms. Sometimes I wondered if they were even allowed to have personalities.

"So, what's the deal, bub?" I asked, looking to my substitute babysitter. There was a harness on each seat, and everyone began strapping-in. I chose to emulate them, safety first, after-all.

"Uh, the deal? Oh, right, the mission." He pulled out his PCD and began flipping through screens. "Okay, we are going to be sending you into a hot-zone."

"Hot-zone? I ain't military, I have no idea what you mean."

"It means you will be entering an area with alert enemies, most likely firing on our position."

"Oh, lovely, I don't feel alive unless someone's trying to kill me." Sarcasm was my shield. I didn't like the idea of being sent into the fray. While I had been running combat trials for months at that point, those were pixels I was shooting. There weren't any hopes and dreams behind those trigger fingers.

"Uhm, sure. Anyway, we will be providing cover-fire until you enter the compound. We want you to infiltrate the compound itself, and it's imperative you remain undetected. The idea is to make them think their base is being assaulted, which they will then repel. This should ensure they don't dump the data in their mainframe."

"And what data am I expected to get from these, wait, who are they anyway?"

"That's irrelevant, you-"

"No, we don't play that game here. Unless you want me to just sit my ass down and do absolutely nothing, you'll answer my question." I crossed my arms and put my back against the wall. I could feel the rumbling of the vehicle as we exited the garage. We were on our way; just beyond the walls of the pillbox was the horizon. It was almost distracting.

"Okay, um, well, they call themselves the Tantillan Liberation Front. I don't really know much about them, it's not my job." The name was a bit shocking. Tantillan Liberation Front? Was the Republic still alive? Could they have survived those past two centuries?

"Alright, fine, whatever, I still need to know what data I'm extracting."

"Of course. You are looking for topographical data concerning supply lines and the locations of other compounds." Another interesting bit of information to learn; the CORPS wasn't omniscient after-all. "Once you have this data, you are to leave the compound and meet us at these coordinates." He held up the PCD and showed a series of numbers.

"How the heck am I supposed to- wait," I squinted at the numbers as an odd sensation came over me, and I suddenly could decipher the coordinates. "What other shit have you inserted into my head?" I asked with a scowl.

"I haven't inserted anything!" He was clearly terrified of me. "Your systems can extrapolate your relative location once you're outside. Even during the day, the sky can be utilized to tell roughly where you are, just look up. From there, your computer can help lead you to the specified coordinates."

"What happens if I do get-" I didn't get time to finish the question as my senses seemed to go haywire for a moment, and I realized we were being fired upon. As soon as the sensation passed, I grabbed a strap that was dangling above me and braced myself. CORPS soldiers rarely reacted to anything, but everyone decided to follow suit. As soon as they did, we were hit by a mighty blow. Whatever had struck us sent the vehicle tumbling. While the harnesses kept us firmly in place, it did nothing for the whiplash effect.

Daylight crept into the vehicle from the side Dr. Langstan was sitting on, and I could see that it was caused by whatever hit us. After only a few seconds, the tank stopped tumbling, and I could hear the sounds of warfare outside. Gunfire and explosions were all around, but I couldn't sense anything beyond the vehicle I was in. Perhaps the armor was interfering.

I got my bearings almost immediately and looked around. Everyone on my side had survived and was beginning to get themselves unstrapped. The others, including the poor young doctor, were lying motionless. Half of Dr. Langstan's face was all but sheared off by whatever had entered the vehicle.

"Poor kid." I found myself saying. By now, the soldiers had managed to get the back hatch open and was fearlessly piling out. The battle didn't sound like it was slowing anytime soon. First, I went to a dead soldier in front of me and stripped him of his sidearm and the two mags he had. It was very similar to the one I used to carry; however, it looked like they miniaturized the kinetic absorption system. He also had a canteen of water and some other supplies that I stuffed into my bag.

Before moving to exit the vehicle, I stopped and looked at the body of Dr. Langstan. It was a shame really; the kid probably didn't have much choice in what life path he took. He lived and died for the most objectively evil organization that had ever existed. I looked down and found his PCD dropped on the floor near him. I stuffed it into my bag and took a deep breath before moving for the opened exit.

It seems every time I got to see something amazing for the first time, such as the local landscape, I wasn't allowed to enjoy it. Nevertheless, I took in as much detail as I was able. We were in a rocky, desert area with dirt and sand everywhere. We were in a valley of some sort with large hills dominating the terrain. The rocks nearby were the size of the vehicles we brought in, with a few larger ones dotting the landscape beyond the valley. The sun was high in the sky, shining brightly. My ocular implants made sure I wasn't blinded by it, and the others ensured I wasn't standing in rapt awe despite feeling it deep within.

The place was an absolute warzone. The CORPS had moved their vehicles into a circular formation and were defending their position fiercely. From the hills, I could see smaller, opened topped jeeps trying to rush into the fray. The CORPS was known for highly accurate soldiers, and several of the enemy drivers were popped off as soon as they were in sight, sending their jeeps crashing out of control. One came rolling down the hill straight towards me, and I calmly stood there as it crashed into the circle of vehicles next to me, debris flying, but leaving me unharmed.

Without looking, I took the sidearm I had found and popped the two enemy soldiers in the head that were trying to climb out of the wreckage and aim at me. From behind, a group of four CORPS Elites formed up in front of me as if to try and keep me safe. Obviously, they weren't briefed on their package as I felt I was in very little danger. I allowed my CIHUD to open and immediately was able to sense the entire battlefield.

The CORPS was losing badly. This was clearly an ambush, which suggested the Coalition had a mole of some kind. That fact alone would have kept me up at night with millions of questions. Ten vehicles were approaching, all with armed passengers, and somewhere beyond the valley, they had been firing artillery. It was probably what initially hit us.

Looking at the soldiers in front of me, I chose a course of action. I raised my gun and, in an instant, shot all four Elites that had surrounded me. After, I immediately took off running. Bullets were whizzing by, but my sensor-suite and ability to anticipate threats allowed me to stay clear of the crossfire. A few shots ricocheted off the magnetic field generated by my shoulder-piece; thankfully, they saw fit to give it back.

I was running at breakneck speeds before my enhanced senses picked up a pair of CORPS Elites behind me taking aim, likely for my legs. I stopped and jumped off with one foot, twisting and turning in mid-air. As my body spun, I fired off two shots, finding the heads of the two who were aiming at me. I finished the move by landing exactly where I was facing before and took off again. I was running towards a rock formation that was just on top of the valley I was facing. I was a sitting duck out there, and my ultimate goal was to obtain some real cover.

Nearing the top, I saw smaller two-wheeled vehicles come jumping over the hill, heading to the melee below. I could easily see as they passed me how the machines were operated and could sense two more on their way. When they drew close, right at the moment their acceleration dropped, near the top of the hill, I dove and kicked the rider closest to me off of their bike. The machine slid across the dirt as its former passenger rolled down the valley. I was already off and running, lifting the bike upright, hopping on, and speeding off.

With the plan changed up a bit, I was hoping I would be home free. I was out of sight of the CORPS troops and soon would be long gone. I was taken aback by the sheer size of the outside world, how far I could move, and yet have so much room. I must have somehow managed to zone-out for a second because I realized I was being shot at when a round whizzed past my head.

I began to weave and bob, trying to keep anything vital out of their sights. I didn't have to look behind me to realize one of the jeeps from the Resistance forces was on my tail, their gunner trying to get a clear shot. I knew it wouldn't be long before they had the bright idea to start firing at the easier to hit bike I was speeding on. I slowed my speed, allowing them to catch up.

"One, two," I counted out loud, bracing myself for the craziest stunt I had ever pulled. I pulled my right leg up and planted my foot on the seat before thrusting hard upward and launching myself several meters into the air. The trajectory and timing just right, I sailed above the chasing jeep and landed on top of the gunner. Catching my balance, I grabbed the back of the gunner's uniform. I violently tossed him off the back, sending him tumbling behind us.

When this occurred, the passenger turned to take aim, but it was already too late. With a quick flick of my sidearm, he slumped dead, bleeding on the dashboard. The driver, seeing all of this, sharply turned the wheel, sending the jeep careening to the side, flipping violently, and tossing us both from it. I was thankful for the kinetic harness as each rolling impact I made on the ground was dampened. It still hurt like a bastard, but I was mostly unscathed. The same couldn't be said for the driver who lied motionless beside the crashed vehicle.

Two other jeeps made their way to our position and came skidding to a stop in front of me. Both passengers and gunners were training their weapons in my direction.

"Drop your weapon and get down on the ground!" I tilted my head to the side, studying them, learning everything I could about them.

"Turn around. My fight isn't with you-"

"I said drop your fucking weapon!"

"This is your last chance. I don't want to have to kill you." I was sincere. While I knew the augmentations wouldn't allow me to hesitate to save my life, I personally had no beef with them. Hell, I was a bit proud of them. Anyone who could catch the CORPS with their pants down was not to be trifled with.

"We're not going to tell you again!" At this point, one of the passengers had hopped out of their seat, training a wicked-looking rifle on me.

"Sir, I think we found the target." I heard one of the drivers speak, probably into a radio. It suggested they had some idea of what they were dealing with. Still, I wasn't about to escape one group of yahoos only to be captured by another.

"And I won't tell *you* again. I don't want to kill you, but if I have to, I will. All of you." When I got to this part, I actually heard one of them laugh.

"What exactly do you think you can do? Just make this easy, and you'll be unharmed." By this point, the one that had begun to approach had gotten close enough. Before any of them could even blink, I grabbed the barrel of his rifle, used it to pull him to me, swung him around and held him in front like a human shield, my gun pressed to his head.

"Last chance. Driveaway, and I'll let him go." I could sense one was taking aim, his heart rate suggesting he was prepared to fire. Just as fast as I had grabbed the advancing soldier, I took aim and shot, striking the hand of the rifle-wielding passenger that was aiming. Quickly I retrained my weapon onto my hostage. "That's a bad idea."

For a moment, the soldiers looked at each other. Somehow, they found themselves in a stand-off when rightfully I should be in shackles on the way to whatever place they called home. One of the drivers stood up, sidearm trained at us, but not preparing to fire. "We don't want to hurt you. The General just wants to talk to you."

"So that's why you fired at me? Well, I don't want to talk to your general. Won't be long before the CORPS has you mopped up. They'll be back any second." I wasn't bluffing either. While I had gotten a decent distance from the fighting, I could tell by the distant weapons fire, that despite the ambush, the fight had shifted against the Resistance.

"That's not your choice. Drop your weapon! If you shoot, we open fire!"

"Then you don't get your quarry, do you?" Almost as if on cue, I saw one of the CORPS armored vehicles begin to climb over the ridge, and when we were in sight, they began firing. The gunners, drivers, and passengers turned around and began to return fire. Those guys were toast, and so was I if something wasn't done. I tossed the soldier I was holding onto the ground.

"Give me your grenade!" He looked at me puzzled before I reached down to his BDUs and pulled a grenade he had hanging from his front. I gave it a good long look, letting my scanning suite analyze the explosive. Yanking the pin and detaching the safety, I turned and looked to the advancing truck. By now, two of the soldiers had been felled, the remaining two frantically hoping to fend off the invader. I waited for a couple of seconds, knowing precisely when the device would go off.

I tried to think of something to say, but honestly, I was too concentrated on the moment. I tossed the grenade. It cut through the air like a low flying comet, sailing towards the advancing truck before going off right in front of the driver-side wheel. The vehicle lurched into the air and rolled several times, eventually coming to a rest in a flaming heap. The soldier I had released was on his hands and knees, staring at the fire in astonishment.

"If I haven't made myself fucking clear yet, turn the fuck around before I end you." With that last sentence out, the left gunner's head exploded in a spray of gore. Two CORPS soldiers had survived the crash and were advancing. With absolutely no effort, I finished their pursuit with two well-placed headshots from my pistol. I looked up to the remaining Resistance fighters. "Now!"

"Get back in now!" I heard one of the drivers yell as the soldier I had been holding onto scrambled into one of the jeeps, and they began to drive away. Self-preservation always wins out in the end. I turned and began to run, clutching the bag I was carrying tightly. I ran hard, and I ran long, not stopping for anything if I could help it. The battle behind me was becoming more and more distant and was slowing.

Eventually, after nearly twenty minutes, I turned. I had cleared several kilometers even in that short amount of time. The battle was just a cloud of smoke reaching into the sky. I couldn't see any real activity from there due to the hills, but I knew that if the Coalition won the battle, it wouldn't be long before they came looking for me. It wouldn't have surprised me if they could outright track me. No, I wasn't out of the woods yet. In fact, I wasn't in the woods at all. I was surrounded by rocks and dirt as far as the eye could see, and my eyes could see very far, indeed. While the occasional bit of vegetation threatened to reclaim the land, it was quite desolate.

I decided I needed to get to high ground. Before me were several rock formations, a few of them looking like they extended a hundred meters or more. I began to jog towards one of the larger ones in the distance, but still traveling away from the battle. While I wasn't as fatigued as I should have been for what just occurred, I was sweating a bit. It was horrendously hot and dry out. If this was Tantil, I was somewhere near the central part of the continent. At least I assumed so anyway. For all I knew, I could be on the other side of the world. Remembering what Langstan had told me, I took a moment to gaze up at the sky. While I didn't have a heck of a lot of reference points, Tantil seemed intuitively correct.

Finding an adequately tall enough rock, I began to scale it, leisurely pulling myself up using footfalls and handholds. The harness I was wearing was self-powered, so I wasn't too worried about falling. Making it to the summit, I took a seat on the peak, resting a moment, admiring the view. Turning back to the battle, I could still see smoke in the distance, but it didn't look like anyone was coming my way. Finally allowing myself to smile, I turned back to the horizon before me.

"I finally made it, Lys. Wish you could see it, kid." Sorrow leaked from my voice, and I gave out a sigh. Despite the depressing thoughts, I couldn't help but feel elation, and it was growing by the second. Eventually, I stood back up, raising both of my fists to the sky and began to whoop and holler. "Yes! Ah, haha! Fuck you, Ronyn, you bald piece of shit! I'm out! Next time I see you again, I'll be gunnin' for ya!" I realized I was talking to myself, but I didn't care. Finally, I was free.

Chapter Thirteen: Civilization

After a few moments of rest, I extracted my CIHUD again in an attempt to gain some sort of bearing. As was instructed, I looked up and concentrated on the sky above, trying not to let the thoughts of awe flood in. Unfortunately, I didn't have a lot of references to work from. The coordinates that had been fed to me weren't very useful without coordinates to other destinations.

I wanted to learn more about the TLF, to figure out how they knew about me and whether their objective was to capture or kill me. I doubt we'd be fast friends considering I treated them like targets.

The CIHUD did its magic. I figured out that I was still a decent distance away from the location of the TLF base I was supposed to hit, at least fifty kilometers out. It would be one hell of a hike with few supplies.

"Well, I guess it's time to test this shit out then." I took a moment and contemplated jumping from the rock but decided to limit the wear on my equipment. Somewhat carefully, I climbed back down and began to walk, making sure to give the battlefield a wide berth. Whoever won would start looking for survivors, and I was hoping to be nowhere nearby when that occurred.

Walking through the arid landscape lost its allure faster than I had hoped, and soon, even I was getting tired. The heat wasn't helping and having to walk a rather ridiculous distance probably wasn't either. While I certainly was less fatigued than I should have been, after the last few months, I forgot what exhaustion felt like. I tried to be very sparing about the water I had managed to bring with me. I knew if I didn't find some sort of civilization eventually, that even I would be a goner.

The air grew cold as night fell. I found an outcropping of rocks and took a seat, admiring the majestic, fiery glow of the mighty guardian in the sky. I had only ever read about our sun as well as seeing it in pictures and old movies. Never could I imagine the rapture it could induce from its sheer scale. For the first time in my life, I truly understood what being small felt like, especially as the first stars began to peek through the atmosphere. Thanks to my new eyes and mind, I was able to pick out the constellations I had only read about and finally had a strong bearing on where in the world I was.

My location was definitely Tantil continent, the central part, a little bit to the northeast. The area, according to historical records, had always been arid, a dust bowl basically. The war did absolutely nothing to help the situation, but I did notice small bits of vegetation dotting the landscape. Cacti, grass patches, and scraggly trees littered the area, giving texture to the picture it created. Nothing I had seen or read about could genuinely prepare me for the size of the world around me.

There were two celestial bodies in the sky, the Children of Gaia as some ancient cultures had called them. One was smaller than the other, a light gray glowing orb. Appearing as if slightly behind and above the smaller moon, the larger gave off a bluish glow. They were both crescent shaped, the larger one somewhat surrounding the smaller moon. I had only ever read about the stars and moons, but to see them was something else. Nothing I had read before could do them justice.

I climbed up to the peak of the outcrop I was resting at and peered across the land. I didn't need the implants to see a viable destination. The sky gave it away at first, the stars becoming dimmer off in the distance, in the direction I had been heading. There were lights, a lot of them, all clustered in an area that, based on the range, was quite large. It looked like a town, and it wasn't very far off the beaten path. I had only gone roughly half the distance to the TLF base, and could use a place to hunker down for the night.

Of course, it did dawn on me that whatever sort of place I was planning to head to could very well be run by the CORPS. I could be heading home for all I knew, all things considered. None of it mattered anyway; thanks to the CORPS, I would probably be aware of their presence well before I was too close to the settlement. To be honest, I was also insanely curious as to what could lie beyond the darkness. What sort of civilizations survived the war?

"Well, only one way to find out," I muttered to myself before grabbing my pack and walking towards the blob of lights on the horizon. For safety's sake, I kept my CIHUD out, so I could have a better awareness of the world around me. If I was walking towards some sort of CORPS stronghold, then I wanted to be somewhat prepared. I was done for if I stuck to the desert anyway.

It was remarkable how my legs had managed to lose much of their fatigue in the small amount of time that I had rested. Whatever gizmos the CORPS placed inside of me, they were truly impressive marvels of scientific engineering. It pained me to think about how the world could benefit from such a miraculous breakthrough, and yet they would most likely never get a chance to experience it. I had my doubts the Coalition planned on distributing them to the sick and disabled. Instead, they would just create more monsters.

The thought made my blood boil, and I savored the feeling. I wanted to be angry, needed to be angry. My bucket list was complete, I achieved my ultimate goal, and now, all that there was left was a little bit of payback for Lys and Ray. What else was there for me? I would breathe my last breath only after Ronyn choked up his. While my mind was wandering, I kept my senses about me, drawing nearer to the lights. As far as I could tell, I was mostly alone out there.

As I got closer, I realized there was a road nearby, not paved, but maintained or at least used often enough that it was still flat and easy to walk across. The only other life that was out and about were little critters scurrying around me. While I couldn't see them, I could sense them. If I was in a better position, I would likely try to find one and study it a bit. There wasn't exactly a bunch of animals chilling in the Undercities.

Once I got close enough to see what I was walking towards, I felt the breath catch in the back of my throat. It was indeed a settlement and most certainly not maintained by the Coalition. The place was large, with a wall that stretched around it. The wall, a cracked and crumbling affair, looked like it had been built in the time when they actually manufactured concrete. It only stood thanks to the scavenged materials found over the years. Gray patches lined the wall, separating some of the larger cracks, and other parts had been reinforced with wooden framing. Where they got the wood was anyone's guess. The area itself encompassed several kilometers and resembled some sort of frontier city, stubbornly withstanding the march of time.

On the corners of the walls were wooden scaffolding structures that looked like makeshift guard posts. I could see people walking across the top of the wall, armed with improvised and primitive firearms, dressed in equally shoddy flak jackets and slacks. The guns themselves were rifles and appeared to be lever-action. One or two even looked like they were old weapons, repaired with whatever might work.

There were two men and two women dressed in the same attire, waiting just outside the gate. The gate itself was large and looked like it opened outward using a pully system, the wheels and ropes peeking up from the other side of the wall. I thought it was curious that they had so many guards moving around. While I hadn't taken any real time to scout the area I was in, it didn't look like they were in much danger of some sort of rival city, and I doubted the CORPS cared about the rabble within.

With a deep breath, I decided I would just walk right up to the guards and present myself, see how it went. Judging by the weapons and their appearance, I wouldn't have a hard time getting away without permanently hurting anyone. I holstered my gun before getting into sight of the guards and casually walked up to the gates with my pack slung over my left shoulder. I also made sure to retract the CIHUD. As soon as I approached the two men trained their weapons on me. One of the women, who had a few doodads pinned to her chest as if she held some sort of rank, approached me. She was of average height with short-cut dark hair, and a scar running down her left cheek.

"Identify yourself." I stopped when she approached.

"The name's John." My voice was calm, lacking any of the nervousness I felt deep down. I wasn't afraid for myself.

"Well, John, what's your business here?" Her voice told me she was all seriousness and that I would do best to show some respect.

"Just passing through. It's a bit chilly out, and I'm hungry, was hoping maybe I could trade some work for a bed and a meal for the night, head right on out in the mornin'." I gave her a simple smile trying to show my sincerity.

"Uh-huh. You Coalition or TLF?" She asked the question as if it had to be one or the other.

"TLF?" I decided to play a little dumb.

"Tantillian Liberation Front, what have ya been livin' under a rock or somethin'?" If she only knew.

"Well, kinda, actually. Long story, suffice to say I ain't part of no Liberation Front, and I hate the CORPS with every fiber of my being."

"So, where'd you get the equipment then?" She motioned with her rifle towards the items that adorned my person. I guess I never stopped to think that I was the weird looking one in the situation.

"Would ya believe I inherited it from my estranged uncle?" I asked, cocking my head to the side a little.

"Don't get smart with me. Ain't no one gonna stop me from puttin' two in ya. Just answer the questions if you want in." I gave her an apologetic nod.

"Of course, been a long day, no offense meant. I found the equipment on some corpses about thirty kilometers or so back that way." I pointed towards the battle, hoping perhaps word of it had gotten out. "Looked like some nasty fight had been happening nearby. Probably found some deserters." My poker face was absolutely perfect as I spoke the half-lie.

"Lucky you. Sure, you can enter, but if you cause any trouble-"

"You'll shoot me yourself," I finished her sentence. Surprisingly this elicited a chuckle.

"Good, glad to see we have an understanding." I tightened my grip on my pack before motioning with my hand at the gate.

"May I?"

"Get now. Don't let me regret this." I gave her a polite nod and walked to the gates, which opened up as I approached, the creaking of the metal wheels pierced the night air. The doors revealed civilization beyond, a bustling population finishing up their day, the sounds of fanfare, and partying coming from various buildings. The buildings themselves looked like they were made from whatever scraps and materials they could find out in the wilderness. The thing that caught my eye was that several of them were made from neatly laid bricks and appeared to have been there for a long time. While some of them were in disrepair, it would seem the place was settled well before the war.

Walking through, I noticed that I indeed stood out way more than I intended to. While I did get a bit dirty, my clothes were clean, almost new looking in comparison to what many others were wearing. It looked like someone had, at some point, brought the tailoring industry back for the inhabitants, but not everyone had whatever luxury afforded them the fancy threads. There was definitely a disparity among the people that I couldn't put my finger on.

Moving through the streets, I got stares from people and occasionally catcalled by what I could only assume were prostitutes, surprisingly of both genders. Whatever they wanted, I didn't have, and I didn't want what they were selling either way. I needed rest, not some sort of weird disease, though I couldn't help laughing to myself when I realized I was probably immune to such things.

"Don't worry, bud, I respect you more than that," I assured myself while looking down. Off in the distance, I could hear what sounded like live music and laughter coming from one of the better-lit buildings down the way. Walking closer, the building looked like a bar of some kind. My suspicions were confirmed when the door swung open, and a rather large and intimidating man proceeded to toss a much smaller, much drunker man onto the street.

"Fine! I dun need yer, hic, shitty swill anyway!" He threw a rock from the ground, ricocheting it off the wall, causing the burly number take a step towards the man menacingly. This was enough to make him scramble to his feet and stumble off into the night. I watched all of this with amusement before approaching the bouncer.

"This a private establishment, or is the watering hole open?" I asked directly. He gave me a quick look-over.

"Sure, cause trouble, and I'll break your legs."

"Wouldn't dream of it." Moving to the side, he allowed me to enter.

The place wreaked of cheap booze and sweat. People were sitting all around the room at various tables. There was a long bar lining the back wall with a couple of busy looking bartenders trying to keep the patrons happy. The place was raucous, and it amazed me that they even bothered with a bouncer at all. I noticed at the bar was an older, balding gentleman, his rotund belly sticking out of the bottom of his shirt, which was stained by grease from an unknown source. By the way he was sitting and chatting, he struck me as the owner. I approached the bar, set my pack down, and took a seat at an empty stool nearby.

"Hey there," I greeted the man who responded with a grunt and a nod. "You own the place?"

"Last I checked." His voice was raspy, yet somehow still loud.

"Fair enough. I'm just passing through tonight and maybe tomorrow. I was wondering how a man gets a room and food around these parts." He looked me up and down, now actually paying attention to the man he was speaking to. A bit of a grin came over his face.

"Coin, just like anyone else, friend." I quirked a brow at the word coin.

"I'm sorry, coin? You mean money?" Just like that, his smile faded. The thought hadn't even occurred to me. While we were taught about currencies in history class, it wasn't something we used in the Undercities. We were paid in privileges for the most part. All our material needs were always met without question.

"Yeah, kid, coin, gold, or copper to be specific. Or, if ya got somethin' else that might peak a man's interests?" He looked me up and down again. I could imagine all of the women this man had made uncomfortable in his life because it sure worked on me.

"Well? I have a few items I might be able to part with." Everything I had was pretty damn useful, and I wasn't sure I was about to enjoy giving any of it up for food and a bed. He was beginning to speak again when my focus faded away, and I realized that something about the place seemed off. I couldn't quite put my finger on it, turning to survey the room as the owner continued to talk about what I must have had on me.

Everyone seemed reasonable given the place we were in, which admittedly to me, meant everyone was weird. So, I began to sleuth their collective similarities, making lightning-fast comparisons to divine what passed for normal. Most were armed with knives and other multi-purpose weapons. A scant few had firearms, though I couldn't tell what type, and I didn't think whipping out the CIHUD would be a good idea. My focus then went to the door, and I sort of glared at it, trying to listen to something I could hear outside. A fight was going on and I could sense the struggle was coming to an end.

The door burst open, and three men waltzed in, the unconscious bouncer laying in a heap behind the door. They walked in with all the charm a pack of thugs could muster. There was an obvious leader and two brutes. The two big boys had bald heads, with a multitude of piercings and grayscale tattoos. Their clothing consisted of what looked to be hide and cloth, loose, but protective against the elements. Most of the color was red. The one on the left had an ammo belt slung around his shoulder and the other was carrying a small sledgehammer like a cudgel.

The leader of the group was perhaps a foot shorter than his entourage but looked like he could hold himself in a fight. He brandished a primitive sidearm holstered at his hip and what seemed like a machete held resting on his shoulder. His hair was short, dark, and unkempt. A few scars adorned his cheek, revealing that he had seen a few scrapes in his twenty-something years. He had a wicked grin on his face that immediately spelled trouble. The owner behind me went silent; he didn't strike me as the bystander type of guy.

"Get a new bouncer ya old piece of shit, ha-ha!" The lead thug grabbed a glass from an occupied table and swigged the drink before smashing it upon the floor. "Woo! Still tastes like piss!" The bar had become silent, and not a person was challenging the man in front of them. I cocked my head a little to the side, studying them and their posture. It was time to mind my own business.

"What are you staring at, pale boy?" Or not. He pointed the machete at me as I remembered how horribly I stood out. I looked like a businessman in a soup kitchen that hadn't heard of sunlight.

"I haven't decided yet." Then an idea popped into my head, "got any coin short stuff?" I had no love for bullies. Truth be told, I didn't look like much compared to the loudmouth and his pals. They probably had every plan of mugging and killing me anyway, so I figured I'd have some fun.

"Oh, please tell me you just talked back. You must be new 'round here, guy. Let me tell ya, I can't begin to say how pleased I am someone finally grew a pair around this place. Strength be praised; this is gonna be good." He and his crew casually walked my way, but I just stood and calmly waited.

"Yep, pretty new here. You seem somewhat important, mind telling me who's supposedly about to kick my ass?"

"Oh guy, we are gonna do way more than kick your ass. Fine, just to remind people here, I'm the first Lieutenant of the Sons of Rellen, also known as the Second." I quirked a brow at his response and remained silent. This seemed to agitate him as they stopped a meter in front of me, and Mr. Lieutenant looked around the room flabbergasted. "You really ain't from around here, huh guy? Let me enlighten you." In a bid to try and remind the room who was boss, he raised his machete and then spun, swinging the blade towards my neck. He probably thought he was slick with his flourishing decapitation attempt, but reality set in quickly. Effortlessly, I raised my forearm, stopping his swing short. I grabbed his wrist and twisted it, snapping his arm in what must have looked like an instant and effortless motion. He screamed in agony.

"Well, nice to meet ya, Mr. Second. The name's John." When the two thugs next to him got over the shock of what just happened, they advanced, the man with the hammer first taking a swing. My expression never changing, I merely arched my back and dodged the attack that, to me, was moving in slow motion. The other man lunged forward, attempting to tackle me. I planted my foot behind me and moved my hands to grab his right arm, moving the planted foot to the side and keeping a hold. As he fell forward, I yanked,

134

snapping his shoulder out of place and bringing him back towards me. I finished the move by using his momentum to flip him hard onto the floor.

"Look, now there are two people on the ground screaming." The guy with the hammer was now hesitant after witnessing the relative ease I dispatched his boss and buddy. It was at this point the Lieutenant on the ground raised the sidearm he was holding, hoping to catch me unaware. Without even looking, I booted him in the side of the head, causing him to grab it and curl into a fetal position. He was dazed and likely concussed despite pulling back as much as I could. "Wannabe next big boy? Pick up your friend and get the fuck out of this bar before I break you too."

It's always a beautiful moment when you get to witness a person genuinely experience an emotion for the first time. With eyes wide like a child, he hooked his hammer to his belt and slung his boss over his shoulder. The third man picked himself up almost sheepishly, and they hurried out of the bar.

There was no cheering when it was all over. Everyone was just staring at me with stupefied looks on their faces like some miracle just happened before their eyes. While the two men were well over two meters tall, nothing about them seemed particularly intimidating or dangerous to me. Then again, my point of reference had drastically changed. I turned calmly to the owner behind me, who had a stupefied look on his face.

"How about that room and food?" He silently nodded, mouth agape before finally shaking it off and snapping his finger for the bartender who scurried out a door behind the bar. I looked at the person sitting near the owner and gestured if I could sit.

"Y-yeah, of c-course." The man was just a wiry fellow, probably a friend of the owner.

"How the fuck did ya move that fast?" The owner finally spoke.

"I'm sorry?" I inquired sincerely. I guess I never stopped to think what it must look like for an average person to see me moving. Relativity was a fascinating thing, and I was beginning to see the effects of heightened awareness.

"Ya moved like lightnin' kid. I barely registered the swing before he was on the ground!" People around us were beginning to talk again, their conversations centering around what they had witnessed. Others leaned in closer, trying to listen in to our discussion.

"You gonna do anything about the guy outside?" I asked, looking to him like it should have been a silly question.

"Bah!" He waved it off. "One of the girls will take care of him." Sure enough, as he said this, I turned and saw a couple of the wait staff heading outside to tend to the man. "Now, where the hell do ya come from?"

"Me?" I asked, turning back to him. "Been livin' under a rock. Came out to get a little sun." In the end, it wasn't exactly a lie.

"Sure seems like it, kid. Well, ya provided a service, room, and board is on the house for the night."

"Barter, huh? I can dig it. Thanks." Soon the man from the bar came back out and handed a plate to one of the female staff. She was scantily clad in cloth garments, showing plenty of skin, which appeared cleaner than several of the people there. She walked over to us and set the plate down in front of me.

"Here ya go, big guy." She gave me a wink and walked away. I couldn't help but chuckle. The place was very different from what I was used to.

136

"Hey, Nicky!" The owner yelled to the barkeep. "Get this boy a glass of the house special." He looked back at me. "Ya look like ya could handle some drink, huh?" I grinned at the prospect.

"Handle? I straight need it at this point. Been a long few years." In a hurry, the barkeep brought over a glass half-filled with a noxious smelling liquid. I picked it up and gave it a sniff. "Huh, interesting." I took a sip, and while it burned at first, like most feelings of discomfort, my little buddies took care of it quickly. After the sip and a shrug, I tilted the glass and downed the liquid, the burn fading as quick as I could drink it. I set the glass down to the astonished looks of those sitting with me.

"Holy hell!" The skinny man next to me exclaimed.

"Damn boy, ya got a death wish? Ya about to go on a trip. Need a bucket?" I looked to the barkeep and then back down at the empty glass. The only thing I was feeling was frustration.

"No, no, this is bullshit. Those pieces of shit!" I exclaimed, almost slamming my fist into the table. My agitation was causing those around me to become nervous.

"What're ya goin' on about, boy?"

"I can't get drunk. Those assholes took my ability to get lit from me. Give me another one, maybe I can overload it." The two men looked at me like I was some sort of crazy person.

"Shit, I'd pay to see that again, boy. Nicky, another round for the tough guy!" I finally decided to look down at the food that had been presented. There was some sort of meat I couldn't identify, roasted, with equally unknown greens on the side. Grabbing the fork and knife in front of me, I decided to dig into the meat first and found it wasn't too bad, not unlike beef. Soon, my next drink came to me, and I once again downed it, feeling the anticipation of intoxication give way to frustration.

"Boy, I don't even think the cattle could handle all of that.." He was watching me with astonishment as I ate the plate before me.

"Yeah, well, at least they would probably catch a buzz."

"Kid, what the hell are ya?" the owner finally asked in bewilderment.

"Just a man with some internal toys."

"W-where do you come from?" The man next to me stuttered.

"I doubt you'd believe me if I told you."

"Well, until tonight, I didn't believe anyone could take down the Son's Second without breaking a sweat, so try me." The owner of the establishment crossed his arms over his chest.

"I come from a giant, technologically advanced underground city built by the Coalition where me and roughly two million others have lived our entire lives." The owner looked like he wanted to say something sarcastic and then thought better of it. His eyes lowered, and his tone became serious.

"Ya, work for the CORPS?"

"No," I answered, meeting his gaze. "Not only do I not work for the CORPS, but it would make me happy to see them crushed beneath my boot." I knew it probably wasn't the best idea to be super honest. Still, at the same time, I doubt the CORPS would resort to questioning randoms from underdeveloped settlements.

"B-but you said you came from them." My lanky tablemate spoke up again. "Where did you get that tech if you don't work for them?"

"Think of me as more of an experiment than an employee. An escaped one at that. I just decided to take some goodies with me on my way out."

138

"Now ya trying to say ya some science project?" The proprietor asked.

"Not trying, am. Look, suffice to say, you're in no danger from me, and unless you're teeming with machines and robots, I doubt the CORPS will come looking for you."

"Fine, fine, fair enough. I won't bother ya about it. Y'know it's too bad ya headin' out tomorrow. Obviously, I could use a new bouncer." I laughed at this.

"Yeah, I doubt big baldy out there is gonna be in for work tomorrow, but I have to give you a hard pass. Nothing personal, it's just that I would prefer to be far away from this place as soon as it's convenient."

"Runnin' away, are ya?"

"For now, until I get my bearings anyway."

"Well, I would hate to be the poor bastards that have to try and pick you up. Then again, the Lieutenant ain't exactly Coalition soldier material either. Guess you do have a death wish."

"Not yet, anyway. So, my turn for some questions."

"Shoot."

"What's around these parts, is this the only settlement?" The two men I was sitting with took a moment and looked at each other with a puzzled look.

"Nah, there are plenty of *settlements* as ya call 'em. Not many places out here to be sure, nearest one is a good day's travel from here by buggy."

"Buggy?"

"Geeze boy, ya really have been livin' under a rock. Them little four-wheeled vehicles you might have seen coming in. They get us around faster." He gave me a look like I was a crazy person. I ate the food that was provided, and it felt nice to finally get a warm meal. While the CORPS fed me well enough, the schedules were pretty erratic and not every day. In fact, I could generally go a few days without eating before any kind of real discomfort set in, provided I wasn't doing much for those days. Now though, it was time to eat.

"Not bad. Good to see civilization survived out here."

"Survived? Were we supposed to die or somethin'?" The owner's expression didn't change with this new line of questioning.

"The CORPS told us the surface was bombed out, that no one could live up here."

"Well, as ya can see, boy, we're still kickin'."

"Yeah, but the war, there are definitely signs of it."

"War? Yeah, mean the time of the Republic? Yeah, there was a war, there were some bombs, but not everywhere got the cloud boy. I ain't no scholar, I just know some stories my granny used to tell me." I finished my meal quickly and looked over to the owner.

"Know any good scholars I could grill for knowledge?"

"Not 'round these parts, boy, but I ain't the man to ask either."

"Fair enough. Well, if you don't mind, it's been a rather long five years, and I'd appreciate some R&R on my own terms." I stood, gathering my things.

"Sure thing, kid." He raised a flabby arm and snapped his fingers three times. Quickly and obediently, a young, blonde woman sauntered over. She was wearing a skirt that barely hid the eye-patch sized garment underneath, with a simple tank top. Her blue eyes still showed a bit of nervousness, but her grin was a little devilish.

"Yeah, boss?" Her voice was perky, but deep within betrayed the nervousness she felt standing next to me.

140

"Show hero boy here to a room upstairs. Make sure he's got whatever he needs." She looked over to me as the old man gave the order. Part of the nervousness seemed to fade, which made me wonder what was actually bothering her.

"Of course. This way, sir." She offered her arm to me, and I couldn't help but smile a little and decided to loosen up a bit. I took her arm in mine, and she delicately led me to a set of wooden stairs at the far corner of the tavern. The stairs were sturdy, but the floorboards creaked anyway, the path lit by electrical fixtures from the ceiling. I had never seen lighting that utilized glass bulbs before, and I had to admit that my look became almost childlike in curiosity.

"You must be new around here." She spoke casually as we walked down a hall with doors on each side.

"You could say that."

"Well, you don't look like the average tourist anyway, but your eyes look like a kid's. It's cute." She gave me a playful grin as we stopped at the door on the far end of the hall. She opened it and let go of my arm, motioning for me to enter. I walked past her and into the room. It was a simple affair with the same dull wooden style as the rest of the place. There was a queen-sized bed that had sheets the cleanliness of which was suspect at best. A small bedside table adorned one side of the bed, and there was a closet for storing personal affects. On the opposite side of the wall was a shuttered balcony window leading to the street below.

"Do people actually live here?" I inquired, putting my stuff down by the bed and inspecting the room all around.

"Some, most people just pass through and are only here for a short stay." She began to walk towards me, provocatively swaying her hips. I had to admit she looked scrumptious, and back in the day, I was a bit of a horndog. At that moment, however, as she made her seductive walk towards me, likely assuming one of my needs, a strange sensation came over me. It was like I was suddenly stricken with whiskey dick and an aversion to anything female. As she approached and placed her hand on my chest, I gently took it and pushed it away.

"Look, I'm sure your boss expects that you take care of my every need, but my needs don't include random one-night stands."

"Oh, come now," she gave me a playful look, "just relax." She placed her lips gently onto mine, but I didn't react in any way. After an extremely awkward second or two, she pulled back. "What are you gay or something?"

"Nah, far from it, and it has nothing to do with you either. Under normal circumstances I would bend you over this bed right now, but-"

"But?" She cocked her head, coyly.

"But it's just not my thing. However, if you wanna avoid work, you can chill in here and tell your boss whatever makes him happy." I took a seat on the bed and looked up at her. She returned my gaze with one of her own that spelled confusion.

"I don't get it." She crossed her arms over her chest.

"I don't mind the company. Hell, I've been spending most of my time locked in a cell or dukin' it out with pixels. A little companionship wouldn't hurt." Her confusion didn't disappear, but then she got a look of curiosity.

"So, uh, what's your name?"

"The name's John. What's yours?"

"Rachelle." She loosened up a bit, realizing she was getting a free break and took a seat next to me. "Where are you from? You obviously ain't from here."

"Nope, I definitely ain't from here. I come from an underground city built by the Coalition." She gave me a look like I was crazy or something. "No, really, I mean it. Check this out." I reached into my bag and pulled out the PCD I had swiped from my substitute handler. I turned it on, and it showed a home screen with documents and basic applications. Her eyes widened a bit, and I handed it to her. She started flipping through screens.

"Wow, this is amazing. What's it for?" She asked, looking up at me almost like a kid herself.

"Data handling mostly. Information can be stored on it, a whole library's worth of books, videos, audio, you name it." As she was flipping through some of the pages, I realized that I hadn't spent much time thumbing through it. Seeing as there wasn't any real security on the thing, I had my doubts it contained any juicy information. Then she made it to the messages Langstan had received. I saw that one of them was from Alonna. I was able to see the entire message as she flipped through it, the words forming in my mind as soon as they came into my periphery.

"Dr. Langstan," the message began *"I wish to extend my gratitude for your offer to assist in the field test of XR001. As you have been made aware, my duties have pulled me away, but I trust you will be able to fulfill your role in this matter. John is gruff, but if you listen to him and respect him, he is also a good man and is not from among the prisoner stock. You're safer that way, and I'm sorry. Best of luck."* Prisoner stock? What the heck did that mean? Did they have some other sort of source of subjects? I shuddered at the thought, but honestly, that wasn't the thing that was bothering me the most about the letter. Why was she sorry? The whole

thing had guilt written all over it, but guilt over what? Did she know we'd be attacked? It wouldn't surprise me given the Coalition's affinity for conspiracies.

"What's wrong?" Rachelle asked, looking up at me. I must have appeared to zone out.

"Nothing." I gave her a friendly smile. I wasn't sure why I didn't just send her away; I had no intention of laying with her. I had to chalk it up to good old-fashioned loneliness.

"So, what was this underground city like?" I gave her a grin and decided to humor the questions. We sat there for at least a couple of hours while I described the underground utopia I had come from, describing the culture, and how life was like. She stared in rapt awe as she listened to the tale. It must have seemed so fantastical to someone who had grown up in a society like the one we were in.

"There's something I don't get." She interjected, "If life was so good, why did you leave?"

"Wait, what do you mean? Life so good?"

"Yeah, you were fed, clothed, housed, warm. No one ever threatened you."

"Well, there was the mutaphorm attacks," I replied, almost defensively.

"I mean, yeah, those sound pretty bad, but weren't you safer there?" She had an incredulous look on her face like I was trying to explain to her that left was right.

"It's not about safety. We all die one day, and chances are it won't be pretty or painless when it happens. I wanted to die free, I wanted to die having seen the sky at least once, to know whether or not it was all lies." I looked down at my hands for a moment before meeting her gaze once more. "You're right though, the Undercities were basically a gentle sort of dystopia. No one ever wanted, people were mostly safe, but it was all built on a lie. You can't force happiness."

"I guess you just don't know what it's like to live up here."

"What is up here, anyway? I see desert, that's not very promising."

"I don't really know much history. I do know that this place is kind of like a waystation between cities. There's an ancient hydro-farm underground that keeps us fed. Lots of caravans come here from the coastal lands. That's where the bigger cities are."

"Huh, what's the closest?"

"I don't know. I've never left here before." She looked down and seemed kind of sad to admit this.

"Well, leave then," I suggested it so simply, not realizing the place of privilege it came from.

"Where would I go? I have no coin, no goods, nothing to trade that will get me from place to place. Besides, until my debt is paid to Owen, I can't go anywhere." I quirked a brow.

"Debt?"

"Uh-huh, debt. My mom owed a debt from a long time ago, and now that she's gone, I owe the debt. I work it off bit by bit, but the interest pretty much ensures I am here for life unless some sort of windfall comes my way." She seemed very upset and was choking back tears.

"You're his slave?" I felt a bit of anger well up inside. After everything I had been through, the last thing I could abide by was slavery.

"His servant. I owe him a debt; if it's paid, I don't have to work for him anymore." At that point, I wish I did have coin, something that could help her. She definitely couldn't go with me; it would be a death sentence. Just like back at the lab, I felt helpless. Is that what the world had become over the last two centuries?

"Look, why don't you rest here for the night. Tell Owen I had you working overtime. No working tonight, huh?" She looked at me, and the eyeliner she had was smearing a little from the tears she was trying to prevent. Obviously, the subject had struck a nerve. No one had probably ever just sat down and talked with her before. The more I thought about it, the more I realized the town was a dark and gritty environment. Everyone looked like every day was a blessing, and our conversation accentuated the point.

"Are you sure you don't want to lay down with me?" Now it seemed a bit less like she was doing her job.

"Call me a bit of a prude, but I'm still not interested in hanky panky. I promise you're certainly hot enough, it's just me. Besides, I don't plan on being here longer than I have to, and I'm one of those sappy romantic types. Can't get attached."

"Can I ask why you have to leave so soon?" That curious look came over her face again.

"I ain't exactly far from where the CORPS lost their newest toy. They'll come lookin' for me, I'm sure, and I would be pretty shocked if they weren't tracking me somehow." I thought about my words as I said them. There was no way the CORPS didn't know exactly where I was.

"If they can find you, how are you going to get away?" A worried tone came over her voice. It felt nice to have someone feel concern over me for the sake of it.

"Oh, I'm not planning on getting away. When the horrors of the

CORPS eventually find me, I'd prefer if no one got caught in the crossfire." My tone was severe as if I was talking about two forces clashing as opposed to one man fighting an army, the actual reality of the situation.

"What if they kill you?"

"It's probably more a matter of when than if. When they finally get their quarry, I will have hopefully done an incredible amount of damage first."

"But why?"

"We all have our hobbies. Some people knit, others foolishly take on tyrants." She giggled a little at the joke and then stretched with a long yawn.

"Well, sugar, if you're not gonna lay with me, I'm taking your offer." She laid down on the bed, laying on her side in what I imagine she thought was a provocative manner. I stood up.

"Sure, get some rest."

"You're not gonna sleep, either?" She looked even more disappointed.

"I don't really do the sleep thing anymore, at least not as often as I used to. Perks of being a monster, I suppose." She laid her head down with this and relaxed. I walked to the balcony window off to the side of the room and opened it up, allowing the cool air to rush into the room. It was refreshing and allowed the stale smell of smoke and body odor from the floor below to waft into the darkened atmosphere. I looked down at the streets below, as it grew late, so did the number of people walking about, but there were still sounds of activity. Like the Undercities, the place seemed to rarely sleep.

My gaze then rose to the heavens, and for a moment, I felt as if all concerns didn't matter. I saw the pinpricks in the sky, my enhanced vision allowing me a clearer sight despite the light pollution of the place.

I stood there for hours, just watching the sky, my legs and neck never growing tired or sore from the action. I was soaking the majesty of it all in. My mind wandered back to just how absolutely tiny we all really were. Even the Undercities were minuscule in comparison to the cosmos. My struggles were all suddenly worth it. I had seen the sky and confirmed the lies of the CORPS.

It was time then, for new goals, a new mission for which to live. It wouldn't be just petty revenge, though; it had to be more than that. Sure, watching Ronyn choke on his own blood was definitely a new bucket list item, but it couldn't be my *only* goal. The CORPS had to pay for what they had done and all of the people they had enslaved. If it took me until my dying breath, I would see the conspiracies of the Coalition revealed, and their machinations toppled to the ground.

I looked back at the now sleeping woman in my bed. "It ain't just about Lys and Ray anymore." I looked back outside. "We've seen the sky kids, now it's time to get some work done." I shut the balcony window to allow warmth to once again overtake the room and took a seat quietly on the floor, grabbing my duffle bag. I snatched the PCD and fished around my things, snagging the creepy data cable I had been given. I looked back up at the sleeping form on the bed before allowing my CIHUD to poke out.

I hooked into the PCD and closed my eyes. I could sense the data flowing all around me, imagining a library in my mind. I found myself in the all-black room once more, the one inside my mind. It was somewhat alarming how real my imagination could become.

"Alright, let's see what ya got." Before me, floating in the air like some sort of hologram, representations of the various files and applications appeared around me, spinning as I willed it to reveal to me the data in the device. The swirling symbols and words would stop whenever I saw something juicy.

148

My senses were still about me in the real world. While a bit dulled, I could accurately tell what and who was in the room with me. I could feel that very little time was actually passing in the real world. My heightened awareness forced me to focus on single bits of data, likely a security measure to make infiltration more effective.

The first thing I came across were topographical maps. First, of the route we took from the XRC facility, then of the suspected TLF base, somewhere to the west in what appeared to be the middle of nowhere. What was truly interesting was what the maps contained that weren't part of the mission. My sleepy companion was definitely correct, the settlement was a sort of trading hub judging by the surrounding areas. According to the documents, I was in a place called Fort Ly'Sihno, which struck me as a F'Rytalan word. It made me curious as to the history of the settlement.

Roughly twenty kilometers to the east, towards the coast, was a series of settled areas, resembling a spread-out city. While parts looked like it had large structures, most of it seemed to be separated into walled-off clusters with roads and paths leading to one another. There were several names for each settlement, while others had designations. I had to assume the CORPS chose to use local names whenever available. Either way, the coast was densely populated, which made me wonder why anyone would want to build a military base in the middle of nowhere. What was in that place that made the Coalition willing to send little old me for?

There wasn't much else on the PCD that was of use to me. It was clear the only information that was provided was need-to-know, such as how to navigate in case things got hairy. It wasn't surprising the CORPS would be wary about their data should I actually escape. However, I wasn't entirely convinced my flying the coop wasn't planned in some way. Alonna's letter seemed to indicate it.

After everything was put away, I decided I would keep the PCD. While I wouldn't have any issues remembering anything in perfect detail, my word wouldn't be proof enough for people. It was definitely a good idea to have a document storage device on me, especially one with a camera. Besides, if push came to shove, I could probably trade it for supplies.

I sat there for the remainder of the night, contemplating my plan of action, how long it would take to make it to the base, and what I would need to get there. The answer to the last bit was "not much," but the walk would still be a grueling one. It would be nice if I could get a hold of one of those vehicles Owen spoke about. It would come in handy to be sure.

I decided I was going to seek out the TLF, see what they were about. If we aligned, they would be my ticket to putting the hurt on the CORPS. Remembering my encounter with them, it seemed very apparent that they were aware of my presence. From everything I witnessed, I was their target, so it stood to reason I may have a foot in the door in speaking with them. If nothing else, we shared a common enemy, and that would have to be good enough.

Chapter Fourteen: The Sons of Rellen

My morning plotting was suddenly interrupted. There was light peeking through the window shutters, and I realized it was daytime already. It wasn't the light that got my attention, but rather a loud, obnoxious series of bells that began ringing out. They sounded like some sort of alarm and true to my suspicions, the working gal in the bed sat upright, looking to me immediately with horror in her eyes.

"The Sons!"

"I'm sorry, what?" I quirked a brow, not sure what she meant.

"The Sons of Rellen! Those are raid bells!" I stood immediately hearing this, grabbing my bag.

"Raid bells? The fuck do you mean by raid bells?"

"The Sons, we're a tributary, but sometimes if they think we've broken their will, they raid! They ride in, they kill and rape whoever they want and take whatever they please!" It was at that point that I heard gunfire in the distance, roughly a kilometer away, while other shots came from a bit further. They were getting closer.

"You mean they make you provide resources and sometimes just take them anyway?"

"Yes! Oh god, I don't know what to do." I then realized the ramifications of what she just described. The Sons of Rellen, the group those fools from the night before belonged to. I figured out that the attack might have something to do with me, and my heart sank. If the raid was my fault, I had to do something about it.

"Stay here, don't open the door for anyone, hide in the closet if you

151

have to." I moved for the window and opened the shutters, seeing people running and scrambling for doors. The ragtag security forces were rushing to the entrance of the city I had come in from. I could see that some others were heading towards opposite end, suggesting the place might be surrounded.

"What are you doing?" She asked while retreating towards the closet.

"Takin' care of business." I grabbed the edge of the balcony and leapt off of it, landing on both legs with a loud thud, dust flying out all around me from the harness's discharge. I began to run through the streets, heading towards the gate I had come in from but stopped when the gunfire ceased. I could hear a voice suddenly roar to life as if being amplified by a speaker system.

"Attention to the Weak of this pathetic town! Your defiance has not gone unnoticed!" I began to move for the entrance again. "Surrender now, and your damage shall be minimal. Bring me the fool who brought this upon you, and we may yet be more lenient!" As his last line came out, the barricades of the gate came into view. There were numerous dead security officers strewn about as well as several corpses in the same style getup as the Lieutenant. Apparently the gate had been opened prior to their attack. The voice continued, but as I approached the gate, the female guard from the night before immediately confronted me.

"You! Why do I feel like this has something to do with y-" She was cut short when I brushed right passed her as if she didn't even exist. With a purpose, I walked to the entrance of the gate, and no one moved to stop me; I was freely giving myself up after all. As I walked past the guards, I gritted my teeth and allowed the CIHUD to free itself from my skull. Everything came into perfect clarity.

I couldn't tell what was happening on the other side of town, but it looked like whatever groups had surrounded the place were not part of the main force. Before me were dozens of men and women, all dressed in the same red styled leather clothing. Hairstyles ranged from shaved, to spikes and neon colors. There were several all-terrain vehicles, the buggies that Owen had mentioned. Some of them sported mounted guns.

Front and center was a humongous machine that looked like it had been cobbled together from scrap. It stood nearly as tall as the city-wall itself. It resembled some sort of ship on treads with a structure sitting on top of a platform. There was a giant, barred gate on the front of the landship that was over three meters tall. The Lieutenant was the one on the mic, standing at the top front of the colossal vehicle.

I walked out with all the confidence in the world, as soon as I did though, two people from either side of the gate lunged out, one wielding a club, the other a long blade. I side-stepped in a quick motion. My hands reached out, grasped the back of their heads and smashed their skulls together viciously. It would have been comical if the situation was better. I looked up at the Lieutenant and pointed.

"Hop on down, coward, and get your round two!" Saying this, I could sense one of the soldiers on top of the hulking machine taking aim at me. When his trigger finger made it to the point of no return, I cocked my head to the side, and the bullet whizzed right on by. "Or you gonna have these chuckleheads fight for you?"

"I want his head!" Came the reply. When this happened, I knew they would open fire and attempt to execute me on the spot. Instead, I dashed forward, knowing the trajectories of the rounds coming my way. Picking a path, I weaved and bobbed. The gunfire came like a torrent of raindrops, whizzing by, sand erupting into the air like morbid confetti.

I must have miscalculated just how many bits of metal were flying my way because one whizzed off my shoulder. Violently, the bullet changed direction behind me, offset by the magnetic field provided by my armor unit. Their weapons weren't powerful enough to penetrate it, and as soon as I realized that, my entire posture changed.

I reached the buggy on the far left of the landship, manned and guarded by two on either side. I let my momentum flow into a punishing fist that slammed into the face of the mounted raider. The raider flew from his seat, impacting the sand a meter or two behind, the force of the punch breaking bones and ending his participation in the fight. His two buddies were firing, using makeshift, lever-action rifles, the bullets whizzing away from me harmlessly. I grabbed the barrel of one of the raider's guns, pulling it from his grasp. My hand deftly made its way to the lever, cocking the weapon as I spun it around and aimed it at the one behind me, blowing his brains over the desert sand behind him.

The Son next to the one I shot barely had time to be shocked. I used the butt of the rifle to smash him in his right temple, ending his fight as well. By this time, everyone had begun firing at me again, now that their friends were dispatched. I mounted one of the vehicles, pulled the throttle, and whipped it around to move behind the group, hoping to prevent any more shots being fired at the city.

No help was coming from the settlement. I was sure they expected me to die gruesomely out there. It mattered little to me as, in a way, I felt like this was my fight and didn't want any more innocents being dragged into it. If the city guards were intent on watching someone take care of their problems, then so be it.

The CIHUD was enabling me to know where the enemies were and how to properly avoid their fire. While my person was protected from high-velocity projectiles, the buggy was not, and I didn't feel like eating dirt at that very moment. Using one hand to guide the vehicle across the sand, I held the rifle in the other, sensing four more rounds available. My first targets were the snipers, who's shots may have been strong enough to penetrate my shield. Keeping my eyes focused on what was in front of me, I raised my arm up. I fired the rifle, the shot striking true of the first moron who dared pull a trigger in my general direction.

As he fell from the tower, I could hear the mic come on again. "Kill this fool! The next one of you that misses ends up on the First's table!" A grin formed across my face as I fired off another round, ending a second sniper on the platform and finally making my way to the other side of their behemoth. Some of the other buggies were starting to give chase, two of them close behind me. As I rounded the corner, I saw four more vehicles and fired my last two rounds with the rifle, knocking out a couple more.

There were still enemies on foot as well, shooting at me, but even their accurate shots were finding no purchase, and most were still trying to hit me as opposed to the buggy. Like a knight on horseback, I sped towards one of them, flipping the rifle around to grasp it by the barrel and used it to smash the sense out of the enemy, riding past as he hit the ground.

A warning blip appeared on the CIHUD, indicating one of the people on the ground were handling an explosive. It looked like a pipe-bomb, spiked all over, with a throwing handle attached. I swung around, as he threw it, dropping the rifle, and reaching down to scoop up the bomb before it could hit the ground. Even a glance told me it was detonated on impact, and thus I tossed it behind me at the pursuing vehicles. The explosion was too much for their respective rides, and they were sent to the sand in violent heaps.

By now, units from around the wall were scrambling to my position, their presence coming in range of my sensors. I knew it was time to get myself off the ground. I whipped around the landship again, driving away, before spinning the buggy in a donut and speeding back towards it. I could see a rock formation protruding out from the sand near the landship and found my mark. I stood up on the buggy, balancing myself. When the vehicle hit the rock, I leapt forward, using the power of my legs and the energy of the crash to send me up. With a twisting flip, I landed on the deck, sliding back from the momentum and placed my hand down on the floor to steady myself.

On the deck were at least fifteen soldiers nearby who had decided to abandon their firearms, charging towards me with all manner of weapons. Whips, chains, knives, machetes, and clubs were all pointed threateningly at me. The first three enemies nearest me lunged, two with cudgels, the other with a steel chain. Their weapons wouldn't be fast enough to set off the EM shield, but I wouldn't need it.

The guy with the chain wrapped it around his arm and then whipped it towards me. I brought my arm up and felt the sting as it struck, allowing it to wrap around my arm, allowing me to yank him forward, spin him like a shot-put, and smash him into his two advancing friends. I let the chain unwrap and fall to the deck.

From behind, someone attempted to sneak up on me with a knife. I twisted mere centimeters from the stab, grabbing their wrist and breaking their

156

arm sideways in one effective move. Yet another thug came from the side, my right leg immediately kicking out and up, finding his throat and sending him off the deck. The one who's arm I had broken had a revolver looking thing. I swiped it and held the trigger while pulling the hammer back with my other hand three quick times, finding the heads of advancing enemies.

I stepped over the bodies I left behind, grabbing a brick house of a woman who lunged at me and flung her right off the side of the deck as if she weighed nothing. My eyes were locked on the Lieutenant who had earned himself a death sentence. He pulled out a gold-plated semi-automatic pistol. It was sleeker than all of the other weapons and different in function. I didn't trust my shield against it.

As he aimed, I stepped to the side, each shot missing me as he fired. When I was finally close enough, I grabbed the barrel, turning the weapon and breaking his finger. Considering the night before, both of his arms were now next to useless. I grabbed him by the throat and lifted him into the air.

In almost an instant, the fighting had stopped, and everyone paused to watch the spectacle. Somehow, someway, one man just walked out to a militarized force, neutralized several fighters, and was now standing on their landship. Their precious Second's life was endangered by that single man. I couldn't help but enjoy my situation.

"Didn't learn your lesson last night, I see. For someone who supposedly worships strength, you're pretty fucking weak to me." To put the cherry on top, I spun, his body swinging with me in my hand like a ragdoll, and then I let him go, tossing him off the deck. As he fell, I finished my spin, grabbing for my trusty sidekick, took aim, and struck his head, killing him before he could even hit the ground.

The air grew silent as his body fell, the impact echoing out. I could see that a crowd had gathered on the walls of the city, jaws agape, people in shock at what they had witnessed. I was expecting the Sons to start to disperse, demoralized by their loss, but I was very wrong about that.

"Impressive." I heard from the speakers of the landship. "He was a blowhard, destined to find his demise at the hand of someone he mouthed-off to."

"Who the fuck?" I looked around, but then was shocked to feel the entire ship lurch for a moment and I figured out where the voice was coming from.

"It has been too long since I have met anyone worthy to demonstrate their might." All of the Sons had begun to back away. They started to cheer and catcall to me about how screwed I suddenly was. I decided to leap off the landship, landing and creating a small crater in the sand before backing up and watching as the gate-like doors in front of the vehicle began to shudder.

"Rellen's First!" One Son yelled. "Show him true Strength!" came another. Finally, the doors burst open, and out came a sight straight out of some horror story. The thing was vaguely humanoid, walking on two meaty legs. It hunched in a way similar to stalkers, looking like it could use its massive arms to run. It was at least five meters tall by the time it was able to get out of its confining space, just one of its biceps nearly the size of my entire body. It was covered head to toe in metallic plates, only able to see by a round opening in its helmet. Its skin was a brownish-green, popping with large red veins all over. In one of its massive mits, shaped like an ape's, it dragged an enormous hunk of metal fashioned into a club only it could wield. The metal hunk itself was also more massive than I was by an alarming amount. One hit would likely

158

kill me.

It approached me somewhat calmly, getting to about a couple of meters away before speaking again. "Not much to look at, are you? I expected more."

"And that's why you'll lose." I wasted no time. I wasn't one for monologues, aiming my pistol and firing for the hole in the helmet. My aim was true, but as it struck, he merely reacted as if stung by a bee. Considering the round he was hit by was a forty-eight, I suddenly realized how much trouble I had gotten myself into.

"Ha, ha, ha, if that's the best you have, you're done for. Fight me like a true Child of Strength!" He swung his massive club at me, but I was barely able to leap to the side just in time, tumbling on the sand. He immediately lifted it back up and swung it around in a spin maneuver. This time I jumped up and managed to land on the weapon itself, grasping onto it and holding on for dear life.

"I'll squash you like an insect!" The voice boomed out. The weapon I was on raised high into the air. I took the opportunity to drop onto its shoulder as the mighty cudgel smashed back down onto the sand. Now on top of him, I planted my feet and tried to pry his helmet off but was shocked to realize it was physically attached to his neck.

A meaty hand made its way up to his shoulder, trying to grasp at me, forcing me to leap from my opponent and roll in the sand on impact. All of this must-have spurned something within the people of the town because the security forces opened fire on the monster battling me. It screamed out in a mighty rage, tossing its weapon at the wall, smashing it violently and nearly toppling a section over. In his distraction, I made my way to a discarded buggy and hopped on.

"Who you fightin' ugly?" I yelled out, and in a rage, it turned towards me and began, on all fours, to run. His size allowed him to keep up, but I wasn't trying to get away. As he dove to grasp me away from my seat, I bailed from the vehicle, rolling in the sand before catching myself and dashing back towards him as he moved to lift himself up. I planned this near a body of one of the fallen Sons, grabbing a pipe bomb she had on her.

The big guy was up again, but I lunged up, managing to grasp a metal plate on his chest, climbing up like he was some sort of moving jungle gym. He pounded at his own chest in an attempt to swat me off, but I found my mark, shoving the pipe bomb into his helmet and jamming the handle in place. Another meat fist moved towards me, so I jumped backward from his shoulders, flipping and landing on my feet. Wasting no time, I raised my weapon again and fired at the grenade, setting it off right in his face.

The guttural scream of pain that came out rang through the hearts of the Sons, the looks on their faces betraying them. The First of Rellen staggered, grasping at his helmet as an almost brown like blood poured from it. He dropped to his knees, still, somehow, not dead. The explosive or perhaps shrapnel must have gotten into his throat because I could hear him trying to speak, but it only came out as a loud gurgle. Silence filled the battlefield, even the people behind me had nothing to say for a long moment.

Casually I walked to the body of the Lieutenant, laying limp and bloody in front of the gate. On him, I found what looked to be a radio and pulled it from his chest. It looked like it still worked and was set on, probably so he could talk into the speaker system at will.

"Alright, let me make this perfectly clear to all of you uneducated savages. I am not having a very good week, and I am seriously not in the mood to put up with you. Disperse now, or I will hunt you all down one by one!" My voice echoed out across the sands, and no one made a response. From the now gathering group of Sons, a uniquely dressed woman approached me. She wore spiked armor and sported half a bald head with hair only on the back, which was quite long and crimson red. She had a wicked-looking blade at her side and held a rifle on a shoulder strap. When she approached, she stared into my eyes with rapt awe before dropping down to one knee, and bowing her head.

"Your Strength is clearly superior. The Strong rule." It was at this time that the Sons all began to gather around me, one-by-one, including the ones that had just arrived from the other wall sections. They all took a knee, and it was quite honestly the most awkward moment of my entire life. By now, the body of their former boss had finally gone still, his blood pouring freely onto the sand below him.

"You've gotta be fuckin' kidding me, oh, shit, oops." I realized I was still being amplified by the radio. I shook my head, tossing it into a pocket, and reached down to lift the woman back onto her feet. "Don't do that shit, it's weird. People behind me are gonna get the wrong idea."

"Wrong idea? You are the First now, the Strongest there is! What could defeat a First if the original was not but a pretender?" She looked at me like I was some sort of religious icon.

"No, no, we don't do that, none of that. Look, I'm just a guy with some sweet toys. What the hell is all of this Strength crap?" As I asked the question, another person stood up, a young scrawny looking thing with one long spike sticking out from the top middle of his head.

161

"Drah Rellen birthed the Sons through his Wisdom. He taught us that the Strong shall rule and that the Weak shall serve!" The others began to nod and grunt in agreement.

"You!" The woman began again. "Are Strong, and we are Weak by comparison. You are fit to rule!"

"Well, well, well, what did you get yourself into?" The voice was of the guard commander from the night before. She sauntered up to us, her rifle resting in her hands, pointed down. She looked sufficiently amused.

"What?" I turned to her, "I didn't get myself into anything. This world is fucked, and that is definitely not my fault." I turned to the Sons, pulling the radio out of my pocket and speaking into it. "Here's the deal kids. You think I'm your boss? Fine! Rulers don't raid their people, rulers don't use them for whatever they want! They use their Strength to protect them!" It was amazing how quickly this entire thought process came to me.

"Wait, what?" I heard the incredulous commander behind me, but I ignored her.

"Anyone can walk up to someone and punch them in the face. It takes real Strength to be the one to get up and face that aggressor! You will not raid these people anymore, and you will respect their laws when in their homes. Show Strength through integrity!"

"But First, how would we eat?" The woman in front of me looked confused by everything I was saying.

"Your people provide for you in return for their defense! That is the point. The Strong defend the Weak, the Weak feed the Strong. Become a symbiote and not a parasite." She turned to look to her people who had begun to discuss this among themselves.

162

"What the fuck are you doing?" The guard commander grabbed my shoulder and spun me around to face her.

"You're seriously gonna argue right now? I was paying attention during that fight, and you know what I saw? I saw a force that didn't crush you because they chose not to." I could see the fury in her eyes, but there was no denying the truth of my statement. "How long before another person like me saunters in and pisses them off, but doesn't have the common courtesy to clean up their mess?" I turned to the Sons again. "You will return to your home. You are never to return here in force, for I fought on their behalf and will do it again if I have to. If you are to return here, it is to send an emissary to begin trade negotiations."

"But First, we have nothing to trade! We do not farm, we do not make things."

"Yeah, you filth, take it all instead!" The Guard Commander spat at the feet of the Sons in front of me. She growled but stopped when I held my hand up.

"You have your Strength, one of the most lucrative trade items. Patrols, scouting, city defense, all of these things are worth their weight in resources." She turned to the rest of the Sons who were staring at me in rapt awe.

"We will do as you say, First. Will you come home with us?"

"No." There was murmuring in the crowd now. "My Strength is needed elsewhere." That seemed to be enough to get the point across. I never really was much of a diplomat. Still, my mental clarity was allowing me to pinpoint the social weaknesses of those I spoke with like it was some sort of tactical tool in my arsenal.

The rest of the Sons stood, the obviously lower-ranking members beginning to clean up the mess. I noticed they stripped their dead of anything valuable and then left them there as if they didn't matter. I could imagine they were considered too weak to care about. I turned to the Guard Commander, who was looking at me with a mix of confusion, anger, and relief.

"Do you know what you're doing?" Her gaze met mine as she asked the question.

"Nope," I answered truthfully. "But do any of us really know what we're doing? Especially these days?"

"Is everything a joke to you?"

"Oh, anything can be funny if you try hard enough. So, what are you gonna do with Stinky here?" I motioned with my thumb over my shoulder behind me, referring to the giant that lay dead in the sand.

"Burn him with the rest. There usually isn't very many Sons bodies to clean up."

"Well." I patted her on the side of her arm. "There's a first time for everything."

"So, what're you gonna do?" She inquired, looking around the battlefield for a moment before meeting my gaze again.

"Get back to work."

"Are you gonna be secretive about that too?" She put one of her hands to her hips.

"Nah. I'm gonna hurt the Coalition, and I'm gonna hurt 'em bad for what they did to me. No big secret there." She seemed a little taken aback by the statement, but only for a moment.

"If I hadn't seen what I just saw, I might think you were crazy."

"Oh, I'm crazy, but that's not my fault." Finally, I got a chuckle out of her.

"Wait!" I heard a man yell from the gates of the city. Turning, I witnessed the amusing sight of a portly, middle-aged man virtually waddling out to where we stood. "Wait, don't leave yet!" He was wearing clothes that were cleaner and nicer than just about anyone I had seen up to that point. He was balding, but the remainder of his hair was slicked back. His tanned skin reminded me of just how different I looked.

My hands were white, almost ghost white in comparison to everyone around me. Having never actually seen the sun my entire life, my skin reflected that. While the light of the Undercities and supplements in our diet mitigated the need for natural sun-light, it did nothing for catching a tan. After taking a moment to look at my hands, I looked back up at the dude who was huffing and puffing.

"Please, we can't let you leave without expressing our gratitude."

"Really that's not neces-"

"Is that thing attached to your forehead?" The Guard Commander demanded incredulously, finally noticing my CIHUD that was still out.

"Nope." I let it retract back into my forehead. "That bugger's lodged in there." Both people jumped, startled from the quick retraction of the CIHUD.

"What are you?" The Commander finally asked.

"Just a traveler who happened to be in the right place at the right time. Lucky you."

"Look, sir," the Mayor looking guy began again. "Please, you must let us at least offer to clean your clothes and feed your belly." I decided to take another glance at my arms, chest, and legs. I was spattered with blood and dirt. I must have looked like some kind of monster. I never gave any thought to how close I was to some of the Sons I shot. I wanted to feel guilty, to feel remorse for being covered in human viscera, but I couldn't. I wasn't allowed to feel something like that.

"Fine, yeah, sounds good." I was ushered back into the city by the man, this time earning myself a guard entourage. At first, I thought they followed me out of paranoia, but then I saw many people gather at the gates, looking for a chance to see the man that stopped the Sons of Rellen. Word was spreading fast. The guards that walked with us kept the crowd at bay as they all asked questions, cheered out, and offered me drinks. Some asked what they will do if I leave, others cried about their lost children and where I was until that point. I couldn't help but keep quiet, somewhat overwhelmed. I doubt walking into a city of desperate, adoring fans was a contingency the CORPS had thought of.

Chapter Fifteen: Kill Switch

I was led to one of the better-kept brick buildings. Inside was fancier than everything I had seen so far; it was clean and tidy. They brought me to a large locker room with a set of open showers, benches, and, most of all, privacy. They left me to my own devices in there and took my clothes to have them cleaned. I was likely getting treatment that only the rich could afford.

I set all of my equipment aside and went to one of the showers. I was surprised to know they had running water at all. Remembering what Rachelle had said about the hydroponics farm, I had to imagine there was some sort of underground reservoir they were tapping into. When the water began to get hot, I felt a little excited. I figured my days of hot showers were long since behind me, but I also couldn't help feeling a little guilty. A lot of people out there deserved to feel the same way.

I took my time washing up, enjoying the shower. To my surprise, I was feeling drowsy and a bit physically drained. I hadn't felt that way since before my augmentations. Turning the shower off, I grabbed the towel they had left me. I went to one of the benches, feeling kind of dizzy and decided to lie down. I had just got done doing more physical activity than the CORPS ever put me through. Perhaps I had found the limits of my machines. I closed my eyes and allowed myself to doze off.

We were running through the tunnel of the giant tram shaft. Lys, Ray, and I, were running for our lives. Behind us were the stalkers, dozens of them maybe even hundreds, their putrid breath stinking of death and permeating the air. I could hear their claws scraping the metal floor, their grunts getting closer. As we neared the end of the tunnel, there was a contingency of Coalition troops, their glowing eyes staring hatefully at us. Ronyn stood in the

167

center of them, smiling with pride. The soldiers opened fire, killing Lys and Ray, before allowing the stalkers to gather and begin devouring.

"Do not fret XR001." I could see Ronyn smile at me. "You are in no danger. They know their own kind."

I stood up immediately, my body covered in sweat while my heart raced.

"Whoa, there cowboy." It was the Guard Commander. She must have come in while I was asleep, and yet I hadn't noticed her. I was still a bit tired, though my body was beginning to return to full strength. "I was just checking on you. You've been in here a couple of hours."

"Really?" I looked at her with a shocked expression.

"Is there a problem?" She asked. I noticed she had a bag that looked like it contained my clothes.

"No, well, kind of. I dunno, I'm tired, drowsy, feel like I could go back to sleep."

"And?" She gave me a look like I was talking crazy. "You should be tired, all things considered."

"Well, yeah, but, oh nevermind. Are those my clothes?" I pointed at the bag.

"Cleaned and pressed. Lucky you." She tossed the bag onto the floor near me.

"Well, I'll be out of your hair soon." After everything I had been through, I didn't care about modesty anymore. I began to get dressed right there.

"I ain't trying to get rid of you, sweet cheeks." She gave me a smirk. "Mayor Sig insists that you have a meal and spend the night at least."

168

"Yeah, and how do you feel about that?" Once I had my pants and shirt back on, I began to re-equip myself.

"Personally? I think you're a troublemaker, but you clean up your messes so I can't complain. Besides, something tells me you're needed elsewhere." I gave her a look when she said that, not quite sure what she meant by it.

"What's your name?" I finally asked, pulling the harness over my shoulders.

"Sheriff Brit." Her voice carried a hint of pride in her title.

"Sheriff, huh? And here I thought you held some sort of military rank."

"Flattery will get you nowhere. You ready yet?"

"All dressed up and ready for war. Lead the way sheriff." Brit turned to walk out the door, and I followed close behind.

"This place was here before you guys, huh?" I wondered, looking around.

"We've always been here. This place was settled by the soldiers that were stationed here two-hundred years ago. We're a trade hub for people foolish enough to travel the desert." We headed to a stairwell and began to head up.

"Is the whole continent a wasteland?"

"Nah, just the central part, where the Tantillan capital cities were. Getting from one end to the other, though, the quickest way is through the desert." We made our way to the third floor of the building and were in a hall that looked like it used to house offices.

"So, what's the coast like then?"

"What'd you grow up under a rock or something?"

"Yeah, that's gonna get old quick. Assume I did." She turned and looked at me with a confused expression.

"Okay, fine then. It's greener than here, some forests, mountains, rivers. It's the place sane people choose to live. A decent chunk of it is under Coalition protection, and even the TLF leaves it alone. They call it the Preserve." She turned back around and went to the door on the far end. "This way, hero." She opened it and motioned for me to enter.

The room was large, with a big, round table at the center. While the paint on the walls began to chip long ago, the place still looked more lavish than the rest of the building. There were ancient paintings of various government officials and soldiers. I walked up to one that I couldn't read the nameplate of but recognized the uniform from history classes.

"This was a F'Rytalan base?" I was asking the group of people that were sitting at the table, specifically the Mayor, as well as several men and women who were all equally well dressed.

"I'm sorry, what?" Sig asked, standing up. "Please, come take a seat." He motioned to a chair next to where he was sitting at the table. I shrugged and walked over, taking a seat as requested.

"Y'know, F'Rytal, they were one of the two major powers that warred centuries ago." I pointed at the painting. "That man is wearing a F'Rytalan uniform. Surprised you don't speak it."

"Whatever do you mean?" One of the older women at the table, attired in a formal blue dress asked.

"This base, it didn't belong to Tantil."

"Oh, you mean the time of the war. Our ancestors were made up of soldiers and local civilians." The Mayor spoke up, finally realizing what I was

170

talking about. "Yes, we're actually a varied group here." Soon a door off to the side of the room opened, and four men came out carrying plates of food. It looked a bit like what I got at the tavern, only of a much higher quality. I suddenly realized how hungry I felt.

"This is something else. To see these paintings, it's like something out of my school days." I must have sounded like a naive kid because I heard Brit snicker under her breath. She was still standing at the door.

"Sheriff, please, come sit with us." Sig requested, motioning to an empty chair.

"No, thanks. I eat with my men." She spoke quite matter of fact like.

"Of course." Mayor Sig sounded defeated, but his smile only faded for a quick moment before he looked back to me. "So, tell us, what brought you here? Why did you help us?"

"Well," I started, taking a bite and smiling at the flavor. "I'm what you might refer to as an escaped experiment. I was just passing through, and I can't abide by a group of assholes raping and pillaging for funsies."

"Someone said you got into a fight in Owen's Watering Hole with the Second of Rellen last night." Another one of the women sitting at the table mentioned, which caused me to snort out a chuckle.

"I wouldn't call it a fight. I like to think of it more as an attitude adjustment." I took another bite, finding myself ravenous.

"A lot of good that did." I heard Brit say with a hint of sarcasm. She was leaning against the door frame, her arms crossed over her chest.

"Yeah, well, sometimes people don't listen so good, so you have to say things a second time." I rebutted with a smirk, continuing to scarf my food down.

"Now, now, son." One of the men, a short, gray-haired affair in business attire, interrupted. "Don't choke, there's plenty of food."

"Yeah, sorry, just never been this hungry before." Before I knew it, my plate was empty, and yet I still felt a bit hungry. As I ate, my fatigue began to fade. I patted my belly. "Still need more little buddies?" I realized I was getting weird looks from across the table, but the Mayor simply clapped his hands. Within moments another plate was brought out. "Oh, hell, yes!" I exclaimed when more food was brought to me.

"Goodness, you eat a lot." A woman noted.

"Yeah, I dunno, guess that fight took a lot out of me."

"You said you were an escaped experiment?" The Mayor finally conjured the courage to ask.

"Yep. The CORPS is apparently playing around with cybernetics these days." I was met with confused looks. "Integrating man with machine. I'm literally swarming with tiny little robots, among other things." The confusion turned to a sort of horror. "Don't worry, I'm not contagious or nothing, though a disease that turns you into a super-soldier would be pretty sweet."

"Sign me up." I heard Brit say.

"But why? What's the point?" A younger-looking man asked, cocking his head to the side slightly.

"Were you hurt or dying?" The Mayor asked.

"Well, no, not as such. I mean that one jerk did shoot me before I went out, but that's because I was about to give Ronyn a piece of his own mind. No, I was never given a choice in the matter. I'm a lab rat with a sense of humor." They were all looking around in astonishment. Had the battle before not happened, not a soul would believe a word that was coming out of my mouth.

172

It was at that moment that the door to the hall opened, and a guard came in to speak with Brit. He was trying to be discrete, but my ears picked up everything.

"Sheriff, scouts say there was a Coalition transport passing nearby. They just got attacked by a TLF ambush." As soon as I heard this, I wiped my mouth with a napkin at the table and stood up.

"Did he just say there's a fight between the CORPS and TLF going on right now?"

"Yeah." Brit turned to me, annoyed. "He was telling *me* there was a situation outside. If you'll excuse me." She began to walk out.

"I'm going too." I walked for the door.

"Excuse me? You better, not b-"

"Try and stop me," I said, meeting her gaze. I could see the frustration in her eyes, knowing there really wasn't anything she could do to stop me from going out there.

"Fine, but I swear if you bring the Coalition or even TLF down on us, I will find a way to kill you myself." She spoke with all of the seriousness her body could muster, and it was a lot. I nodded to show my understanding, and she began to head out with me following in tow.

"Well, uh, good luck?" I could hear Sig saying behind me, but I was on a mission. The CORPS was probably looking for me, it would explain why they were close by. I couldn't stay if that was the case for precisely the reasons Brit had alluded to. The CORPS had no compassion, and I didn't want to think about what they would do if they thought these people knew of my existence. I was hoping to catch another nap, but the food and sudden emotions woke me right up.

Brit led me back outside and to the western wall of the city. We climbed a ladder up to where a gathering of guards was standing. As Brit got up, she took a pair of binoculars from one of her men and peered out into the distance. I could already see what she was looking at, and as I focused, my vision became my own set of internal binoculars.

They were kicking up a lot of dust, but I could see a CORPS convoy, a transport that was at least as heavily armed as the one I escaped from, if not more so. The TLF had surrounded them, but from my perspective, it didn't look like their ambush was going as planned. Besides having superior technology, Coalition soldiers were cold-blooded monsters. They didn't know fear, and even their privates were tactical experts.

"This is gonna end badly for the TLF," Brit commented. "Idiots, why would they even try? I never understood it."

"I need a buggy," I virtually demanded.

"Excuse me?" Brit was incredulous. "Look, you might be some hero, but you don't get to just take whatever strikes your fancy. Trying to live up to your new title Mr. First?" I pursed my lips, getting a little pissed, but then remembered she didn't know the gravity of the situation.

"Let me make myself clear. That convoy is probably looking for me, and if the CORPS find me here or think I was here for an extended period, your people will suffer for it. Let me leave and assist the TLF. I'll be out of your hair for good and can make sure the CORPS doesn't give two shits about your little settlement." She stared at me for a long moment before shaking her head and looking to one of the guards.

"Give him one of the scout bikes." She grabbed my arm and looked into my eyes. "I don't want to see you back here. Between the Sons and the

174

CORPS, you ain't worth the risk."

"On that, we agree." She released my arm. I followed the guard she ordered to assist me, down the wall. We walked to a small concrete garage that held one of the two-wheeled vehicles that were like the ones the TLF had been using. It looked like it saw heavy use, and I wasn't sure I entirely trusted my life to the thing, but there was no time to waste.

I took a moment to analyze the bike, running my hand over it and letting my CIHUD come out, learning about its make-up.

"Do you know how to work this thing?" The guard asked as I mounted the bike. I used the kick starter, getting the engine to roar to life.

"I do now." I gave him no time to reply as I sped out of the garage and immediately made my way out of the city, speeding through the desert towards the battle ahead. The dust kicked up behind me like I was some sort of tornado carving a path towards my targets. Honestly, I wasn't sure what I was doing; all I knew was I couldn't stay in that town any longer, and I sure as hell couldn't let the opportunity pass.

I left the CIHUD out, allowing me to get a feel for how the battle ahead was faring. I was amazed at how I was able to drive the machine through the sand and rocky areas. The augmentations ensured I was always confident in my abilities and thus took the necessary risks for success. Besides that, I was rarely off-balance, but I was still a little drowsy. Luckily, the adrenaline was beginning to take care of that.

As I grew closer, I became aware of what I was dealing with. The TLF came prepared, as if whatever it was the CORPS convoy contained was really important. There were several tanks and other vehicles I hadn't seen in the previous battle. What shocked me was when I began to hear the noises above.

Zooming around was a machine with fast-moving propellers on the top and what looked to be jets on the side. It was coming in hot, guns firing into the line, and I realized the flying machine was part of the Coalition. Its missiles fired, taking out a tank, but I was still a good kilometer away.

I thought the flying machine would do them in, but then I heard something else, a fast sound, also coming from the air. Looking, I could see what appeared to be a metallic arrow, screaming through the sky at mind-boggling speeds. Before I could even close half the distance, it was there, slamming into the gunship and sending it spinning out of control. The jet that fired it zipped passed as if it hadn't even been there.

The CORPS had an answer, of course. Now within full view of everything, I could see it was an armored convoy, and they had tanks of their own. One of them had a strange, boxy, swiveling head. It turned, pointing in the direction the jet had flown. There was no sound, no light, or any sort of fanfare. As it aimed, the jet that was coming back around suddenly caught fire and took a nosedive, smashing into the ground with a mighty explosion. The CORPS were employing energy weapons; this fight was not going to end well.

As my bike drew closer, I realized that I was coming into sight of some of the Coalition troops that were surrounding the center vehicle. An Elite took aim and fired at my bike, but I swerved out of the way of the first shot. When others began to fire, I wasn't so lucky. I knew the bike was toast, so I waited, letting a round hit my tire, causing the bike to lurch from the back. I was promptly launched into the air, using the momentum to sail forward and somersaulting when I impacted the ground. As I did, my hand found its way to my sidekick, and I fired off five fast rounds, ending the ones shooting at me.

176

I dashed to the side as the hail of fire came my way, using the terrain and vehicles to weave through cover. I could see TLF soldiers taking the distraction I was causing to start advancing. I might have been one man, but now the Coalition was flanked. Continuing to run, I was making my way to a unit of six CORPS troopers when suddenly I could sense one of the tanks had taken aim at little old me. I leapt high into the air, quickly clearing five meters. The concussion from the impact of the tank round added to my momentum, shrapnel flinging away harmlessly from my EM armor.

I landed directly behind the unit that was about to blast one of the TLF armored vehicles. One of the Elites had a large cylindrical weapon, and I had a feeling nothing good would come out of it. Two of the Elite soldiers noticed me, one taking a swing with a bayonet, which I easily avoided by ducking under it. I came back up with a punch to his face, spinning his entire body with a bone-crunching thud. Using the momentum, I twisted and kicked another next to him in the side of the head. In mid-spin, I grabbed the massive weapon of the Elite in the middle, ripping it from his hands.

Like a mighty bat, I swung the cylinder around, smashing the original holder and the guy next to him. One of the soldiers came at me with a knife while the other remaining member of the unit aimed his rifle. I dropped the cylinder, grabbing the wrist of the knife-wielder and spinning him around violently as his buddy pulled the trigger. The human shield I held, violently rocked and spattered blood before I tossed him to the ground. I lunged at the remaining soldier, grabbing onto his shoulders and kneeing him in the stomach with enough force to lift him several centimeters up. When he was back on the ground, I finished it with a kick to his head.

I heard an ominous whistling coming through the air, my CIHUD flashing warnings about explosives coming from the TLF side. I watched as bombs arced through the atmosphere, but then the laser tank quickly turned its sights. There was no firing again, but all of the mortars were blasted out of the air.

By now, I had made a spectacle of myself, causing the CORPS armored units to begin focusing on my location. My CIHUD had managed to analyze the weapon I had used as a bat, and I learned precisely what it was. I grabbed the rocket launcher and quickly took a knee, firing at the laser tank. My shot was accurate, as a jet of flames fired out from both ends of the weapon, sending an arrow of righteousness to end the wicked. It struck a weak spot in the armor, sparks, and flames spewing out, immediately sending the tank out of commission.

I began to dash again having become a target, and the TLF took the initiative. There was a loud series of piercing whistles, and my CIHUD began to flash warnings about incoming explosives. I ran harder than I had ever run before. The bombs sailed through the air, striking three of the armored vehicles, leaving the one in the center, likely their target, completely unharmed.

I, on the other hand, was not so lucky. Some of the explosions sent me forward and into the dirt. While I was only hit by the concussive force, it was still enough to launch me a few meters. My harness absorbed the blow, causing little explosions of sand to jet out each time I rolled on the ground. Finally stopping, I stood up, ready for more until the strangest sensation came over me. I was dizzy, and the drowsiness was somehow getting worse.

"C'mon, not now." I tried to run forward, but then tripped over my own two feet and fell back down. Every part of me ached and I was exhausted in ways I couldn't even begin to describe. All I wanted to do was sleep, despite everything happening around me. Vehicles whizzed by as the TLF took advantage of the opportunity I had provided them. Things were fading, and I couldn't sense everything around me anymore. I felt naked and even a little scared. Eventually, I passed out.

Chapter Sixteen: Still Human

"You found him." *A familiar and distant voice said. Was it Lys?*

"Him? He's what you pulled this stunt over?" *A man's voice, could it be Ray? I'm sorry.*

"Yes, he is. You'll find out soon enough." *As the voices faded, my mind wandered to many places. I could float around the Undercities on the outside, seeing the structure, observing the monsters. I bobbed up and above, beyond the mountains, sailing higher into the waiting sky above. All I wanted was rest, was this finally it?*

I woke up to the rudest bucket of water ever invented. Someone had splashed me, and I realized my arms were chained to a wall. My eyes opened and saw a darkened room with a light shining on me. A soldier in TLF fatigues tossed the bucket he had splashed me with aside. I was shirtless, my equipment missing, and my pants were my only attire. The room wasn't very big, and there were a couple of guards stationed at the door to my left.

In front of me, I saw a man standing with the bucket wielder. He was average height with short, well-kempt blond hair. His piercing blue eyes were accented by a scar running down his left cheek. Despite this, he seemed to have an approachable air to him. It was his uniform that struck me. It was heavily decorated with medals, honors, and his rank was one I hadn't seen before. His shoulder sported a patch that contained five stars circling a shield.

"Well, glad to see you're awake. Can you understand me?" I quirked a brow with the question, unsure of what condition they had found me in.

"Yep, loud and clear boss. So, is this how you treat everyone who saves your asses, or am I special and get the kinky treatment?" Surprisingly, I got a chuckle out of the well-dressed man.

"You're a special case. I am General Delantil of the Tantillan Liberation Front. You are John, yes? Known to the Coalition as XR001." I wanted to roll my eyes, but I realized that the TLF were more resourceful than the CORPS would ever like to admit.

"You have me at a disadvantage, but yeah, that about sums it up. Care to explain how you know all of that?"

"We'll get to that in a couple of minutes. First, I have some questions if you don't mind." I was surprised by his politeness all things considered.

"Hey man, I'm just hangin' out, as you can see. Go for it."

"Why did you assist us in the battle four days ago?" I couldn't help my shocked reaction to the question.

"Did you just say four days? Yeesh, figured my arms would be more tired." I tried to get back to my nonchalant attitude. In all honesty, though, I wasn't tired at all. I felt like I was at full strength.

"We only put you here twenty or so minutes ago. You have to understand our position." He donned a sympathetic look, and it seemed somewhat genuine.

"Well, I think we both could benefit from that. To answer your question with a question, why not? Does anyone who actually knows what the CORPS is, like them?" The guard that had splashed me chortled at this. The General shot him a look, and he quickly clammed up.

"That's fair, I suppose." He turned back to me. "But that's not what I want to know."

"Fine, I hate the CORPS with every fiber of my being. I want to expose them for the evil that they are, to go home to the Undercities, and free everyone's minds." My voice was laden with seriousness, getting rid of my

181

humorous attitude.

"While you and I certainly share a goal in that, I don't think I'm making myself clear. Why *that* convoy, why then and there?" He kept a professional tone and posture. Honestly, I had met many people that could learn a thing or two from the guy.

"Honestly? I was in the right place at the right time. I know that sounds like a cop-out, but well, I was nearby, saw the fight and decided to lend a hand. I figure it would be a better way to meet you than what the CORPS had originally planned." He quirked a brow at my comment.

"And what would that be?"

"Well, about a week ago apparently, the CORPS sent me out on a little field test. They were sending me to a base of yours not too far from that walled settlement I was at. I was supposed to steal some information from you." He seemed to think a moment, and then his eyes shone with realization of what base I might be referring to.

"What sort of information?"

"I don't know. I was supposed to copy everything onto a datacard for a PCD. It should have been with my stuff."

"We found it. Are you aware of what was on it?" Clearly, he knew but wanted my answer.

"It was blank, wasn't it?" I asked with all honesty. He seemed to accept my ignorance.

"No. It contained a worm virus. Our techs believe it was designed to infect out communication network for monitoring purposes." His candidness surprised me. There was an ace up his sleeve, and he was keeping it very close to his chest. Considering I left everything behind, I couldn't imagine what he thought that was.

"Well, you clearly know more than I do."

"Then you were unaware of the purpose of the facility you were being sent to."

"I'm gonna point out that whole thing about you knowing more than me. Nah, man, I had no idea. It's not like I was ever given a choice in literally anything involving the CORPS."

"What happened to you during that battle? By the report, you came in like a storm of destruction, taking out an air defense tank and an entire heavy weapons team on foot. The report said you used weapons you found on the field. When we found you, you were seemingly unharmed. Our medical examiners, were quite astonished by their findings." He held out his hand, and the guard that had splashed me produced a manila envelope and handed it to him. He opened it and pulled out what looked to be medical scans. He held one up in particular that showed the storage container the CORPS had replaced my stomach with.

"Oh geez, I didn't want to have to see it," I said honestly. Delantil held up another, revealing my skull, the CIHUD tucked neatly inside, leaving very little space. There were distinctly metal components from the scan.

"To be honest, we had to pull out all the stops for these images." He handed the folder back to the guard.

"Why's that?" I was genuinely curious.

"Your body was giving off a weak magnetic field. Enough to disrupt a lot of our medical devices. We figured an MRI would be a bit dangerous. The Coalition did a number on you it would seem."

"That's an understatement in terms." My sarcasm was positively dripping from my mouth.

"What was your purpose? Why did you volunteer for this project if you hate the Coalition?" I had a feeling we had finally made it to where he was in the dark. Despite his ignorance, the question still managed to offend me.

"I didn't volunteer for jack shit, bud." I nearly spat out the words.

"Really?" He seemed somewhat surprised. "You mean to tell me that the Coalition forced these enhancements on you?" Somehow it felt like he didn't believe me.

"That's right General, I was an escapee."

"Escapee?"

"Yeah, escapee. I lived in a place we called the Undercities. I'm not quite sure where that is because I was captured at the end of our journey." I looked down dejectedly. How did my life end up like this? Chained to a wall, forever haunted by phantoms, and being questioned by someone who was just about as in the dark as I was.

"You lived in an underground city?" Delantil seemed astonished at this news, but not because he had never heard of such a thing. I felt as though I confirmed a suspicion.

"Yeah. There were millions of us down there, everything built and run by the CORPS. We've been down there since the end of the war two-hundred years ago." He looked to the guard who had an equally shocked look on his face.

"The rumors are true then. What do you know about Dome City?" He had a gleam in his eyes like maybe he had hit the jackpot.

"Dome City? Besides that being a super lame name, nothing, why?" The gleam left his eyes as quickly as it appeared.

184

"We've heard about these Undercities. We were aware the CORPS had ushered in a lot of people to several locations a couple of centuries ago. We also know they somehow relocated some of those people just a few of years ago." It took me a moment to process what he had told me.

"You mean to say they opened them up? They let people out?" I was looking back in the General's eyes. All of a sudden, it felt like my journey may have been for nothing.

"No, not exactly. We think the Coalition may have some sort of tunnel network they use to move people about." I felt a weird sense of relief from his words.

"Okay, so where were they supposedly moved to?" I asked, feeling like he should already be answering the question.

"Dome City."

"Okay, what the fuck is Dome City?" I really couldn't get over the name.

"Well, to be fair, I doubt that's what the Coalition calls it, but suffice to say the term is accurate. In the South-Central Wasteland, over twenty years ago, the Coalition began construction of what we call Dome City. Since its completion five years ago, it has been the center of their research, development, and military production. It's a monster of a construct. We estimate it at around one thousand meters tall at its top center." This was all very shocking to me. I had never heard of any other city, but five years seemed like too much of a coincidence to me. They said I had been sleeping for five years. Did Dome City have something to do with the XRC Project?

"Why are you telling me all of this? I'm chained to a wall; shouldn't I be telling you things?"

"Yes, quite right. I wanted to know what you knew, and I am fairly certain it's not much where Dome City is concerned. So, you escaped this underground city. Why?" He got right back to business. The man was professional but firm. I couldn't help but sort of like the guy.

"Well, it wasn't like I was suffering down there. Life was pretty decent, actually. They told us the surface was unlivable, that we couldn't go back and see the sky. We all lived our entire lives underground. By now, no one alive had ever seen the sun." He tilted his head a little, studying me.

"That explains your complexion. Go on, please." I was cooperative, so he was cordial.

"One day we were attacked by, well, monsters. We called them stalkers, a big mean cross between an ape and a canine." The guard and the General exchanged looks for a moment.

"I believe I am familiar with them."

"Yeah, well, they killed my family and a few others too. We came to the conclusion that the surface can't be dead and support super predators."

"A logical assumption." His voice betrayed his curiosity.

"Well, it turns out we were right. Long story short, myself and another had made it to the exit but were met by CORPS soldiers. Said I would make history before shooting me and taking me prisoner. I woke up a few months ago, and that brings us to today." I tried to give a little shrug despite the chains.

"How long has it been since the Coalition took you?" His voice now revealed a bit more sympathy. I felt like the questioning was to tell if I was a friend or foe.

"Five years." I met his gaze, hoping he might see some sort of importance in that.

186

"Interesting. So then you wouldn't have been around when the Coalition began moving people from the Undercities, as you called them."

"I guess not. So what are we doing here, General?" I let my impatience shine through my tone.

"Talking for now." The only door in the room opened, and a guard came in, walking over to Delantil. Like others before him, he tried to be subtle, but I could hear his words as if he was whispering them to me.

"The woman is getting impatient. She insists he could be in danger if she's not allowed to perform her tests." I glared at the two men.

"Who exactly are you referring to?" The General turned to look at me, seemingly not surprised I was able to hear them. He then looked back to the guard who had entered the room.

"Bring her in with her equipment. I want it locked back up as soon as she is finished." The guard immediately gave Delantil a salute.

"Yes, sir!" He hurried out of the room. Delantil began to pace for a moment, lost in thought.

"The Coalition has begun making cybernetically enhanced soldiers." He spoke, seemingly to himself.

"That's about the half of it." I watched Delantil pace, curious as to what was going through his head. I had to appreciate that it was all a lot to take in for more than just me.

"Effective ones at that. This could finally be the end of the war, and freedom is about to lose out to whatever dystopian image they have." He looked at me again. "I want you to appreciate my position here. You represent the greatest threat we have ever known."

"I'm no fool, I can see that plain as day. Make no mistake, though; I

187

also represent the greatest threat the CORPS has ever unleashed upon itself." I met his eyes as if to somehow transmit my honesty to him. The moment was broken when the door slid open again and in walked Dr. Alonna LyRul, the absolute last person I expected to see. As soon as she came into view, my lips pursed in annoyance.

"Ah, so, I see. Just another test, right?"

"I beg your pardon?" Delantil asked, obviously confused.

"Not this time John." Alonna made her way over to us, the guard from before standing close by. "We're both captives here." She had the medical scanner she had frequently used in the past and approached me with it.

"Well, *you're* a captive anyway." I was unable to hide the grin. Something about the concept brought glee to my heart. I allowed her to scan me. "So, what the hell happened to me anyway?"

"Your nanomachines expired." She spoke in that matter-of-fact way that used to drive me insane. She never looked away from her scanning device.

"Why do you always make me ask you to elaborate?" I asked in a huff. She finally met my gaze, seemingly satisfied with her readings.

"You were somewhat of a prototype, John. Once you escaped, you were deemed expendable." She explained this with a hint of sadness to her voice, but then it changed to triumph. "But I have changed all of that, thanks to the TLF." Delantil stepped forward to be part of the conversation.

"Plan to elaborate on that doctor?"

"I knew where he was, we were tracking him. I knew how long before his nanomachines stopped functioning properly. The plan was to simply let him die, but well." She looked at me again. "I pulled in a favor."

"Okay, I'm confused," I finally interjected. "What the hell is going on here?"

"Dr. Lyrul here made contact with us a few months ago, feeding us intel. Originally, we attempted to capture you a little over a week ago, but you managed to escape. Then we were," he looked to Alonna, "conveniently alerted that a high-value Coalition scientist would be traveling in the area." He looked back to me. "We had no idea you would be there."

"She did." I shook my head. "That's how they work General. Plans upon plans, conspiracies hiding conspiracies."

"I'm well aware. That is why she is being kept as a prisoner." He gave me a look that showed we saw eye-to-eye.

"I do not understand why that's necessary. I have done nothing but help you." Alonna still had that haughty confidence about her. If I didn't loathe everything she represented, it might even be attractive.

"He's not stupid obviously," I answered her comment for the General. She shot me a look, and it was the first time I genuinely frustrated her. It actually spoke volumes to me, and suddenly I believed for the first time she was going by the seat of her pants. None of her situation was planned, which meant she really was at the mercy of the TLF. "You really are helpless."

"Really now?" Delantil inquired. "What makes you say that?"

"She isn't prepared." My eyes were on her, analyzing every inch, and for a moment, I could tell she was uncomfortable. I felt no sympathy, she could drink in what it felt like to be nothing more than data to analyze. "She really did escape. I've never seen this woman scared and to be honest with you, it's starting to make a little sense. What do you have to say about Langstan, Doc?" She looked down when I spoke his name.

"It was my hope you would keep him safe." I scoffed and rolled my eyes.

"Please, he was dead as soon as the first round hit our transport. Would've been you y'know." The day just kept getting weirder. Delantil was letting me grill her. I felt like he was getting the same sort of satisfaction out of hearing it as I was getting saying it. Here I was, chained to a wall, and yet I was the one in control. The chains weren't anything more than a formality really; the bolts would've popped easily.

"That may be so, but you," her gaze met mine again, "would certainly be dead had I not acted. You would have died upon your return and been dissected like an animal." Her voice was tinged with anger, though it was hard to tell what it was directed towards. Her fists were clenched, and she shook lightly from the stress.

"Did it ever occur to you that sometimes dead might be better?"

"No, it did not. I am a doctor; dead is never better." Her haughty confidence returned to her quickly. "If I may change the subject. You no longer have an expiration date for your nanomachines. They will self-replicate indefinitely. When we have time, I would like to ask some questions about how you felt prior to losing consciousness."

"You just don't give up, do you?"

"This has nothing to do with the XRC Project. Knowing the effects failing nanomachines had on your system will allow me to better detect and treat you should the Cybernetics Division devise a way to disable or damage them."

"Okay, fair, go on." I gave her a look as if to say she had a good point.

"Thank you. I did successfully manage to shut down the tracking systems that were installed into the nanomachines. I have also made their signals invisible to CIHUD technology."

"CIHUD technology?" Delantil asked, and I gave him a smirk, allowing my CIHUD to open over my eye. I noticed him shudder a little as it happened. "As professionally as I can, that is creepy as all hell."

With the CIHUD out, I could sense everything much more clearly and know that we were underground somewhere, dozens of meters at least. It felt like a bunker of some kind, the ventilation system allowing my sensors to escape to other areas, but the range and clarity wasn't as good.

"So Doc, what's the point of making me invisible to me?" I wondered, not realizing my own ignorance.

"Surely at this point, you must realize that you are not the only, for lack of a better term, completed unit." The General shot a look at Alonna.

"Do you mean to tell me there are more of him out there?"

"Yes, and that is exactly why I told you we should never have brought him here. The tracking signal was only prevented when you allowed me to inject him with the new nanomachines. They had two days of tracking data sent out." Almost as if on cue, I felt a strange sensation wash over me. I could sense thousands of tiny little signals in an almost bubble-like area, moving at its center, changing in size as it traveled. It was snaking through the ventilation system as if the dust itself were holding little transmitters.

Another guard entered the room, this one looking much more severe than the others. I couldn't tell her rank as it seemed that the uniforms had changed over the years, but she seemed somewhat important.

"General, security reports that we've lost contact with levels A and B." The General turned, and his face showed concern.

"Has the engineering section checked the comm system?"

"Yes sir, they report that no malfunction appears to be present." I looked to Alonna.

"You're being tracked," I snapped accusingly.

"No you fools, I just told you this! They didn't let me examine you for nearly two days after your collapse. Retrieving your body was part of the original project parameters." I turned to Delantil.

"I can't blame you for not trusting a CORPS scientist, but she's right. Something's here."

"What do you sense?" Alonna took a step closer, and light entered her eyes as the scientist crept back out.

"There's a bubble of thousands of tiny signals moving above us. It's hard to sense though, the walls are interfering with the CIHUD." I didn't realize I had become accustomed to answering her questions in detail.

"That sounds like a CIHUD signature. We have to leave this place now." Alonna suddenly looked frightened. She was a fish out of water, and a bear was nearby.

"The only way out of here is up." Replied the General. "There must be another explanation; if we were assaulted, we would have known."

"Trust me when I say this," My gaze met Delantil's. "Everyone on level A and B are probably already dead. You don't realize any assault because you aren't experiencing one. It's likely just one person." I mustered all of the seriousness I could imbue my tone with, trying to get the point across.

"So, what do you suggest, doctor?"

"I suggest," I spoke again, not letting her answer. "You make a decision to either let me out of these chains or force me to rip them out of the wall. You have one option General, and it's currently half-naked and

192

unarmed." I could see a grin grace Alonna's face. She always did appreciate my humor better than the other stiffs.

The General of the TLF looked down for a long moment, many calculations seemingly running through his mind as he considered my words. Finally, his gaze rose once more. "Release him."

"Yes, sir!" The obedient answer came, and the guard released me from my chains. I gave my wrists a bit of a rub before addressing the General.

"I need weapons."

"What you need is to prove your usefulness to me. If you're as amazing as you and the doctor here claim, then show me." He reached to his side and pulled a six-shooter from its holster, checking the chambers before twirling it and offering it to me. I took the weapon and gave him a nod.

"Fair enough, you've already proven yours."

"John!" Alonna's worried voice came. "There is no telling what they armed them with. They could be in armor or even have an EM shield like the one you had."

"I'll figure it out. We have little other choice. Do you honestly think the TLF has even ten soldiers that could fight one of us?" The question was rhetorical, and she knew it.

"Do I need to worry about security on the doors?"

"No." Delantil walked to the door, motioning for me to follow him. With a purpose, everyone exited the room revealing the tight metallic hallways of the bunker. Lights lined the ceilings, which were barely a meter taller than I was, and pipes were running along the side of the wall accompanied by electrical conduits. I walked behind the General, and his presence ensured no one questioned us.

"I want all levels below B sealed off." Delantil spoke while holding his right ear; clearly, he had some sort of comm attached to it. "I will be sending someone up from level D, he is to be given full access as needed. Sound an intr-"

"No." I interrupted him. "I want to keep the element of surprise. Make him think his infiltration is still successful."

"Cancel the alert. Give the man access and move all security teams to the lower levels." We walked through the corridors as soldiers scrambled about to get to their various positions. "Begin evacuation protocol alpha. We are to be gone from this base in four hours." We finally stopped at a set of sliding doors, and Delantil faced me.

"That should be plenty of time for you to eliminate the threat. After that, we'll talk about how we can help each other."

"John!" Alonna had followed us, her guard in tow. "Be careful. While they will not be able to sense your CIHUD, they will still be able to sense your movement, sound, and smell. Hiding will still be next to impossible."

"Good to know. So what's the point of hiding my CIHUD then?"

"If you get an opportunity, it could provide the element of surprise." Her tone conveyed her seriousness, and she seemed genuinely worried.

"Fair enough. General." I motioned for him to open the doors. He waved his hand over a small box next to the elevator, and it dutifully slid open.

"Four hours, if we haven't heard from you by then, we storm our way out and blow this base to kingdom come." I gave him a nod and turned to enter the lift. I could see buttons leading to the various levels and hit the one marked B. The doors slid shut behind me, and I thought about how crazy everything was, going in with no shirt and six rounds. Then I thought about
194

everything I had personally done up to that point and realized that very little would genuinely help me that I didn't already have.

The lift was agonizingly slow, but when it reached its destination, I gripped the revolver tighter in my hand. The elevator slid open, and I was greeted to a grizzly sight. There were TLF bodies strewn on the floor, all neatly executed with single shots to the forehead. A lot of them likely didn't have time to react. I felt like I was walking through the aftermath of one of my own incidents.

I had to keep my wits about me. At any moment, the fight would be the most real thing I had ever encountered. I could sense the bubble the XR unit was making more clearly now, indicating he was close. There were others, my CIHUD pointing out movement, all running to a central point of the level. From the looks of things, the area consisted of quarters, and the larger center room was likely a mess hall. I began to head for it. It wasn't long before I could hear gunshots, almost like panic fire coming from the center room. Something was in there with them, moving fast.

I was dashing through the corridors when I finally made it to a set of metal double doors with a push latch. I kicked the handle, letting the door fly open and moved inside. I could see in the far corner from me were three soldiers, all firing in a panic at a figure that was running at breakneck speeds. Typically, most people moved slowly to my sight, but this man was quicker than any I had seen before.

I took the opportunity, seeing that he was about to fire at the group, and took a shot, forgetting my own methods for avoiding that sort of thing. In a flash, the XRC soldier spun to the side. He landed with his knee to the floor, and one hand in front of him. Though narrowly dodging the round, it left a cut on his cheek. He stood, his eyes on me now.

"Accurate." Was his only word. He stood a little taller than I, sporting a crew cut and clothes similar to those I wore on my first time out. He held in his hand a wicked-looking SMG with a long barrel, what I thought was a suppressor at first, but then I realized it was a magnetic rail. The rounds would be silent by their nature, and their velocity would make most high caliber ammunition seem slow.

The TLF in the corner were reloading their weapons, but I yelled out to them. "Evacuate to the lower levels, General's orders!" Now in a standoff, the soldiers realized this was their only moment to survive. They scrambled to another set of doors on the other side of the mess hall. I kept my weapon aimed, ready to fire if he tried to shoot at them, but he was studying me and clearly had a new target.

"So, you're awake." He began to walk sideways, watching me, looking for an opening. I did the same, making sure he didn't get a chance to find one. The CIHUD likely gave me away, but I couldn't let him slaughter anyone else.

"Seems so. It was a nice nap. Do we really have to do this?"

"Why not? I haven't had a good fight since the surgery. Everyone else is like beatin' up toddlers." He stopped for a moment, studying me, analyzing my reactions.

"Not a problem for people who aren't psychopaths. This could be your chance; walk away from the CORPS, make your own way."

"And why the fuck would I do that? The CORPS gave me these wonderful machines! Machines I plan to use to end you!" He aimed his weapon and began firing. Fingers only move so fast and I was able to judge his aim. I ran to the side, avoiding the spray, sliding as he lowered his weapon, deftly dodging his planned trajectories. It wasn't long before his mag was empty, and he tossed the gun to the side.

"Good, it'll be more fun this way!" As he spoke, I swung my arm around, taking aim and firing one of the rounds from the revolver. He had mastered my own secret to dodging, deftly weaving out of the way of the shot while dashing toward me. I stood as he closed in and tried to pistol-whip him upside the head, but he ducked under it, using the motion to come up with a left upper-cut. I leaned my body back, dodging the blow, but he was already bringing his right fist for my head. I spun with the motion and crouched low, avoiding the punch and attempting to trip him, but he merely leapt over my leg.

"Stand still!" He yelled as his foot came up to try and stomp me, but I rolled and got to my feet. I used the rolling motion to gather momentum and attempted to kick for his head, which he dodged by jumping back. He stepped in, throwing a flurry of punches, each I was able to anticipate and move out of the way of, knowing even just one would send me to the ground like a ragdoll. I ducked under a right swing, bringing the revolver towards his chin, but he cocked his head out of the way as I fired. I jumped back when he tried to follow with a swing and a headbutt.

We were at a stalemate, but my opponent was having none of it. He moved over to one of the tables and lifted it like it weighed next to nothing. He spun, sending nearby objects careening wildly, letting the table loose in my direction. As it flew towards me, I leapt, taking two steps off the table as it flew by and sailed towards him, hoping to land a flying haymaker. He moved to the side as I landed on my knee, my fist smashing into the concrete, leaving a bloody, fist-shaped crater.

His leg came up high in an ax kick, and I decided to try something different. I waited for his leg to come down, grabbing him by the ankle. Pulling hard, I tossed him several meters, crashing him into a nearby table and making more of a mess of the place. As he landed, he kicked back up to his feet immediately and grinned.

"Well, well, this *is* going to be a good fight." He stood, and we went back to watching each other. Clearly, the impact had no effect, he was wearing a harness. The stalemate wasn't changing anytime soon. I wasn't going to take him down in a typical fight. I had to find some sort of an advantage. I thought the revolver might give me an edge, but I might as well have been throwing loud punches with the thing. I looked around, trying to survey my surroundings.

The place was a disaster, and there were a few bodies. The three people were likely only alive because the guy wanted to toy with them. He seemed sick in the head as if the CORPS had given him the tools to continue on with kinks that deserved to be shamed. Luckily for me, a quick glance left and right was like taking my time. There was a kitchen area and a lot of pipes moving from the ceiling to the grills, probably fire-safety devices. At least one of them looked like a gas line of some kind.

My thoughts were interrupted when my opponent lunged forward. Having jumped from a table, the extra height enabled him to touch the ceiling before crashing down with his leg. He only found the floor as I spun to the side and followed up with a kick. My nemesis quickly twisted, grabbing my ankle, but he had to let go as I jabbed at his head, my balance unaffected when he released me to dodge the blow. He knew as well as I what getting hit meant.

I began to run, heading towards the kitchen area. Reaching the kitchen,

I hopped forward. The aim of my jump allowed me to move my body sideways and squeeze through the opening just above the sneeze guard.

I knew he could pull the same tricks, so I acted fast, quickly diving behind the prep table in the center of the kitchen. I opened the cabinet that was at the bottom, hoping to confirm what my CIHUD was indicating. Yes, there was a natural-gas tank at the bottom. The place was a temporary installation, they had things they could move and use elsewhere. The cabinet was small and enclosed; if the tank were punctured, it would hit explosive air ratios almost immediately. "Tanks and hoses don't dodge" was my thought process. It wasn't long before I had company.

My opponent wasted no time leaping in, ready to cause havoc. While I was the one to discover fire, he apparently discovered tools. The psycho found all manner of sharp objects, including a wicked-looking butcher knife, and proceeded to hurl them at me. He was laughing as I dodged each one, some of his throws lightning fast enough to cause me to have to get creative about getting out of the way.

"Yeah, hide you little bitch!" He was laughing in between words. "What'cha sound like gettin' stabbed boy?" We were standing now, both hands on the prep table, staring at each other from the other side. "I can do this all day, and I know you can too. Maybe in a bit, some friends will come by, and we'll play a different game."

"You're a suck fuck y'know that?" He actually gave me a look like I should already know that.

"Aw, let me guess, *I didn't do it, it wasn't me,* right? Please, we all belonged in that hole!" He grabbed a ladle and tossed it at my head. I cocked my noggin to the side and turned to watch the ladle bend against the wall from the impact.

I knew he wouldn't take the time to explain anything to me, which was a shame because I sure as shit wanted to know what hole he was referring to.

"Who the fuck are you?" He gave no reply as he moved to try and run around the table to get me. Instead of meeting him, I played along, moving so he was now on the opposite side. I positioned myself, putting the serving table behind me, while he faced the center cabinet.

I jerked my body forward, faking like I was going to jump at him and then pushed back from the table, jumping up and sliding just above the glass. I twisted and aimed the revolver, shooting at the prep table where the gas line entered, easily severing it. The sudden release of gas was ignited by the pilot lights when it traveled down. Before he could react, I fired at the table where the tank was, managing to puncture it. What followed was spectacular. First, the tank began to rocket out of the table. As soon as the doors were flung open, the flames lit up and blew out both sides of the cabinet, causing a mighty reaction that brought a ringing to my ears.

My opponent was not nearly as lucky. We were fast, but not fast enough to outrun a blast that was mere centimeters away. Before I was tossed into the tables, I could see him slam back against the wall before the smoke and flames masked him from my view. Not long after, I could hear alarms that sounded like a fire system, and sure enough, the pipes from the ceiling began spraying flame-retardants everywhere.

I first took a knee and then stood, putting my finger into my ear and wiggling it a bit. My hearing quickly began to clear, and I walked over to the ground zero the kitchen had become. There was debris and glass everywhere, but I walked in barefoot, able to mostly see through the smoke.

The XRC soldier laid broken in a heap, surrounded by destruction. He

200

was missing one of his legs outright, likely struck by the tank. His face had been mangled, the CIHUD looking bent and broken against his forehead. Blood was pouring from the shrapnel wounds that weren't immediately cauterized. Miraculously, he was still conscious.

"What was your name?" I asked. He coughed and sputtered, looking up at me and then spoke.

"XR102." He seemed to think for a moment, then met my gaze, hacking and wheezing, bringing every ounce of strength he had left. "Reginald. T-they called me Reggie." At that moment, we both understood one another. Whether he was a psycho before or after the CORPS got to him, something in his eyes told me he finally realized he was still a prisoner.

Having one round left in the barrel, I took aim at Reggie's head. "I'll always remember your name." My voice carried the weight of an oath. While he may die, at least someone will remember him. I pulled the trigger, the shot echoing like a mighty crescendo.

I walked out of the kitchen, moving to the far end of the mess hall, my feet lightly slapping on the floor below. I walked out of the room and made my way back down the corridor to the elevator I had initially come in from. I stepped over the bodies, feeling like I was in some sort of fugue, the picture of reality a mere background image to my perception. Entering the elevator, I hit the button and made my way back down to the waiting General and Doctor.

Chapter Seventeen: Strange Bedfellows

The doors to the elevator opened. I let the revolver drop to the floor at my feet and put my hands up. My face was mostly expressionless. As expected, I was met by the barrels of four rifles held by masked soldiers. When they saw me, they lowered their weapons.

"Where's the General?" I inquired.

"The General is in the security station. We were instructed to escort you there if you returned." I lowered my hands and kicked the revolver over to one of the soldiers who reached down, picked it up, and tucked it into his belt.

"Lead the way." My feet had finally stopped aching as we began walking down the corridors. I was being led to an area of the base I hadn't seen yet. Many soldiers were running around, frantically moving, preparing to leave as soon as possible. To most, it might have seemed chaotic, but there was a method to their madness.

Finally, we reached another nondescript security door. It dutifully slid open, and the blue light from within spilled out into the hall. The room was somewhat dark, with an extensive computer system lining the back wall, many camera feeds being shown on rows of screens, the controls to operate them just below. I could see several of the screens showed only static or broken images, likely from Reggie destroying them during his infiltration.

Standing near the screens was Delantil, two soldiers were sitting at the controls, and Alonna was sitting in a chair off to the side, an armed, masked guard watching over her.

"That was the most remarkable fight I have ever witnessed. We honestly had a hard time seeing some of the moves you two were making." He was clearly impressed, but I wasn't feeling any sort of ego boost. The only good I could get myself to feel was that one last psychopath had left the world.

"It would have been quicker if you had properly equipped me. Ever walk through broken glass barefoot?" I tried to pretend I was mad at someone other than myself.

"Judging by what we saw of the cameras he didn't manage to disable, you had yourself handled. Besides, every minute we waited was another of my soldiers that died. I can't have that." I met his gaze and saw his sincerity. He was making it hard to dislike him.

"Fair. It got pretty dicey for a minute," I remarked. Alonna had stood and looked to the guard behind her.

"My scanner, please" She requested while holding her hand out. The guard looked to the General, who gave him a nod. Alonna took the scanner when it was held out for her and moved over to me with a purpose. She waved it up and down slowly, circling around me in a manner that never stopped being uncomfortable.

"Miraculously, you are mostly unharmed." She took the hand I had smashed the concrete floor with and examined it. "It looks like you fractured one of your knuckles. It is amazing you are as in good a shape as you're in." She was talking to me like a mother scolding her son or a girlfriend upset about the antics of her lover; both irked me.

"Yeah, I keep getting unlucky and surviving all this crazy shit." She gave me a stern look, but I just turned back to Delantil.

"I don't think he was here to bring me back. I think he was here for the doc and to put an end to me." The General looked down for a moment, thinking before looking back up.

"What makes you say that?"

"He didn't seem surprised to see me. In fact, he seemed to expect me to be comatose or, at the very least, not up to full strength." Delantil seemed thoughtful, and I looked to Alonna. "Any ideas?"

"Not particularly." She looked down at the floor, I could tell something was bothering her. She looked back up after a moment. "It is possible they predicted my betrayal."

"If that were the case doctor," Delantil began, "why would they allow you to succeed at all?" She seemed distressed as if a great conundrum was confounding her in some profound way. I couldn't help but laugh at her expression. "What's so funny?" Delantil asked.

"Her." Alonna cocked her head to the side, giving me an annoyed look. "She knows what it's like now, to be wrapped up in one of their elaborate schemes. Alonna, Are you sure about this?"

"I see no other way for the soldier to have any idea that you were alive. The last signal your nanomachines sent would have indicated a dying unit."

"So that settles it then," I concluded. "They knew what you were up to or, at the very least, planned for it as a possibility. I, for one, think we should operate under the assumption things are going according to plan for them." It was Delantil's turn to give me an annoyed look.

"You're telling me that you killing one of their units, in one of our bases, was part of their plan? That seems over the top, even for the Coalition."

"Nah, it really doesn't, man, look at the information." It never occurred to me as I spoke that my ability to connect the dots was superior to theirs. The strange look of admiration from Alonna helped me realize this, so I took a

204

breath and tried to think down a little. "Okay, so this one here has been watching over me for five years or so, right? If she developed any sort of affection-"

"I think the augmentations have made you a little full of yourself." Alonna crossed her arms over her chest, her eyes slit in frustration, but her cheeks were flushed from embarrassment, and I could feel her heart rate increase.

"Whatever helps you sleep at night, doc. Any who, true or not, the CORPS thinks she has some sort of infatuation."

"Go on." The General had an impatient look on his face.

"They decide to run with it, see where it goes. I mean, they're running all sorts of experiments with the others, they have to be if my experience is any sort of an indication. I don't doubt for a second that the kind of data they could get from me being free would be invaluable."

"Yes, but John, as I said, I prevented them from receiving any more signals from your systems. They are not receiving any data."

"That's true, but think about it, it's a coalition of eggheads. Psychology experts have got to be a thing among the CORPS. They know I ain't just gonna sit down, I didn't back at home after all. That's why I'm here." Alonna suddenly seemed thoughtful. Her hand moved to her chin, and she turned away, muttering to herself. I could scarcely make out her questioning of whether unnamed things were true.

"General." she finally spoke up, looking to Delantil. "Is there a private place we can all talk?" He chuckled at the question, and it seemed like he found her never-ending sense of authority amusing.

"Sure doctor." She shot him a look that indicated her seriousness.

"Fine, of course." He motioned for us to exit the room. I walked out first, waiting for Alonna and Delantil to follow. Delantil took point, walking down the halls, the two soldiers from before following us out. We were mostly quiet as we moved about the base, eventually using the elevator to go to a lower level.

This level seemed smaller than the others and appeared to be some sort of command section. Delantil led us down to the end of the hall the elevator was in, and we walked through a pair of sliding doors into a conference room. It had a large oval table with several comfortable-looking swivel-chairs. The soldiers that had been escorting us waited just outside. Delantil took a seat.

"Please, sit." He waited for us, Alonna sitting opposite of me and Delantil at one of the heads of the table. He was leaning back, relaxing a bit. "Go on doctor, explain yourself."

"I think John is right, there is more going on here than meets the eye."

"Duh," I said, crossing my arms and leaning back so I could put my grimy and bloody feet up on the table. I picked a piece of glass from my right foot I had missed and flicked it across the room.

"Please, John, hear me out." Alonna looked between the both of us as she spoke. "General, do you recall the conversation we had about the prison stock?" I raised an eyebrow.

"Prison stock?" I asked, knowing I wasn't going to like the answer.

"I recall. You said that the candidates for the XRC project were chosen from different populations." Delantil answered.

"Wait, time the fuck out, what does he by mean different populations?" I was incredulous. Everything was getting crazier by the minute.

206

"What I mean is," Alonna started again, "that there were multiple variations of what you know to be the Undercities. Yours was designed to be a sort of utopian society, populated specifically with genetically healthy individuals from skilled backgrounds." I looked down at the table a minute; even with the machines, I was a bit dumbfounded.

"That explains a lot actually. So, this prison stock?" Delantil pressed.

"Right, one of the other populations was specifically taken from prisoners, often violent, from around the world. We even populated them with criminals from the other habitats." I put my feet down and leaned forward, listening intently. A lot of things were beginning to make sense about life in the Undercities.

"So, why do all of this?" The General asked, looking to Alonna. "This seems extremely elaborate to breed stock for a cybernetics experiment."

"Because it is," She answered frankly. "The Undercity projects were, in fact, many different experiments. Sociological, psychological, biological, you name it, there was an experiment for it. For the XRC Project, it became apparent that we would glean better data from subjects from all walks of life. There are even people from various settlements that have been taken for the project."

"So, you wanted to see how these machines would work on different people, maybe even fix existing ailments?" I analyzed her words, trying to get a bigger picture.

"Precisely. There were many specific reasons. You, for instance, were chosen as the first model because of where you come from. Genetically speaking, your people are likely the healthiest and strongest on the planet. That was due to the nature of one of the experiments of the habitat you came from."

"Forgive me, doctor, but what is your point? None of this seems relevant to our current situation."

"It is completely relevant!" She was frustrated again, likely due to her inability to get her point across. "John's relationship to the Coalition could best be described as a scientific control. His genetic background, education, and physical health mean there are minimal chances of rejection or complications. If he were to be freed and allowed to make his own decisions, while simultaneously knowing he was no longer being tracked, he would be ripe for study."

"You know, doc, we really need to work on your tact," I hated these sorts of conversations.

"What you're saying is that we were allowed to capture you and John?"

"Keep thinking I'm here against my will," I said honestly, but unable to hide my smirk.

"Fine, either way, allowed us to procure you for the sake of running experiments? That's insane."

"No, it makes sense," Alonna insisted. "Think of John as a sort of enemy, a threat to be dealt with. As he goes out, doing what he does, they can observe the effects of his passing, gathering data that way. When he encounters another XRC soldier, the data from that encounter will be sent. Every encounter he survives will be valuable, and each soldier likely more capable of being the last he encounters."

"Fuck," I muttered. "Uhm, yeah, the effects of my passing, you say." I got a slit-eyed look from both of them, but it was Alonna who asked the question.

"What did you do?"

"Well, I may have pissed off some dude from the Sons of Rellen who decided to attack the walled settlement I found you guys near." I looked down, feeling somewhat sheepish about everything.

"Why do I have the feeling that's not the end of the story," Delantil joined the interrogation.

"Because it's not." I sighed deeply for a moment. "I may have, kind of, stopped the attack, killing both the dude I pissed off and this big monster guy who called himself the First." I saw the General's eyes widen at the last part. "I may have also killed a dozen or so of their men in the fight." I wasn't a murderer, before or after my surgery. While the augmentations were preventing the effects of things like PTSD or a crippling amount of guilt, I still felt terrible about the whole ordeal. Except for the Lieutenant, he had it coming.

"So, you interfered in a local conflict." Alonna sounded like a disappointed parent, and it was somehow creepier than her usual scientific mannerisms.

"No, I caused the conflict. Kind of. They rolled into this tavern I was chilling at like they owned the joint."

"That's the general MO of the Sons," Delantil offered plainly.

"Yeah, well, he tried getting uppity with me. He regretted getting physical and decided to come back with a hundred of his friends and that ugly-ass boss of his. In the end, the Sons literally bent their knees to me, like I was some sort of demi-god or something."

"Considering you're claiming you took on a hundred or so soldiers, including a genetically modified living weapon, that isn't very surprising."

"Who are the Sons of Rellen?" Alonna looked to Delantil with a curious gleam in her eyes. There was a hint of pride in there too, masked by her disappointment in how overt I had been.

"The Sons of Rellen are a nomadic group of religious militants. They worship some sort of ideal of the strong being lords over the weak. They often force weaker settlements to hand over their goods and crops in exchange for them not slaughtering their people. A rather sordid bunch to be sure."

"That name Rellen, it sounds familiar." Alonna lost herself in thought for a moment.

"Something important?" I asked.

"No." She answered, looking back up. "Just a historical reference I can't quite put my finger on. The reason I asked we discuss this privately, is we have no idea who or what may be listening to us and reporting back."

"Of that, I am very aware." Delantil gave Alonna a sort of death glare.

"I assure you, I am not that person, and neither is my equipment. You checked it yourself for transmitters."

"Yes, doctor, that is true, but considering the circumstances, the transmitters could be in your body for all I know. Suffice to say, this base is being evacuated in less than four hours. You're coming with us." He looked at me. "I would appreciate it if you came with us too. I think we can help each other unravel mysteries and prevent what could be a serious problem."

"You seem to be assuming a lot about me, General." I crossed my arms again and sat back. "Just what do you expect our relationship is going to be?"

"I hope one of mutual benefit. We have a common enemy in the Coalition. You have the abilities to take on their newest weapon, and I have the resources necessary to help you realize any goals you may have."

210

"Well, you're right about one thing bub, the XRC soldiers are a threat I need to deal with because no one else can. Yet anyway."

"Yet?" He quirked a brow with an interested look. "Do go on."

"I can't be the only XRC soldier that has it out for the CORPS. Prison stock? No way all of them came out happy, and I refuse to accept their selection process is omniscient. Sure, I'm probably going to have to fight and kill some of them. We should also be open to the possibility of liberating them."

"I have a feeling you're about to say something I am not going to like."

"I have a feeling he is about to say something I will like." Alonna had that cocky look back on her face.

"Yeah, you're both right. Alonna, are you able to produce more of the nanomachines that gave me my freedom?" My tone was now serious, and my posture became more assertive, almost without my own effort.

"Yes, if I am allowed access to equipment. I can use clusters from your own body and modify them to other subjects."

"You can't seriously believe I am going to allow her, of all people, access to anything other than a cell." Now the General was beginning to posture himself, realizing he was in for one hell of a negotiation. I wasn't budging though, having the benefit of immunity to anxiety.

"Oh, I do believe it General, and I do believe she will not be leaving my presence if it can be helped either." Alonna gave me a dumbfounded look, my demands apparently being the last thing she expected. "At this point, she's the only one that can help me if something goes wrong. She's my handler as it were, therefor she's in *my* custody. You don't have the soldier that will be more vigilant over any fuckery than me."

"I can't argue with that, but this isn't exactly mutually beneficial right now. You're asking that I give up control of one of the greatest assets to ever fall into our laps. Dr. Lyrul's knowledge of the nanomachines could do wonders for our people beyond a military scope."

"I would be happy to provide that knowledge freely." Alonna's voice had a hint of passion to it. She always did seem like the only CORPS doctor that actually gave a shit about people.

"I ain't stoppin' her."

"Okay, I can agree with that. Cooperation makes this much easier for all of us. What of you, though?"

"To the point then. I will help you. As long as you don't cross any lines and you really are a man of freedom, we'll get along. I'll need your help and your resources. Not just equipment, but your forces. We need to find others like me, and we have to figure out what the CORPS is up to. We need to expose them to the people they have been lying to these last couple of centuries."

"Well, my friend, that is exactly what we have been trying to do. I will agree to these terms. Doctor Lyrul will be in your custody, and you are responsible for her actions. We will cut off any help the second you become a liability."

"Fair enough." I stood and reached over with my hand to shake his, meeting his gaze. He rose from his own seat, straightening his uniform before taking my hand in a firm grasp.

"So, it is agreed then. I'll send you down to the quartermaster who will retrieve everything we found on you and provide clean clothes and new equipment."

"If you do not mind my asking, where are we going?" Alonna inquired.

"To the Capitol, of course." He said with a smug grin.

"General, forgive me, but the capitol of Tantil is a somewhat irradiated ruin." Alonna retorted.

"Yes, it is. There are a few things we've managed to keep from the Coalition over the years. It will be a long trip with a few stops along the way." Delantil gave me a look. "So you're aware, wiping out random bands of marauders is not on our schedule."

"No promises it stays that way, General."

"She doesn't leave your sight." He reiterated.

"Dude, I ain't watchin' her shit," I joked with a smirk.

"Oh, John." Alonna put her palm over her face and shook her head.

"Figure it out." Delantil shot back, and I couldn't quite tell if he was serious or not. He motioned to the door. "Let's head out, we need to get you equipped before everything is packed away."

"C'mon doc." I walked towards the door. "Role reversal time." With a frustrated sigh, Alonna stood and moved over to me. We waited for the General to walk over and head out the door. He looked to one of the soldiers who were posted by the conference room.

"John here is responsible for the doctor. Take him to the quartermaster, she'll have a recommended list when they arrive."

"Yes, sir!"

"If you two will excuse me, I have to attend to my people. We'll meet later." Delantil took a moment to glare at Alonna, before walking down the hall and disappearing into one of the rooms. I could hear a lot of clicking, and it was likely a Control Room of some kind.

"This way." The soldier led us back to the lift.

Chapter Eighteen: Making Plans

The elevator ride, and walk were uneventful. Alonna stuck closer to me than I was necessarily comfortable with, but I could tell she was extremely anxious. The role reversal felt satisfying, to see her not knowing what was going to happen next; to be under the influence of others felt like some sort of karmic justice. Too bad it had to happen to admittedly the most compassionate CORPS scientist likely in existence.

The armory we were led to probably looked better when it wasn't bustling with soldiers busy packing and getting ready for a sudden haul. I had to admire the focus of everyone there. Their morale seemed unshaken.

"You the cyborg?" I heard a female voice ask as we entered the room. She walked up to us and was a fascinating sight to behold. Her hair was blonde and put back into two braids. Her face was young, but dirty, as well as her hands and clothes. She wore fatigues like the rest, opting for the undershirt as her top. She stood tall in a mechanized suit, her body resting in a metallic frame that moved along with her. Either she was disabled, or it was designed to help with moving large objects. I noted one or two others in the same getup and figured it was the latter.

"That's me." I walked over and offered my hand. She gave it a firm and dirty shake.

"I have a list from the General. Woo boy, you don't look like much considering." She clicked her tongue with a headshake and pulled a PCD from a large side pocket, flicking through some screens. "You must be one special buddy."

"My mom always said I was special." Alonna giggled.

"I bet. Well, big guy, you're in luck because I happen to have this stuff unpacked. Follow me." The machine she was wearing made whirring sounds as she turned and walked behind a steel cage, shutting the door behind her. I could see an open desk window and approached it.

"Does everyone here have such an attitude?" Alonna asked under her breath.

"My kinda folks," I replied. She shot me a look, and I just kept facing forward with a smirk. Eventually, the quartermaster returned with a large crate. She set it down on her side of the desk. Reaching down, she pulled out a magnetic shield like the one I had before, though I noticed it appeared to have glass panels on it.

"What are these?" The quartermaster quirked a brow like I asked what a chair was or something.

"Solar panels. All of our equipment is self-powered."

"What the hell is a solar panel?" I was genuinely confused.

"John, on the surface, people utilize the power of the sun as one of the many ways they generate power," Alonna had a hint of sympathy in her voice.

"Oh, neat."

"Right. Anyway, back to business." The quartermaster dug back into the box and produced a kinetic harness. "You know what this is, right?"

"Never leave home without one," I replied. With a nod, she grabbed more equipment, placing some clothes down, fatigues similar to what the others were wearing though not necessarily a uniform. The boots seemed rugged and made from sturdy materials. They would probably last several treks through rough terrain.

She then produced another belt that looked like it was made to fit over my shoulder and had several grenades attached to it.

"You've got yourself the full complement here." She began pointing at the different grenades, each labeled with a colored stripe. "This one's your run of the mill flashbang, and this is the ever-useful frag." She then pointed at one with a gray label. "Two more utility grenades. One is nasty to hang out in for very long, but it creates a lot of ambient heat and smoke, making IR sensors pretty useless. The second one is an EMP grenade. Not sure if you wanna play with one of those."

"I'm a big boy, I'll be alright." I was beginning to understand things a little better. "Is that all of it?"

"Not quite. Your gun they found you with is here, I was told you wouldn't need much else for weapons. We have a new knife, your PCD, and everyday survival stuff, tools to make fire, the works. There were two other items the General specifically mentioned. First, this: it attaches to the front of your harness." She produced a small rectangular box. It had some hefty hooks that looked like they would attach to the harness pretty tightly. Pressing a little button on the front, it popped open, and I could see a spool of very thin cordage that was almost transparent.

"That's three hundred meters of incredibly strong cordage. Stuff is extracted from a worm I'm told. The tinsel strength is close to a ton. There's a climbing hook in the bag to go with it."

"Where the fuck do you find a worm that shits out one-ton cordage?" Honestly, I was astonished.

"You breed em, duh. Anyway, the last little goody." She pulled out a pair of insulated, yet very thin gloves. They had a small metal rod coiled around them and sewn into the fabric, which was a type I couldn't identify.

217

"Work gloves?" I picked them up, quirking a brow, and meeting her eyes. She had a broad smile on her face.

"Oh, you bet your sweet ass they're work gloves. Those are coil gloves, and they can be charged by your harness. They can release an electrical discharge into anything you touch. Usually, more than enough to destroy most electrical equipment and give someone a nasty headache."

"Now we're talkin'. How long do they last?"

"Well, you'll get a dozen or so discharges out of it at full blast, twice that much at half strength, though you won't be knocking out any electrical grids that way. You can discharge it all at once, which is not recommended."

"Why's that?" I inquired.

"Because, you foolish man," Alonna interjected. "That much energy will seek the path of least resistance, and that, likely, will be you."

"The egghead is right. A good way to have a coronary. Well, that's it, big guy. Don't make this a waste of good equipment." I wanted to roll my eyes but thought better of it.

"Thanks." I felt like a kid in a candy store. There I was, being armed by a group of people who hated the CORPS as much as I did. Things seemed to be looking up for once, though, of course, I was having thoughts of ruining it.

The TLF was a scrappy group and one not to be underestimated to be sure. I watched them bustle around, getting ready to upend themselves, unsure as to just how many times they've had to just up and leave. The issue was, I wasn't in this to fight a war. Truth be told, the CORPS was a secondary enemy. My heart yearned for the demise of two specific members of the Coalition, Mick and Ronyn. Who knows how I'd feel after that.

"Well, doc, let's go find the General and skedaddle out of this joint."

"Yeah, sure." The doc was obviously distracted. There was something on her mind, and I had a feeling it had little to do with our environment. She was plotting, contemplating some sort of exit strategy. At least that was my assumption anyway. I still didn't entirely trust that she wasn't some sort of trap, even unknowingly. Alonna seemed to have a knack for keeping some of her feelings private, even to my senses. She was useful though, and even Delantil knew that.

The pack-up was mostly uneventful. We met back up with Delantil and helped where I could. It was remarkable the speed and efficiency everyone worked, but it was nice to work with people again. They joked, they talked, they worked, and it was refreshing. It was the small things that counted in the moment.

Everything was packed into a convoy, many armored personnel vehicles, tanks, jeeps, bikes, and even some aerial vehicles like the ones I had seen before. Everything was kept in a massive hangar-like structure just below the surface. The platform everything rested on was capable of rising; the ceiling would open up when everyone was ready.

Lights flashed and a siren wailed, signaling the beginning of the journey. The massive ceiling opened, allowing sand and debris to fall below. The sounds of jets could be heard in the distance, air support called in for the dangerous adventure ahead. They were prepared to fight their war on the move if need be.

We were set up in an armored command vehicle with Delantil. It wasn't as cramped as other tanks like it, actually containing walking room. It was a beast of a machine, shaped almost like a wide bullet with a pregnant middle. Inside were computers, sensor readouts, and communication systems, allowing the General to be in direct operational control of the entire convoy. Even the soldiers manning their various stations seemed a cut above the rest.

The convey began moving when we made it out of the hangar. I couldn't exactly tell what was going on outside the vehicle I was in, but I decided it didn't matter. I could relax for a little bit. Sitting off on a bench near the back exit, I put my hands behind my head and leaned back. Delantil walked over and stood in front of me.

"This trip will take a couple of days with frequent stops. I would like it if you could help keep our perimeter safe whenever we stop anywhere." I gave a shrug and a nod.

"You got it, boss." Alonna was sitting next to me, and I could feel her eyes studying my form, an almost goofy grin on her face. If she were a teenager, she'd probably be twirling her hair and giggling too. It was somewhat creepy to me. Was this how women felt most of the time?

"John?" She finally spoke. "Could you describe your current condition. Feelings, anything strange?" I shot her a look and then shook my head.

"You're gonna be at this until you're old and gray, huh?"

"Somehow, I think you'd be disappointed if I wasn't." She gave an almost playful smirk. "Come now, help pass the time, hmm?"

"Fine. I feel fine, nothing weird to report. A little anxious to get some shit done. Getting a little tired of running y'know?"

"You haven't been running for that long." I think she was trying to be optimistic, but it was lost on me.

"Long enough. I don't plan on being on the run for much longer. If I can help it, I won't be the one running away." Even I couldn't help but realize how dark my statement sounded. I was beginning to sound a bit obsessed, and part of me didn't like that. "Someone has to push back against the bullies."

"My sentiments exactly." Delantil interrupted, approaching us. "And we will be doing just that. Come with me for a moment." He motioned for me to follow him over to one of the soldiers sitting at a terminal. I stood and walked over, crossing my arms across my chest, looking to the screen. "Bring up Project Needle."

"Yes, sir." My lips frowned somewhat as I gave the General an almost silly look.

"You guys really gotta work on your naming conventions." Alonna, who had followed us, snorted out a laugh, and even the soldier sitting down appeared to be putting effort into a straight face.

"Anyway." The General interrupted the fun. "Project Needle is our plan to penetrate Dome City."

"Poppin' the balloon, huh? I've been thinking about this Dome City thing you mentioned." He looked over to me. "You said there's a ton of civilians in there?"

"Of course, there is," Alonna spoke up. "It would appear that I am not going anywhere anytime soon, so there is no reason for secrecy." While work was still being performed, the room fell silent, almost deafeningly so. I could see Alonna looking at the screen. "May I?" She asked Delantil.

"Something tells me I am going to be quite interested. Corporal." He spoke to the soldier in the seat who immediately stood, giving a salute before standing at attention. Alonna took his place and, in a very cliché manner, cracked her knuckles. She seemed to know her way around computer systems because she quickly began navigating the files and brought an image of the massive dome up. It was an aerial shot, presumably because the TLF couldn't get very close. "We'll have to chat later on how you know our OS." Alonna gave an almost sheepish shrug.

The Dome was a greenish color that seemed to resemble the stuff powering my new gear as if the entire structure was made of it. The Dome itself was surrounded by buildings, which definitely looked like military installations. Vehicles could be seen in various images moving in and out of the area. The place was swarming with gun emplacements, soldiers, anti-air weaponry; it looked like a veritable army was stationed there.

"This is Habitat Zero-One, the first of five planned installations, the final stages of Project Shepherd." The General was patient, listening to the information, but I could tell he was somewhat excited. His heart was racing, and he even seemed to be salivating a little. There were times I wasn't fond of the ability to sense minute bodily functions. People turned out to be nasty walking bags of meat, sloshing around, and being generally gross.

"Project Shepherd, huh? I feel like project naming is, universally, an entry-level job. Bunch of nerds coming up with metaphors." Alonna turned and rolled her eyes at me before pointing at the screen.

"Everyone you ever knew is there, John." My eyes widened, and I looked to the screen. "Good, now that I have your attention, allow me to explain. Project Shepherd started before the War two centuries ago."

"Centuries long projects." I heard Delantil say under his breath. I couldn't tell if it was shock, horror, admiration, or all of the above.

"Indeed," Alonna continued, looking to him and then back to the screen. She navigated a few pages of data before finding a topographical map of the Tantil continent. She zoomed in on a section in the southeast,

222

surrounded by mountains, which seemed to be the source of a large river. "That's home John, the Undercities."

I couldn't help the wave of emotions I felt looking at the screen. While I could control them, I still felt them, and part of me yearned deeply to go home, to be done with all of the nonsense. That part was small and weak, a mere fleeting thought of rest.

"Project Shepherd was essentially a preliminary project, setting the stage for nearly every major project that would come after. Well, more accurately, it was one of two major projects. This particular project had one goal, which was to procure, secure, and cultivate specific populations for later use."

"You were raising lab rats," I spoke through snarling teeth, my fists suddenly clenching.

"John, I was raising nothing." I looked to her, and she had a sympathetic look on her face. Her reminder was an appropriate one. Sometimes I forget that in many respects, she was also a slave. Did it really make a difference whether you were setting the table or tilling the field?

"Just go on."

"Fine. The entire idea should be obvious by now. The Undercities were designed to survive the War, even if it went nuclear."

"Which it did in many places," Delantil added.

"Indeed. The Habitat you crudely call Dome City was designed after the war, drawn up by some of the most brilliant scientists among our test populations. It was designed to allow entire populations to live and grow within, to augment and grow the installation as necessary, and to ensure the genetic purity of the people within."

"Geeze, genetic fucking purity, are you serious right now?" I was a little shocked, considering the CORPS never demonstrated any form of bigotry before. Everyone was equally fodder to them.

"Yes, John, very serious, but I do not believe we are thinking the same thing. By genetic purity, we mean free of defects or reduced enough risk to be nearly free. By defect, I mean anything from mental to physical ailments and deformities."

"What do you do if someone is born within these populations, that doesn't fit your criteria?" The General asked, crossing his arms.

"We sterilize them through non-invasive means, both to preserve the populace and to ensure the experiments are not tainted by unnecessary knowledge." Her nonchalance was making my blood boil.

"Do you ever just listen to yourself talk?" I incredulously asked, glaring at her. She seemed almost sheepish, remembering she actually had a shred of empathy.

"Look, as you would say, it is what it is. All I can do is explain to you the facts." Her voice was diplomatic and patient.

"Fine, go on," I grumbled.

"I would like to know how this is all relevant to us?" Delantil seemed to be losing a bit of his patience. Alonna turned to him.

"It is relevant for a variety of reasons if you claim to be a man of ethics and morals." She looked back at the screen. "That Habitat installation is housing millions of innocent civilians. Civilians that very well could be friends or family of John's." That was when I saw Delantil glare, and for the first time, I saw his angry face. He said nothing though, and Alonna looked back up to meet his gaze. He likely saw her explanation as an attempt to manipulate me.

In reality, she was doing him a favor.

"I'd like to point out that if I had helped you kill a bunch of people from the Undercities, *you* would've become a target," My voice dripped with absolute surety.

"And what precisely makes them more important than everyone else?"

"Nothing, that ain't the problem. It ain't about whether one group of people is more important than the other, but whether you're on the same moral level as the CORPS. With all due respect General, you wouldn't deserve victory if it meant spilling all that blood."

"If I may continue, gentlemen." Alonna interrupted. "The Undercities were built into a massive cave and tunnel system, some parts natural, some parts dugout. At no point did the Coalition plan to transport the people via the surface; they did so underground."

"You saying there's a way to the dome from the Undercities?" I suddenly was losing my desire to go home.

"Precisely. The entire idea was to not only keep any renegade factions in the dark but to also ensure the safety of the populations we were moving."

"Are you privy to whether or not the entrance to these Undercities is guarded?" Delantil was weighing his options and was beginning to realize how important the information really was.

"I would think not. It would be more logical to guard the inside of the tunnels. Having any sort of base on the outside would make factions such as yourself more likely to uncover the project. Better to make you think the Habitats were independent." Delantil grimaced and turned away for a moment. His mind was obviously racing, his demeanor that of deep thinking, pondering the information.

"General," I spoke up to get his attention, and he turned to me. "This Project Needle, what was your plan?" His grimace faded for a moment and leaned over, hitting a few spots on the touch screen panel. A series of windows appeared on the screen revealing topographical maps marked with the trails of supply lines and scouting parties. There were also aerial photos of installations and settlements. Combined, everything on the screen coalesced into a coherent map of CORPS operations in Tantil.

"As you can see, we have been watching the Coalition for some time," The General began. "When we discovered Dome City, we began to realize it was a central hub of all operations in this region. At first, it seemed like everything was going towards building the city itself. We quickly realized the efficiency of the Coalition, however."

"Efficiency?" I was curious as to where he was going with his train of thought.

"They completed factories and local mining operations first. Soon they had all of the materials they needed right where they were sitting. It's likely why they chose the spot they did. Tantil has always been rich in just about any resource on the planet. It wouldn't be surprising if they stumbled upon mineral veins laced with valuable materials. Suddenly what was easy to disrupt became a self-sufficient foxhole."

"You tried attacking them?"

"Several times. We probably slowed their project by a few years, but they planned the entire thing around constantly being under attack. Once they were finished with the initial phase, it became nearly impossible for us to outright attack them without experiencing heavy losses or resorting to measures that, quite frankly, put us in this position to begin with."

226

"I'm a little bothered by something." My hand moved to my chin as I looked up thoughtfully, hundreds of scenarios racing through my mind. My eyes met Delantil's. "Didn't the Republic have a space program? A lot of these shots don't look like they were from high enough up. Shouldn't you have better intel than this?"

The General looked down a moment, a flash of anger, or perhaps regret came over his face before he composed himself. "During the war, the Coalition used their people installed in the F'Rytalan government to knock out our satellites with EMP blasts from their own in orbit. Joke's on them, of course, the Coalition eventually turned on everybody."

"You have not spoken with those in F'Rytal?" Alonna looked up at the General and cocked her head curiously.

"I think you know very well, we haven't." He didn't even look at her. Instead, he seemed more to be explaining things to me. "The Coalition setup signal jammers on the coastline and land borders. The network is widespread and requires multiple hits to have any meaningful impact. We haven't had contact outside of Tantil for nearly a century. Anyone we physically send has yet to make it back."

"Your plan, General?" I asked, trying to get things back on topic.

"Of course. Dome City is protected by a robust defense network." He began pointing at maps and images. "You see the points here, here, and here? These are ALBs, anti-air laser batteries."

"That's a decent distance away to be protecting a giant-ass, glass balloon."

"It isn't made of glass." I wanted to call Alonna a nerd when she corrected me but thought better of it.

"Indeed. A single ALB can offer adequate protection of the air surrounding the Dome. Missiles, VTOLs, you name it, it won't get close without an overwhelming amount of them."

"Like a crapshoot."

"Exactly. It isn't worth the resources until they come down."

"They look surrounded by defense installations," I commented, looking at the screen.

"That's because they are. Just taking one offline would take a heck of a lot of manpower."

"I see where I come in, but what comes after that?"

"An aerial-raid to crack the Dome was the original plan. First, we would bomb out the surrounding areas, hopefully before the Coalition can scramble their own response. There's still a step missing, of course."

"What sort of step?" I crossed my arms again, wishing he would just get to the point.

"The dome itself is surrounded by an energy field, a magnetic one at that. Unless we start making bombs with all plastic parts, anything we launch at it will ricochet away from the structure itself. While it would wreak havoc around the surroundings, the dome wouldn't be harmed, even with bunker-busters." He began to point at various images again. "There's two main power generators on opposite ends of the dome that power these four field generators. Just like everything else, it is an efficient system. If one goes offline, the other picks up the slack. They would have to both be taken down, likely at the same time in case they have unknown contingencies."

"Cracking the dome," I said, shaking my head. "That's where you lose me, but I have a better idea anyway."

"I'm listening." Delantil gave me a stern look. Clearly, he thought I had better say something useful. "Well, as the doc said, there's a way into the dome from under it. Inside that thing are millions of people who have never done a single thing to harm you. They are just as much victims in all of this as you are. Sounds like possible allies."

He perked up hearing the idea. "Go on."

"The CORPS's been lying to the people in there their whole lives. It's a dome, I'm willing to bet they've convinced them the air is toxic and unlivable."

"Almost certainly," Alonna interjected. "The Habitat's dome structure can project images from the inside and the outside acts like a massive solar panel, powering the city within."

I motioned to Alonna with my thumb. "What she said. If I can get in there and prove to these people that they've been lied to, we can bring their installation crashing down from the inside." The General rubbed his chin, pondering the possibilities.

"How are you, one man, remarkable of a man though you may be, going to accomplish capturing an entire city?"

"I ain't. I'm ridiculous these days, but I ain't stupid, no delusions of grandeur here. Nah, we still need the rest of your plan sans the wrecking the dome bit. If the dome is surrounded and dealing with its own problems on the inside, you'll stretch em thin."

"You forget that the Coalition has a military force of their own." Delantil reminded me. "It won't be a quiet fight on the outside of the dome, nor will it end once we claim victory. They will retaliate, and they always send more forces than necessary."

"They may also neutralize the Habitat," Alonna spoke up again. "While I am honestly not privy to such a contingency, I must admit that it is not out of the realm of possibilities. They may choose to wipe out the entire area to prevent their secrets from being divined."

"Hmm, well, that is a doozy." I knew damn well she could be right.

"Then, we take the ALBs as opposed to disabling them." The General's mood seemed to lighten with the idea. His gears were turning as he spoke. "We'll need someone within the Coalition, a software engineer, or even a coder who can take control of the ALBs onboard computer systems."

"How in the fuck are we doin' that?" The General's typically controlled expression formed into a grin. "Oh, right, me. Kay, but where are we going to find one of those?" As I asked the question, we both looked at Alonna, who suddenly seemed like a rat that got tossed into a snake pit.

"Wait a moment now. While my programming skills are top-notch, I have no experience with Coalition security protocols and machine language. We do not use universal languages."

"So, the Coalition is not all about efficiency?" The General asked, almost sarcastically.

"Efficiency comes in many forms, General Delantil. By making our systems run under highly specialized languages, it increases their overall security. Just having compatible software would be a challenge in and of itself, let alone knowing how to hack a system once you could make an attempt. Of course, you are in luck." Alonna had an almost proud smirk when she looked to me. I was a bit confused, though, because it didn't feel like she was entirely honest about her ability to hack security systems. She knew more than she let on.

"I don't follow. No offense, but John doesn't strike me as the hacker type."

"Usd to be lucky to run solitaire bub." I shrugged but knew what she was referring to. "She ain't wrong, though."

"John here was fitted with a new type of computer interfacing system. He can interface with machines using his own mind as a processor. It can adapt to most forms of machine language and has a database to work from. He doesn't hack, it would be more accurate to say his brain does."

"It's sub-conscious?"

"Nah, man, more like a video game. I ain't gonna lie, it's pretty uncomfortable, but I can think my way into systems. It was part of my training." Delantil took a deep breath, taking things in.

"We would of course need to find a way to bypass any biometric security measures. I will have to work on that one." Alonna mused.

"There's obviously more to your idea." He motioned with his hand for me to continue.

"Right again. Knocking out their defense systems is good and all, but I noticed that there's no obvious control center."

"You think they are being controlled from within the dome?" The General scratched his chin, thinking.

"Yeah, it makes sense."

"He is probably correct General. Their weakness is likely the assumption that nothing will get into the dome. You may not even be able to control them from the outside."

"That's a problem." Stating the obvious, Delantil looked to me patiently, knowing I had already thought of it.

"Like Alonna said, there's gotta be a back door, a way in that bypasses all the dudes at the front door. Time for me to go home and find it. If I find a way into that dome, I can wreak havoc from within, maybe even knock out their exterior systems."

"And if you can't control them from within?"

"Then I find a way back out and hit them from behind. Either way, sending me into that dome is our best bet." Delantil took a long moment and turned his back, deep in thought. The intel was lacking at best, we were rolling the dice on the entire situation, but finding a way to nuke the place wasn't any better. Delantil knew he needed my cooperation if he was going to turn the tide of the war or even just having a solid chance at defending themselves. I knew I wouldn't have any closure until I hit the CORPS where it hurt: their lies.

"So be it." Delantil finally spoke up looking to Alonna and then meeting my gaze in a sort of man-to-man fashion. "We'll bring you to the site the doctor informed us about. We'll give you time to find a way into Dome City. In the meantime, we'll begin planning an assault against their main defenses. The problem, of course, is communication."

"Of course," Alonna muttered under her breath, looking down thoughtfully before looking back up at us. "You have likely not seen any signals coming from within, have you?"

"Negative. We have observed signals going to the outer bases, but nothing ever originates from the Dome itself."

"Indeed. This makes sense to me. The defensive field likely also blocks all transmissions in and out of the Habitat. However, the Coalition would not leave itself unable to send signals in case of an emergency. While the Coalition exhibits hubris, they are not stupid. There will be a way to send a signal from within the habitat itself."

"Even more reason for me to get in there. General, we have to hit these bastards because it won't be long before a line of mes are knocking at your door. Going toe-to-toe with a cyborg might as well be any two of your guys getting into a fight. I can't guarantee a win." The General nodded and then took a moment, looking down at the table, lost in thought. Finally, he looked back up, surety once again gracing his demeanor.

"Lieutenant!" Delantil's voice carried the authority of his station, and one of the soldiers sitting at the helm stood up and saluted, meeting the General's gaze as he turned to her. There was a lot of respect in her eyes, and I could tell the loyalty Delantil instilled in his people ran deep.

"Yes sir, General!" Came the dutiful reply.

"Scatter the convoy, leash the dog and send the kids to school." I gave a weird look, hearing all of the code.

"Yes sir, General!" She sat back down and pressed her finger onto a spot on the panel before her. "Big Daddy says leash the dog and send the kids to school. I repeat, send the kids to school." Laughter escaped my mouth, I couldn't help it.

"Hey man, you should get the guy who names your codes to name your projects." Even Alonna had to cover her mouth, giggling. The General turned to me again, but his demeanor seemed unshaken by the humor.

"I'll keep that in mind. I'll be leaving this convoy to head back to our capitol. You will be left behind with a smaller convoy who will be under the command of Lt. R'yalax over there." I looked back over to the one he had given the order to. She had ebony skin, an extreme contrast to my own, her eyes shined with confidence, betraying the slight smirk she had hearing the General's orders. She was tall and well built, obviously suited for whatever Delantil tossed her way. Something about the look on her face said we'd get along just fine. "They'll bring you to where you need to go and take what you say under advisement, but she is in charge, and I don't want you forgetting that."

"Fair enough. I wasn't one for takin' the blame anyway. Leadership ain't my bag." I shrugged. R'yalax seemed capable enough.

"As long as we're understood. You'll have access to our network for a time, but eventually, you will be out of range. Take the opportunity while you have the chance."

"Networks?"

"Yes, historical records, technical and training manuals. It stands to reason your ability to learn new information is likely heightened, considering everything else."

"Extremely so," Alonna proudly remarked.

"Great, I'll go sit and be a nerd, I guess." I felt the command tank come to a stop, and the General calmly moved for the exit.

He turned as the door opened, revealing another transport with an opened hatch right outside, complete with a guard detail. "We'll be in contact, there's more planning to be done, but that's for my people. For now, you're being redirected to the tunnel entrance the doctor showed us. Good luck." He turned away once more and exited the command tank.

"Alright, folks, we're headed out," R'yalax declared before sitting and getting the command tank underway.

Chapter Nineteen: Kindred Spirits

The trip itself would take at least a couple of weeks with planned stops. Our convoy was small, only containing a couple of troop transports and the command tank. Our course was not straight forward, taking many detours, and it wouldn't stay in a desert landscape forever.

I spent my time being a nerd, scouring over information on the TLF's network. It wasn't always available. According to some of their data, they had network relays set up all over the continent. Sometimes they got taken down by man or nature, so its reliability was sparse. I wanted to spend some time on their historical data to see what happened directly after the war, but I had better things to occupy my time with.

The General wasn't lying about technical and training manuals. Combat, equipment maintenance, even how to make improvised bombs and weapons were all available to me. At first, I sat there, reading the screens, and then decided it wasn't enough. The information was valuable and would be necessary for the trials ahead. I used the fancy cable and my CIHUD, connecting with their network in a way I doubt they would've been comfortable with.

I spent almost my entire travel time hooked into their network when it was available. It wasn't that I didn't realize what a freak I must have seemed like, never getting up to rest, eating occasionally, and just constantly hooked into a terminal. Nah, I knew how ridiculous I appeared, I just stopped caring. Maybe I always had that attitude, perhaps it was given to me, but all I could think was, "it is what it is."

The soldiers around me could never understand. While I always thought such sentiments were ridiculous and selfish, in my case, what I was doing wasn't in the realm of most people's imaginations. It sure as shit wasn't in mine. What they truly didn't get was, their data was turning me into a weapon. I not only had the reflexes and enhanced abilities; I now knew how to use them with deadly precision through the study of several martial arts forms. I could disarm and build nearly any explosive device with minimal ingredients and knew precisely where they belonged to topple a reinforced structure. Not only could my internal computers hack systems, but now I could do it with my fingertips. I had become knowledgeable in fields experts needed to carry manuals in. The next fight I got into was going to be far more frightening than the last for my foes. While I shuddered at the idea, I knew my path would intersect with many enemies.

We often found places out of the way to camp for the night. The soldiers enjoyed the time to stretch their legs, chat, and generally be somewhat off duty for a while. During these times, I would find myself a secluded place to stare up at the stars. Part of me thought that even if I had been born under them, I would still marvel at their majesty. We were nothing more than a grain of dust on the sands of the universe.

"Is this what you do every time you disappear?" The voice was that of R'yalax. I was standing on a large rock, looking up at the sparkles above that shined on the landscape below. We were drawing towards a livelier region, with green trees beginning to pop up on the horizon. Still in a desert, the arid landscape became a bit rockier.

"Something like that." I didn't look away from my stargazing. She stood next to me and looked up.

"See something interesting?" She turned to me, studying my reactions.

236

"Everything." She looked up once more.

"I suppose that's accurate. I can't imagine what it would be like, to never see the stars. I guess I don't blame you." I finally adjusted my gaze and looked to her. She turned back to me as well. "We'll be leaving the wasteland soon. We'll make a scheduled stop at a nearby settlement for some supplies and a little R&R for the troops."

"Fair enough. Anything I should know about the place?" Seeing more of the surface's civilization seemed like an enticing pit stop.

"Yes, there's a Coalition base located within it." My heart sank at the idea.

"So, they run the joint?"

"Not exactly. Their presence is tolerated because it keeps raider bands away. When we get there, it would be best if you kept a low profile."

"Uhm, why?" I was a bit dumbfounded on why either of us should be showing our faces in some sort of CORPS tributary.

"Because none of the rest of us are being hunted. Besides, it's a neutral zone. While the Coalition could probably crush the city, they have their own purposes for adhering to the laws of the people there." She used air quotes when she said the word laws.

"Something tells me there's more."

"It's a libertarian state bordering on anarchic. It's why they don't allow the CORPS to do anything other than be there."

"Well then, I suppose-" We were promptly interrupted by one of her subordinates.

"Lieutenant!" She turned to meet the youngish looking soldier.

"Yes, Private? What is it?"

"Homestead intel reports we have a tail." I quirked a brow listening in.

"A tail? Speak plainly, soldier." She crossed her arms over her chest.

"Yes, ma'am. There's a small group from a local raider tribe, staying back and watching our movements. According to Homestead, they're on their way to our position." R'yalax looked to me and then back to the soldier.

"Show me." He immediately turned to head back to the mobile command center, R'yalax following, so I decided to tag along. Once inside, he led us to their comms officer.

"Who's this tail we've got? Pictures?" The woman sitting at the terminal nodded and punched a few spots on the pad before her. Soon some images came up on the screen, and I felt my eyes roll back in my head almost as a reflex.

"Dude, really? This is like having a high school stalker or something." R'yalax looked over to me.

"Is there something we should know?" R'yalax seemed unamused by my reaction.

"Well." I rubbed the back of my neck, thinking about how to word it. "It's the Sons of Rellen."

"I can see that." She gave me an expectant look, like a mother ready to scold her son.

"Right before I met up with you kids, I had a run-in with them. I kind of, sort of, maybe killed their two leaders." Apparently, the Sons were a big deal because everyone stopped their activities to look over at me.

"Their leaders? Are you aware of who those actually are?" I looked away a moment before meeting her gaze.

"Big, ugly, metal headed dude who goes by the title *the First*?" Now there was murmuring.

"Cut the chatter!" R'yalax gave everyone a stern look. "After what we have witnessed, I won't doubt you. So, they're hoping for some sort of revenge then."

"Well, no, actually, not exactly revenge against me no. More like worship me." She gave me a quizzical look. "Look, apparently they dig strength to the point where you school their boss in front of them, and you become the new boss. How far away are they?"

The comms officer spoke up. "A few minutes."

"I'll go meet up with them, in the meantime, probably best to consider a location change." R'yalax thought about this for a long moment before coming to a decision.

"Agreed. You're taking an escort, though. I want an early warning if something goes wrong." I thought about protesting, but clammed up, knowing it wouldn't do any good. R'yalax was the epitome of strength and calm in a commander. I could definitely see why Delantil left her in charge; even I didn't like challenging her half the time.

"Fine, but if things get hairy, have them stay back. The Sons ain't shit to me in a fight." With that, I moved to get suited up and headed out. R'yalax discretely found me six infantry she trusted the most. While she began the process of waking up the personnel and moving the camp, we moved out to intercept the incoming Sons before anyone could ask where we were going.

"We ready boys and girls?" I asked, looking over the people that were given to me as an escort. They looked tougher than a lot of the other soldiers we were with, and I could see their insignias were different.

"After you, boss." A brutish woman in both size and demeanor stated before motioning for me to lead the way. By the looks of it, she was the squad-leader.

"Right." We began to move across the sand. I started jogging, deciding to stay slow enough to let my entourage keep up. I wasn't sure what we were going to find when we got there, but somehow, I knew it wasn't going to be anything I expected.

It took us a good couple of minutes of jogging to finally make visual contact with the small group headed our way. It was two jeeps followed by a raggedy looking personnel transport. I wouldn't doubt if they hadn't built the vehicles themselves out of whatever scraps and spit they could find.

"What's the plan, boss?" The squad-leader asked, but I didn't stop, instead offering a suggestion.

"Stay here if you want. This might get hairy." I paused a moment before adding, "For them." With a motion of her hand, the group split up, three to one side, and two the other of the quasi-road we were following; it was clearly a well-beaten path anyway. As I got close enough for the group to notice me, I pulled my sidearm and stopped, waiting.

The convoy of raiders slowed to a stop, their lights blasting my shadow against the arid landscape behind me. As the last vehicle came to a halt, one of the men in the jeeps hopped out, and while I could tell the others wanted to join him, the man merely put his fist up, and they stopped where they were.

He was a somewhat short, but athletic looking affair with a short, dark hair. His brown eyes had an almost mischievous gleam to them, his mouth cocked in a sort of grin. He carried a rifle over his shoulder, walking casually towards me. His face had an old scar on it that likely been there for years; it ran down his right cheek from top to bottom.

240

His clothes immediately put me on the defensive. They resembled mine in many ways, including the EM shield and the kinetic harness strapped to his torso under his clothes. As he drew near, my fears were confirmed as a CIHUD extended from his forehead. He stopped a mere meter from me, seeming to think a moment before his grin grew.

"Just six, huh? Well, that'll make this easier." I rolled my eyes.

"Good god, are all of you cliché pieces of shit?" I crossed my arms over my chest and studied him.

"Pretty much, buzz. This is between you and me. Keep your little cronies out of it." He tossed his weapon to the side. "I wanna see firsthand if the report was true or not."

"The fuck you doing rolling with the Sons anyway?" I inquired incredulously. He looked behind him before looking back at me.

"Those clowns? They knew where to find you. They've been fawning over their new messiah for a bit now. It sure helps the CORPS find your dumbass." I gave him a confused look.

"The CORPS used the Sons to find me?"

"No, I did. Just watch the fallout of the shit you pull and follow the breadcrumbs. Really, you don't need Supertech to find ya."

"Man, why be their lapdog? You're the least annoying person they've sent my way. To be fair, you're only the second-"

"Yeah, heard you put down a mad dog, but just let me say, fuck you. I ain't anyone's lapdog." I waved my arms out in frustration.

"Then what the fuck do you want then?"

"A friendly sparring match. I wanna see how good the precious prototype is." I suddenly dropped my arms to the side, now really confused.

"Spar? Just a friendly fistfight? Why?"

"Why not? You gonna sit there and run your mouth or we squarin' up?" He put his fists up in a fighting stance, his leg moving back. From my recent studies, I could tell he was employing some sort of F'Rytalan martial-art style. It was known for its brutal takedowns and offensive maneuvers.

"Y'know what? Fuck it." I donned a stance I had never tried before, yet finding myself pulling it off quickly and easily. It was a form from a nation once known as Prytok. They were known for their spiritualist ideals; it was a purely defensive form.

"Well, well, it looks like the CORPS doesn't know how resourceful you are. Let's go, buzz!" He lunged forward with a fake swing and then attempted to sweep at my legs, but I switched my feet position back and forth, dodging it like a weird game of hopscotch. He moved up from the sweep, his body arching and spinning into a kick, which I quickly blocked.

A flurry of blows came my way, but I was able to anticipate and block each one. He was pushing me back and gaining ground. As a left haymaker came my way, I reached for his forearm and twisted, bringing him closer, but his reaction time was as good as one would expect from a cyborg. He brought his neck back and brutally attempted to smash his skull into mine. Our CIHUDs retracted and extracted in time with the possible impact. I let him go, pushing back as I did, narrowly preventing the attack.

By now, we had a circle around us. The Sons had all piled out of their vehicles, hooting and hollering about the spectacle before them. I had no idea what he had done to get into their good graces, but it likely involved a lot of bodies. To these freaks, they were witnessing two gods battle it out. I could sense my escort taking positions around the group, ready to ambush should the need arise. Luckily, I wasn't sent with idiots, and they knew to stay back.

"You can't deny you're having fun." He said, walking sideways as we circled around, keeping each other in front.

"I mean, I'd be lying if I said there wasn't a little entertainment in this."

"That's the fuckin' spirit!" He lunged once more, but I was prepared, stepping to the side with each attempted blow. To the others, it must have seemed like he was making a near-instant dash attack, at one moment behind me, another in front, and yet another on my side. Each time I was able to anticipate and move, knowing the damage he could easily inflict. Was there really such a thing as a friendly sparring match between cybernetic monsters?

I decided waiting for him to attack was getting old and switched up my stance to a mixed style, my feet shuffling positions back and forth, almost like some sort of dance. He mirrored the image, a grin of recognition forming as he advanced towards me, and the blows began again. I threw a right hook to his face, which he blocked and attempted to follow with a sucker-punch to the gut, but this was turned aside by moving my arm and body sideways to meet the blow with a block. He tried for a headbutt again, this time, however, I grabbed for his head and tossed him behind me. He tumbled against the sand, his harness sending waves of debris from the impacts as he rag-dolled several meters away. Somehow, he managed to catch himself and land with one leg behind him, the other knee touching the ground as his hand scraped the sand below, slowing his momentum.

There was no hesitation, and he pushed forward again, but instead of a strike, he moved his arms out in a tackle and managed to catch me with his speed, trying to brutally send us both to the ground. I managed to catch one arm, using my leg to lift him up as I fell backward, utilizing his mass to toss him behind me.

After a moment of tumbling, he picked himself back up and grinned, brushing some sand from his clothes. "Why do you fight?" He asked, squaring up again as we once more started our circular dance. "What's the point of rolling with the TLF?"

"Is that a serious question? You actually like what the CORPS did to us, or did you get lucky and got picked from a hat?" As I asked this, his smirk faded a little, and several blows came my way, but as usual, neither of us seemed capable of harming the other.

"The CORPS's been fucking me since day one buzz. What made them dumb enough to give me these goodies is beyond me."

"John!" I heard from a rock behind me as the squad-leader revealed herself. "The LT wants a report! What the fuck are you doing?" I turned to the confused soldier in frustration.

"Tell her to keep her pants on I'm fuckin' busy here." I turned back just in time to see a flying roundhouse aimed for my head, which I narrowly ducked under. "Listen, ya cheap prick!"

"Hey guy, ain't no such thing as a fair fight!" I took a few steps back while he remained stationary, watching my moves.

"Y'know what? You're right." I twirled, letting my body sink low, snatching up a large rock in the process, gaining momentum, and hurling it at him as hard as I could. He simply bobbed his body to the side, the rock sailing passed him, smashing into one of the jeeps with enough force to savagely dent one of the doors.

"Oh ho ho, sly mother fucker aren't ya?" He grabbed up one of his own and attempted the same thing, getting a similar response.

"We gonna be at this all day?" I was getting more frustrated. I had more important things to do than some strange version of a friendly spar, but something intrigued me about my adversary. This all felt like some sort of a test.

"Nah, man, we can make a decision." I saw his hand reach for his sidearm, but I could tell he wasn't aiming at me, instead, drawing and shooting the squad-leader's weapon as she attempted to aim, sending it flying from her hands. "Next one's true if you try that again."

I watched the spectacle before turning back to him. "About what?"

"Us, of course. Let me ask you something. You grew up in the paradise, you're the lucky one, why do you hate them so much?" I cocked my head to the side, no longer in a fighting stance.

"They took it all, man. My family, my friends, everything. They lied to us, and they're still lying to those poor bastards under the dome. Someone has to stand up to them, might as well be their new weapon." He seemed to think about it a moment, processing some unknown equation in his mind. From my own experiences, anything that makes us pause is some serious thought we're putting into the situation.

"Good enough for me." He held out his hand. Part of me thought it was some sort of clever trap, but the other, more logical side knew, somehow that this was how this guy shook hands, with a closed fist first. I took his hand into mine, and we both gave a firm shake.

"What's your name?"

"Arcibald, friends call me Arc. You're John, right?" He seemed to understand as well as I that our CORPS designations were meaningless.

"Yeah. Alright, man, what the fuck gives, huh? What's the point of all of this hubbub?" I crossed my arms once more. The Sons seemed somewhat confused at our lack of fighting, but none of them were prepared to try and do something about it either.

"Couple reasons, really. You can't really know a person until you see 'em under pressure in a fight, y'know?"

"Not really, man, but I'll take your word for it."

He looked down a minute, almost sheepishly before meeting my gaze again. "I also heard you found a way past the expiration date." I thought about this comment, realizing immediately what he was talking about. "Yeah, we all get one once we escape."

"Incidentally, you ain't wrong. Dr. Lyrul is with us, she invented our little swimmers." He grinned at this.

"Well then, it looks like I came to the right dude."

"Time out now, we still ain't done talking this shit out." I looked behind me and in the direction of the other soldiers of my entourage, making sure they didn't get any other ideas.

"Fair. If it makes ya feel any better, I hate the CORPS too, have since I was a kid. Do y'know what it's like to grow up in one of their penal colonies?" That's when it struck me, he was from the same place as Reggie. Was I the only one from the Undercities?

"No man, I don't. I lived a pretty privileged life, but it didn't stop them from tearing it all to pieces." We both suddenly had sympathetic looks for each other.

"That's what they do, give, take, give, take. Sometimes they take without giving too, and I was *that* poor bastard."

"John!" I heard the frustrated voice from behind.

"Calm your fucking jets!" I demanded while looking back and then turned to Arc again. "So, what's your goal then?"

"Bring the hurt back to them, of course. These assholes have been screwing with people for centuries, someone's gotta teach them what for." Arc crossed his arms over his chest with a look of confidence in his statement.

"Is that why you came to find me then?"

"You got it buzz. There isn't any point in me fighting those crazies by myself, and there sure as shit isn't any point to you doing it either. You help me live past their little fail-safe, and I'm in." I didn't have to think about this. I couldn't have hoped for a better outcome. I wasn't a cold-blooded killer, no matter how hard the CORPS tried. Having two of us around would be an incredible leg up.

"You've got yourself a deal." Once again, we shook hands, each giving a nod of approval. "So, what about your pals?" He looked back to them, and they suddenly took knees realizing they were being noticed.

"Hey!" He yelled, turning to them. "Keep your distance, I'm sure the TLF doesn't need you cramping their style. Keep up, and you'll get a chance for glorious battle." They looked up and then to each other, as if a god had come down and personally bestowed some sort of blessing. I stopped and thought about the events that had occurred so suddenly. I wasn't entirely certain my new buddy was going to be well received by the TLF. R'yalax was smart, that couldn't be denied, but that might be the problem. In all honesty, it could've all been an elaborate trap.

I took a moment to, in a sense, scan my surroundings. Unless the CORPS had methods of hiding them from me, there were no signals I did notice a faint tracking signal coming from Arc. It was being received by an object in his pocket.

"Are you tracking yourself or something?" I pointed at his pocket. He looked confused for a moment and then got an expression like he remembered something.

"Yeah." He pulled a device that opened up into something very similar to what Alonna carried around. "This thing. My handler kept it on her."

"What happened to your handler?" He looked down for a moment, seeming to wince in pain before looking back up.

"She didn't survive my escape. Before you say anything, I didn't kill her; she was hit by a stray round meant for me. Sometimes wonder if she got in the way on purpose." The last bit struck me as important somehow. Alonna definitely had some sort of powerful infatuation with me. Arc's handler having the same kind of behaviors could mean it's part of the program.

Finally, I motioned for the commander and her troops to join us as the Sons began to disperse, heading off into the night. The commander approached in only what I could describe as a huff. She wasn't impressed by anything she just witnessed, which, in a way, felt somehow insulting.

"The LT isn't going to go for any of this, you know that right?"

"The LT or even Delantil, for that matter, can shove it. I have an agenda, and they don't have to be a part of it." She glared at this statement, but honestly, I wasn't worried about it. The TLF had their backs against the wall with the completion of the XRC project; they could either join up or finally fade to dust.

The walk back was mostly uneventful. The Sons did their job well, staying out of range of even my scanners. Something told me they were likely expert trackers; they had to be in the world they grew up in and the lifestyle they chose.

When we began to get within sight of the convoy, Arc suddenly arched his back and gave off a pain-stricken sound before dropping to his knees. He started dry heaving, curling up into a ball.

"You alright?" I moved to his side, using my CIHUD to get a detailed scan of his systems. The signals emitted by his nanomachines were erratic, and it looked like whatever he ate last wasn't meant for human consumption. He was exhibiting signs of poisoning. I decided not to wait and picked him up, quickly getting him onto my shoulders, and started jogging toward the convoy.

"I thought you guys were superhuman or whatever." The commander and her troops were keeping up, and she was moving alongside me.

"We are, but the CORPS don't like rebels. His body is literally shutting down, and apparently, he ate something that would've probably already killed a normal person."

"T-the zer, of, of, worth." Arc was babbling incoherently. When we approached the convoy, which was now packed and ready to leave, we were met with the sight of gun barrels pointed our way. The guards and scouts quickly recognized us and moved in to offer assistance.

"Get Dr. Lyrul!" The squad-leader ordered one of the guards who didn't take time to salute, instead, turning, and moving for the command tank. I followed and entered the open hatch with my newly found and unconscious friend over my shoulder. The whole night was surreal, but I was beginning to get used to that sort of thing.

Upon entering, a tired-looking Alonna saw what I was carrying and looked to R'yalax who was standing there, waiting patiently with her scanner in hand.

"Lieutenant, may I have my scanner please?" Alonna held out her hand, and R'yalax pondered a moment before handing it over. I set Arc down, laying him on his back on one of the benches set up near the exit hatch.

"Who is this?" Alonna asked, taking a knee in front of the bench. She pulled a syringe from the side of her scanner and stuck it into Arc's neck. The syringe turned red with the blood it extracted, and then Alonna plugged it into her device.

"The better question is: why is he here?" I looked over to R'yalax and shook my head.

"If you or your boss think I am fighting entire armies of mutant soldiers on my own, you're out of your collective minds. We need allies, and I think I may have found one."

"How do we know he's not a Coalition plant?"

"How do we know I'm not a Coalition plant? This whole plan could be an elaborate way to send a massive amount of your forces into a huge trap. You don't fucking know, do you?" She rolled her eyes at my rhetorical line of thinking.

"You have performed actions to prove your worth and trust. While I don't doubt the Coalition is capable of next level conspiracy, my gut says you're one of the good guys." R'yalax was trying to be diplomatic.

"Yeah? Well, what does your gut say about this dude? Because mine says, I need help. I saw the hatred in his eyes, and you know what I'm talking about." I met her gaze, hoping to convey my feelings.

"Fine, we'll go with your little experiment for now, but I'm reporting this to the General. You can appeal to him." She turned and moved to sit with the comms officer.

"Whatever, I ain't scared of him either." I turned to Alonna, who was dutifully attending to the man before her. She was waiting for some sort of information to pop up on her scanner.

"There it is. Yes, just as I suspected. The expiration protocol was triggered. His nanomachines are failing, but something is accelerating the process. Some sort of poison he ingested. His augmented digestive system seems to have slowed its spread." She was studying the readout intently, seeming to be thinking at speeds typically meant for folks like me.

"What's the verdict doc, can we save him?" She looked up at me with grave concern.

"Is that what you want? The Lieutenant's points should be heeded John, this man could be our undoing." Hearing her words taught me a little bit more about the state of mind of the handlers. She obviously wasn't as concerned with his safety as she was with mine.

"I'm not an idiot, I understand the risks. Imagine if I'm right, though; what could we accomplish with two of us? What happens when I get into a fight with two of them? Or more?" She looked into my eyes, almost longingly and the grave concern remained, but shifted gears. The idea that she could protect me better with another cyborg around struck the nerve I was hoping for.

"There is a way. The nanomachines were all designed to be interchangeable with the others. This machine allows me to take existing nanomachines and imprint them with the DNA of the intended host. I essentially brought blank ones with me to help you."

"So, you just need to do to him what you did to me."

"Precisely. I already have the sample here. It will take an hour for the data to transfer to his nanomachines, and then probably a few days before they can replenish their numbers, but there's a problem."

I rolled my eyes. "There's always a problem."

"Whatever he ingested will likely kill him before the new machines can replenish their numbers. I am unfamiliar with the compound he ingested."

"Probably the Elixir of Worth." R'yalax came back over to us. I could hear bits and pieces of the conversation she just finished, mainly her end of it. The General had reached some sort of decision.

"What the hell is the Elixir of Worth?" I asked, putting my hands to my hips.

"It's a poison the Sons of Rellen use, both in rituals and when raiding settlements. Any who survive are said to be worthy and part of the tribe. That's just a dart; apparently, there's some other ritual involving drinking a whole glass of the stuff." I gave a disgusted look.

"How do people end up believing in shit like that?" I was incredulous over the entire affair.

"That makes sense." Alonna finally stood back up. "Had he ingested a large amount when his nanomachines began to expire, they may not have been able to keep up with the spread." I got a puzzled look on my face.

"Sort of off-topic, why does the expiration happen over time? Wouldn't it be smarter to just shut them all down at once?" I inquired.

"There are a few reasons for that. One of them is that the process is supposed to be subtle, helping to prevent curious parties before the body can be recovered. Besides this, it may be prudent to prevent the process should it be triggered accidentally, having a time window allows for that. Finally, and this is perhaps the biggest reason, the nanomachines, while they do work in clusters, are mostly independent. If but one is present within your system, it will be able to replenish all of the clusters. Because of this, it's more practical to shut them down in the same manner that a virus kills healthy cells."

"So, they can just shut me down then?" I was genuinely curious, as opposed to afraid.

"Theoretically, yes, but my meddling here fixes that."

"How so?" It was R'yalax who asked the question.

"I added an algorithm that searches for foreign code and executes an elimination protocol on the infected machines. Your healthy bots essentially act like a secondary immune system, preventing not only disease, but even computer viruses." I couldn't help but grin at the news. I was reasonably certain she wasn't lying to me, and besides that, it meant something significant. The CORPS was, for once, in the dark where I was concerned. With her meddling, I really had become a Wild Card of sorts, and soon, there would be two in our deck.

"Sounds to me like you would be executed if they ever found you again," R'yalax crossed her arms over her chest and seemed to be lost in thought. Alonna looked down at her scanner and gave a shrug, which was the sort of gesture you wouldn't expect out of someone like her.

"It is what it is, I guess. Right, John?" She looked up at me, and I couldn't help smiling back at her. I reassuringly patted her shoulder.

"You got it, doc. So what are we doing about the poison in his system?"

"We have that covered," R'yalax interjected. She tossed me a small vial attached to a quick injection mechanism. "We keep antidotes around in case we run into those yahoos. The General agrees with you, but he's your responsibility. Anything he does is on you." I wanted to roll my eyes at the statement, as if they could actually do something to me if he did fuck up. It didn't matter much anyway; if they were going to be agreeable, I wasn't going to fight about it.

"Fair enough. So, where we headed, boss?"

"A few kilometers from our current position to set up a new camp. The boys and girls are tired. Besides, I'd prefer you to be briefed on where we're going more thoroughly before we get there." I finally did rolled my eyes.

"Look, I get it, I'm some scary one-man wrecking crew to you, but I can behave. You know I had almost no criminal record in the Undercities."

"Almost?" Alonna inquired, looking away from her work for a moment.

"Look, petty vandalism as a kid doesn't count. The point is, we'll be fine."

"You had better be. It's my ass if you do something stupid. You know when one of my soldiers does something dumb, it doesn't end in a pile of bodies and wrecked armor." She was finished with the conversation, accentuated by her turning and walking to her station.

Alonna completed her work an hour after we found a new place to camp out. She gave Arc an injection of swimmers and an antidote. She claimed we would have to wait possibly a day or two before the new machines could repair his body. It was interesting to see someone else in the position I was in a few days ago. It must have been surreal for the others to see a failing body miraculously come back to life. Performing a ritual, though, why? What had Arc been through?

Chapter Twenty: Not So Dead

"I thought you said I was a prototype?" I asked abruptly while Alonna, myself, R'yalax, and a few others sat around a fire under the night sky. We had made it to a sort of plains and forest-like area with a ton of vegetation. Somehow, someway the world hadn't entirely fallen during the war.

"You are," Alonna answered, delicately taking a bite from a bowl of stew she was holding.

"Okay, so where did Arc come from then? What about that dude in the base a week ago? If I was brought online recently, how are these guys popping up, some of them looking like they had more training than me?" She set her food down and wiped her mouth with a handkerchief.

"Well, it's because you were the first. This will likely not sound very pleasant, but we had to spend a great deal of time and effort just trying to keep you alive, trying different sets of nanomachines, fighting your immune system almost hourly due to rejection syndrome. It took us nearly three years just to stabilize you, but once that happened, the rest was comparatively easy." Some of the soldiers sitting with us were on the edge of their seats, others looked like they had lost their appetite.

"So, in other words, the first three years was working out the kinks and once you did that-"

"We were able to produce more units, yes."

"Units? Aren't those people you're talking about?" R'yalax asked the question, and I could've kissed her for it.

"Yes, you are right, but I get enough semantic guilt trips from John."

"Can't say I blame him." The conversation that was growing more awkward by the minute was interrupted by Arc, who emerged from the command tank. Everyone grew quiet as he sauntered over to the group.

"Mind if I join ya, buzz?" He asked after approaching me. I nodded and motioned to the ground nearby. He took a seat and looked over at everyone, seeming to study them with an unnervingly calm gaze. His eyes settled on Alonna, who looked away, rubbing the back of her neck nervously. "I hear I have you to thank."

"Yes." She looked at him and gave a polite nod. "You now have the benefit of liberty."

"Yeah, bud, CORPS can't track ya now, and they can't flip the off switch anymore." I gave his back a hearty pat, and he responded with a grin.

"Good, so I owe ya then, just like we agreed." He had a reassuring tone to his voice, though I don't think it was directed at me. The people around us clearly were very distrustful of his presence, and honestly, who could've blamed them?

"How is all of this actually possible? How do we know the Coalition didn't place some sort of fail-safe in your machines?" Alonna gave R'yalax an almost haughty look when she asked the question.

"To allow myself a moment of ego, I invented them, Lieutenant. I know every part of the nanomachines and how they run. Even if other Coalition scientists attempted to add some sort of a fail-safe in other components, the nanomachines would hunt the errant code down." Alonna had a prideful grin on her face as she explained this.

"It sounds to me like the nanomachines are the key to the entire system," R'yalax observed, pondering the possibilities.

"That would be an accurate description of their importance, yes.

Without the nanomachines, the body would reject all the augmentations wholesale, killing the host in a most slow and painful manner. It is their job to regulate the system, install new firmware, repair damage to both body and augmentations, provide scanning systems with data, and enable the host to exert conscious control over otherwise sub-conscious functions. Because of this, the only real way to shut an XRC unit down remotely would be to shut down every single nanomachine in their system."

"Y'know, I've always wondered about that." Arc chimed in. "I mean, why would the CORPS make something that could so obviously fuck their shit up if it stopped liking them? To allow the nanomachines to be hacked in a way to thwart any real fail-safes. Shit seems dumb."

"Well sure, if your intention is to merely create soldiers for war. That was a mere side effect of the actual goal."

"And what is your goal?" It was one of the soldiers who was sitting with us, a low-ranking officer. She and others tended to watch Alonna with great suspicion in their eyes. I was reasonably confident that if I wasn't around, she wouldn't be either. Alonna simply looked to them with an almost diplomatic visage.

"Beyond the incredible amount of data such research would glean? The Coalition's singular purpose has always been one of scientific discovery. Much of the research is centered around improving the survival capabilities of our species. In that sense, the XRC Project is probably the greatest achievement towards that goal."

"Are you trying to tell us that the lunatics that blew our civilization to hell are somehow trying to improve us?" I could see the frustration in the eyes of the officer, but Alonna had a very surprising defender.

"That's exactly what she's saying," R'yalax spoke up and looked to Alonna. "Isn't it doctor?" Alonna's cool demeanor lost a bit of its luster.

"The unfortunate reality is that the Coalition will do anything for their research, up to and including conditioning the environment." The officer was about to speak up again, but Alonna waved her hand and interrupted. "It is one of the many reasons why I can no longer abide them as an organization. At no point in my life did I become a doctor to harm others." She looked to me, and I got that all too familiar, creepy feeling. "I became a doctor to improve our condition."

"And just like that you became a goody-goody all of a sudden." Arc rhetorically commented. He stood and walked over to a nearby table where bowls and stew sat. He didn't look over as he retrieved some sustenance. "Please, I know kids that fib better than that." He walked back over. His words had created a lingering silence among the others. Even people who had been engaged in nearby conversations stopped their gabbing to take a listen. He took a bite, gave a bit of a grin, and looked over to Alonna. "Now I ain't doubting for a second that you really do wanna help people. I buy that shit. What I don't buy is that being your reason for walking away. I can only imagine the sick shit you engaged in before this. Nah, there's more to it than that." He took another bite of his meal, but never took his gaze from Alonna.

"Well, if you must know." Alonna looked down, and her expression changed unexpectedly. She took in a deep breath as if preparing some sort of confession, and something told me I probably wasn't going to like it. "Five years ago," she looked back up to meet Arc's eyes, "a patient was brought to me. He was in bad shape, had been shot in non-vital areas, but was nevertheless quite injured. I had a singular duty: To fit this man with the machines I had created, to begin the single most important project in the Coalition's history."

As Alonna wove her tale, others began to gather, find seats, and listen. "My job would be more than just introducing the nanomachines. I would be this man's handler, and it would be my job to learn everything I could about him, to observe him, to know him." She looked to me for a short moment and then to the rest who had gathered. She was addressing everyone, it seemed. "The first thing I did was watch the footage of his capture." For a moment, I was looking at the fire, just listening, but I slowly looked back to Alonna as she began that part of her tale. My gut feeling was proving to be accurate, as it always did.

"In my time with the Coalition, I had witnessed many-" She looked down. "-atrocities." She looked over at the group again. "Things I will have to live with until my dying breath, but I am ashamed to admit, I was always disconnected from it all. I always knew there was little I could do to change anything, so I built a shell. When I saw this man's footage, knowing my task would involve becoming close to him, my emotions came through. I saw-" she stopped herself, looking at her hands a moment, seemingly searching for words. She looked up once more. "Pain. True pain, the pain that comes from the loss of a loved one. I saw for the first time, humanity, and was presented an opportunity to perhaps do something this time. So, I did."

I had finally had enough of the story. I stood up quickly, knocking over a cup of water I had next to me and walked away from the group. The people who had gathered parted for me, giving me a wide berth.

The last thing I ever wanted to hear was a CORPS lackey, former or otherwise, recount the most painful moment of my life. The control the machines imparted to me only fueled my anger. I wanted to be mad, to yell at

259

her, to remind her that the pain had a name. Lys deserved better than some speech from a CORPS doctor.

I knew he was approaching before Arc placed his hand on my shoulder, and I did nothing to move away. "Need a tissue, buzz?"

"You're an asshole, you know that?" I spat, giving him a glance, but was unable to help the chuckle that came out after. He was a real charmer at times.

"Nah, man, I'm a dick."

I gave an incredulous look. "What's the difference?"

"I do the fucking, not the other way around." His hand left my shoulder, and he moved around, so he was facing me. "Can we trust her?" The question was simple, but the context complex.

"Maybe," I answered sincerely.

"Y'know, that's a better answer than I was expecting."

"She wouldn't sell us out to the CORPS, I dunno why, but I feel like I can guarantee that."

"But?"

"But I am also certain there's some other agenda. I don't know what it is though, can't tell if it's personal or something else entirely. I'm also fairly sure it ain't necessarily harmful."

"To us." He had a creepy knack of reading my thoughts.

"Yeah, to us. While Alonna doesn't seem to get the same creepy stalker vibe over you, I got a feeling she'd save you before any of these TLF kids."

He gave a chuckle. "She ain't my type anyway. We're about to have a visitor." We could tell someone was approaching. I turned and saw R'yalax walking towards us.

"Mind I if I interrupt the girl talk?" She asked with a somewhat stern look on her face.

"Hey, don't let me fuck with your vibe." Arc shrugged and began to walk away.

"Stay, I want to address both of you." Arc and I looked to each other and then gave the Lieutenant our attention. "As I explained to you earlier, John, we will soon be heading to Libsal, a scheduled stop. The city has a decent population and is quite large. It's imperative that both of you keep a low profile."

"I sincerely hope you ain't tellin' me what to do." Arc crossed his arms over his chest.

"I am actually." R'yalax kept her admirable, icey look on her face, which even Arc seemed to enjoy. "Our goal isn't this city, it's a stop. We want this to go smoothly."

"Y'know, I ain't exactly privy to our goal here." I looked to Arc and realized he was right. This all seemed very rushed.

"We're goin' to Dome City."

"Dome City? Lame name."

"That's what I said!" I shook my head and refocused. "Look, the Undercities may have been evacuated to this big ass Dome in the middle of nowhere. The CORPS is apparently based there these days, production facilities, research, the works."

"Sounds like a target." He mused, getting what was becoming his signature grin.

"Not quite. Instead, we're gonna infect their sterile environment and wreak havoc."

"You don't strike me as the terrorist type."

I shook my head and waved my arms. "Nah, man, nothing like that! If it really is the Undercities that populates the bubble, then they're a bunch of lied to sheep. I know, I was one. I wanna sow anarchy, bring chaos to order. Shed some light on the truth."

Arc waved his hand dismissively. "Alright, alright, enough of the metaphors. It sounds like it'll put a hurt on the CORPS. I'm in. Be good while in Libwhatever."

"Libsal," R'yalax spoke again. "Thank you. We will be obtaining new equipment for the operation. It's vitally important that everything goes smoothly while we're there."

"We get it, you already gave me this speech." I replied. "We'll be good boys."

"What about the Sons?" R'yalax asked, and we both looked to Arc.

"Look." He gave a shrug, "I don't exactly control them per se. He does." He motioned his thumb to me.

"Don't fucking tell me that was what the fight was about?" I asked incredulously.

"Kinda? I didn't lie to you, man, but I mean had I won, I'd be the First." His grin was more like a smirk.

"So, what do I do then?"

"Really? What are you dumb? You gotta address 'em, give 'em orders and shit." I thought about this for a moment, and both of my companions were silent.

"Y'know," I started, "these Sons could be an asset. A sort of Wild Card style backup if things get hairy. Some extra guns couldn't hurt."

262

"While I would not argue the logic in that, the Sons are not allowed in or near Libsal. Libsal doesn't allow standing armies." R'yalax informed us.

"So how the hell do you and the CORPS get special treatment?" My question had merit, a lot of this wasn't making much sense to me.

"Mainly respect. The people know whatever troops either have there won't suddenly attack. They also limit the number of personnel we have stationed there."

"Let me guess, cybernetic freaks aren't on your manifest?" Arc gave a chuckle at my guess.

"No, not exactly, so, the dogs stay in the garage." With that, R'yalax turned and went back to the fire. Arc and I looked at each other, and both shook our heads.

"I didn't exactly agree to tag along to be cooped up."

"Quit your bitching. The sooner we get to where we're going, the better. If we gotta be good little kids, then so be it." I gave him a pat on his back and walked away to my perch on a tree I had chosen for stargazing. I didn't watch where Arc wandered, instead, taking in the sky and catching up for lost time.

Our journeys eventually brought us to an area I was just as shocked to see as I was the sky. First, the sparse patches of grassy plains and prairie gave way to hills and dense forest. Trees, as tall as buildings, reached for the clouds, standing proudly in stoic positions. Perhaps two centuries was enough for mother nature to start taking over again. Maybe the War hadn't caused as much damage as the CORPS had led us to believe. Whatever the answer, the world was far from dead. It somehow seemed less lush than it could have been. Everything had clearly gone wrong with the world, but the world still existed.

263

Libsal was built into a mountain valley, with forests and mighty hills providing foundations for the walls of the city. As the convoy traveled through the well-kept roadways into the wilderness, the main wall itself came into view. Built into the mountains themselves, the wall seemed to take the shape of a gigantic, half-eaten doughnut. It was made of concrete, likely reinforced with metal, and looked somewhat new in the grand scheme of things.

While the forest had plenty of trees, it wasn't continuously thick either. There were plenty of bare patches dotting the landscape, looking like a ghost of forgotten homes and places of work. I could see the old roads in how the plants grew, with the new roads demonstrating our ability to overtake nature with ingenuity and gumption.

I spent a lot of my time outside of the command tank at the protest of R'yalax and Alonna. I spent my entire life cooped up in confined spaces; I wasn't about to make a habit of it on the surface. There was something liberating about the idea of having no walls around you. Either Arc felt the same way or had his own reasons for not staying inside the command tank.

We sparsely spoke since he joined. We joked and shared stories at night about old friends and places we had seen, but there felt like there was a barrier of some sort, forcing us to keep certain feelings to ourselves. It was ironic really, because no one else could truly understand our problems and yet we refused to discuss them. Then again, not every issue needed addressing. Sometimes, trash belongs in the trashcan. No need to pick through it.

Another thing I noticed was the attitude towards Arc and I coming from the TLF personnel we traveled with. I expected some sort of distrustful air to come from everyone, but anything like that seemed mostly directed at Alonna. As far as the soldiers were concerned, it seemed, we were victims. Just

264

like them, we were looking for retribution. It probably helped to imagine having super soldiers on your side. Who wouldn't buddy up with a walking weapon in a time of war?

Poor Alonna. As more time passed, my suspicions waned, and I began to honestly believe she really was a defector and trying to make good for her sins. It didn't make me forgive her, let alone warm up to her, but I wasn't apathetic. Watching the life she was living among the TLF was rough. No one wanted to speak with her, and they would often discuss among themselves what they would do should she ever show her *true colors*. The paranoia ran deep.

Chapter Twenty-One: A Promise Kept

The ride to the actual wall was a suprisingly long trip, a testament to its size. As we drew closer, it was almost like entering some sort of frontier town one would read about in ancient folklore. There were homes clearly made from wood, fashioned from the surrounding landscape. The area was even more sparsely wooded than the others. There were mountains rising-up on either side of the city.

The road was wide, and while our convoy was the only vehicles traversing it at the time, it clearly saw a lot of traffic. It was early morning, and it seemed like things would likely be much busier later in the day.

It was interesting to see such organization in a place that was described to me as being somewhat anarchic in nature. Spirits seemed high, the homes well-kept, and there were visible signs of commerce all around. Civilization was alive and strong there and apparently all under some sort of mutual benefit as opposed to a centralized government. I was curious to see how it all worked and had a feeling I might end up disobeying R'yalax's request in some innocent fashion or another. At the very least, I took the time to snap pictures using the onboard camera of my PCD. Photographs are still more fun than photographic memory.

I could tell by the reaction of the locals that we were some sort of spectacle to behold. While the roads showed clear signs of vehicles crossing day-to-day, it became immediately apparent that a military convoy was not the usual visitors to the area. It also looked like we were coming from the road's end as opposed to where it led to. It explained the lack of traffic from where we were coming from.

People exited their homes to watch the small parade, and it almost felt like going back to earlier times. It seemed the majority of people there were self-sufficient workers. Men, women, and even children were all busy with some sort of homesteading.

I was walking alongside the command vehicle with a smile on my face. I imagined what Lys and Ray would have thought to know the world wasn't dead, but was actually thriving in some places. Even their memories weren't upsetting the pep in my step. Of course, it wasn't long before someone had to ruin the party. The convoy came close to the entrance of the massive wall.

"John, Arc!" I heard my name coming from the command vehicle. R'yalax had come out the back and was beckoning us.

"Oh come on, what can we hurt just walking around?" She crossed her arms impatiently at my question.

"Too many people have already seen you as it is. Come now, we are on a schedule."

"Sure thing, ma!" Arc exclaimed, walking towards the back of the command tank. "Wouldn't want to break the curfew or anything. Can't promise I won't trash the place." R'yalax rolled her eyes, and I walked past her before stopping and turning back for a moment.

"Just a quick reminder. I ain't one of your lackeys. First thing that piques my interest I'm checking it out." She began to protest, but I held out my hand. "Not one of your lackeys." I turned and walked into the vehicle. I saw Arc sitting and leaning back on the left bench just near the exit door.

"Comfortable?" I inquired.

"Fuck, no! This is a load of horseshit. They're treating us like animals." I took a seat across from him.

"No, they're treating us like we're wanted because we are." Arc's face only seemed more frustrated by my explanation.

"And who exactly is gonna take us in? The CORPS? What are the chances we run into one of their new pets?"

"Extremely high." Alonna, who had been relaxing inside the command vehicle, walked towards us. "Libsal is considered an important location for sociological research."

"What the fuck does that have to do with cyborgs?" Arc gave Alonna his signature pissy look, complete with the tone to go with it.

"Since the first units began waking up prior to John being revived, they have been sent to various research locations. It was part of the initial testing phases. Some came as guards, others to assist with the actual work. Besides all of this, Libsal laws almost guarantees that the Coalition would seek other security alternatives."

"One-man armies would fit that role real good." I thought out loud about the implications.

"Y'know I still don't get why the CORPS would give fuck one about Libsal and their laws." Arc's point echoed through my own mind. I was curious about that too.

"As I said, it's a hub of sociological research. The Coalition abides by local laws when it fits with their plans. Why crush the city when it freely provides a wealth of data?"

"I don't buy it," Arc interjected. "There's gotta be something more to it."

"Well, let us be fair a moment; if the TLF or Coalition chose to, they could individually wipe Libsal from the map. This would obviously go against

TLF ideals, and the Coalition sees no reason to waste resources on something they currently gain knowledge from."

"I guess that makes sense. So, it's a benefit to just leave them be then?" As I asked the question, I could feel the vehicle come to a stop. We must have arrived at the wall.

"Basically, yes. Libsal itself is open to all who wish to make a life or profit. They do not engage in war or politics." The entire idea of the settlements seemed surreal to me. When I thought back to my history lessons, it seemed unreal that a continent-spanning civilization, with enough tech to choose what their babies would look like, could all but disappear from the world. Sure, the TLF was still around, but they were a mere shadow of the Tantillan Republic. What once was a mighty empire was now reduced to quarreling city-states dotting the habitable areas of the landscape. Going further on those lines, it was also surreal anything was there at all. While the entire world wasn't bombed out like the CORPS had claimed, some places were. Even two centuries later, there were likely barren areas laden with radiation infused dust, and glowing water with three-eyed fish. That's assuming anything survived in those places at all.

The command vehicle had finally come to a full stop after reaching some sort of checkpoint. We must have arrived at the TLF compound. As soon as we did, R'yalax approached Arc and I, sitting in the back.

"We don't plan to be here very long if we can help it." She said, looking to both of us.

"Gonna share what we're doing yet?" I asked, leaning back, crossing my arms over my chest.

"We're picking up a new piece of technology recently developed by a

Coalition defector." I looked to Alonna, sitting just across from us.

"So, it would seem the doc here ain't the only one then." Alonna gave a surprised look and stood.

"Who?" She was eager to learn and only got a scoff in return.

"With all due respect, doctor, you are the last person I would give that information to. It's also information I don't have. If you'll excuse me." Saying this, the hatch in the back opened on cue, and she confidently marched out of the vehicle. Before the hatch closed behind her, I could see a bit of where we were. There were soldiers on patrol in what looked to be a walled-off yard. I couldn't see the other buildings, but logic dictated the basic idea of a square, walled compound, with buildings on the inside of the wall sections.

"I wonder what new toys we're gettin'?" Arc wondered with an almost child-like smirk on his face.

"What makes you think we're getting toys?" I asked.

"Just a hunch. I mean, c'mon, why else would they interrupt your all-important mission? Speaking of, you haven't exactly told me a hell of a lot about your plan." I shrugged my shoulders and opened my mouth to speak, but then the comms officer approached us.

"John. You have a message on the line, high priority." I pulled my head back a bit and gave her an incredulous look.

"Me? Who the fuck is calling me? Here?" I stood and walked up to the comms officer. "Who is it?"

"I am unable to answer that question. This way, please." I looked back to Arc and Alonna and got an unhelpful shrug from both. I shook my head.

"Fine, lead on." She led me over to the communications panel and offered me an earpiece before sitting down. It was a small affair, and I couldn't see a mic on it, but assumed it must have had one.

"John's Butcher Shop, where the competition just can't beat my meat." I had no idea what to say honestly, and humor was always my go-to stress reliever. Surprisingly, I got a chuckle out of Delantil, who was on the other end.

"Glad to see you're okay so far. I am going to dispense with the pleasantries and get right down to it."

"Go on."

"I am sure Lt. R'yalax has done her job and chained you to the fence, so to speak."

"Yeah, we're in the doghouse, dad." Sarcasm was positively dripping from my lips.

"Good. In about ten minutes, Lt. Syahl will enter the command vehicle and take Alonna out for questioning. Allow this to happen. Do what's necessary to keep your new friend under control." My lips pursed in irritation.

"I ain't fucking down for this espionage crap."

"Don't worry, I don't plan on leaving you in the dark. On the contrary, she can't succeed without you, but it's absolutely imperative everyone else not involved stay out of the loop." I took in a deep breath before letting it out, signaling my feelings.

"Fine, go on."

"R'yalax is retrieving an engineer, one with information about technology vital to our final mission."

"What kinda tech?"

"Honestly, that's not important right now and would take more time to explain than you have. Suffice to say we need that engineer alive. The

Coalition is well aware he is in Libsal and that we're looking for him."

"Well, sounds like they're about to not even spit on it then."

"Charming but accurate. The Coalition will take him out without a second thought. According to our intel, this technology is extremely sensitive."

"In other words, you want a technological leg-up on them."

"Essentially, yes. Alonna is going to be briefed on a bogus mission, and she will be used as bait. She is going to meet with the engineer for us." The way he seemed to emphasize the word meet signaled to me that he was lying about the last part, and I felt like he wanted me to know that. "The Coalition will most certainly attack with everything they have available in Libsal in an attempt to kill two birds with one stone."

"Then Arc and I make them regret their decisions in life," I replied firmly. The plan sounded like a good one, and Delantil seemed to be learning how to talk me into action without even asking.

"Alright, bait, and switch. I'm down, and I'm sure Arc will be too."

"Arc? Is that the XRC Unit you found?"

"More like he found us."

"Do you trust him?" His tone made it clear it was the only thing he cared about.

"Against the CORPS and as far as the mission goes? Yes, implicitly." I could almost sense him giving me a nod.

"Good enough then. Be discrete, no one is to know of what you're doing."

"They're not going to let us leave the command vehicle," I pointed out.

"Make them. I'm sure you'll figure something out." I rolled my eyes, though he was right.

272

"Fine, we're on it." I took the earpiece out and set it down on the panel. I very simply, but directly, put my hand on the comms officer's shoulder. "Open the hatch." My voice was severe.

"Sir, I don't-"

"That wasn't a request." I waited to end my sentence before slowly meeting her gaze and letting my CIHUD pop out. By now, every single person in the tank had stopped and looked over at the commotion I was causing.

"Y-yes, right away." She stood, and no one moved to protest. I was banking on their fear of the technological boogeyman in the room.

We walked to the back of the command vehicle, and I looked to Arc. "C'mon, we've got shit to do." The comms officer walked to a wall panel and opened the hatch. Arc leapt up as I said this.

"Oh, hell yes, you don't have to tell me twice." He gathered his equipment, and I also made sure to suit up, grabbing the grenade belt and my sidearm; I was already wearing my harness. Alonna began to get up, and I raised my hand to stop her.

"You stay here." She cocked her head in confusion. "I'll explain later." The hatch was open, and I left her standing there, as dumbfounded as the rest of the present crew. As we walked out of the vehicle, I could see that some of the guards took notice and began to approach, drawing their weapons.

I looked to Arc, and he gave me a nod. One of the wall edges wasn't very far, maybe ten meters from the command vehicle and only a little more than three tall. In a flash, we both dashed towards the wall, leaping into the air, and vaulting right over it. We both left small craters when we hit the ground. Debris and dirt flew, masking our view momentarily, allowing us to dash away from the compound. We didn't go very far, however, just far enough to hide behind a tree and take a seat for a moment.

"Uh, the fuck are we doing? I thought this was an escape or something." Arc took a seat behind a tree next to mine. We could hear the commotion behind us of several soldiers mobilizing for a search.

"Nah, this will be more fun. Apparently, they're about to take Alonna out of here and to meet some CORPS engineer they're getting fancy new tech from."

"Okay, so what's this gotta do with us being out here?"

"This shit is covert, my friend. No one's privy to our involvement, not even the doc." I couldn't help but chuckle at the idea. Something about lying to the liar felt somewhat poetic. As we sat there, we could sense the patrols drawing near as they came looking for us.

"Time to go, buzz." Arc was right, so I got up and moved from my position, heading closer towards the wall, but first moving away from the patrols. Arc followed but didn't seem to enjoy being in the dark. I had no plan on keeping him there, but a man deserves a little fun once in a while.

"So, are you gonna tell me what the fuck we're doing?" We had made it to the concrete wall of the compound. From our position, I could see that Libsal was made up of several such compounds. City-States within a broader community.

"Yep." I finally answered his question and pointed to the corner of the wall one-hundred meters away. "Head over there, use your CIHUD to keep an eye on the command tank inside the wall. Keep distance, we need to follow Alonna."

"These things don't exactly differentiate people." With the CIHUDs, we could easily follow the positions of the patrols. They would likely be called

274

off the search sooner than later anyway. I had a feeling Delantil was keeping tabs on this particular situation.

"We won't need it to. It should be obvious. They're taking the doc to go meet the CORPS defector, but the dude's a fake. The real rendezvous is happening elsewhere." Arc seemed to ponder this a moment before a sly grin came across his face.

"She's bait, a fuckin' distraction."

"Basically."

"So, what the fuck are we doing then?" He crossed his arms over his chest impatiently.

"She's the bait, we're the trap. We'll rough up any fool who shows up and make it look real. Give the other group the cover they need to collect their man. Apparently, they're getting some-"

"Dude, you had me at roughing mother fuckers up." He turned and walked over to the position I had indicated. Watching my CIHUD, I could see that after only a few minutes, the search party for us was called off.

"Smooth move General," I muttered and watched the radar layout before my eye. We were just close enough to the command tank to be able to tell when people entered it. Soon enough, six people walking in formation behind a seventh, approached the vehicle. The leader entered the command tank and, after a few minutes, exited with another person in tow. I looked over to where Arc was.

"There's our marks," I spoke as if he was next to me, knowing Arc would be able to hear it. "Keep the radar net, follow em with me." I saw his hand stick out from the corner with his thumb sticking up. "Good man." I waited and watched as the group approached the compound's main gate, causing Arc and I to move up along the wall and keep pace. When the group got to the gate, my CIHUD picked up a vehicle coming from deeper within the compound, stopping at the group, who promptly entered.

Realizing that they were about to be moving a bit faster than we could, I found the tallest nearby tree and proceeded to climb it. I couldn't help but take a split second to marvel at what I was doing. If someone had told me five years ago that I was going to be climbing trees on the surface, I would've said they were drunk. Now there I was, climbing a tree on the surface, actively participating in some never-ending war.

Arc decided to follow suit, finding himself a tree nearby and climbing up for a better vantage point. From there, we could watch the convoy for a long distance, keeping up by going from treetop to treetop. The terrain was to our advantage as the roads wound around it.

The convoy left and drove down a winding dirt road, deeper into Libsal's territory. They weren't the only vehicles riding around either. Many powered and unpowered travelers moved about the infrastructure, like ants through a colony. People traveled between the various compounds, trading with one another.

The convoy seemed to take a road that wasn't as well-traveled as the others, likely going to a more secluded place to conduct business. We watched them for a long while, using the gift of our enhanced sight to keep track of their direction. At some point, several more vehicles came from the TLF compound, as well as a couple of small squads on foot. They all moved in different directions, some seemingly preparing to leave Libsal, others visiting other compounds. None went in the direction of our target, and this seemed glaringly deliberate. They were really hamming up the bait.

"Time to move," I observed out loud and stood on a branch strong enough to hold me. My scanners allowed me to tell the structural integrity of tree branches, which meant we could stay on the treetops. Like some sort of arboreal version of parkour, we started moving, sometimes running, other times base jumping from tree-to-tree. Occasionally we would land back down on the ground, only to find a new set of trees to climb. It was a liberating experience, just moving freely as if all of the obstacles didn't even exist.

Alonna's vehicle had finally come to a stop in a circular clearing on top of a massive, hill surrounded by trees with a cleared out area at the peak. There was a large, but at that moment, empty firepit surrounded by wooden bleachers. The place was absolutely gargantuan, looking like some sort of an arena in which plays, parties, and various shows took place. The firepit itself had a radius of nearly ten meters, and the bleachers themselves could easily fit hundreds of people. It wasn't part of any compound, leading me to believe that this was neutral ground.

The vehicle was parked just outside the bleachers, and next to it, I saw the squad I had met before when we found Arc, plus a couple of extra soldiers. Standing in front was Alonna, who seemed a bit confused judging by the expression on her face and gravely concerned. She likely thought herself too valuable to be sitting out in the open like that. The irony was that it was her value that put her in the situation to begin with.

Arc swiftly moved around the other side of the bleachers, finding his way up a large, green needle covered tree. I did the same on the opposite end and couldn't help the grim thoughts of gratitude that I wasn't the poor bastards about to be flanked by cyborgs. From our vantage point, we could hear the conversation below.

"I do not understand what you expect from me." Alonna's voice was laden with protest.

"You don't have to understand, you just need to verify the identity of the engineer before we can bring him back to the compound." The commander of the group, the squad-leader that was with me when we found Arc, was just as salty as ever. Her rifle was slung over her shoulder, her disdain filled eyes watched Alonna's every move.

"But that makes no sense!" Alonna waved her arms out in protest. "The Coalition knows the location of your compound. Everyone in Libsal does!" It was at this point the squad-leader got right up into Alonna's face, with an icy look in her eyes.

"It doesn't have to make sense to you. You just need to do your job. I don't make the orders; I carry them out. It is absolutely nothing to tie you up and gag you until the engineer arrives. Am I understood, or do I have to demonstrate?"

"I-I-, um, yes, I understand you just fine." She crossed her arms in an almost teenaged manner. If I wasn't concerned about giving away our positions, I would have fallen from the tree with laughter. At least they were keeping it entertaining, though I wouldn't have been bored for very long.

Mere minutes after our arrival, another vehicle approached the amphitheater, parking on the opposite end of Alonna and the gang. This seemed really coy to me. Somehow I think no one present actually knew what the hell was going on because even the commander of the squad seemed impatient at the situation.

From the other jeep, a wirey looking guy and two well-armed men approached Alonna. It wasn't long before her incredulous voice could be heard complaining. She had no idea who those people were, as expected.

I didn't have time to pay attention to the comedy. From the road the fake engineer had come from, we could see two CORPS transport vehicles screaming towards the gathering grounds, with another just minutes behind it.

The arguing quickly came to an end as the first two armored personnel trucks literally came crashing into the amphitheater, smashing two of the bleachers into splinters. I looked over to Arc from my vantage point, who looked right back at me and we both nodded, knowing the plan without having to go over it.

The TLF had no time to react as the CORPS Elites came piling out of the trucks, ten apiece. Just before either side could speak or open fire, Arc and I both dropped twenty meters from our treetops. Our harnesses made our entrance even more dramatic.

My hand was already on my pistol as soon as I hit the ground, and I fired off five successive rounds, as did Arc, dropping half the group in almost an instant. The TLF troops immediately moved to whatever cover they could find, though there really wasn't much. Panic fire came from the TLF, while the calm Elites turned their attention to the true threat and began firing at Arc and me. Ever ready for this sort of assault, we both bolted to the side in opposite directions, drawing their fire away and narrowly escaping being turned into confetti ourselves.

As soon as everything looked clear, I reached for the grenade belt the TLF had provided and pulled one of the two frag grenades. I stopped running, quickly turned, and heaved the hot potato towards the enemy vehicles. Arc must have sensed this, because instead of waiting for the grenade to go off, he waited until it was in the air next to the trucks and fired at the explosive. The grenade went off spectacularly, sending shrapnel flying and the remaining Elites to the ground.

"We've still got one more!" I yelled out and pointed to the road behind Arc, who gave me a nod of understanding. While the entire attack was thwarted in mere seconds, something told me the second one wasn't going to be so simple.

Arc moved to his original vantage point and climbed back up. When he was high enough, he turned and called out, "We have a lot more than one more buzz! I see three others not far behind this one!"

"Fuck." I cursed under my breath and looked to the TLF soldiers.

"We'll get her out of here." I heard the commander say.

"No! She stays!" I called back.

"What?" Alonna was beyond incredulous, having meandered her way into grim astonishment, but we had a job to do. I couldn't let the bait leave the trap. There wasn't any time for protest, because the third vehicle had made its way to the amphitheater ground and came careening to a stop just ten meters away. This vehicle was a bit different than the others, smaller, but more heavily armored. The doors opened up and a woman leapt out, holding a monster of a weapon in her hands.

She stood tall and proud, despite the nearly two meters long barrel attached to the beast she was holding. Her long black hair flowed behind her, and her attire was something very similar to my own. The CIHUD protruding from her head was a dead giveaway, and I knew the fight had suddenly got real. For all we knew, the other vehicles contained more.

The barrel of her weapon began to spin, and I heard a loud, almost whining sound coming from the devices attached to the monstrosity. My

CIHUD began to scream warnings at me and just in time. I dove straight to the ground, avoiding the weapon's trajectory, but nothing came out of it despite the barrel becoming red hot. She flicked the weapon side-to-side, and as she did, chaos followed. The weapon fired an invisible energy beam. Trees in the direction of the discharge began to immediately catch fire and then fall as if some flaming saw blade had sliced right through them.

The squad-leader was not as lucky as the rest of us, the beam cutting right through her, bisecting the poor soul at the waist yet leaving no spatter or sign of blood. The wounds were instantly cauterized, leaving the victim on the ground, screaming, attempting to crawl away helplessly.

Alonna had the good sense to hit the dirt, but upon seeing what happened, tried to rush over to the fallen soldier. As the woman took aim again, I pointed my sidearm and fired the remaining rounds in her direction, causing her to twist and move behind her armored transport.

Unfortunately for her, Arc leapt onto her back from his perch on the tree. Her weapons bulked prevented her from evading. He reached to punch her in the side of the head, but she instead moved so his back was against the armored vehicle and violently slammed herself back, denting the hull and dropping Arc. He was dazed, but not out.

I gave her absolutely no time to finish him off, dashing towards her as fast as I could. Her weapon trained on me, but it took time to fire a shot, giving me a moment to sidekick the barrel, sending it out of her hand. It came to a stop a mere five meters away, its bulk making it exceedingly heavy.

She was stunned, but only for an instant. Our adversary grabbed a knife from her belt and violently swung it at me. Arc attempted to trip her, but she stepped over his attempt as if it hadn't even happened. I found myself weaving and bobbing out of the way of her knife. She was somehow a bit faster than I was, managing to find purchase with a downward stab into my shoulder. Clearly, the CORPS training paid off better than my DIY attempts.

Arc was the game-changer, grabbing for his own blade he had procured from the Sons, a wicked and serrated beast meant for causing pain and suffering before death. He swung at her back, and she managed to dive to the side, somersaulting away.

"This doesn't seem very fair to me, boys." Her sentence was followed by the crescendo of transport vehicle engines. Two more came flying into the area, coming to a stop, the soldiers hopping out and training weapons on us. "How's about an equalizer?"

The TLF squad was not about to go down without a fight, their commander's near-death steeling them with the thirst for revenge. They took up positions and began firing at the CORPS troopers.

I took this opportunity to head into the fray of lesser foes. Dashing away from my adversary and heading towards one of the transport vehicles. I dove into the air, my fist held high, finding purchase in the skull of one of the troopers. His melon smashed into the ground, the blow killing him almost instantly. Using my foot, I kicked his rifle up from the ground and into my hands. I immediately began firing at the CORPS Elites near me, leveling several of them before diving behind cover.

Arc was wasting no time with the big bad. I had to thin the ranks, leaving him to battle the monster. He was hurt, but not out.

"You remind me of my ex; she was a crazy bitch too." I wish I could have seen the look on her face when I heard his line, but I was too busy dealing with my own problems. I could sense the scuffle, though, and knew I had to get back to him sooner than later.

The TLF soldiers had managed to cut down a few of the new players, but they had already lost two more of their own to crossfire. Alonna had managed to drag the squad-leader behind one of the intact sets of bleachers but was pinned down. The fake engineer had made their way to her position, trying to hide from the gunfire.

With four remaining soldiers near me, I used the rifle as a bludgeon, smashing one in the face and tossing it into the chest of another. The force was strong enough to damage the barrel and send the soldier back a couple of meters. The other two took aim, but even with their heightened abilities, they were too slow. I simply danced around them, physically taking both of them down with my bare hands. As soon as they were neutralized, I dashed back across the battlefield.

Arc was locked in combat with the XRC soldier. They were holding onto each other's shoulders, trying to break each other's hold. When I drew closer, I put all of my weight onto my left foot, spinning once for a vicious sidekick to her spine, but her reflexes were on point, and she let go of Arc twisting to the side. She stood there a moment, backing up and staring us down.

"Two on one doesn't seem nice, boys." She waggled her finger at us.

"She's stalling." It was the only words to escape my lips as Arc, and I charged towards our newfound nemesis. As we both swung and kicked for vital areas, she moved with the grace of a hummingbird, sliding to and fro as if we were children attempting to take down a martial-arts master. However, the odds were in our favor, and when she finally stepped in to take a swing at me, forcing me to dodge, Arc managed to land a blow, his fist slamming into the side of her ribs. The audible cracking sound was nothing compared to the spectacle of her body being launched into the air a couple of meters up and several more back. Though her harness protected her from the fall, the decisive strike left her on the ground in a fetal position. A regular person may have been folded in half by such force, but she wasn't quite dead.

"No!" I heard a very familiar voice scream, and the passenger side door of the vehicle the XRC unit had arrived in swung open.

"Mick," I growled through gritted teeth as the scrawny, lab-coat wearing form of the number one man on my list appeared. Ronyn was a cock-sucker to be sure, but Mick was personal. His face was full of both pain and rage. He ignored me and ran over to the defeated soldier between us. She was struggling to get up; Arc likely broke more than a few ribs.

Mick's reaction was more than a little curious. He was personally upset by the turn of events. He was shaking, with tears running down his cheeks. Reaching into his coat pocket, he pulled out an injector with who knows what sort of revitalizing concoction. I marched towards him and kicked it out of his hand.

"You dead mother fucker." I was preparing for a moment of personal enjoyment when I heard two more personnel vehicles making their way up the hill. The whole affair made me question just how closely the CORPS followed the laws of Libsal. I wasn't afraid of more troopers or even another XRC unit, as far as I was concerned, we were on a roll. My mind was singularly focused on my quarry. Then I heard *her* voice.

"John! We have to leave!" Alonna was calling from her rapidly deteriorating cover, only three TLF soldiers remained from the original escort. This whole plan went to hell in a handbasket, and I somehow think Delantil thought we would prevent casualties. Arc and I were good at keeping ourselves alive, but I couldn't dodge bullets for other people. As much as I wanted my revenge, it had to wait.

"Arc, we're taking the truck," I spoke without looking at him, instead, grabbing Mick by the back of the collar and dragging him behind the cover of the armored vehicle. As we neared the truck, I one-armed tossed him into the back, causing him to cry out in pain from the impact, his arm bending in ways arms weren't meant to bend. He immediately began moving towards the exit, as if to get back to the woman I ripped him from. Arc was already in the driver seat and brought the truck around the bleachers, the moving vehicle causing Mick to roll about the floor.

Inside I found a rifle rack with a couple of weapons still present. Grabbing one, I aimed outside the back, which was still open. Arc drove towards the survivors, giving me a clear view of the soldiers that were piling out. I noticed they weren't too keen on firing at me with Mick in the back, which gave me ample opportunity to start picking them off. Simply flicking my head side-to-side and even swaying my body was more than enough to dodge the trajectories being fed to my senses.

By the time we reached the survivors, most of the troopers had been neutralized, allowing me to provide cover when they clamored into the back. Two of the soldiers carefully carried the remains of the bisected squad-leader, her top half still screaming in pain, somehow still alive. I smacked the back of the wall leading to the cab to let Arc know it was time to leave, who dutifully drove away from the carnage.

"Do we have any painkillers, perhaps anesthetic from a medkit?" Alonna asked frantically, finding herself with a patient.

"Just fucking shoot me!" The squad-leader cried out, her head thrashing back and forth from the pain. Grimly enough, the remaining soldiers had remembered to bring back her lower half. It was the most gruesome thing I had ever seen.

One of the soldiers took a knee and slung their pack onto the floor. He reached in and grabbed a red zip-up bag, producing from it a medical injector. Alonna quickly took it and only examined it for a moment before jamming it into the commander's neck. Soon her cries of agony subsided, her eyes rolling back into her head before she slowly lost consciousness.

"What the fuck was that thing?" One of the soldiers who was standing next to the opened back asked, advancing towards me momentarily before thinking better of it.

"I dunno, I've never seen a weapon like that before. According to my CIHUD, it was putting out some kind of energy beam." I gave a simple shrug, it was all I could offer.

"Directed energy weapons are usually mounted to vehicles." Another soldier decided to join the discussion.

"Well, assuming she had the kind of strength I possess, I wouldn't doubt if she was carrying a mounted weapon. None of that matters, though." I turned to the cowering form in the corner, his lab coat stained with blood as he nursed his mangled arm. "Micky, I've missed ya, buddy."

"Just get it over with freak." He spoke between whimpers of pain. "I won't give you the satisfaction of begging."

"Begging? You think I want you to beg?" I was angry all over again and advanced towards him in the blink of an eye. My fist clenched the front of his shirt, and I lifted him so that his back was touching the ceiling.

286

"John!" I could hear Alonna's voice behind me, but I was ignoring it.

"No, I want to deprive you of your ability to breathe! You know, the shit you deprived Lys and your own brother of?"

"I never killed anyone and you-" I extended my arm up and shoved his back into the wall, knocking the wind out of him and preventing him from continuing.

"You lied to us! You knew at least most of us were fucking doomed you piece of shit!"

"John!" At this point, Alonna had moved up to me and put her hand on my shoulder, but I shrugged it off. "John, we could use him! Think about what the General would think if you let such a valuable target die!"

"Fuck Delantil and his merry band of misfits, this is between old Micky and me." I moved my arm again, so he was forced to stare into my eyes. "You know what fucks with me the most?"

"What?" Mick's voice was defeated but still stricken with the struggle against pain and my grip.

"You mourned that freak out there more than your own brother." I tossed Mick back onto the floor, but I got an unexpected reaction. First, Alonna went quiet, and then, despite what he had been through, Mick began to laugh. It wasn't some cliché villain laugh. Instead, it was genuine humor. "What the fuck is so funny?"

"You've come this far, and you're still at square one. I'll say this, Xavier had higher hopes for you." My lip moved up almost in a snarl, and I tossed him to the side, causing him to groan and roll around.

"I'm done with these games."

"No, John." Mick was picking himself up so he could sit with his back to the wall, looking up at me almost pathetically. "You aren't." He began to chuckle again. "We've barely just begun."

"John." Alonna put her hand on my shoulder again. "We could use him. If the Coalition have devised any new upgrades, he would know about it. His knowledge is valuable." I didn't look at her; instead, my eyes looked directly into Mick's.

A curse of my condition was the ability to remember everything with perfect clarity. I could hear Ray's screams as the stalkers ripped him to shreds, his eyes begging me to be spared such a horrible fate. I could feel the warmth of Lys's dying body in my arms. I could hear her labored breathing and see the smile on her face when she got to see the sky.

At that moment, my path was clear. I walked over to Mick, and with one arm, I picked him back up and brought him face to face. "Fuck his knowledge." With a quick motion, I brought my other hand to his face, and with the ease of snapping a twig, I twisted his neck, filling the room with a horrible cracking sound. I let his lifeless body drop and just stared down at it.

"No! John!" I could hear Alonna cry out in protest. Tears were streaming down her face, and I doubt if she would ever be able to sleep with the horrors she had witnessed. The TLF soldiers just watched quietly. Perhaps they understood, maybe they just didn't want to be next. Either way, they knew enough to leave me alone. "John, why?"

I turned to Alonna, my face cold and emotionless despite the maelstrom of feelings I felt inside. "Because he deserved it. His little games caused the death of his own brother and the best friend I ever had. We had our lives robbed by the CORPS, but Mick? Mick pretended to be my friend, promised a pipedream, and delivered a nightmare. If I could bring him back and kill him again, I would." After this, I sat down on one of the benches on the side, running a hand through my hair. My shoulder was throbbing from the horrendous wound, and my chest hurt from its depth. Truth be told, I was lying somewhat. I'm not sure if the man I was five years ago would've been capable of the same thing.

"John?" I heard Alonna's soft voice and looked up at her. She sat down next to me and looking down for a moment, seemingly searching for words. "I need to see that wound." She finally declared.

"Yeah, alright." I allowed her to pull back the sleeve to get a look.

"That looks very deep. If the blade were longer, or you any slower, she might have been able to pierce a lung or even your heart." She produced her medical scanner, which had been left with the squad-leader, pulling from it a small syringe that she used to take some blood from my arm. She took a moment to review the information the sample was providing. "Just as I thought, very lucky. No major arteries were hit, the infection seems to already be maintained. You will definitely make it through the night." There was a hint of humor as she tried to lighten the mood, as if that was easy with one dead fool and a half-dead soldier only a few meters away.

"Thanks, doc," I rubbed my shoulder around the aching wound. Alonna got up to check on the squad-leader.

"You can tell all of that just from a blood sample?" The soldier who had been tending to the fallen squad-leader had asked.

"Well, not precisely. The nanomachines provide their diagnostic data to this device which interprets it. John is essentially his own medical scanner."

"Convenient."

"Hey, assholes." Arc's always friendly voice came over an inter-comm inside the truck. Despite his joking facade, I could hear the pain in his voice. He must have taken a harder hit than I thought.

"I prefer being called a dick, thanks. What do you want?"

"Always fucking things without thinking it through, huh?" he chuckled. "Alright, dicks, we're almost home, get one of your TLF buddies to make sure we don't get a mortar for a welcoming party." With that, the soldier currently in charge pulled a comm device from a vest pocket, dialing a knob before pressing a finger to his ear.

"This is bravo team, we are approaching the compound in a Coalition transport vehicle. Lower security measures, clearance code 13374873." He seemed to listen to a response before nodding his head and speaking so Arc could hear through the intercom. "You're clear to enter."

Chapter Twenty-Two: Horrific Machinations

We drove into the compound and were soon met by an entourage of security and medical personnel. Upon entering, they immediately pulled the squad-leader, the pieces of her anyway, onto a stretcher. Some of the medics then took her to a separate section of the compound. The others tended to the wounded, and I was met by one of the security officers with Arc following behind. He was a middle-aged man wearing a heavy combat uniform.

"Sir, you and your friend here need to come with me to be debriefed." I ignored the man and moved over to Arc, placing my hand on his shoulder. He had his hands on his hips, slouching forward. He looked like he was in pain.

"You gonna make it?" He met my gaze and shrugged my hand from his shoulder.

"Don't worry about me, buzz. A little back strain." Alonna moved from behind me, as if she was going to attempt to examine Arc, who held out his hand in protest. "Business first."

"This way." The officer said and motioned for us to follow two subordinates while he and another trailed behind. It felt more like a prison escort, and it was clear that they still didn't completely trust us.

I was finally able to get a good look at the compound. It was decently large, looking like a hundred armored trucks could fit within the central courtyard. The concrete walls contained the various buildings that kept the place running efficiently. Soldiers were patrolling everywhere, on the walls, on the grounds, and likely within the buildings themselves. I couldn't see R'yalax or any indication that the other team was successful. Judging by the general air of attitude around us, it felt like recent victories had occurred.

We were led into one of the buildings in the back of the compound and ushered into its lower sections. We used a stairwell instead of an elevator to head to a tight set of corridors, eventually leading to a conference room.

The conference room resembled a war room. There were holographic displays on the walls, showing various bits of data on critical locations in Tantil. The table itself was round, containing its own holographic display that could be manipulated by those sitting around the table. It was surprising, to say the least. Everything I had seen up to that point seemed so ragtag and temporary. The Libsal compound was obviously permanent and important.

Delantil was sitting there as well as four other heavily decorated officers of varying ages. It seemed all but one was a lower rank than Delantil. The highest-ranking member was a middle-aged man, grizzled looking, complete with untrimmed white whiskers adorning his chin. I could not tell his rank or his importance in the grand scheme of things, but I could tell Delantil was uncomfortable around him. Our entourage stayed outside when we entered. Alonna had followed us, and no one objected to her presence.

"Ah good, I was hoping you brought the defector with you." A man sitting next to the grizzled leader spoke up. He was young and appeared to be the lowest rung on the ladder before me. He motioned for us to take a seat at the table.

"I take it you mean the doc?" I asked, motioning with my thumb towards her.

"Indeed, we have many questions. For the record, what do we call your friend here?" He looked to Arc, who gave a grin in response.

"Early to dinner if you're smart. Otherwise, the name's Arc." I could see the man was entering in data into the panel on the table before him.

"I understand the Coalition have designations for individual members of their special project. John, you were XR001. Arc, yours was XR171, is that correct?"

"Sounds about right." Arc was trying to act nonchalant, but I could tell he was nervous. We could likely escape if needed, but it wasn't conducive to any of our plans.   "So it would seem our intelligence is accurate."

"Thank you, Colonel." Mr. Bigshot spoke with a very deep and serious-sounding voice. "General Delantil?" He looked over to the General, who gave a nod and looked back to Arc and me.

"This meeting was called to serve a few purposes. One purpose is to familiarize senior officers with our two new allies. Another purpose is to discuss some recent developments we feel may be good for you to be informed of. Finally, we will discuss plans on assaulting Dome City. Everyone on the same page so far?"

"Get on with it, buzz, I ain't getting any younger." Arc crossed his arms over his chest.

"If Doctor Lyrul here is to be believed, you aren't getting any older either. Allow me to introduce everyone." Arc rolled his eyes, but otherwise stayed quiet. "Arc and I have not had a chance to meet, so I will start. I am Brigadier General Ron Delantil. To my left is Lieutenant General Millar Rointal, next to Dr. Lyrul is Colonel Dylon Myceron. Finally, to my right, it is my esteemed pleasure to introduce Commander-In-Chief Tolan Del Tantilla."

"Well, don't I feel underdressed," I commented, wondering why they left the safety of their capital.

"Thank you, General," Tolan spoke with the authority his title imparted. Things seemed out of whack to me, why was he here in Libsal instead of wherever their current mother base was located? What was so important that a man like that would be dragged out into the open?

"So, let's get down to business." The Colonel began to speak again and punched a few buttons on the screen before him. In the center of the table, a man appeared before us. He had a short goatee moving around his mouth and wore the jumpsuit/lab coat combo of a CORPS engineer. "Alpha Team made contact with a one Engineering Chief Robin Miorillo less than one hour ago. If you had not explained this to Arc, your mission, deemed a success, was to distract the Coalition long enough to allow us to make contact and take the defecting engineer in."

"If you call nearly losing the entire unit with their commander being sliced in-half successful than sure, yeah, it was a success." I could feel Alonna's eyes move to me when I said this and could sense her agreement.

"The casualties were unfortunate. We believe if your presence wasn't there, we would have suffered a total loss of the unit."

"Whatever helps you sleep at night." The Colonel seemed lost for words for a moment before clearing his throat.

"Anyway, we learned a great deal from this Robin. Besides providing us with the necessary schematics for new technology, he has also offered his services to us as an engineer. He will assist us in implementing the new tech into our forces."

"So, what fun new toys did ya get, buzz?" Arc was suddenly interested. He probably thought that whatever it was they managed to get a hold of, was probably going to be for us.

"Well, the first is trivial to you. A new communication array that will make our current communication net obsolete. A single array that could encompass the entire continent."

"Boring." Even Delantil could not help but grin at Arc. He got a glare from Tolan and adjusted his look.

"If I may continue." The Colonel looked like he was a bit flustered. He probably wasn't used to such casual conversation for things so serious. "This communication array will allow us to monitor Coalition activity and, according to Robin, will also allow us to receive signals from beyond Dome City's superstructure." He punched up a new image of a satellite dish looking device with an almost web-like structure just inside the dish. The structure had a multitude of metal forks protruding from it.

"We also managed to get schematics as well as ten units of these." The Colonel reached below the table and pulled out an intricate-looking rectangular box attached to a belt. It seemed so simple yet somehow extremely complex at the same time. "These are personal shielding devices, I believe the engineer referred to them as PEKS or Personal Energy and Kinetic Shield. This creates an energy field around a user, providing direct protection against kinetic and energy-based attacks."

"Holy shit, I needs me one of them!" Arc exclaimed, reaching over and snatching the device to inspect it.

"Indeed." The Colonel continued. "There are drawbacks to this system. While it can withstand many small arms impacts and a few heavy impacts, it will drain its power very quickly. While it does protect against directed energy weapons, there is a strong possibility any significant energy impact will short out the system."

"Sounds untested." My voice conveyed my doubts. Arc handed me the device, and I looked it over. It seemed so simple. All of the technology was safely locked away within the box at the center of the belt.

"It has been thoroughly tested, it just takes a god-awful amount of power to keep the shield running. The Coalition is supposedly working on this issue."

"Thank you, Colonel," Delantil spoke again. "We planned on giving you both a unit. We feel keeping you as well-armed as possible is in our best interests."

"Fuckin-A right it is," Arc spoke matter of fact-like.

"May I ask a question?" Alonna's voice was soft, full of fear, and something else I couldn't quite pinpoint.

"Of course, doctor, considering our deal, I expect your input." Delantil gave her a serious look.

"Thank you. When did the Coalition become aware of the defection?" I could see the men look at each other as if that question seemed unexpected.

"We aren't entirely sure, but we do believe it was around the same time he contacted us for extraction." Delantil continued to speak for the group.

"I feel it is important to inform you of Coalition protocols. When a defector is discovered, they generally are not informed of this discovery. Instead, one of two things happen: One, they are executed immediately. Two, they are allowed to defect, giving the Coalition a possible unwitting mole. I recommend caution with any defectors."

"Such as yourself?" The Commander-In-Chief spoke up, studying Alonna.

"Yes, actually." Impressively, her demeanor did not change with this question. "Obviously, the Coalition is not perfect, but often times defectors
296

are furthering their goals, sometimes knowingly, sometimes unknowingly."

"And which one are you?"

"My agenda lies solely with the well-being of my patient." Her eyes moved over to me before meeting Tolan's gaze again. "If John sees you as an ally, so do I."

"So, John," his gaze fell upon me, "do you see us as allies?"

"I see you as the enemy of my enemy, and you know what they say about those." I met his gaze with my own unshaken visage, and he gave me an approving nod.

"Good enough."

I spoke up again, "If I may, while the shield technology is understandable, it seems like this operation had a lot of risks to it. There's more going on."

"Astute as always, John," Delantil answered. "General?" Delantil looked over to the middle-aged man who hadn't spoken yet. His head was bald, his skin light, but his eyes seemed much darker. He appeared to be studying everything around him at all times.

"I have been in command of intelligence operations in and around Dome City for some time now. We have been unable to send signals that penetrate the Dome's material, and thus, we cannot gain any information on what exactly is inside. A lot of our information is based on conjecture and observation of supplies." The Colonel across the table hit a few keys, and an image of Dome City appeared before us. There were dozens of compounds and defensive structures all around it. Several green lines appeared heading to and away from either side of the Dome. "These are the known supply lines. Up until six months ago, these lines were two-way. Now only things come out of the Dome; we haven't observed anything entering it for some time."

"Then they really are finished," Alonna interjected and looked down in thought. For a moment, I thought I saw dread in her eyes.

"Finished with what, doctor?" Tolin's voice carried the suspicion of his question. Alonna looked up surprised as if she hadn't realized she had spoken out loud.

"The Habitat, Dome City, as you call it, once finished and operational, was meant to be completely self-sufficient in every way."

"If I may continue." Millar seemed a little impatient, like he had been waiting eagerly to give his report. "The array technology that we have procured will allow us to not only penetrate the dome but finally attempt to decrypt Coalition codes. Up until now, we haven't had the technology to even listen to their transmissions, let alone decode them."

"So, a team wouldn't have to go in blind and could basically report back." I pondered out loud.

"Precisely. The problem, however, is that implementing this technology could take weeks, and we do not feel we have weeks. We have reason to believe that the Coalition is gathering resources and troops from within Dome City itself and is preparing for some sort of large offensive."

"Do we know their possible targets yet?" Delantil asked.

"No, while there are obviously prime targets, none would require the kind of firepower they have mustered."

"Wait, wait, I thought you just said that they haven't been getting shipments and shit? Which one is it?" Arc was getting impatient, and so was I. They were trying to keep us in the dark for no real reason it seemed.

"The last two months of shipments before they stopped included large

298

groups of personnel, weapons, manufacturing equipment, and a massive amount of materials to go with it."

"In other words, they're hunkering down and building up." I concurred with the assessment.

"Exactly. One of our major priorities is trying to figure out what their targets are when they're finished, though we believe we should move on Dome City whether we learn that or not."

"I-I." Alonna began to speak up and seemed to be struggling internally with something. Apparently, she won the battle. "I know their target."

"Out with it then," Tolin commanded impatiently.

"The entire continent of Tantil. Every settlement, every tribe." There was a moment of silence as the senior members of the TLF looked became uncomfortably silent. Delantil finally spoke up.

"I think you should elaborate, doctor."

"I-I will try to keep it brief. The why isn't necessarily important to you."

"It is to me." I interrupted, giving her a stern look.

"Fine. The whole story." She looked over to me and met my gaze. Despite being at the table, it was almost as if she was talking to me directly.

"You may or may not be aware of the Coalition's goals." She finally looked back at the group. "To elevate our species to the point that we can survive any situation, any environment. Essentially they wish to ascend our race to higher states of being."

"What the hell does that have to do with them waging war on everyone around them?" Tolin's impatience grew.

"I am getting to that. The Habitats were being built as a final stage in essentially cultivating certain types of civilizations. John and Arc here are examples of what they plan to do to the various populations under their protection. Within the Habitats, you will find, quite frankly, genetically superior people, free of defects, diseases, and most of all, cultural strife."

"The opposite of the real world," Arc spoke under his breath.

"The real world is their target," Alonna replied frankly. "Once the Habitats were finished, they would begin the final stage of that project. The systemic destruction of all surrounding civilizations, no matter how small. They plan to kill everyone not within the Dome." I slammed my fist on the table, suddenly stricken with rage at her words.

"Those bastards are trying to keep up their lie!"

"Explain yourself." Tolin addressed me, though he seemed less stern about it. My gaze met his.

"The citizens of the Undercities were all told the world was a blasted wasteland, that no one but us survived the war. We already know they have an underground way into the Dome. I bet they still have the people convinced that the world is unlivable."

"That's the fuckin' key, buzz!" Arc exclaimed, suddenly standing, resting his hands on the table in front of him. He pointed to the image of the Dome. "We expose the lie."

"Indeed, they are correct." Alonna took over once more. "It is almost assured that they have sections that are separate from the populations. The people likely do not know the state of the world beyond the dome."

"Why have you neglected to give this information to us until now?" Tolin's face became ever more irritated. It was like he was looking for a reason to condemn her.

"Honestly? You would have never believed me without seeing the might of XRC soldiers and of the extent the Coalition is willing to go to achieve their goals. Until you met John, the Undercities were just a rumor, and cybernetic super-soldiers were pure fantasy." With this explanation, the Commander-In-Chief seemed to calm. I had to admit she had an excellent point. After everything they had seen, it would be hard to doubt any plan the CORPS might cook up.

"For my own sanity," Delantil started again, "let's break this down. You hypothesize that the population within the Dome is unaware of the state of the world beyond?"

"Yes, General." Alonna's confidence was returning. The truth will set you free as they say.

"And you believe that the military portions of the CORPS, possibly including production facilities, are separate from the civilian population?"

"Very likely, yes."

"That makes sense actually," I spoke up again. "Tier E in the Undercities was extremely secure, only CORPS personnel of certain ranks would be allowed in or out of the area. I couldn't even tell you how big Tier E actually was because I only saw part of it from the outside during the escape. It wouldn't surprise me at all if they had an entire army just chilling up there." The officers looked among themselves a moment before Delantil continued.

"Then there's enough evidence to suggest that the assumption is likely true. Our intel does confirm a massive build-up of military power within the Dome. There is one piece missing: While it is true that John and Arc here are impressive, to say the very least, I do not see how the Coalition has the ability to essentially purge the continent."

"That is because you have never experienced the full extent of the Coalition's power General." Alonna stood and put her hands behind her back, turning and thinking. She was fighting something, and I think everyone in the room was aware of her turmoil. The CORPS assuredly conditioned her in ways we could only begin to imagine. For once, I couldn't help but admire the strength it took to fight whatever horrors she was subjected to.

Finally, she turned around. "General, Commander-in-Chief, you have to understand something. You and the Coalition are not fighting a war in the conventional sense. They are studying warfare; you are the mice they have placed into conflict." She held up her hand as Tolin was about to speak. "Please take no offense, but this is the absolute truth of the matter. Any skirmish before John and Arc came to you, was won because they chose to let you win. Tell me," she turned to the Lt. General, "what are your actual estimates of Coalition forces on this continent?" She emphasized it in a way to demonstrate they had barely half a picture.

"Well." He looked over to Tolin, who gave him a nod. "We estimate Coalition forces to have at least one hundred thousand ground troops, two-"

"Stop. I can already guarantee the rest is as inaccurate as the first. The Coalition, on this continent alone, has access to nearly three hundred thousand mutaphorm troopers alone. At any time, they could access a civilian population of well educated, highly-skilled, very healthy people, and create yet another army that outnumbers your forces more than two to one. I assure you, any fight you have won to this day was a victory the Coalition allowed." Finished with her speech, she smoothed out her coat and sat back down, taking in a deep, calming breath.

The officers before us looked to each other, and even Tolin's face had become ghost white. It wasn't the news they wanted to hear. Alonna basically told them they were fighting a losing battle. There was no clear way to win in any conventional sense.

By now, I had plenty of time to take everything in, and I looked over to Arc, who met my gaze. We both had the same grin, and I gave him a nod. I stood this time and crossed my arms over my chest.

"If we're done being all emo about the news, let me say a few things. First, I feel like this should have been obvious a long time ago. Second, in two-hundred years of fighting, you guys haven't even cracked their communications network without meeting a defector. Face it guys, this is a war without end. It's time to change the rules."

"And what precisely do you suggest?" Tolin looked to me with a silent rage in his eyes though I couldn't tell who or what it was directed towards.

"Well, obviously, you need more charming buddies like me and this dude over here." I motioned my thumb towards Arc. "Finding the XRC facility on the way to the Undercities has to be a priority. If we can convince more of us to join up against the CORPS, we might be able to even the odds. Just one of us is realistically worth hundreds of their freaks. Then we have to deprive them of their option B."

"Revolution." Arc murmured.

"Exactly. I grew up in the CORPS's care, and while life is comparatively good under the heel of the Coalition, people still chafe under heels. Lys, me, and the others couldn't have been the only people the CORPS lured out of there or even the only people to try on their own volition. If we could expose the CORPS for what they are to the people in the Dome, we might be able to cripple their production in Tantil. They've invested a fuckton into it, losing it will have to hurt."

"John, this plan is good and all, but you forget about the problem posed by Arc," Alonna spoke up looking to me, gesturing with her hand towards him.

"And what exactly is the problem with Arc?" Tolin asked.

"I don't come from some hoity-toity underground utopia like some people here. Me? I came from a penal colony. The CORPS gathered up the world's scum and stuck em in a technologically advanced hole in the ground. Life was rough growing up there, and I promise you, no one bought any lie about a blasted surface."

"Where is this penal colony?" Delantil steepled his fingers.

"Across the pond buzz, in F'Rytal. Out of your reach these days."

"Would the Coalition be able to muster forces from F'Rytal?" Tolin was leaning forward now, intent on hearing the conversation out.

"No, Mr. Tolin," Alonna replied. "While I was never privy to the projects in F'Rytal, I do know that they would also be participating in the Habitat project," Alonna spoke with grim surety.

"Meaning they will have their own purge to carry out," Delantil spoke frankly.

"Most likely."

"Then, our plan of action is clear." Tolin finally spoke with finality, and I retook my seat.

"General Delantil will provide you the necessary resources to make your way into Dome City. The secondary task would be to find and attempt to recruit any XRC soldiers and eliminate any others that remain loyal to the Coalition. They cannot be allowed to use them to murder the populace. John,

Arc, I am not your leader, I cannot command you to do anything, and I understand you have the power to leave at any time." Tolin had become impressively diplomatic. The truth was the truth either way. "It is my sincere belief, however, that we cannot accomplish these goals without your direct assistance. In that vein, I am willing to commit the resources needed and provide you with autonomy regarding our security protocols."

"Mr. Tolin!" Millar began to protest.

"Remember your place," Tolin snapped to Millar quickly and then turned back to me. "If you accept, we can begin immediately."

"Well shit son, I'm down for a brawl or two. I'm in." Arc extended his hand.

"Considering this is my own goal? I'm in." I extended my hand as well. Tolin stood and shook each of our hands. If you had gone back in time and told me that I would suddenly be given control over military forces for the purpose of sticking it to the CORPS, I would have asked for whatever it was you were drinking. The list of impossible things was growing that day. Tolin seemed to understand his situation. The man knew when he was backed into a corner.

"I will begin assembling a team and squads for your mission." Delantil took over. "We'll make sure you're well-stocked and armed. While Mr. Tolin has given you autonomy, I ask that you proxy orders through our officers."

"Don't worry, General, I won't harm their egos." I gave a grin and sat once more. We began to hash out the plan, who would be assigned, what equipment we needed, and how long it would take to get to the suspected site of the Undercities. The TLF leadership soon realized the benefits of our enhancements. While we were monsters in the field, behind a desk, we were computers that could make decisions on the fly. We offered our brains and our brawn.

When the meeting had ended, we were treated to a hearty meal and a warm bed. Getting rest sounded like the best of ideas, giving my shoulder time to heal and Arc a chance as well. Apparently, he had nearly broken his spine, cracking a couple of discs. The Doc said he'd be fine in a few days. She didn't seem to take the same kind of care for him that she did for me.

Later that night, Arc and I were sitting in a mess hall, eating with the rest of the soldiers. Alonna approached us, holding the medical device she used to work on our enhancements. "J-John, I uh, I believe I have come up with a little boost for you and Arc's nanomachines. Nothing permanent, just something to accelerate your healing process to deal with your wounds from the previous fight."

"You okay? You seem a little shook up." Beyond the stutter, an unusual thing for her, her hands were shaking a little.

"Looks like she just jacked someone, and they're in the room," Arc spoke, but never looked up from his plate, working on his third helping.

"Well, I feel like it honestly. This place makes me nervous. I am not exactly well-liked or trusted here."

"Who's fault is that? Sorry, sorry, uncalled for. Take a seat." I motioned for her to sit across from us. She declined the seat and instead tapped at her device before pulling the syringe.

"This will make you both feel drained and drowsy as your body allocates energy to your healing processes." She went to Arc first, who didn't even flinch as she plunged the syringe into his neck. Though we had the table to ourselves, the people around us looked rather disgusted by the scene. One

306

even walked away from their table, likely to report the incident, not that it would mean anything.

Alonna prepared the syringe once more before producing it again.

"Dude, I ain't sharing needles," I sounded incredulous. She rolled her eyes.

"Well, it's a good thing that this device breaks needles down and rebuilds them as part of the sterilization process. N-now hold still you big baby." Her humor seemed strangely forced as she plunged the needle into my neck and gave me the injection.

"Ow."

"Don't be a bitch." Arc smirked.

"Shut up, Arc."

"Well, I'll leave you two to your banter." She stared at me for a long moment in a way that went beyond creepy, even for her, before turning to leave.

"Must be weird sharing quarters with her."

"We leave in a few days. No one trusts her still, so I get to be her CO." We saw that as she left, she handed her device over to a soldier that seemed to be her escort. "At least I get substitutes from time-to-time."

We sat there quietly and finished our meal. Alonna wasn't lying when she said the injection would make me feel drained. It wasn't long before I felt like I ran a marathon without the implants, minus the muscle aches. Arc seemed to be feeling it too.

"Y'know, if that bitch wasn't so obviously in love with you, I might get suspicious." He suddenly remarked.

"A little sleep sounds nice. It's been a couple of weeks. What's the worst that can happen in the middle of this base?"

"We get attacked while we're passed the fuck out?" I thought about this for a moment.

"Why do you always gotta be a buzz kill? We'll be fine." I stood and stretched a bit. "I'm heading off to bed, slash, babysitting."

"Have fun, buzz." He stood and went to take care of our trays. I walked through the barracks to our assigned quarters.

Our quarters were a cramped affair, with room enough for a desk and bunkbeds. When I got to the room, the guard stationed by the door gave me a nod and then left his post. The doc got no trust, but apparently, I was the golden child. I nearly stumbled into the room, ready to fall asleep right there.

"Oh!" Alonna exclaimed as I moved from the door. She stood and rushed over to help steady me. Normally, I would've brushed her off, but face-planting didn't seem worth my ego.

"Thanks. Man, you could've been clearer about this." She led me to the bottom bunk, and I laid down with her sitting on the bed next to me.

"The guards have my scanner, but nothing seems alarming to me." She was suddenly very calm, her nervousness had utterly disappeared. "Experiences may vary. Arc may not fall asleep while you do, for instance."

"That doesn't-" I stopped to yawn, my eyes starting to close. "-sound like your usual mode of operation." I could barely lift my limbs. I would have been alarmed a long time ago, but between the mental enhancements and how dog tired I felt, I wasn't able to muster the motivation to care.

"No one's perfect." She replied with a shrug and a smile. "Now, you sleep, let the wound heal. I will tend to you in the meantime." I remember trying to give a smart-ass remark, but I couldn't find it in me. Barely a minute later, I passed out.

Part Three:

Home Again

Chapter Twenty-Three: The Hunt

The world was covered in a hazy mist. The landscape before me was reduced to grayscale, though I retained my own color. I was on a long winding dirt road, walking to an unknown destination. My stride was calm and slow.

Eventually, I came upon a fork in the road, branching off to dozens of places. Suddenly I felt the presence of people as they began to pace around me, disappearing and reappearing from my view as they moved.

"Still playing games?" Lys walked around me.

"Never could settle for less, could ya?" Ray moved in the opposite direction of Lys.

I was startled by the sudden appearance of Mick, nearly flying into my face. "They've already won dumbass! She really took you for a ride, didn't she?" He moved away, laughing maniacally.

"I don't give a shit about your protocols, I'm going in there!" *Arc's voice, distant, somewhere strange.*

"It's complete." *Alonna's voice, whispering into my ear.*

"I said, I'm going in there!" My eyes opened slowly, and I found myself drooling on the pillow of my bottom bunk. The door slid open, and Arc was standing there, at first angry and then sheepish, seeing me awake.

"What are you doing?" I heard the feminine voice demand above me on the top bunk.

"Checking on him. I trust you about as far as the guy behind me could throw you."

"Arc! I'm fine, fuck." I sat up, rubbing my face, feeling the grogginess quickly fade into the ever-ready energy I usually felt. "The hell is wrong with getting some shut-eye?"

"Shut-eye? Buzz, you've been asleep for two days." With his reply my eyes widened a bit, and then I yawned, giving a stretch, which seemed to be a disappointing reaction to Arc. I scratched at my sides, coming to the realization that the only thing I was wearing was pants, though I didn't remember getting undressed.

"I warned you both I was unsure of the side effects, but that you would be safe. John is safe." Alonna's voice sounded annoyed, but otherwise, nothing suspicious in her reaction.

"Whatever. You're awake, we're out real soon, not my idea either. I'm gonna go get some eats and pack up." He turned and walked away, the door sliding shut behind him.

"What a paranoid man," Alonna spoke almost absentmindedly. She often seemed to be in many places at once.

"Wouldn't have it any other way. Someone needs to be the naysayer in all this shit." I stood and gave another stretch before looking up to face her. Boy was I in for a sight. She was dressed in only the barest of terms, clad in nothing but undergarments. Her coat hung from the top bunk's frame, her shirt and pants were neatly folded on the desk nearby. She wore a black and somewhat tiny ensemble leaving very little to the imagination. I immediately turned away to be polite.

"Shit, sorry, didn't realize." I couldn't help but notice the grin she had on her face. I began to gather my own clothes, which I apparently had hastily discarded under my bunk.

"Oh, come now, we are both adults here. You know, I am very doubtful this is the first female body you have ever seen."

"Yeah, well, that's fair." I listened as she delicately got up and hopped from the bed, moving to gather her clothes. The man inside of me just couldn't help but sneak a peek at her form. She had a fantastic hour-glass figure, and her black hair usually kept back, flowed neatly down her back, accentuating her light, slightly tanned skin. I had to admit, considering her intellect, that the woman had won the genetic lottery. I looked away again to give her some privacy.

She dressed and cleared her throat to indicate she was finished. I turned to look at her, and she gave a little twirl, posing for me. "Better?"

"Yeah, you wouldn't want to distract all those poor guards out there."

"Are you sure it's the guards you're worried about?" She gave a coy grin.

"Alright, alright, that's enough of that. We have a lot of work to do."

"You're no fun." She swatted at my chest playfully.

"You're suddenly in a good mood. Well, I guess I shouldn't complain. C'mon doc." I motioned for her to follow me out.

I left her with Arc in the mess hall and went for a shower and fresh threads. I was surprisingly calm, even the situation wasn't bothering me as much as it should have. Every cliché claims that revenge makes nothing easier, but knowing Mick was gone, his brother and Lys avenged, made me quite content indeed. With that loose end tied up, I felt ready to face Ronyn and my people. I wondered if anyone who knew me was still around.

After the zen-like contemplation I missed so dearly, it was time to get ready and depart. We had a long journey ahead of us, and I still had the feeling that this was a one-way trip, though now I didn't seem to dread it so much.

The Commander-In-Chief of the TLF was a man of his word. He delivered on everything we needed. We were given an armored scout vehicle with an anti-materiel cannon attached despite its small, maneuverable size. The command tank was requisitioned to us again, as well as R'yalax and her crew. With the scout command vehicle and several jeeps to ride alongside, our numbers were roughly one hundred. A small group in the grand scheme of things, but we weren't aiming for subtlety.

All in all, we didn't ask for much. I was already leery about having such a big group moving about. We were a perfect target of opportunity.

We had no planned stops between Libsal and the mountain range the Undercities entrance was said to be located in. On our way, TLF intelligence would be searching for the lab I had escaped from. Our destination was a few days away if we went straight there, but we planned to take an erratic route in the hopes of misleading anyone who might be dumb enough to follow. This was in exception to the Sons of Rellen, whom Arc contacted shortly before we left. They would be scouting behind and be ready to provide back-up to us or the TLF if it was needed. It still felt weird having the Sons follow us around, but it felt good having allies so close by.

Our journey was somewhat uneventful for the first three days. We plowed through the land with the passion our mission required, making great time as Arc and I trained in the interim. I was a little worried that if we got there too fast, we would have to wait for the array to be completed while we were inside the Dome itself, but that was increasingly becoming a moot point. Every day we waited was another day closer to whatever genocidal plans the CORPS may have had.

On the fourth day, things got interesting.

"Commander, we are receiving a priority transmission from Homestead." I was connected to the network computer, studying the geography of the area around the Dome. I hoped we could find some way out of there that didn't involve going back the way we came; not that I thought the mission was anything but one-way.

"Patch it through to my comm." R'yalax put a finger to her ear, listening intently. A grin formed across her face as she looked over to where I was sitting. "Of course, General, we'll divert immediately. Send the coordinates to our nav computer."

I pulled the cord from my CIHUD. "Where exactly are we diverting to?"

"A few days out of the way, but intelligence believes they've found that roaming lab of yours."

"The XRC Labs?" My voice was almost giddy.

"We believe so. I trust you agree with the decision then?"

"Any way we can get there sooner?"

"Unfortunately, no, it is quite a way out of the way, and five days is as direct a route as we're willing to risk. It's not exactly paved roads, and truck stops out there."

"Fair enough, I suppose," My words came out as a shrug, then I felt Arc's hand slap onto my back.

"Gonna go get us some friends buzz!" He laughed heartily and sat back down next to Alonna. They were seated on one of the benches near the exit. He put his arm around her, and she looked sufficiently uncomfortable from it, which I am sure was his goal. "You're gonna have all the patients you could want." He said, gesturing outward with his free hand.

"Lovely." She shrugged his arm off and stood, walking over to me. "John, are you sure this is a wise idea? There's no telling how many combat-ready XRC units will be there." Her eyes were gazing into mine like she was a wife urging a husband not to do something stupid.

"Nothing we are doing could be classified as a wise idea, but who else is capable of pulling these missions off? I mean no offense to anyone here, but this would be a suicide mission for anyone other than me and Arc

"This could be a suicide mission for you too!" She exclaimed incredulously. "You're not a god."

"Look, your worry is honestly touching, but my mind is made up. Arc and I might be one-man armies, but we need way more than two to pull this off. Even just one more person would tip the odds in our favor."

"I hope you're right." She sat back down, though not near Arc, pulling out her PCD and fiddling around with it. Sometimes I wanted to take the thing from her, to see if there was more she wasn't telling us. There had been something on her mind ever since we left Libsal, but I couldn't quite put my finger on it. I never paid it much thought as simultaneously she was in better spirits than she had been since allowing herself to be captured. Hell, she wasn't even like that at the labs if I stopped to think about it. Either way, I welcomed it.

"Think we'll actually find a buddy, buzz?" I walked over and sat next to Arc, leaning back to get comfortable.

"Dunno man, but what I do know is that we might be able to strike a major blow by tearing that place up."

"If I may." R'yalax approached us. "While it is not among my orders for a variety of reasons I don't necessarily agree with, what are the odds you can extract research information on your enhancements?"

"To what end?" Alonna looked up and demanded, trying to inject herself into the conversation. I looked up at R'yalax with a suspicious gaze.

"And why would I wanna do that?"

"Those enhancements could give us a leg up, we would turn the tide not just here, but everywhere." As she explained this, I stood and walked so that we were standing face-to-face.

"Let me make one thing very clear to you. No one and I mean no one, not even me, should have this level of power. You're not talking about handing new guns to soldiers; you're talking about making super weapons with legs. If I find any vital information about the XRC projects, I'm destroying it." With that, I returned to my seat. R'yalax's ever-powerful poker face was what I was met with.

"Very well, then." Disappointed, she turned and went back to her duties.

"You just wanna keep this shit to yourself," Arc said with a smirk.

"Shut up, Arc." He met my comment with a laugh and slapped me on the back.

"Me too, buzz."

Suddenly things felt more serious than I intended. I hadn't given a whole lot of thought about trying to destroy the XRC Project itself. It honestly felt like the project was basically finished, and every new monster they turned out was just gravy. What was surprising was how easily the place was found. The lack of subtlety on the top side of the surface seemed extremely suspicious to me.

We were making our way back into arid lands, places that nature hadn't reclaimed yet after the devastation of the war. It seemed the CORPS preferred locations most people with two brain cells to rub together would avoid.

320

After a few days, we had managed to catch up with our target, finding its tracks heading in a favorable direction. While we had to deviate course, it would seem the lab had begun to move towards our original destination. We were still days out, but it was a welcomed, if not also suspicious, development. I couldn't shake the feeling that the CORPS knew exactly what our plans were.

"Lieutenant," I called out, walking towards the nav computer where R'yalax was standing.

"What can I do for you, John?"

"I think it's a bad idea to have the convoy approach the labs. Even if we managed a sneak attack, the doc's point about an unknown number of battle-ready freaks means any ambush from us could be quickly reversed."

"I assume you are about to suggest that you and Arc go in alone?"

"Well, not exactly. To the facility itself, yes, but we need a plan of escape, possibly for more than just two of us. Can you bring up a map of the area?"

"Of course. Corporal?"

"Yes, ma'am." The navigator replied before punching up an image of the landscape around the labs.

"Here." I moved my finger around the perimeter of where the labs currently rested. "It's vulnerable from all sides. I want to send the Sons in to make it look like a raid. Over here," I pointed to a spot two kilometers south of the labs. "This will be a good extraction point. We can use this small canyon here to box in any pursuers."

"I see you've been studying up on tactics and strategy." I gave her a nod. Anything I could pull from their database that might be remotely useful became a subject of study for me. For me, studying was as easy as glancing at the words.

"So, you agree with the strategy then?" I inquired.

"Indeed, I do. I take it you will use the cover of the raid to infiltrate the facility?"

"I'd like to be in before they get there. Chances are they'll send the XRC units out for a little practice, but I seriously doubt they'd go after them if they retreated."

"The Sons are not known for retreating," R'yalax stated wisely.

"Oh, don't you worry buzz, they'll do whatever the fuck we tell them to." Arc had walked over moments before, listening in on the plan of attack.

"He's right. The plan is, Arc and I go into the facility and try to extract one or more friendly cyborgs." I refused to refer to them as units, it felt so cold and inhuman to do so. "We're in, we're out, no fun," I said, glaring at Arc "and no data extractions." My glare moved over to R'yalax.

"Well, lucky for me, this whole fuckin' thing will probably be lots of fun." I couldn't help but laugh at Arc's comment, though part of the humor was the nervousness only I could detect in him. He knew we were about to go all-in on very little intel. Arc walked over to the comms officer. "Hey toots, do me a favor, hail this frequency." He reached over and typed in some numbers for her.

"Yes, sir." She replied dutifully, though I could hear the disdain for his attitude in her voice. She entered the frequency, and there was a double beeping sound after a moment as she put us on speaker. "You're on." Arc motioned for me to come over.

"They're gonna wanna hear from their First big man." With a sigh, I walked over.

322

"Uh, this is the First?" I looked over to Arc shaking my head and shrugging my shoulders. He was holding back laughter.

"May Strength never leave you First! We thirst to test our might!" Some of the officers around us turned to listen to the shocking conversation. The Sons weren't known for revering random dudes.

"Right, uh, good. Well, your First has a mission for you. We're going to send you the coordinates of a CORPS mobile lab. I want you to take a portion of your forces and hit them hard. You must be there within one hour." I looked to Arc, who motioned for me to ham it up some more. "Show them your Strength." I allowed my last words to sound dark and sure, trying to stir up the religious fervor.

"Yes, my First! It shall be done!"

"Good, the Second and I shall be there, attacking from within. When we leave the lab, you are to follow, even if more enemies still stand. Got it?"

"Yes, my First!" I gave a nod to the comms officer who understood and ended the transmission.

"You know John, there is a solid chance the Coalition intercepted that transmission," Alonna spoke from her seat.

"I'm counting on it." Saying this, I looked over to Arc, and his grin only grew as he quickly understood.

"We need to get there before the Sons. The CORPS will be expecting us to hit them during the distraction, but we're gonna hit them before and use the distraction to escape, using the Sons to cover our way."

"Dirty pool. I'm down." Arc began to gather his things, getting ready for the assault.

"On foot, it will take nearly an hour to get there!" R'yalax protested.

323

"Maybe for someone who can't sprint indefinitely." My voice carried the confidence our abilities deserved. "Get to the canyon Liuetenant, we're gonna need to boogie on out real fuckin' fast."

"We'll be there." Her voice carried worry, but she knew we could handle overselves. I gathered my own equipment, much of it being the same as what we had during our previous encounter. Arc was about to put on his brand-new shield belt when I held my hand up to stop him.

"Nah, man, remember training a few days ago? We can sense that thing from an unhealthy distance away."

"Goddamnit." He set it back down again.

Once prepared, the convoy came to a stop, allowing Arc and I to leave for our mission. We wasted absolutely no time with banter and planning, instead, sprinting through the sands. It was evening, and the stars were shining spectacularly above us, watching the pitifully small events of our world.

Chapter Twenty-Four: Two's Company

We made it within visual range of the lab with more than twenty minutes to spare, giving us time to survey the situation before attempting to strike. We had made our way to the top of the canyon we would come back to for our escape.

The labs, like everything else the CORPS did, was not small, its off yellow color somewhat blending in with the landscape around it. The construct was more wide than tall and sectioned off into four rounded yet flat-topped structures, each with their own engines and treads underneath for mobility. I wasn't sure if the thing traveled as a unit, individually or both, but it likely didn't move very quickly.

Surrounding the labs were four transport vehicles and ten jeeps, all swarming around the structure, keeping an unusually close perimeter around the building. I was surprised at how small the forces on the outside were considering the importance of the facility. That revelation made me worry about just how many active XRC soldiers they were sporting. It could've also been yet another ploy at subtlety; having hundreds of soldiers swarming isn't exactly stealthy.

"Looks like they have a garage on the right side," I noted, seeing one of the jeeps disappear into the building and another coming out moments later.

"Looks pretty busy too," Arc commented.

"Still probably our best chance of getting in."

"You're a crazy fuck y'know that?"

"Wouldn't have me any other way." I began to move down the canyon, heading towards the labs. Arc followed suit, and despite the terrain, we were able to swiftly and quietly make it down. We both had our CIHUDs out, which allowed us to monitor the vehicles surrounding the base. While the CORPS's security was usually on point, people like us could see the holes in their patrols. Finding the first safe opportunity, we ran for the building itself.

Successful in our stealth, we made our way around the facility, propping ourselves against the wall before making our way to the entrance of the garage. The garage itself was open, allowing shift changes on the fly. I also noticed it was sparsely guarded by two Elites on either side of the door, as well as some other guards waiting deep within the garage itself. It wouldn't be long before we ended up running into the roaming patrols.

Arc pulled his knife out and looked to me with a smirk. I gave him a nod, understanding precisely what he meant. We both made our way to the entrance guards, eventually coming into their sight. As we did, the knives left our hands, slicing through the air, both landing near-simultaneously in the necks of the two Elites. They dropped silently, and we quickly moved towards them, recovering our blades.

We grabbed the two bodies, making sure the entrance of the garage was clear before dragging them inside. The garage itself seemed sparsely packed. Most of the machines that were left behind were large transports and various command tanks.

Arc and I moved up along the sidewall, spotting two more guards standing at a sliding door entrance to the labs themselves. Getting passed them in a manner that wouldn't alert the entire base would be difficult. I looked over my CIHUD, and I could see that security cameras were watching the door, likely hooked up into an automated system. As soon as they saw us, the base would be alerted. Strangely, the Elites were watching the door itself, as if more concerned about something coming out than in.

"This isn't exactly gonna be quiet if we go through them, buzz," Arc noted, seemingly coming to the same conclusions.

"Well, the way I see it, we have two options. One, we wait for the Sons, use their attack as cover, but then we lose time to get this shit done."

"Or we wreck some shit and blow fuckers up?"

"Basically." I saw a sly grin come over Arc's face.

"How's about Plan B?" I gave him a quizzical yet expectant look.. "You got those 'nades?" I took the bag off my shoulder and reached in, producing the grenade belt. I brought it with me as a just in case, but I didn't feel keen on wearing explosives. "Alright, here's the plan: I saw this place is run on solar power from the roof. We'll use one of these frag grenades and run like hell out of here, blow up a vehicle or two. While they're all discombobulated, we get to the roof and drop both EMP grenades. If those CORPS bastards did their job, the EM field the nanomachines put out should protect us. Plus, we got magshields anyway." He gave my shoulder-pad a tap.

"We could short out their electrical grid, possibly for hours, provided the CORPS hasn't built some defense against that."

"Exactly."

"Oh, hey, here." I reached in and pulled out one of the electrical gloves I was given during my first encounter with the TLF. "Good way to knock these bastards out on the hush-hush." He gave a nod, put the glove on, and pulled one of the frag grenades from the belt. We moved back towards the entrance of the garage, using our CIHUDs to track the vehicles outside, waiting for our window. As soon as it came, Arc used his teeth to pull the grenade's pin, flicked its safety off, and under-hand tossed it beneath one of the smaller vehicles parked inside.

We didn't wait for the grenade to go off, instead, moving out of the garage and to the outer wall of the facility. We leapt into the air, catching the edge of the roof and pulling ourselves up. As soon as we did, the explosion went off inside, unexpectedly causing a few others when the fuel tank blew. The entire building shook, but our balance was unaffected.

"You go left, I go right." I pulled the EMP grenades out, handing one to Arc. "One, two, three!" We tossed our grenades to opposite sides of the roof. For as simple as the weapon seemed, it caused quite a boom when the casing blew. Sparks were flying in every direction from the surrounding equipment. The two EMPs did a little more than short-circuit equipment; much of it would have to be outright replaced. As soon as the spectacle was over, we could hear the low-pitched sound of the machines below us shutting down. The exterior lights were the first to go, except for any not attached to the building itself. Lighting wasn't our goal, though, as CORPS troopers could naturally see in nearly no light situations. Just another perk of their genetic engineering.

"Won't be long before they know where we are. Gotta get ourselves inside somehow." When I turned after speaking, I saw Arc was exploring the roof, kneeling and looking over to me. He pointed at the floor below him.

"Maintenance hatch. I'll bet the security system is offline up here."

"Don't get cocky, I would be shocked if they didn't have a backup generator."

"Sames, but up here? There ain't nothing working now, I promise." He reached down, grabbed the handle of the hatch, and began to pull up. It budged but wouldn't give. "Get your lazy ass over here and help me." I rushed over to assist him.

There was pandemonium underneath us as troopers scrambled into and out of the garage. Some tried to make their way to the roof. Oddly enough, the patrols began moving as if to prevent things from exiting the labs instead of entering it.

Gripping the hatch's handle tight, we both lifted, our immense strength prying the door right off its hinges. Arc looked like he was going to toss it aside, but then thought better of it, instead gently setting it down.

"Easy." His voice was filled with confidence.

"Let's get in there." I began to climb down the ladder, entering the labs themselves from the maintenance hatch.

"Ladies first." Arc quipped before beginning to climb down as well. Before he got too far, he grabbed the broken hatch door and, as evenly as he could, placed it over the opening, giving it the at-a-glance appearance of being closed.

The hatch led down a narrow access-way, the ladder going far enough to seem like it was on ground-level. We hopped off and found ourselves in a maintenance storage room. There were random crates of materials and workbenches with various tools. It looked like it saw frequent use but was dark and void of people. Only our implants allowed us to see.

There was a lone double sliding door leading into the room. Arc and I put our backs to either side of the door and paid attention to our CIHUDs. I could barely sense power emanating from the door, suggesting it was still operable.

"These fucking things are useless," Arc growled in frustration.

"Geeze, how long has it been since you've been here? The walls block our scanners, but they'll be useful in whatever room we're in. Buck up bud, can't rely on their shit for everything."

"I guess. Ready?" He had his hand to the wall panel that would open the door. I gave him a nod, and he punched it, both of us waiting to hear if anyone was nearby. When the door opened, my CIHUD was flooded with information from beyond the hall.

"No one's out there," I remarked. Arc confirmed what I saw, and we both slowly walked out into the hall with our sidearms aimed and ready. The lights were dim but on, and it seemed, judging from both the door and the lights, that some sort of emergency power was in play.

"Think they're occupied with the diversion?" I asked without looking over.

"I dunno. To be honest, I thought there would be more alarms and shit."

"Yeah, same. Might be a silent alarm." As we slowly made our way through the labs, we came across an intersection moving onward and also to the left. When we approached, I could sense two guards down the left corridor and two more ahead of us. The ones ahead were moving away from our position. Several meters down the hall to our right was another set of sliding doors. We both looked to each other and gave a nod, quickly moving for the doors to our right. The doors still had some sort of security lock-out and were forced to pry it open. We were able to provide an opening large enough to both squeeze in before the door promptly shut behind us.

There was no movement inside the room we found ourselves in; it was empty of people but full of stuff. I looked around, taking stock of where we were, and my heart jumped with glee.

"This has to be the storage part of the facility." I observed.

"My favorite kinda storage." Arc commented. We both looked to each other with similar smirks.

"The Armory." We spoke in unison. We found ourselves in a weapons and equipment storage room. Given the shape of the halls behind us, I had to guess that the room's location was part of its security. There were rifles, sidearms, and even explosive launchers of varying types, all adorning walls and racks throughout the large chamber. There was also a myriad of machines to help keep the weapons in tip-top shape, the tables littered with a multitude of broken and busted guns ready to be worked on.

"Oh-ho-ho, fuck yes!" Arc had moved to the rifles and then to smaller arms, finding an open case on one of the workbenches. He pulled out a wicked-looking pistol, sporting a wider than usual barrel, with distinct electronics surrounding the firing mechanism.

"What is that thing?"

"Them fuckers went and did it buzz!" He tossed one over to me. "Magnetic sidearms, like the rail rifles. They miniaturized it." He took aim at a random target at the back of the room. There was a small firing range, likely to test the weapons. The first thing I noticed when he fired it was the tiny thwip sound when the bullet exited the barrel. It met its target at break-neck speeds, but otherwise left no sign of it ever being fired. There was no flash, and there was no bang, not even a muffled one.

"I saw the rifle version at the TLF base Reggie attacked." I reminisced.

"Shut up weirdo, and let's grab some mags." He picked up one of the magazines for the weapons and emoted happily again. "Du-u-u-ude. These things hold fifty rounds a pop."

"Makes sense, bullets can be smaller. Grab a rifle too." I suggested, though Arc was already on it. He grabbed a rifle and more ammunition. Luckily, we brought the bag.

"Alright, I say we move on out of here and-" I was interrupted by a sound from the other side of the closed doors. I gestured to Arc to move for the doors and he gave a nod. We both walked and waited on either side of the exit.

By now, two of the Elites had made their way to the entrance of the armory. As soon as the door opened a crack, we could sense them. Both of us were out in the blink of an eye. As the doors opened, we each reached out towards the nearby enemies with our coil-gloved hands. Sharp crackling emanated from the gloves as we grasped our enemy's arms, sending shocks through the surprised guards. In the same moment we aimed our pistol-wielding hands at the other two Elites down the hall, quietly firing our two new toys. Near simultaneously, all four soldiers dropped.

We were moving quickly now, knowing that as soon as their primary power was restored, we would probably be discovered. We went left, moving down the halls only another thirty meters before we came to what looked to be a massive security door. It was shaped like an iris and twice as large as the one we had exited coming out of the maintenance room. Its size seemed to have more to do with stopping power than large things going through it.

"We technical bypassed this shit, huh? Do we just open it?" I asked, putting my hand to the door, inspecting it as carefully as I could.

"Do we have any other choice?"

"No," I declared, slipping the pistol into the back of my pants and readying the rifle. Unfortunately, when we hit the switch to open the door, it made a frustrated whining sound but never budged.

"Fuck, there ain't enough power," Arc gave the door a kick. I looked around, scratching my chin, trying to find some way to get the door opened. "Think we can use the gloves?" Arc wondered.

"We'd have to be really quick and gentle about it. Might end up frying the damn thing." I took a deep breath, shook my head, and pressed my gloved hand up against the terminal for the door. I flexed, allowing the electrical discharge to flow out. The door roared to life, and Arc readied himself, as it opened centimeter by centimeter. Finally, it opened wide enough for us to pass through before the glove shorted the whole panel out. "Well, that's that."

"Sense anything out there?"

"No, not really. What the fuck gives? You would think this place would be hopping with security by now."

"Something's wrong," I muttered under my breath, but we decided to press on. We now found ourselves in familiar territory. It was the system of halls that led to the various simulator rooms. Walking to the entrance of the simulator I had trained in, we came face-to-face with why everything seemed so relaxed up to that point. The hall was filled with the shot-up corpses of at least a dozen Elites and even a scientist. There was an escape attempt going on.

"Arc, do you think this was happening when we got here?"

"Could be, might also be a seized opportunity."

"I agree. Let's be careful." I decided to use my prior knowledge of the facility to begin navigating the various halls, where we were met with more corpses. Eventually, we made our way to the computer mainframe section, something I was banking on running under its own power. The information stored in it would be as valuable as any soldier we brought out. While I had told R'yalax I would destroy any data we found, I thought it smart to check it first.

Quietly making our way to the mainframe room where Mick and I had had several encounters, I silently wondered just how successful we were about to be. For all we knew, the escapees were utter psychopaths or even already long gone. The mainframe room was sealed when we got there.

"Well, it looks like I was right." I was examining the door as I spoke.

"What's that?"

"The mainframe is running under its own power. We can't get in without explosives or something." I saw Arc get thoughtful for a moment and look to the biometric scanner on the side of the door. He promptly disappeared for a moment, reappearing with the body of a CORPS scientist. He held the body up by the neck and shoulder and had it "approach" the door, letting the scanner attempt to do its thing. With a satisfying clicking sound, the door opened.

"No fucking way." I was incredulous.

"Yes fucking way. He's only been dead for a minute or two. Don't knock it, it worked." With a shrug, I stepped over the body and walked into the room that was now spilling light out into the dim hallway. The machines inside seemed active.

"So, what the fuck is the point of this?" Arc asked, standing point at the door as I sat in a chair at the front of the extensive computer system. I reached into my bag and pulled out the data cable.

"We need to know about any upgrades we might be contending with or even fit ourselves with. We also need to destroy this place, and I have a

334

feeling this will tell us how." I also desperately wanted to find Ronyn.

"Destroy this place? Wasn't on the agenda, buzz!"

"Since when are you against gratuitous violence?"

"Well, when you put it that way, get them boom booms goin'! I guess I can see the merit in blowin' this place to kingdom come."

With us both in agreement, I set to work. Upon hooking myself into the machine, my senses were flooded with an incredible amount of data. While I was aware of the room around me, I let my thoughts delve as deeply into the machine as I could, trusting Arc to keep me covered. There was so much to take in that it was challenging for me to sift through everything. I was looking for the relevant pieces that would help our cause.

The CORPS had come a long way on the XRC Project. There was a lot of information that would take too much time to sift through, but it would seem that the first field test occurred three years before my awakening. Apparently, I was used to help learn how to speed up the process. It would also seem that new algorithms had been developed to increase the capabilities of the nanomachines communicating with the rest of the equipment. I took in as much information as I could.

"Uh, John. We've got a problem." I suddenly heard and opened my eyes. I looked to my CIHUD and found three XRC sensor suite signals heading directly towards us. Two from the left hall and one from the right. We were cornered like rats. There was a pause in their movement before a lone signal moved closer to the still opened door.

"What's your designation?" I heard the voice call out, feminine in quality, yet a bit deep.

"Certified badass, what's yours?" I heard Arc reply. There seemed to be confusion over the response, and then bravely, the form emerged in front of the door. She held a sidearm in her hand that she likely picked up from one of the troopers. She was of average height and slender build, her hair short and only just growing back from the procedure. She seemed somewhat recent in the grand scheme of things. Her skin was a dark and smooth complexion, indicating her ancestors originally hailed from somewhere other than Tantil.

"I won't ask again." I rolled my eyes at Arc's posturing before I finally spoke up, not sure how it would be received.

"XR001. Calling me that usually earns a smack." I quirked my brow, giving her a look to indicate I awaited her response. I was still sitting down, hooked into the mainframe.

"That's the one!" I heard a male, gruff sounding voice call from the hallway beyond.

"So, we killing each other or what?" Arc inquired as I heard the footsteps of the other two approach the room, though their pace didn't seem to indicate hostility. Finally, two men appeared from the hall, both looking like they spent most of their time at the gym. Their bulging muscles were visible through their clothes, though one was a bit shorter than the other. Their heads were freshly shaven, indicating they preferred them that way.Their light skin looked like it got real reflective in the day with haircuts like that.

"Didn't plan on it." The taller of the two men spoke. He was sporting a sleeve tattoo on his right arm, visible because he intentionally ripped the sleeve from his shirt. It depicted a surreal scene of a beautiful field, giving way to sterile gears and machines. He held the tattooed arm out to shake my hand.

"Been wanting to meet the guys who actually managed to escape. If you're John, then you're XR171, Archibald." Arc gave him a disgusted look hearing the full name.

"Arc will do buzz." We both shook his hand, accepting the friendly gesture. I was still hooked into the computer system and was only half paying attention, sifting through data. I came across two encrypted files, one entitled Project Kill Switch and the other, Project Perfect Conception. The latter had way more security than the first. Pressed for time I, dove into the more frightening sounding of the two: Kill Switch.

"We want out, we want to join you." The woman said plainly.

"How the hell did you hear about us anyway, buzz? I mean shit, this isn't gonna turn into autographs, is it?" Arc did the talking as I did the hacking.

"Word gets around to any of us who have been in the field. It's hard for the story of two men battling the Coalition and coming out with W's to stay secret for long." The tattooed man spoke. "I'm XR059, Vern, this is my brother, XR060, Riley, and this is our new friend XR107, Reya."

I finally broke through the encryption while the introductions continued. Project Kill Switch was apparently incomplete, a retrovirus of some sort that would be used to take down the XRC units in the event of a worldwide takeover. An interesting read; they never had time to finish the virus from what I was able to gather. I also had my doubts we'd be taking over the world anytime soon.

"Why'd you do it? Escape I mean?" The taller, less tattooed brother, Riley, spoke up.

"Is that a real question?" I asked, making my mental way into the bowels of Project Perfect Conception, at least I was trying to. The encryption was clearly designed to lock the likes of me right out of it, and I was only able to get bits and pieces of information. Apparently, it was the final phase of the

XRC Project and was deemed successful roughly three weeks prior.

"Of course, it is!" Vern protested.

"Well, why are you escaping?" Arc asked, crossing his arms over his chest.

"Freedom from the Coalition, freedom to live our lives how we want. I was never a killer and still don't want to be." This time it was Reya speaking.

"Then, you have your answer already." My voice was almost trailing off, concentrating on the encryption, but I knew I had to stop. Instead, I pulled a PCD from the bag we brought and hooked it into the mainframe. I could always try to break into them later. I only copied the two projects and a few files I thought Alonna might make use of.

"What exactly are you trying to do?" Vern cocked his head, watching my every move.

"Me? Trying to blow this place to shit now." When the file transfers were complete, I dove into the security protocols and didn't have a hard time finding exactly what I wanted; a self-destruct mechanism. It would be more shocking if a place like that didn't have one. The whole building began to shake, and we could feel other light tremors. The Sons had started their attack.

"Oh, fuck!" I suddenly exclaimed, ripping myself free of the cable, stuffing everything back into the bag. "Look, kids, this is a great conversation, good to meet you and all, but we have barely three minutes to get the fuck out."

"Why did you set it to only three minutes?" Arc was incredulous.

"I didn't set shit. Either it's silent, or we knocked out the alarm, but it was already set. If you three want out, let's go, I feel a lot more comfortable making our exit with five as opposed to two." I pushed passed them out of the corridor. "Out the way we came."

"What crawled up your ass?" I heard Arc ask behind me as all five of us began running through the hallways. I was visibly upset about a bit of the information I was able to find.

"Ronyn ain't here." It was, unfortunately, true. According to the personnel information, Ronyn had left a couple of months ago shortly after my escape. He was assigned to oversee the science division in the Tantil Habitat. He was in Dome City.

"Ronyn, you mean Xavier Ronyn, the head of the project?" Vern seemed to be the leader of their trio, asking all of the questions for the most part.

"Yeah, that walking corpse." We didn't meet any resistance, making our way back to the hatch we had entered from, all of us scurrying up the ladder as fast as we could, keeping the count in the back of my mind. We had twenty seconds by the time we made it to the roof. It would seem any Elites who had made it up to the roof had quickly jumped back down when the Sons attacked.

"Fuck John, they don't have harnesses!" Arc pointed out. I kept running, heading for the edge.

"They'll survive six meters!" I had finally made it to the ledge and was treated to the sight of the Sons who had the place surrounded. They were taking heavy casualties from the troopers and vehicles that had been mobilized from the facility. It seemed strange to me they would be defending a doomed facility so fervently, unless, of course, they didn't know it was about to blow.

We had thirty seconds before I had jumped, landing in an explosion of sand. Without hesitation Arc and the others leapt from the roof. Our acquaintances rolled as they hit the ground, their reinforced frames and enhanced abilities allowing them to easily weather the drop.

By now, the nearby Elites had noticed us and attempted to take aim. All five of us had no intention of getting shot, and we began to fire our weapons while running across the field. Seconds felt like minutes while we blasted our way through the battlefield, leveling an impressive number of enemies in the blink of an eye. With the final tick of my internal clock, the facility began to go up most spectacularly. First, a raging inferno burst forth from the garage, every vent on the roof suffering the same fate as well as any other place the pressure could immediately escape. To the average eye, this was all an instant as the pressure became too great to contain the explosion.

We all leapt as fast and as hard as we could, having already cleared a great distance in the few seconds we were able to run. I could feel the force of the shockwave behind me, throwing us all back and into the sand. Arc and I were well protected from such an event; our friends, however, tumbled violently, being tossed like ragdolls.

Most of the surrounding vehicles were toast from the shockwave of the blast. The Sons were luckier, having a strategy on their side. When they attacked, they came in two waves. The first wave was sorely defeated by both the CORPS and the self-destructing labs, but the second wave was screaming in as fast as they could.

Arc and I moved over to our fallen comrades, checking on them. Although shaken and bruised, they managed to escape the explosion with only minor injuries, a testament to their augmented state. A normal person would've been lying in a broken heap.

My CIHUD began to scream at me as I was helping Reya to her feet.

Heading towards us at breakneck speeds were four XRC signals. Looking behind us, I could see them, two men, two women, looking dirty and ripped up from the previous battle, but more than ready for a real fight. I pulled my new sidearm and began to fire towards the group, as did Reya. It was fruitless as they weaved and bobbed out of the way, not even slowing their advance. Arc and the others joined us, creating a cybernetic firing line.

"Focus on one at a time!" Vern yelled out, and I decided to oblige his callout. We began to fire at the man on the left, alternating our trajectories, and surprisingly it worked. As he dodged the first three, the other two were aimed for where he would need to move to avoid the shots. The rounds violently sent him to the ground, but the other three were undaunted and nearly in melee range.

"First!" The gruff sounding, loud-speaker enhanced voice called out. A sizeable open-top transport vehicle was barreling towards us. Honestly, it was a beautiful sight at that very moment.

"They're friends!" I said both to the Sons and our new allies. Without fear, several of them leapt from the vehicle, tucking and rolling, seeming to wear makeshift armor made for that sort of maneuver. As they piled out and attempted to take on the advancing cyborgs, all five of us found an appropriate spot and managed to leap into the vehicle as it screeched by. I grabbed a rail attached to the chassis and was hanging off the side of the truck.

"Out," I said to the driver, moving my thumb to tell him to get into the backseat. Very carefully keeping it steady, the passenger held onto the wheel, and the driver got out of their seat. I quickly jumped in and took over, pushing the vehicle to its absolute limits.

Looking into the side-view mirror, I could see that the XRC soldiers had already made short work of the Sons, but even they couldn't run as fast as our machine could go. Of course, they weren't stupid either and would find a way.

"The day is ours!" I heard the driver I just evicted cry out, and the remaining two other Sons in the vehicle hollered their agreement. Other Sons trucks had begun to follow us and exactly what I was worried about happened. The three remaining soldiers commandeered a jeep from the Sons and began to drive towards us. Quickly, they started neutralizing transports with well-placed shot.

"Any of you boys got them spikey bombs?" I asked, concentrating on the sand dunes before me. I headed straight for the ambush point, hoping the TLF would be ready to hold off the freaks behind us. We had finally entered the canyon where our trap would be sprung. When our enemies approached, my worry of them became stark reality as my right shoulder exploded out in pain and a spray of blood; one of them managed to hit me.

"Gah, fuck! Time to bail kids!" I yelled out, using my good arm to turn the vehicle hard to the side, causing it to roll. I wasn't sure if the Sons would be able to handle it, but they seemed like a tough lot. We all jumped and tumbled onto the sand while the Sons transport rolled a few meters away. We had made it, though.

The canyon walls were surrounding us now, just as planned, and I could see the TLF squads already in position, aiming their weapons. It all seemed like some sort of a slow time moment. Our vehicle was rolling away, with the cyborgs closing in. The TLF soldiers opened fire from the canyon while my new-found friends managed to tuck and roll like acrobats. Eventually, they also opened fire when they became stable. Even the Sons managed to scramble for safety, their bulky armor softening much of the impact.

For all of the power the implants imparted to us, the three pursuers didn't stand a chance. Their vehicle was ripped to shreds, and the cyborgs were cut down as they tried to bail. There were too many trajectories, five of which could nearly anticipate their moves. As the dust began to settle, the shooting stopped, and all that could be heard in the distance were the approach of surviving Sons of Rellen jeeps.

Finally, able to realize what had happened, I knelt down and grasped my shoulder in pain. The bone had managed to mostly survive, but it was bruised, and the muscles heavily torn. Even for me, it would take a few days to heal it all, though I wasn't prepared to take another one of the doc's concoctions. The brothers lifted me to my feet and led me to a nearby transport truck, ready to drive me to safety.

"I'll take care of the Sons, buzz. Get some R&R, huh?" I felt Arc pat me on the back while I was loaded into a TLF truck. If the other approaching vehicles had been full of enemies, they likely decided falling prey to the same trap was inadvisable. Only five Sons jeeps returned. They suffered heavy losses, and yet I could see their expressions as the door to the transport closed. They were elated, absolutely ecstatic about the entire affair. In a sense, I envied their pure love of a good fight.

"You look hurt. Here." The transport had a field medic within, who was coming at me with some sort of painkiller laced needle. I brushed it away.

"I'll be fine. Give it a minute, I'll be pumped full of more drugs than I know what to do with." The male medic gave a confused look and looked over to Reya and the brothers who had joined me.

"It's the nanomachines," Reya explained. "They provide us with all that we need, including pain relief."

"Fair enough." He shrugged and moved away. R'yalax had apparently decided to join the operation and was inside the transport. She approached me, using a handhold rail to steady herself.

"What happened? Was the mission successful?"

"You tell me," I said, motioning to my newfound allies.

"Can we trust them?" She had no qualms about asking right in front of our guests.

"Do you trust me?" She was silent, giving me a look that conveyed her answered. "Okay, well, if that's the case, then trust *them*. We found them in an area covered in bodies, and I'm going to assume they weren't just lucky to avoid the murderer."

"Fair enough. They did clearly open fire on their own."

"They're not our own," Riley spoke up, glaring at R'yalax.

"Calm down bro, she doesn't know our story." Vern offered his hand, and R'yalax shook it professionally. "Don't mind my brother, we have no love for the Coalition."

"That is all I needed to hear. We'll debrief all of you when we return to the Command Tank. I am sure Dr. Lyrul will wish to see your wound." R'yalax turned and retook her seat. Riley peered at me, studying my reaction before his brother spoke up.

"Dr. Lyrul? Dr. Alonna Lyrul? The woman who invented our nanomachines? You're working for the Coalition?" He suddenly seemed angry, but all I could do was roll my eyes and leaned back to get comfortable.

"That's insulting. No, I don't work for the CORPS in any capacity, and as far as I know, neither does she."

344

"That thing you said, as far as you know." Reya pointed it out and awaited a response.

"Can anyone be absolutely sure when it comes to the likes of her?" I asked rhetorically. "She helped me escape. As much as I hate to admit it, if it wasn't for her, both Arc and I would be dead, and the same would go for you after today's stunt."

"So, there *is* a way passed the fail-safe." Vern scratched the back of his neck, pondering out loud.

"Yep, otherwise, we wouldn't be chatting."

"What did you do about the conditioning?" Reya was still on the offensive in her interrogation, but I was suddenly confused by the line of questioning.

"What do you mean?" All three of them looked to each other with the same exasperated expression. Clearly, they knew more about the project than I did.

"She was your handler, wasn't she?" Reya crossed her arms over her chest, and I didn't like where everything was going.

"Yeah, why?"

"The Handlers, there guy," Riley took over, "are conditioned to become obsessed with their respective charges. At least, we assume they are. They'll do anything for their charge, as long as its within the bounds of the project. I remember watching a handler take bullets for the unit they were in charge of during a field exercise one day. Never saw either of them after that."

"The brothers here filled me in, and it made a lot of sense considering." Reya seemed to be thinking out loud.

"Yeah, well, she's definitely clingy and frequently creepy, I'll grant you
345

that, but if I had to be objective, she's been invaluable so far. I guess you can say the TLF here has been helping me with her conditioning as you call it."

"What's the deal with them anyway?" Vern asked.

"The TLF? Our deal honestly; freedom from the CORPS. They've been fighting for centuries against these clowns, and we're here to give them a leg up."

"Centuries, you say?" Reya finally decided to take a seat. "So, they really did lie. We could have lived above at any time." My eyes moved over to Reya, and in her, I suddenly found family in a sense.

"You were born in the Undercities?" She looked up and nodded.

"All three of us were, though not all of us obviously knew each other."

"Two million-plus inhabitants, that's not entirely surprising." I mused.

"What about Arc?" Riley questioned.

"Arc? He was apparently born in a similar place that started as a penal colony. He doesn't talk a lot about what life was like there, but I assume there was a similar lie or something about it he doesn't want to tell me."

"That doesn't bother you?" Vern quirked a brow, watching my reaction.

"Nope. For the same reason, I don't talk about my escape very much. Some memories are better left buried." They gave a look of understanding, and I knew right then and there that I had found close friends. My confidence in our task grew at the rate the pain in my shoulder faded; slow and steady.

Chapter Twenty-Five: Adopted Family

The rest of the ride was mostly quiet while we made our way to the rendezvous point. The command vehicle and a good two-thirds of our allotted forces had stayed behind to ensure we had a place to go in the event our mission fell apart. Arc had rejoined us shortly before getting back, and we all decided it would be best to find a place to hunker down for the night.

The area seemed very odd to me in the way the terrain was laid out. There was erosion in many places, but at times it felt like the roads we walked were once rivers and the dunes at one-point forests. It would seem the CORPS dealt in half-truths and obfuscation than outright lies. Many places of the surface really had been bombed out or otherwise been scorched in some fashion. Rivers and lakes dried up, forests withered, and animals perished over the petty fighting of nation-states. I had to wonder what role the CORPS had played in the war. It wouldn't surprise me if they started it on purpose, instigating every slight and salting every wound. It was frightening and at the same time, impressive. Could science actually be used to manipulate people so totally? Is it even logical to blame the tool?

I was mostly quiet that evening, contemplating our next move and running those philosophical thoughts through my brain. My new friends were a lively bunch, full of life and fervor. Apparently, Vern and Riley were picked for some sort of sports enhancement experiment in the CORPS Research Section of the Undercities. They were promised fame, that they would become the greatest athletes anyone had ever known. Such things were coveted in the Undercities; in a place without currency, your merits were all you had. When it became clear that the CORPS had lied to them, that no such glory was coming, they eagerly awaited their escape. They listened to reports of Arc and I's antics across Tantil even though we really hadn't done much from our point of view.

Reya was a different case altogether and turned out to be a more valuable find than we could have anticipated. Reya came from Dome City, having transitioned with the rest of the people more than five years before our meeting. She was able to give us a detailed account of how the Undercities were emptied and what went on under the Dome.

"Let me get this straight, there's literal office blocks and real as shit buildings under that thing?" Arc was fascinated by the entire affair. We all were really. We were camped out in a small canyon we had found, providing cover and good vantage points to keep safe the needed R&R.

"Yep, that's the gist of it. The Undercities are honestly plain in comparison to the Habitat. There's room to grow too, we barely took up half the available space when we got there."

"And how did you get there?" I asked, curious to see if we were wasting our time heading for the Undercities.

"The CORPS Engineering Section apparently built a whole new set of tunnels and refurbished the ancient tram system that brought us underground to begin with." Reya talked with her hands as she spoke, and I found myself admiring her upbeat attitude.

"So, there is a tunnel then." I was rubbing my chin, staring off in thought.

"Yes, there is, and it's doubtful they've sealed it."

"What makes you say that?" Alonna decided to join in the conversation, having returned with her second helping of soup that evening.
348

She took a seat on the ground next to me.

"Well? It's how I got to be in this situation." Reya answered, pointing to her forehead where the CIHUD comes out. "I uh, well, I had a thing for getting into places I didn't belong, and one day I got curious about shipments."

"Shipments?" I inquired, giving her an inquisitive look.

"Yep, shipments. The Coalition has a lot of factories making various items and materials for the Engineering Section, but a lot of it disappears into the restricted zones and never comes back. If my basic elementary geometry is still on point, the restricted zones are huge." Arc, who was sitting on the opposite side of the fire from me, looked up, and we met each other's eyes at the same time. That wasn't the sort of thing we wanted to hear. I looked back at Reya.

"So, what'd you find?"

"I found a weapons storage facility as well as an assembly yard." My look became grim.

"So, it looks like you were right doc, they're planning on doing a whole ton of murdering." She didn't look up at me, instead, concentrating on her meal.

"Wait, what?" Vern looked up from across the fire, Reya was sitting between the two brothers.

"I'll explain in a second. Reya, I guess just like with Vern and Riley, I have to ask, what gives? Why fight the CORPS?" I studied her now, eagerly hoping for a juicy answer.

"Are you kidding me? When they found me, they gave me two choices. Execution or take part in a new project, never again to see my friends or family. I had a fiancé." She nearly choked up for a moment, then took in a deep breath.

349

Vern put his hand on her shoulder, and Riley rubbed her back a bit. She nodded to them, composing herself, and I suddenly understood precisely why everyone was there. We all lost something to the CORPS, something precious we can never have back. We were family. We didn't need to be together for very long to realize what was true between us.

"What about you, Arc?" Reya looked over to him with interest. "What happened to you?"

"Me? Pfft, nothing half as dramatic as you yahoos. Nope, I was picked, knew exactly what I was getting into."

"Wait, really?" I asked with shock. He hadn't told me that.

"Yeah, buzz, really. Look, the CORPS does all sorts of fucked up experiments on people across the globe. Us? We were taken from the dregs of society to provide breeding fodder for their mutant military. Yep, some of those freaks you kill are probably kinsman of mine." We all looked to each other, unsure how to take that, but then Arc laughed. "Relax! They weren't nice people, I assure you. Not all of us down there were bad to be sure." He held his arms out to indicate himself. "Look at me! Genetically superior like you Undercity kids, somewhat educated. Oh yeah, I was ripe for their new special program. They wanted some of us that grew up in the Pit. We knew how to handle ourselves and weren't afraid to get our hands dirty."

"So what gives then?" Riley asked. "Why give a shit at all?" Arc's look grew dark as he met Riley's eyes.

"You guys are all about what the CORPS took from you. Me? I'm all about what they never let me have." And suddenly, it all made sense. Arc was robbed of the utopian life we took for granted, denied a humane existence, knowing from the very beginning he was nothing but fodder. They took it all
350

before he ever had a chance to have it.

"Alright, John-boy, you're the last one," Vern said, looking to me. "We all shared buddy." I sighed and looked away for a moment before running a hand through my hair.

"Really, it's a lot like all of you. Me and some friends got it into our heads that we could escape the Undercities. We were gonna use the old maintenance access-ways to make our way out, and see the sky. We didn't care if it was livable or not."

"So, what happened?" Reya asked, and I suddenly realized that all eyes were on me, even Alonna was taking an interest. I took a deep breath and continued.

"It was all a CORPS ploy. Someone I thought was my friend, Mick, put the escape plan into our heads. We were super naive, he had blueprints, knew exactly where to go; we followed pretty fucking loyally. Ray," I could never help the guilty feeling I felt whenever I spoke his name, "was lost pretty early on, and Mick managed to fake his own death. Lys, she uh, she died in my arms, but she got to see the sky." I looked down for a moment, my fist clenching before looking up. "They're going to get theirs; I fucking promise you."

"That's why you killed him," Alonna spoke softly, almost cautiously. I looked to her with an affirmative glance.

"Now, you understand."

"Alright, enough of this shit. Let's talk shop." Arc interrupted the uncomfortable silence in a way I always appreciated. We did exactly as he said, beginning to discuss the ramifications of our plan. We informed our new friends of Alonna's theory that the CORPS was planning mass genocide, and that we might be the only thing standing in their way.

When all was said and done, a remarkable thing happened around the fire. We all had a reason to wreak vengeance against the CORPS, we all wanted to get even, but when it came down to it, that's not what we were in it for. When people are abused and harmed, sometimes they lash out at the world around them, but some people decide that they could never allow another person to endure what they did. That is what we became. The CORPS gave us the power to move mountains; it was a moral imperative that we used it.

We all took some time to get some rest. My wound healed up nicely, and strangely enough, Alonna didn't offer me any new concoctions. I chalked it up to the lack of resources we had on the road considering the Libsal compound had actual medical facilities. Still, it seemed odd, nonetheless.

Chapter Twenty-Six:
Conspiracies Within Conspiracies

We ended up having to backtrack a little due to the exposure the open terrain was causing, adding an extra week to our journey. After the fiasco at the XRC labs, none of us wanted to chance whether or not the CORPS was actively hunting us down. Things still seemed out of place, and I almost couldn't help thinking we had somehow done the CORPS's bidding by annihilating any chance of someone copying their work. One thing that bothered me the most was the absence of Ronyn. It struck me as odd he would leave his pet project to the hands of others. One morning, only two days from our destination, I decided to question Alonna about it.

It was early, and I wanted to wake her up before we headed off for the day. We usually slept outside on bedrolls or in tents, but when I got there, she was missing from her camp. I popped my CIHUD out and found her a few meters away behind some rocks. Walking over, I could hear retching and vomiting. Turning the corner, I found her wiping her mouth, her skin extremely pale, and her body feverish, according to my sensors.

"You okay, doc?" I tilted my head, showing genuine concern.

"I uh, I'm fine." She gave me a smile looking up, but her looks betrayed her feelings. She was sick. While the CIHUD wasn't meant for robust medical scans, I could tell she had foreign bodies coursing through her veins.

"Don't lie, you're all fucked up right now. Are you infected? Something is swimming around in your blood."

"Nanomachines." She said confidently. "Disposable ones. I think I may have eaten something that didn't agree with me, so I gave myself an

353

inoculation this morning." I gave her a puzzled look, not entirely convinced by her explanation, but I didn't see a point in pressing it. It's not like her being sick was a problem for anyone other than her.

"Fine, fair enough. Look, if you're feeling up to it, I have some questions."

"Of course, let's sit, you know I am always here for you, John." She forced a smile, took my hand, and led me to a place where we could sit and talk.

"When I was in the XRC labs, I uncovered some information."

"Yes, you showed me. I have already begun integrating the upgrades you downloaded into my next inoculation for you all."

"Is that why you haven't given our three new friends their injection to prevent the fail-safe?"

"Yes, I plan to incorporate it all into one shot for them." She was starting to improve, though her fever still seemed unabated. "Besides, the fail-safe takes longer if they aren't straining their bodies."

"That's good to hear. So, there's some information I have neglected to share. One thing before I get into that: Ronyn wasn't at the facility anymore." Alonna's eyes widened for a moment, she seemed to catch herself however and regained her composure.

"That is unfortunate, I presume?"

"Very."

"You did not come to ask me about Xavier, did you?"

"Not exactly, but it just seems weird he wasn't there."

"Well, what else did you find? Perhaps we can find clues?" I thought about this for a moment.

354

"Well, I found two projects, one that looks unfinished, some sort of virus, a new fail-safe, I guess."

"V-virus? For XRC units?" She suddenly seemed very alarmed.

"Yeah, why?"

"What about the other project?" She suddenly grabbed one of my hands, seeming desperate for an answer.

"I really don't have anything on it, just the name and that it was completed super recently. It was Project Perfect Conception." She let go of my hand and looked down, suddenly laughing lightly to herself.

"So, nothing really is good enough for them."

"Alonna, you wanna start making some sense, please?"

"John, did you get any information about the virus?" I didn't like her sudden attitude about things. She was scared, and I couldn't tell if it was for me, for her, or all of the above.

"Yeah, just about everything, but what does this have to do with Ronyn?" I was getting frustrated.

"Well?" She took a deep, calming breath. "If Project Perfect Conception has been deemed complete, then the XRC Project itself was deemed a success. If that's the case, Xavier was likely promoted to the Council of Consensus."

"Council of Consensus?"

"Yes, you see, the Coalition is not run in a governmental fashion the way you are used to. Instead, the brightest minds of the various divisions come together to form a governing body. They always reach a consensus, regardless of the situation. Together, they choose how the Coalition will realize its goals. The Arbiter, as you know them, is merely a figurehead, a person we place at the head of various civilian governments. It allows us to keep tight control over their growth."

"So, Ronyn's a hotshot now?"

"Yes, which means you will likely cross paths with him yet. Now John, please, I must see everything you have on the virus."

"I mean sure, but I told you it wasn't completed, looked barely half-finished."

"Do not be naive, John!" She was suddenly angry, and I was taken aback by it. She was always the picture of emotional control, but now she looked like she was a second away from hysterical.

"Whoa, chill out."

"No, I will not chill out! How many times must the Coalition prove to you their ability to mislead? I must see that virus!" She stood now, looking ready to scream at me.

"Alright, alright, relax. It's on my PCD, it's in my bag next to my bedroll." She didn't say a word; instead, she marched over to my stuff to get the item in question. I just let her do her thing, not moving to stop her or protest. Something was bothering her to be sure, but something else was preventing her from handling it.

From there on out, Alonna was a ghost. She wouldn't speak to anyone, barely eating and definitely not sleeping. She had become obsessed with the virus I had uncovered. Though she did find the time to prepare inoculations for all of us, it consumed every other second of her time.

Eventually, we drew close to our final destination. The mountain range itself was quite impressive, and we were able to see it from a decent distance away. It was sparsely filled with vegetation that only seemed to recently try to take hold of the land once more. This mountain range seemed like it suffered more from the surrounding fallout than it did from any sort of direct attack, showing no signs of previous civilization. It was also an eerily quiet trip. We expected resistance, a real fight on the way up the mountain, but instead, there was nothing.

Finally, we reached out target, and I found myself stricken with awe from the memory I tried to keep hidden away. A colossal glass structure stretched up into the sky, nestled into a deep valley of the mountain. The glass was popped with broken shards and ancient grime, and I knew then and there, we had found the entrance to the Undercities. It, just like our journey, was void of any signs of the CORPS. We decided to make camp nearby and form a plan.

Most of us were gathered just outside the command tank with soldiers patrolling nearby. Alonna was conspicuously absent.

"We really don't have time for this, buzz." Arc sounded frustrated. With a roll of my eyes and a shrug, I marched inside the command tank. I found her fixated on one of the computer screens, continuing her research.

"Alonna, we might need your input. Alonna?" I walked over and put my hand on her shoulder, realizing she was sweating. She jumped, startled by the contact, but then her hand found its way to mine on her shoulder, gripping it lightly. Her skin was clammy and cold.

"Yes, of course John, my apologies." I knelt so I could look into her eyes.

"Alonna, you look really sick." For once, I felt an actual concern for her. I wasn't sure why, but it was like watching a good friend suffer. She had started to grow on me.

"I will be fine John, really, you worry too much. Come on, let's begin." She stood, and I led her out of the command tank. As soon as we stepped out, I could see R'yalax's face grow as concerned as mine.

"Are you alright, doctor?"

"Yes, yes, please, you must really stop, I am just fine." She took a breath and smoothed her coat.

"Alright, then," I started. "So, I've been thinking about this for a while. I know what those tunnels are like and a little of what we can expect down there. I've come to the conclusion that the TLF should turn back and leave this to us." R'yalax put her hands behind her back, taking this in before replying.

"With all due respect, how do you plan on getting out of there when your mission is a success?" That's when me and the four other cyborgs looked to each other before I looked back to R'yalax.

"We don't expect to make it back out." Alonna's eyes widened, and I felt her hand grip my arm.

"John, no, you must make it out, this does not end with just the Habitat." I looked at her.

"You're right, but Alonna, the chances of us even succeeding are slim enough, the idea we won't end up martyrs down there is almost laughable. Every person we bring with us is one more we have to worry about."

"Besides doctor, you look like you're in no shape to be going anywhere." R'yalax's concern grew, and Alonna's condition did look like it was worsening.

"There's a plethora of bullshit we might encounter down there, and it may take days before we even find our way. Food and water will be scarce." I concluded.

"Then, it is settled. We will set up an encampment here, a small one, perhaps request some communications equipment. You will need this." R'yalax handed me a small box with a simple touch screen interface. "When the array is built, we will use this to attempt to contact you. If you find a way to contact us first, then do so if you can. We won't do anything brash until we hear from you. It will still take a couple of weeks for the array to be deployed, but once it has, General Delantil has indicated he will begin mustering troops around the Dome." I gave R'yalax a nod and offered my hand, which she took in a firm shake.

"You're a one of a kind R'yalax."

"If I may," Alonna spoke up. "How are the enhancements functioning?"

"Kinda weird to tell you the truth." Vern replied. "I was used to being able to sense my buddies."

"Do not worry, only similarly enhanced XRC units will elude your senses."

"I, for one, wish we had these enhancements before going into those labs," I said, giving my shoulder a roll.

"To sate my curiosity, what exactly did she do to you?" R'yalax was the only one who seemed comfortable asking questions about our condition. Alonna responded with a proud, yet somehow weak grin.

"Their awareness and reaction time has been enhanced by nearly two factors due to a very simple enhancement."

"That doesn't sound very simple." R'yalax retorted.

"On the contrary lieutenant. All the Coalition did was increase the efficiency and speed in which the nanomachines communicate with the rest of their equipment. When your reaction time is as fast as theirs, even a small increase in such areas can translate into huge gains."

"As long as the fail-safe is gone, then I'm happy," Reya remarked.

"Alright, alright, enough of the chit chat. Let's grab everything we might need and get this done. I don't see any reason to lollygag." Arc had his usual get it done attitude, but it was well placed. Wordlessly, we moved to begin preparing for the possibility of a one-way trip. Alonna grabbed my arm again to stop me.

"John, you have to come back." She was searching my eyes, for what, I wasn't sure.

"Alonna, I'm just a man, albeit a powerful one. My life isn't more important than anyone else's." I tried to pull away, but her grip on my arm tightened.

"To some, you are very important. More than you know." She was acting strangely and still feverish. I shrugged her hand away from my shoulder.

"If I don't do this, there might not be anyone to come back to." My face was serious, showing for once a stoic sort of conviction. She searched my eyes for a long moment before walking back to the command tank.

"She's acting weirder than usual, buzz." Arc was standing a few meters away, his arms crossed over his chest, watching as she left. He looked back over to me. "A lot weirder."

"She's sick." My tone was basic, as my mind focused on the mission at hand.

"She's sick, alright."

"You know what I mean, Arc."

"And you know what I mean, John. Even her being physically sick seems a little fucked up. How come no one else is sick?"

"Who knows man, she was a CORPS scientist. I can only imagine what shit she's been subjected to. Could be some weird form of cancer for all we know."

"And she could be harboring some sort of virus."

"Well, it ain't gonna matter much to us in a minute, will it?" I walked passed him, but he moved back in front of me.

"Why are you defending her? What the fuck is all this affection lately? Don't forget what she is." Fed up with the conversation, I moved towards Arc, nearly touching noses.

"I know damn well what she is, and I will never forget that, but don't you forget that you're alive because of her and that just like us, she's fighting this war."

"You care about her." I scoffed in response.

"So what if I do? Is it so wrong to have a little compassion? Quit fucking around, we have work to do." I stormed off, leaving Arc to prepare for the journey ahead. I wasn't sure who I was angrier with, him or myself. I couldn't adequately explain how I felt about Alonna, if I hated her, liked her, cared for her, wanted her dead. It all seemed like some sort of blur of emotions, but I do know one thing: I wasn't enjoying watching her suffer, and selfishly, I was glad I wouldn't have to. Whatever was wrong with her seemed far more severe than she was letting on. None of it seemed to matter in the grand scheme of things. My course was laid out, and I was set on it.

Chapter Twenty-Seven: Into The Breach

We packed lightly for our journey, grabbing a couple of canteens of water each, some rations, and other basic survival equipment. We each took a grenade belt, kinetic-harness, and a couple of shield belts, the only two we had. We'd find a use for them somehow. Each of us had our own pet sidearm. Arc and I had fallen in love with our rail weapons. Due to the specialized ammo, however, they would eventually become deadweight. We took everything we thought we would need and be able to carry without much encumbrance. I insisted we take rifles as well, worried about the mutaphorms still lurking within the bowels of the Undercities.

We decided not to wait to enter the lobby. Daylight would be a moot point, so there was no real reason to hesitate. No one saw us off. Instead, we chose to make our exit quietly as soon as we were finished packing, informing only R'yalax of our departure. It was easier that way.

Walking through the main entrance of the lobby brought back a flood of memories I didn't want. Seeing the CORPS troopers filing out of doors, Ronyn's smirking face, and Lys's dying smile. I was thankful for the artificial composure I was gifted with. The place looked positively untouched since I had last been there, which made a lot of our intel come into full focus. Lys and I were likely the last civilians to occupy the space

Arc let out a whistle. "Look at the size of this place."

"It was designed to usher in hundreds of thousands of people, nearly all at once," Reya commented as she too looked around in wonder.

"This the place you ended up, John-boy?" Vern looked over to me, holding onto the straps of his backpack.

"Yeah, unfortunately. This is where we ended up."

"Fucking crazy, man." I couldn't help but chuckle at his wonder. When we moved to the central processing area, I found myself confused at the state of the massive door. It was gone, leaving only the twisting, winding tunnel beyond.

"That seems off," I spoke absentmindedly.

"What does?" Reya asked.

"That tunnel. There used to be a big-ass security door just chilling right there, but it's gone now."

"Maybe the Coalition took it down when taking people out?"

"But why would they?" None of us had an adequate answer to that question, but it didn't matter because we had to press on. We moved into the outer depths of the Undercities.

The first thing I noticed stepping into the tunnels was that the security checkpoint with the gun emplacements had been removed. Whether it was originally part of the trap that ensnared Lys and I or, like the door, was moved for some other purpose, I didn't know; we were going in blind. The only one who didn't seem bothered by everything was Arc, who I had to assume spent his whole life riding by the seat of his pants.

"When you guys were going through here, did you encounter mutaphorms?" Riley inquired. He was looking all around, his CIHUD already out and scanning for possible intruders.

"Oh yeah, we did. Stalkers and these weird, bat things. Who knows what else is lurking considering the menagerie we found."

"Menagerie?" Reya asked.

"Yeah, they were keeping stalkers as pets, studying them for something." I took in a breath. "It's where we lost Ray." No one questioned it any further, thinking about the implications of dying at the claws of stalkers.

"So, who do you think made them?" Riley broke the silence as we walked.

"Mutaphorms?" Arc asked, joining the conversation.

"Yeah, do you really think it was the Tantillans?"

"Does it really matter?" I asked rhetorically. "Either they did, and they're scumbags, or the CORPS manipulated them into it, which would make them dumb scumbags."

"Fair," Riley replied. We kept up the idle banter as we walked through the kilometers long tram tunnel. We took the time to learn about each other; hobbies, interests, hopes for the world. Sometimes I forgot I was a regular old person when all was said and done, and such conversations helped to ground me in the real world.

"Used to be a good card counter back in the day. Bet I'd fuckin' kill it these days." Arc mused, and I laughed at the thought.

"I'm surprised. You? Math skills?"

"Fuck yourself." He said but was still smiling. "Nah man, games of chance were a big deal in the Pit. I mean, we had all the regular entertainment amenities. The CORPS weren't completely cruel, but there was something about high stakes and big risks that got most of us going."

"You think a lot of the ones from the Pit joined the CORPS happily?" I was honestly curious; if it were so bad, why weren't there more Arcs.

"Honestly? More than I wanna admit."

"Really?" Reya commented. "You would think if it were as bad as you say it was, they would jump ship in droves." Arc surprisingly laughed at this.

"That's exactly why they'd join up. When the surgery was done, I was promised everything under the sun for cooperation."

"So, what's your excuse then?" I asked.

"I be what I wanna do." Arc said this as if it was the most sagely wisdom he could impart on the subject and declined to explain it further.

The massive tunnel twisted and turned as we continued to traverse through it. Finally, we made it to the point where Lys and I had managed to enter tram tunnels. I pointed at the now-closed hatch we had crawled through.

"That's where we came in from."

"Wouldn't that just lead us back to the Undercities?" Reya inquired, curious as to my plan.

"Yep, that's where I think we need to go. I mean, what are the chances the CORPS brought the civilians this way?" My companions looked at each other and seemed to agree with my assessment. "There is a problem, though."

"What's that?" Vern inquired.

"Well, we exited from damn near the bottom of this barrel. I think if we follow this all the way back, it will cause problems."

"So, what's the point, asshole?" Arc crossed his arms over his chest.

"It will lead us to the outside of the superstructure, and we can probably find our way from there. I mean, look at the bright side, at least we won't be going in completely blind." No one seemed to agree with my bright side. Riley didn't waste time, walking over to the hatch, he reached for the handle and gave it tug, but it wouldn't budge. He grasped the handle with both hands, and still, it wouldn't move.

"That fucker is sealed up real good." He said factually. I walked over to inspect it myself and could see the seams had been completely welded shut.

We might have been able to pry it open, but it would've taken a lot of strength and a durable lever. We only had one of those things.

"What do we do now, fearless leader?" Arc asked expectantly.

"I guess we continue down these tunnels. They gotta end somewhere." With the group in agreement, we set off once more, hoping we would find some sort of sign we were going the right way. We had been walking for a couple of hours, and it didn't seem like the tunnel was getting any smaller.

Frustratingly we came upon a fork in the proverbial road. It continued on in the direction we were going, and the other one veered off to the left. It was the same size as the original, but this tunnel seemed new somehow, the metal barely touched by dust and debris. The paint while not fresh, wasn't old either.

"I've got a hunch." I thought out loud.

"Out with it buzz."

"Right. This tunnel definitely goes to wherever in the Undercities people were originally loaded off from. Which would make this tunnel." I pointed towards the one that went left. "Most likely in the direction of Dome City."

"Makes sense," Reya confirmed. "They either built it recently or completely refurbished it."

"I'm banking on refurbished." I looked in the direction we had come from and pointed. "That monster of a door was missing, and it had a decent amount of tech in it. Knowing the CORPS the way I do, they reused it."

"Y'know, it's almost sad." Vern started. "For all the bullshit the Coalition pulls, they seem to have quite a few right ideas."

"Anything is a weapon in the right hands, buzz."

"Arc ain't kidding, bro," Riley replied. "But we aren't exactly making progress right now guys, let's get it going." I gave Riley a nod and knew why I liked the brothers and Reya as much as I did. They had their eyes on the prize. It also put me at ease to have others from the Undercities with us, which at the same time made me feel pity for Arc. There were times it seemed like he was simultaneously alone in the universe and just another guy. Honestly, I think he liked the personal solitude.

We began to walk down the near-pristine tunnel. It was hard to describe how immense and powerful the seemingly simple structure was. We were like ants scurrying down a sewer pipe. The walk was incredibly long. To be sure, Dome City was only a day away from where we had entered the tunnels, if you had a vehicle and didn't stop for anything. On foot, even if we ran, we were in for a long hike.

Spirits stayed surprisingly high, especially Arc, who always had a joke or two around the corner. Us cave dwellers suddenly felt at home. Sure, the surface was beautiful, and I had plans to die up there, but being back home and possibly seeing people who knew me as a normal man, filled me with delusions of hope. The reality was, the odds were not in our favor, and even if we did succeed, it would not be pretty by any means. The CORPS would see to that.

The first day of walking went by much faster than I thought. My entire adventure felt like some sort of personal field test of everything I could do, and I was still learning about my capabilities. While our awareness was heightened, our perception of it was only present when it was needed, which felt like natural instincts with technological enhancements. Even animals become more aware when threatened, but it would seem our ability to be

367

patient was somehow increased as well. Time passed, and we were aware of it, but we didn't care, which made it go seemingly faster.

We did not rest, and we did not falter, continuing down the kilometers long tunnel at an even pace. We ate rations and drank water on the move, but only rarely. We ate heartily before our adventure, and that energy would last us quite a while.

"Can I address the elephant in the room now?" Reya began to speak, looking forward, her thumbs nestled under both straps of her pack on either side. Somehow, I knew who she was addressing.

"I got a feeling this won't be pleasant."

"Probably not, but Johnny, it has to be asked. What's with Alonna?"

"Yep, knew it. She's a nutjob CORPS scientist, what about her?"

"Is she, though?" She tilted her head a little but didn't actually look at me. I glanced at her a moment and shook my head.

"This is why Arc's the favorite. Just come out with it, please." I was never a fan of beating around the bush.

"Well." She seemed to think about it for a long moment before nodding to herself and finally looking over to me. "All the handlers were likely conditioned to have feelings for us, right?"

"Old news," Arc interjected.

"Well, it just seems, I don't know, different with Dr. Lyrul. Every once in a while, I would be seen by other handlers for one reason or the other, and they generally treated me like a precious object like all the others."

"Okay, what's the point?"

"Well, Dr. Lyrul was, shall I say, less than cordial with me. She was almost cold, like she wasn't fond of my existence at all."

368

"She gives me the same fuckin' vibes," Arc replied, seeming to be enjoying my interrogation.

"You know now that I think about it, she was nothing more than professional with my brother and me too, though we met her before you even woke up." My face scrunched with curiosity and I stopped, turning to Riley. We had been walking for over a day; no one objected to resting for a moment.

"You knew the doc?"

"Yeah," Riley answered. "She was something else to deal with when compared to the other handlers. She felt like she didn't even want to be there most of the time, but with you-"

"With you, she looks like she's ready to jump your bones every instant." Vern finished his brother's sentence who nodded in agreement.

"Hey! It's not my fault I'm sexier than you." I smirked, but Reya clicked her tongue, rolled her eyes, and crossed her arms over her chest.

"Nice. It's more than that, and you know it." She gave me a stern expression.

"Look!" I tossed my hands up in exasperation "I don't know what you want me to tell you. I have done everything in my power to make that bitch hate me, and she still won't leave me alone."

"Have you though?" Arc, who usually had my back, was on their side.

"And what does that mean?"

"Give me a break buzz, you care about her. She's kept you and your dream of bending the CORPS over alive. She helped you escape, saved your life on at least one occasion I'm aware of. It's not like it's a big fuckin' deal you like her."

"Is this necessary?"

"Yes, it's necessary buzz, I still don't trust her. She's been fuckin' with your head, and I can tell. You don't have to sleep in the same quarters as her, but you do. You don't have to be her babysitter, but you are."

"The TLF feels more comfortable that way," I said it, but it sounded like a weak argument to my own ears.

"Yeah, okay buzz, whatever you say. I think you're more worried that someone else would mistreat her."

"So what? I give a fuck, alright?" I started walking again, and everyone followed suit. "What else am I supposed to do? I might be more machine than man these days, but I'm still a man."

"Look, buzz." Arc put his hand on my shoulder as we walked. "I ain't judging you one little bit. We just need to know you realize it too. Hey, if she does end up being trustworthy, fuck, she's hot, smart, and gives a shit about you."

"Always the silver lining with you." I couldn't help but smile at his attitude and somewhat at the thought. Then I shook the idea out of my head as quickly as it came. "I must be getting desperate."

"This wasn't my point, though." Reya once again offered her wisdom. "Think about it, if it were her conditioning causing how she feels about you, wouldn't she act like all the other handlers?" That thought struck me as somehow relevant, but I couldn't explain it either.

"You're saying she's actually in love with me on her own?"

"No woman looks at a man like that unless she cares, but it's toxic Johnny. How's she been the last week?" That's when I had to think about it for a long moment.

"Cold, but somehow, a forced kinda cold. She cares, but it's almost like she doesn't want to."

"Like she's finished something," Arc muttered under his breath.

"You say something?" I asked.

"Nothing buzz, just more conjecture, which ain't very helpful."

"Fair enough." After the conversation, we were all quiet for hours after. The further we got, the closer to home the feeling of dread became. We could've been walking to our execution, or worse, we find out we've been helping the CORPS all along. Nothing seemed capable of suppressing the paranoid thoughts. The CORPS was real good at making a man question himself.

After another day and a half of travel, we finally came across a familiar-looking kind of turn in the tunnel. It was the same shape as the entrance to the surface lobby. We had to be getting close. When we rounded the bend, we all could hear unsettling noises. Vern put up his fist to signal a stop and pointed at the right side of the tunnel, revealing an open hatchway which had been torn asunder. The claw marks were unmistakable.

"Stalkers," I said quietly. Riley, Vern, and Reya nodded in agreement. Arc looked between us with confusion.

"Okay, what the fuck are stalkers?" We all looked at him with our own confusion. "What? The monsters were your neighbors where I came from. No boogeymen and shit. I've only read about mutaphorms."

I began to explain. "Big-ass, hairy, hulking monsters, complete with metal rending murder mitts, teeth that will bite you in half, and oh, hey, did I mention that they communicate in ways people can't fully perceive?"

"You left out the infrared vision," Reya mentioned.

"And the likely sapient level of intelligence," Riley added.

"Okay, okay, I get the po- wait, what's that sound?" Arc stopped, and I listened close, hearing it too. It was the chittering sound I remembered hearing, but there were other pitches to it, extremely high, though difficult to make out. We all looked to each other, and almost simultaneously, our CIHUDs came out. Rifles were at the ready, and we quietly began to advance. The sound got louder as we completed the bend. Our CIHUDs had picked it up first, though any normal ears would have caught what came next.

First, we saw movement on our CIHUDs, moving just outside the tunnel. I could see that there were other similarly wrecked maintenance hatches. Quickly, five of the creatures poured out of one of the hatches. The next thing we heard was gunfire echoing through the tunnel. We began to run towards the sound.

When we came within visual range, we could see what looked to be an outpost built into the tunnel. Behind it was the massive door I remembered from my first trip through the Undercities. There were a dozen CORPS Elite troopers standing behind concrete barriers, who were most certainly going to win the fight against the five mutaphorms barreling towards them. It was stalkers, alright.

"We help the monsters," I said simply and took aim with my rifle. Everyone understood my logic that the ones with the guns and training were the more dangerous foes. We began to fire our accurate rounds, finding even small slits in the cover the troopers were using. It took mere seconds to cut down the soldiers, and as soon as the creatures, three left, turned their attention to us, it was already too late for them. I let my rifle hang by its strap and pulled my sidearm, stretching my arm out straight. With three quick shots, the beasts hit the ground, each with a smoking hole between their eyes. I twirled my gun

372

and holstered it.

"Get positions, no way they don't know we're here now. Disable one, leave 'em alive." Following my plan, we all dashed towards the massive door at the end of the tunnel, two on one side, and three on the other. First, there was an electronic whine while the security system did its thing. Then, as predicted, the smaller part of the door opened, allowing five Elites to rush out. They came out guns blazing, but their reaction time was nothing compared to ours, and we cut four of them down almost as soon as they came out.

The door immediately slammed shut, nearly catching the fifth one inside of it, and to be honest, he likely wished it had. Arc and I fired on the last guy, ripping his arms to shreds and sending him uselessly to the ground. I casually moved to the writhing form and forced him to his feet. Like most CORPS Elites, he was silent, waiting for whatever it was we were about to do to him. I placed him in front of the door, holding him there as the security device I remembered from my escape stuck out and bathed him in blue light. As it did, the door began to open, and we pushed right through it.

There are times in one's life when a snap decision must be made. Running by the seat of their pants, people eventually make a misstep. This was one of those times. We had no idea what to expect on the other side of the door. Whatever thoughts we might have had sure as shit wasn't what we got.

Upon entering, we found ourselves staring at an immense garage, sporting at least one hundred different military vehicles. Tanks, jeeps, personnel trucks, you name it, we were looking at it. The place was tall enough to encompass three levels of catwalks, which were likely used for maintenance. At that moment, they were being used as firing positions.

"Oh, fuck." My voice was somehow calm, and we all looked at each other before scrambling to run in different directions. We were dodging bullets like raindrops, the entire garage becoming inundated by the explosions of gun barrels, and the call outs of CORPS Elites. While it looked like the place was always full of soldiers, it seemed like more piled in when the stalkers dropped outside. It suggested huge numbers because there were scores of them at the ready, firing at us.

"This wasn't part of the plan!" I heard Riley yell out.

"What fuckin' plan?" Arc asked rhetorically. We had all managed to find some cover on either side of the garage. While we could undoubtedly dodge gunfire, none of us were going to take their chances with the torrential downpour of metal.

"I don't sense any cyborgs here!" Reya called out.

"They weren't expecting us then," I concluded, and it was true, our entire presence there was based entirely on a guess, a guess with a lot of evidence, but it was a shot in the dark. "Let's use the advantage, Reya, Vern, fire on the right, Arc and I got the left, Riley run that middle ragged!" I got nods of approval, and we stood, planning our firing lines, crossing our trajectories, and making it difficult for the soldiers to gain an advantage over us.

We were popping Elites left and right, but they seemed to be coming from an endless source of bodies. Every five we took out, six took their place. We moved from cover to cover, trying to find a reliable exit when I realized something strange coming from the very end of the garage. There was sunlight peeking through an opening at the end of a long ramp.

"Is that daylight?" I called out.

"Looks like it!" Arc replied.

"New plan!" I waited for a moment for the deluge of lead to stop so I could make my way to the side of one of the transport vehicles. I ripped the door open and climbed into the driver's seat. Acting as fast as I could, I reached into my pack and pulled the CIHUD cable from it, hooking myself into the truck's onboard computer while keeping my head low. In a matter of seconds, the engine roared to life.

Arc was providing cover fire from the outside, picking off the Elites that noticed my move and keeping them from wrecking the vehicle before we could even get to it. While every shot we made was clean and accurate, our ammo wasn't infinite; we had to do something fast.

"Come on!" Arc yelled out as I commanded the back hatch to open up. Quickly, my companions ran to the truck and managed to make their way into it. For the moment, our enemies were only firing small arms and couldn't penetrate the armored hull of the transport truck. It would only be a matter of time before they wised up. We weren't waiting for that to happen.

I heard the knocking on the back wall, indicating that everyone had made it inside safely. Slamming the accelerator, I drove the transport towards the ramp, just in time as the onboard computer's sensors detected anti-vehicle weaponry being brought to bear. I activated a flare system, causing small rockets to launch in every direction from the truck, attracting an oncoming, guided RPG. Undeterred, the truck barreled up the ramp, leaving the others in our dust.

Nearing the top of the ramp, my eyes gazed upon a sight I couldn't adequately explain. We were outside for all intents and purposes, but we had definitely made it to Dome City. The inside of the dome's wall seemed to stretch an impossible distance into the air. It included a simulation of the sky,

375

with a sun facsimile shining brightly overhead.

"Johnny!" I heard Reya's voice come over the vehicle's intercom. "We gotta lose our tails!"

"No, shit! This place is fucking teeming!" We were in a base of some sort, built like a small town. It was marked with barracks buildings, storage facilities, and the roads were anything but empty. I still saw no signs of civilians from where we were, but there were plenty of jeeps roaming around and what looked to be trucks for hauling goods from one site to another. The buildings were all generally the same off-white color, and from here, it looked like everything was military or production based.

"If we can lose them, I know how to get into the city itself," Reya called out over the intercom.

"Sounds easier than it is!" We had more than just a few tails from what I could tell. Vehicles were making their way out of the garage we came through, though I was surprised that they stuck with small arms. It seems they were more willing to use explosives inside than out. I used it to our advantage. I took the truck through different streets and roads, circling around and trying desperately to get away from our pursuers.

"You've got harnesses, right?" I asked, seeing a narrow alley between two large white buildings. It wouldn't be big enough to fit our truck, which is what I was hoping for.

"Yeah, what the fuck you plannin' buzz?"

"Bail from the truck!" There was no argument because there was no time for one. I concentrated on the information being provided to me by my CIHUD, getting as much physical data about the truck and its surroundings as I could before disconnecting. I cut the wheel hard to the side and sent it into a controlled roll. I leaped from the driver's seat, rolling when I hit the ground, though the kinetic harness made it a mostly soft landing.

My allies had had the same luck, successfully bailing. We wasted no time picking ourselves up and dashing towards the wrecked truck, which had landed on its side, blocking the entrance to the alley. We all jumped over the transport and took cover behind it. Right behind us, we could hear the many jeeps and transports coming to a stop, soldiers spilling out and preparing to pursue.

"Won't be long before they get through," I commented, and no one was ready to argue. Looking at our surroundings, I could see a door off to the side on the other end of the alley. It led to the building on the right, which was much larger than the one on the left.

"Through the door!" I heard Vern yell as he ran over to it and pried it open. Though locked, it didn't stand a chance against one of us. Of course, a broken door can't be shut, so we knew we weren't home free yet. As soon as we passed through the doorway, we began to look around for ways to barricade it off and found one. We were in a warehouse storage facility and by the sounds of things, also an automated factory of some kind. In the distance, there were likely dozens of machines running, doing whatever it was the CORPS needed of them. We spotted a three-meter high metal container that actually took all of us to be able to move to the door in time. It was big enough and certainly heavy enough to block anything trying to get in.

"Geeze, this was not a good idea!" Riley exclaimed.

"Never is," I replied while surveying my surroundings. There was no one inside, and it seemed like a lot of the machines could run indefinitely without much inspection. The only machines we could see from where we entered were automated lifts, organizing the large containers which were strewn about the place in ordered lines. The lifts themselves traveled on a ceiling-mounted rail system.

"Uh, guys?" Arc decided to get curious and had managed to get on top of the container we used as a barrier. I moved over and jumped up, holding onto the edge to get a look. It was full of ammo, separated by weapon type; bullets galore.

"Holy fuck, that's a lot of ordinance." I whistled in astonishment. "You could do a lot of shit with this sort of firepower."

"Like murder a continent," Reya commented to herself, having climbed up to see the contents.

"Look, I appreciate the insight," Vern started, "but we really can't stay here. They're probably piling into the back by now or worse, sending cyborgs soldiers our way." Vern spoke worriedly as I hopped down from my spot.

"Keep your shirt on, we'll be fine." Arc hopped down and gave Vern a pat on the back.

"I think I know of a way out of here." Reya suddenly spoke, and none of us were prepared to argue.

"Lead on then." I motioned with my hand for her to take point, and she began guiding us through the warehouse. The warehouse led to a factory floor where dozens of automated machines performed all of the processes necessary for bullet production. We were moving quietly and rightfully so because off in the distance, we could see a squad of CORPS troopers storming into the building. They were likely coming in from the factory's front door. We could also hear banging at the entrance we had barricaded, indicating that we had very little time to act.

378

"Where exactly are we going?" I was curious as to what Reya's plan was.

"To the wastewater facility. All of these factories have one."

"Sewers? Really?" Arc was surprisingly the one to start complaining.

"Yeah, it's how I found the military section of the dome." We were moving through the facility, cutting the chatter to prevent them from finding our location. The factory was loud and covered up a lot of the sounds we made. Reya led us through the building, eventually finding stairs to the lower levels while successfully escaping the sight of our enemies. They were beginning to turn the factory upside down, looking for us, but even motion sensors would be hard to make use of in an automated factory.

The stairs led down to a basement hallway, containing five doors. Two doors on the left, two doors on the right, and a final middle one, which was colored red, unlike the other gunmetal hues.

"That's it." Reya pointed to the red door. The door was heftier than the others, sporting a very solid structure, and some sort of security system that kept it closed. There was no real place to get a grip to try and pry it open. It seemed to open by sliding down, and judging by the seam, the door actually went slightly further down than the floor itself. Reya, however, did not waste time, knowing exactly what to do. She pulled out a wall panel that was just to the side of the door itself, revealing the computer electronics that controlled the door's security systems and what looked to be an emergency lever. Reya grabbed the lever and pulled it down, letting it slide up again and pulling it down once more. Slowly, the door slid open with each pull.

"Let's go." She replaced the wall panel before we moved into the door. Paying attention to my CIHUD, I could tell our pursuers were getting closer to our location. They had found the stairs and were beginning to slowly descend. They were trying to be stealthy as if they really had a choice in the matter. On the other side, Reya found a similar panel and hit a release button that caused the door to shut. Before us was a dark and dank underground tunnel. It was warm, humid, and definitely had a stink about the place.

"Great, we narrowly escaped death, and now we get to slog through some fuckin' floaters." Arc almost seemed like a kid who just had their toy taken away.

"Buck up, buckaroo, we survived." I gave him a pat on the back, but he seemed unconvinced we were in the clear.

"Well, now all we have to do is navigate our way to an exit into the city proper." Reya began to walk down the tunnel, which ended pretty quickly into an enormous chamber. The roar of running water was all around us as we stood on the edge of what was essentially a balcony overlooking a massive network of pipes and water treatment systems. It looked like it went more than twenty meters below, but the ceiling was a mere five above us.

"How the hell did you end up finding that section again? I'm dying to know how you did it without a CIHUD." I was looking to Reya, honestly astonished at everything I was seeing. There was no way the CORPS started building this recently. This was obviously a long time coming.

"Well, to be honest with you, I worked down here."

"Really?" Vern seemed surprised by this.

"Yeah, I was a municipal engineer. I spent a lot of time exploring when we first arrived in the Habitat."

"Then you found a big red door you just had to open, right buzz?" Arc asked.

"Well." She seemed somewhat embarrassed by the story. "Yeah, basically. Curiosity killed the cat."

"Or turned it into a cyborg." I joked, still taking a moment to marvel at the place we had found ourselves in. "I wonder where it's all going." I thought out loud.

"Well, some of the wastewater will be recycled, but anything that can't be will get dumped underground," Reya spoke factually, and then Vern pointed down the cistern.

"Hey, is that what I think it is?" We all looked down to see a stalker corpse that looked a day or two old, riddled with holes. It rested on a balcony similar to the one we stood on. We all took a moment to look at each other.

"There's gotta be other ways in here," Riley spoke absently. We all silently agreed, taking a moment to ponder the possibilities before I finally interrupted.

"So, where to now Ms. Sewers?" I asked.

"Yeah, that's not sticking."

"It might," Arc gave his smirk.

"Alright, alright, seriously, where to?" Riley inquired as well.

"There should be a maintenance shed somewhere nearby that leads to the surface." Reya finally answered.

"It doesn't look like anyone has followed us," Vern remarked.

"They may have not thought to check down here yet, but we really should be moving." Reya was still taking point. I was still in a bit of shock that the dome existed at all. I wasn't sure what structure was more implausible, the giant, nigh-impenetrable dome with a city in it or the giant, nigh-impenetrable underground city.

Reya led us to a catwalk which she indicated would lead to a maintenance shed and then the surface of Dome City. I couldn't help but laugh at the fact that I kept finding myself escaping to one surface area or another. We came upon a considerable gap between us and the catwalk leading to the shed Reya had mentioned. We were all able to make the leap, clearing an easy twenty meters and landing one-by-one safely.

"This way." Reya had confidence in her voice, and thus we followed. We walked across the catwalk, getting a moment to marvel at the technological might of the CORPS. It was a sad state of affairs that such power wasn't used for the greater good, but rather some twisted idea of scientific advancement.

Finally, we came to a standard metal door that slid open as we approached. The maintenance shed itself wasn't much to look at, containing basic computer systems for regulating the machines in the sewers as well as some workbenches and lockers. When we walked through, four men were standing around in a circle, cups in their hands, all wearing blue worker's jumpsuits. Their conversation stopped when they saw us. They stared in silent confusion, and it was then I realized our CIHUDs were still out. I allowed mine to retract.

"Heya fellas," I started with a peaceful tone. "Just giving the old machines an inspection. Don't mind the piercings, all the rage with the kids these days." One dude literally dropped his cup, and another, with purpose, walked to one of the wall terminals. What must have seemed like a flash, Reya moved over to the computer and grabbed the hand of the worker before he could do whatever it was he was about to do.

"That won't be necessary." The move caused the other three to back up into the wall. It was then I remembered their expressions had more to do with our heavily armed state than some bit of metal protruding from our foreheads.

"Look, fellas, sometimes those mutaphorm fucks get out. We're just here to keep you safe, buzz." Arc gave the men a wink, and they seemed unconvinced.

"A-a-are you gonna kill us?" One of the men standing with their back against the wall asked. He seemed young, maybe in his twenties at best. "I have kids, a family, please, I'm n-" He was interrupted by Arc's laugh.

"Buzz, if we wanted you dead, you wouldn't have even known we were here." I gave Arc a look of disapproval. These were the people we needed to get on our side.

"Reya?" One of the other men spoke her name, bravely stepping forward to get a better look. She studied the man and let her own CIHUD retract, which seemed to be enough to allow the man to identify her. "It is you! But you died."

"Died?" Reya let the other man's hand go, who slowly moved to rejoin his friends. "What do you mean?"

"You know this woman?" The one who had moved to the computer spoke up. He was a portly old fellow that clearly had an air of authority about him. He was likely the superintendent.

"Yeah, surprised you don't. Remember the engineer they found dead in the sewers?"

"The one that fell?"

"Yeah, that one."

"Wow, those Coalition assholes don't know when to quit, do they?" Reya usually spoke somewhat professionally, like a person of higher class, but

383

clearly, she was annoyed.

"W-what do you mean?" The begging daddy was getting a little braver.

"I never died; the Coalition apprehended me."

"More like kidnapped," I muttered.

"Fine, kidnapped me."

"But I saw the body." The worker insisted.

"You obviously saw a body buzz, not her body." Arc offered some insight.

"Look, we don't have a lot of time for this, we have to lose the troopers." Riley was ever the voice of reason, keeping us focused.

"No, we'll be fine here, I think." Reya offered more wisdom. "I don't think the Coalition would risk exposing their base."

"Base? There's no Coalition base down there." The super sounded incredulous.

"How do you explain us then?" Vern moved his hands down his form, indicating our heavily armed state and then pointed to his CIHUD, which was still out. They seemed to accept this, but for a reason I couldn't put my finger on.

"Look, we ain't winning hearts and minds this way." I dropped my pack and rummaged through it, finding my PCD. I flipped through a few screens before finding some pictures I had taken in my spare time of the outside world. I handed the device over. "This is where we came from." The PCD was displaying an image of Libsal from the perspective of a treetop.

"What is this?" The older man seemed taken aback. They all gathered and looked at the images, beginning to flip through them. Various pictures existed, pictures of the soldiers we traveled with enjoying some R&R, others of desert landscapes and signs of civilizations once thought lost. "These have to be fake!"

"Are we fake?" I asked.

"You look normal to me." The super was the one fighting us, but the younger men were staring at the photos with wonder.

"Oh yeah?" Arc spoke up and walked to one of the workbenches. There he found a clamp that was bolted to the table and, with his bare hand, ripped it right off with minimal effort. He then grabbed the clamp by either side and bent pieces that would be impossible for an ordinary person to bend. One of the younger workers almost dropped my PCD in astonishment.

"Why are you here? What do you want from us?" The superintendent asked. His tone almost felt like he was asking a CORPS representative as opposed to random strangers. I decided it was my turn to take over again and answered the question.

"To stand up to the CORPS. People live outside the Dome, and if the CORPS have their way, those people will all be put up against a wall and shot. They lied to us, they lied to everyone. What we want from you is to tell people what you saw and heard today. They won't believe you at first, but trust me, it won't be long before we prove it to everyone."

"What if we run to the authorities, tell them we found you?" The super asked, somewhat puffing up his chest.

"They already know we're here. You do what you think is best. C'mon guys, it's time we skedaddle." I picked up my bag and retrieved my PCD, putting it away. I gave the men a polite nod, and we all pushed passed them. I wasn't sure if we had any impact with those people, in fact, I highly doubted it, but it wasn't a bad idea to get a little practice in.

Part Three: Home Again

Chapter Twenty-Eight: Dystopia Realized

The maintenance shed opened up into the city itself, and had I been a normal man, I may have collapsed from awe. We stood on a busy street that looked like it was part of some sort of maintenance district. There were all sorts of different buildings, and unlike the sterile look of the CORPS base, the civilian area was very colorful. It felt even less sterile than the Undercities ever had. There were quite literally hundreds of people moving throughout the streets, driving in various electric vehicles, walking, talking, working, and just trying to get by. In the distance, we could see towering high-rises reaching to nearly the ceiling of the dome itself. The city was oppressively large, and it looked like we would spend days just getting the lay of the land.

One thing I couldn't help feeling was that I had finally come home. While the Undercities had no real way to simulate day and night in the way the dome seemed to, the people all looked the same. Talking, playing, working, fighting, and just in general, living. Styles hadn't changed much in the five years I had been gone, and I realized right away there was more of a law enforcement presence than the Undercities ever had. Likely, it was harder to keep order in what was, quite frankly, a bigger place. There was room to grow, and I could imagine there being somewhat empty districts popping the landscape of the dome's interior.

We had decided to ditch the rifles in a nearby alley and conceal our sidearms within our bags. We wouldn't need them. We were walking weapons in comparison to most of the people there. People didn't seem to pay much attention to our presence. We appeared to be mostly ordinary folks, allowing us to blend in well. Coupled with the fact that we couldn't be differentiated as cyborgs, we were very well camouflaged indeed.

"So, um, what the hell do we do now?" It definitely seemed like Riley wasn't used to flying by the seat of his pants. It was understandable, many who grew up underground often craved order.

"Well, I suppose we need to find some friends, like-minded folks. We also need to secure a base of operations, somewhere we can meet up, rest, and chill when things aren't so busy." We began to walk the streets, exploring the city proper, and trying to get our bearings. While Reya had lived there and possessed a photographic memory, even she had only seen a fraction of the city itself.

People seemed to be moving about almost obliviously. Once upon a time, I would think nothing of it, but now they looked like sheep to me, a flock that was successfully herded into the safety of the CORPS's embrace. Simultaneously the people also felt like children to me; children living in an abusive home. It wasn't long before my feeling was confirmed.

"Work allows us to function." A man suddenly appeared on screens all over the place. It became apparent that many buildings and walls sported displays for blatant propaganda. The man himself, to my eyes, seemed like the biggest snake imaginable. His hair was smoothed back, his piercing blue eyes seeming to stare into one's soul and pull back the truth. He appeared a little older than me, and his clothes were neat, pressed, and professional. Flanking him on either side was a male and female XRC soldier, their visible CIHUDs were unmistakable.

"The Arbiter," Reya declared, looking up at one of the screens. "When did they start doing this?"

"Probably around the time, they started hiring cyborgs for security." I commented on the Arbiter's entourage.

"Work allows us to band together as a community, and it will be work that allows us to retake the surface. Our ten-year plan was set into motion when we entered this place and sooner than later will come to fruition. We will find a way to restore the world to bring it back to its former glory. We must work towards this goal." Oddly enough, people moved about, as if oblivious to the PSA. They all acted quite dismissively to the overt fascism before them. Then we heard the magical phrase that would lead them astray.

"Go fuck yourself!" The male teenager who said it fruitlessly tried to spit at a nearby screen, and the sight made me grin. He wasn't very large, skinny with an average height and build. His hair was spiked up, and he wore all black clothes. Chains loosely hung from his pants and shirt; everything was baggy and big, and he seemed interested in projecting his teenaged angst in any way possible.

"I bet this place is full of kids like that." I mused to myself. I couldn't lie, it was kind of amusing to watch. Right up until the point when uniformed men made their way to the youth. They weren't CORPS troopers, at least not all of them. Like some sort of overseer, an Elite stood off to the side while three normal-looking men in blue uniforms, packing heat and various law enforcement devices, approached the kid. None of us were talking, instead, moving well out of the way of foot and vehicle traffic to eavesdrop on the situation.

"What? I know my rights!" The kid protested.

"Yes sir, you do have rights, and so do the people on this street. They have the right to a normal day-to-day routine that doesn't involve someone yelling obscenities." The shorter of the three and obviously in charge, or so he likely thought, was doing the talking.

"I wasn't yelling!" The kid ironically yelled out.

"Brat's gonna get arrested." Arc said, giving a "tsk-tsk" sound afterward.

"Maybe we can prevent that." I had a grin on my face, a plan formulating in my mind.

"What? You can't be serious." Reya looked incredulous, and I just shined my grin her way.

"Reya, you're gonna learn real quick that I don't say anything I'm not serious about. Look, we're wanted, as soon as any troopers or CORPS lackies get a chance to get us alone, they're gonna pounce. So, what's making a little disturbance gonna hurt?" I raised my brow with the final question, and begrudgingly, Reya shook her head and agreed.

"Alright, fearless leader, what's the plan then?"

"Make a scene. We need to start weavin' a legend."

"Oh dude, I'm so fuckin' down. I just remembered why you're my favorite, buzz." Arc gave a friendly punch to my shoulder. I shined my grin his way, and we both looked to the scene, which was escalating.

"I'm not going anywhere with you sheep! Don't you see what's going on since we came up here?" The kid was becoming frantic, and the two silent officers were struggling to restrain him non-violently.

"Reya, you and the brothers secure an escape for us, somewhere we can get someone slower than us through." Reya gave me a nod.

"I'll carry his ass if I have to," Arc said matter of fact-like.

"You got it." Reya started. "Try not to do anything stupid."

"Sorry, kid, that's kinda my schtick." I gave her a wink, and Arc, and I began to march towards the civil disturbance. "Non-lethal Arc, we can't be seen as monsters."

"I'm good at lying, buzz." He gave his signature smirk. People had gathered around the scene, which under normal circumstances would have ended with the CORPS restoring order to their happy little lives. We were the unknown element of chaos about to disrupt their world.

Arc was smart and began marching right towards the CORPS trooper who, as expected, recognized the threat. We were wanted men after-all. The Elite was fast, his enhanced reflexes allowing him to draw his weapon and even fire off a round before Arc could close the distance completely. Arc was quicker, and we were lucky no one got hit in the cross-fire. Once close enough, Arc grabbed hold of the gun barrel and wrenched it violently out of the Elite's hands. Within the same moment, Arc's other hand stretched out, grabbing the trooper by the throat as he stumbled forward. Well trained and powerful, the Elite didn't grasp at the hands around his throat like a normal victim would, instead, reaching for a knife to gut Arc with. Unfortunately for him, cyborgs were far faster, and he found his arm caught by Arc's powerful grip, which was easily snapped like a brittle twig.

This moment immediately fueled the reactions of the crowd. People began to scatter from the gunfire, but not all could pry themselves away from the spectacle. As I approached the three ordinary officers, they had zero time to react. The leader went for his sidearm, but before he could even take aim, I grabbed his arm, squeezing just hard enough to make him release the weapon, which I quickly took with my other hand. Releasing the guard, I disassembled the sidearm and tossed the pieces to the ground. To me, this took a few moments, but to the crowd, my motions were a blur.

"I wouldn't," I said, looking to the two other officers who were reaching for weapons. "Since when do the people not have the right to free speech? How far have we fallen?" The men before us had no idea what to think. In mere seconds they went from authority figures to powerless.

"Holy shit!" The kid we were rescuing had fallen on his ass when the first shots fired and had finally picked himself up. "Who the hell are you?"

"Can it, kid!" Arc called out, still holding the CORPS trooper by his throat.

"Walk away now before this gets worse." One of the officers on the left demanded. He reached for his ear, obviously containing a communication device. Ever ready, I advanced before his arm could make half the journey, grasping it enough to cause pain, but not actually break his arm. The new enhancements Alonna gave us had made our reflexes near god-like.

"Ah! My arm!" He cried out in pain, and I looked to the others before releasing him.

"Walk away now, and you don't get hurt."

"Who the hell are you?" The leader of the trio asked.

"The name's John. You'll be seeing a lot of me soon enough, neighbor." I gave him a wink, but our troubles were just beginning. As expected, someone had alerted more authorities, who were likely nearby to begin with. They rounded the corner of a nearby block and were screaming for everyone to get back, which just about everyone dutifully did. Six more normal officers and two Elites were training weapons on us, waiting for the crowd to disperse and Arc's hostage to be released.

"John, fifteen meters south of you, there's a door, enter it." I heard Reya's voice enter my ear, using the basic comm system we brought with us from the TLF. We had maintained radio silence up until then, but something tickled me about the idea that the CORPS was about to pick up a TLF signal within their precious Habitat.

"We're outta here, Arc. C'mere kid." I held my arm out to the youth who took my hand, and I pulled him towards me, slinging him over my shoulder. He didn't seem too impressed by this, but I wasn't about to let him get arrested over our antics. Arc, like a rag doll, one-arm threw the CORPS trooper towards the group that were aiming weapons at us. Bystanders gasped and looks of shock formed on the faces of civilian and law-enforcement officers alike. We were making it clear we were not average people, accentuated by our CIHUDS as they extracted from our foreheads.

"Lead the way, buzz!" We began to run, and as soon as we were out of range of civilians, they began to fire on us. Apparently, they didn't care about the kid, but luckily for him, we had the habit of not getting hit by bullets.

"What the fuck?" The kid cried out in both exhilaration and horror. The door that Reya spoke of was easy to find, leading to an apartment complex. It was labyrinthine with its many apartments on each floor, the complex seeming to stretch up for at least ten stories of hallways. Reya and the brothers were waiting, and we all ran up the stair-well she had found, racing to the top of the building.

"Going up is your escape plan?" My voice sounded exasperated.

"I'm willing to bet we're the only ones on the block who can leap across streets from rooftop-to-rooftop!" Vern answered, and I had to admit he had a solid point.

"Jump across streets?" Our new friend definitely didn't like the idea.

"I can leave you here, and they can arrest you." I made the most valid argument I could think of.

"Please make the fucking jump!" He got the picture. It was nothing for us to pound-feet up the steps, making our way to the top before our pursuers could get a quarter of the same distance. "Dude, I'm gonna be sick." The kid protested.

"You puke on my back, and I will punch you." We continued to scramble, Reya smashing through the roof door, nearly taking it right off the hinges.

"This way!" She called out, and we all followed. She indicated the edge of one of the rooftops, which was slightly higher than ours and across the street.

"Are you insane?" My slightly willing passenger screamed out.

"Probably." My comment did not seem to reassure him. There was no pause, no moment to catch our breath, or get a running start; we were already running anyway. We all leaped, using the ton of force our legs could produce to launch ourselves high into the air. We landed on the middle of the roof across the street.

The people below were not expecting this turn of events. While some troopers attempted to fire up towards us, most didn't want to risk the collateral damage that could cause. We were now running from rooftop-to-rooftop, leaping and even crisscrossing from street-to-street, easily leaving the rag-tag posse in the dust. When we had traveled a solid kilometer deeper into the city, we found a high-rise to let our friend rest. He had indeed vomited, but only after I set him down.

"Oh fuck, oh my god. What the hell just happened?"

"We prevented you from being arrested for speaking your mind," I spoke with the grace of being right.

"Gee thanks, what the fuck do I do now?"

"Repay the favor," Arc said. We were all kind of standing around the kid who looked incredibly overwhelmed.

"How the hell do I repay people who can leap fucking streets and buildings? Break CORPS soldier arms and disarm weapons in the blink of an eye? Wait, what the hell is sticking out of your forehead? It's like those guys on the recordings!" He was starting to panic and was obviously experiencing shock. Vern was the more compassionate one of the group and knelt in front of our new charge.

"Let's take this one step at a time. What's your name?" His eyes were frantic, but Vern's voice was calm and patient.

"I uh- I'm- my name is- I mean, it's Terry." He was stammering.

"Alright, Terry. I'm Vern, this here is my brother Riley, the lady over there, is Reya, that one there is Arc, and the one who carried you out is John. Now, we all know each other."

"Why did you help me?" He was starting to calm down.

"We're here to shake things up, kid," I spoke up again. "We agree with you; that crap on the big-ass screen was shit."

"Y-yeah! Yeah, it is." He nodded in approval of his own words.

"We're here to tell people the truth, Terry." Vern began again, keeping his tone level and understanding. "You see, the Coalition's been lying about what's out beyond the dome, and we think they plan to hurt all the people living outside of it."

"People are living outside the dome?" He had a look of shock on his face, yet at the same time, it seemed as if he was expecting that sort of

395

bombshell.

"Guys, we ain't got time for Reality one-oh-one." Arc's voice sounded off a warning. "We've got company." My own CIHUD began to throw off warnings about two XRC sensor suites nearby. With a loud thud, two augmented soldiers landed on the rooftops along with us. They carried batons in their hands and pistols at their hips. They both had shaved heads, which seemed odd to me. Usually, that was a sign of a newbie, one fresh from waking up, though they didn't look fresh. Perhaps it was just a style the brothers. One was dark-skinned, the other a little lighter, and the lighter-skinned one looked like a wall of a man, having more muscle than not.

"We've found the renegades." One spoke seemingly to no one, likely communicating with outside individuals.

"Reya, you and the brothers get the kid out of here. Arc and I will handle these clowns."

"Strength in numbers, bro!" Riley protested.

"Which is why you need to go with the kid. Go now!" I hated giving people I felt like were equals orders, but logic was the authority figure in this situation. Arc and I turned to our foes and began marching towards them.

"Cross the bastards?" Arc asked, and I nodded in agreement. We walked only within a few meters of the monk-like adversaries and stopped. We studied their faces, which held mute expressions. There was no malice in the direct sense; instead, there was only silent dedication to whatever orders they were given. It was somehow the scariest thing I had seen in a long time.

"Release the divisive and submit." The one on the left spoke in a monotone voice, apparently referring to the kid.

"Not happenin', buzz," Arc spoke, but it almost felt like they didn't hear it. They were looking passed us to our compatriots who were carrying their charge away from the rooftop we were on. Quickly, the two in front of us moved to intercept, but Arc and I were prepared. We both took swings at our machine like foes, each of us attacking the one opposite of where we stood, crossing our attacks. Their reaction was swift and passionless, quickly blocking and attempting to deliver their own blows.

Arc and I were forced to assume defensive postures, utilizing the fighting styles we had learned. Their attacks came fast and hard, but it was less difficult dodging their strikes and more so keeping ourselves between them and the rest of the crew. If we had allowed it, they would abandon the fight and head straight for our retreating friends.

After swiftly dodging a barrage of blows, we began to slowly back pedal, trying to buy some time. Suddenly I was struck with an idea and looked to Arc, who seemed to get the same plan. We immediately rushed in for another assault, this time ganging up on one of the two targets at the same time. Arc got there first, his fist slamming towards the head of the enemy on the left in a powerful hook. The emotionless foe ducked down, but as he did, I was already moving in with an uppercut, connecting with a gruesome sounding crack. The force of the blow sent him flying from the rooftop, but I would soon follow as his friend managed to slam his shoulder into me, launching me off the building and nearly into the wall across the street. I fell to the ground in an explosion of dust, my body aching from the blow. Arc was suddenly fighting alone.

Standing, I felt an aching pain in my arm and realized my right shoulder was dislocated, but something had to be done sooner than later. I was struck with an idea to try something I hadn't done since my training days in the XRC labs. My CIHUD was able to detect both combatants despite their fast movements. I had a hunch and took aim at a metal post next to the rooftop they were on. The shot ricocheted, its trajectory finding the head of the final enemy on the roof. While I didn't see the strike, my CIHUD told me the shot was true.

"Geeze, buzz!" Arc was looking over the edge of the rooftop down at me with surprise. I had figured that the combatant would be too distracted and the vectors too extreme to react fast enough. Something told me I wouldn't get away with a stunt like that very many times before they got wise. People had gathered around, watching the display, and I knew it wouldn't be long before there were more bogies on our position. With a quick and mighty leap, I jumped back onto the roof with Arc. Without hesitation, we took off running.

"Where are ya, Reya?" I pressed my finger to my ear, activating the comm.

"T- id is leadi- to -ome club or some-." The signal was getting hit by some sort of interference, but we managed to discern Reya's directions. Arc and I followed as quickly as we could. They either couldn't or wouldn't scramble more XRC soldiers, and thus none could keep up with our movements. We had successfully caused a kerfuffle that people wouldn't soon forget.

Once Arc and I had lost our tail, we disappeared back into the crowd of people. The city itself was built like those before the war. Massive blocks of buildings made it feel almost cramped, and everything seemed separated into specific districts, much like the Undercities were divided into tiers and sections. We entered what looked to be an entertainment district of some sort. Music was heard from many places, and there were people enjoying meals in outdoor patios.

We made our way to the building Reya had barely been able to describe. It wasn't as tall as the others and was a bit blockier. There was a densely packed line of people waiting to get in, though I didn't see our friends. The crowd was all dressed in attire that brought back a lot of memories. The Undercities used to have clubs where the more young and rebellious members of society would dwell. Those in line sported multi-colored hair, spiked clothes, mini-skirts, and outrageously long socks. It was somehow comforting considering the sterile conformity we had witnessed earlier. The more pessimistic side of me, however, knew that the CORPS were Masters of Social Engineering; one must release a little pressure now and again. The place that was lamely called *Dystopia* seemed like a good enough pressure valve.

"You don't expect me to wait in line with those freaks, do you?" Arc was almost pleading. After all we had been through, he was more worried about having to mingle with the posers.

"We really can't afford to. Reya, we're here, but it's a little busy." People were already beginning to comment and point. While I was reasonably certain no one had seen us jump down from the roof, we still stood out in comparison to the crowd. Our clothes were ragged and dirty from our exploits.

"Glad you made it out, boys. Head to the back. Apparently, Terry here has some way to get you in." The signal was a bit clearer with the proximity, yet still had a lot of static in the background.

"Sounds good." I looked to Arc, who was still balking at the scene in front of him. Somehow, punk clubs didn't strike me as something he had seen before. I nudged him along, and we walked around the building, making our way to the back via a side alley. The back area was dingy and likely where they dumped their daily refuse. A metal security door in the back kept us out, as well as a freight door off to the side. The security door opened, and Terry's head stuck out. He beckoned for us to hurry inside. Arc and I both looked at each other, and then with a shrug, we walked into the club.

The first thing I noticed was the vibrations from the bass. There was a lot of music coming from the front of the building. When we entered, I saw a man standing right behind Terry, who hadn't noticed the guy yet. As soon as Terry turned, he nearly bumped into the mystery man's chest. He stood tall, his shoulders broad and made more so by the black leather-like jacket he wore despite being indoors. He sported a pair of black cargo-pants and equally black combat boots. His hair was long (also black), and his hand was covered by a tattoo that likely went up his whole arm. It made his hand appear crafted out of wires and machinery, which seemed somehow ironic. Thinking about Riley's sleeve, it seemed like a trend.

"Terrance, not this again. We talked about this, I thought?" His voice was calm, his demeanor suave and collected. His curious eyes made their way to us, scanning the weirdos the cat had dragged in. "Well, at least they look of age this time. Sorry fellas, but this isn't a soup kitchen."

"I thought you said they didn't use currency here?" Arc looked to me, utterly ignoring the scene in front of him. It seemed intentional, a sort of subtle power flex. I played along, giving him a shrug.

"Doesn't mean everyone's a winner bud. Some people are just useless." I answered.

"This is cute and all, but it looks like Terrance, and I need to have the Talk again. You clowns can just leave my establishment." I decided to take a step forward, putting my hands up in a peaceful gesture.

"Look, man, I don't need your club or permission for that matter. What we need is a drink and to talk to someone important and who gives a shit." He raised his eyebrow curiously at my words.

"Gives a shit about what?"

"Life, the world, everything."

"World's a thrivin' buzz; we're just trying to tell everyone." This whole thing really did seem sort of lame. We had no idea what we were doing, and I was beginning to feel like a stooge. The man, unimpressed, glared at Terry.

"Now, you're bringing me crazies?"

"L-look, Mikey, I'm telling you, you don't want to miss this opportunity! These guys beat the shit out of Elites, man! They jumped buildings!" Terry was frantic, babbling, and obviously frightened by the man.

"Jumped buildings, Terrance? Are you drunk?"

"I wish!" Arc and I spoke in unison.

"John, need us to take care of the guy?" I heard Reya's voice in my earpiece. Figuring she was watching from somewhere within, I shook my head no.

"Listen, I'm just here to meet up with a few friends and then leave. They're already inside." Mike was beginning to look more and more frustrated with our presence. He reached into his coat, and I immediately knew he was about to draw a weapon. From his posture and look, I doubted he was going to just shoot us right there, so we let him draw his small, semi-automatic pistol.

"I said lea-" He didn't get the last word out. My hand had reached for the gun at my hip, my arm taking aim at a blistering speed, blasting his weapon right out of his hand. I suspected that the music going on in the dance area would prevent people from hearing the shot, and from the lack of reaction, I assumed right.

"Fuck!" Mike exclaimed, holding onto his hand. I gave the gun a quick twirl before holstering it again.

"Wanna start from square one?" I asked, making Mike's expression change. I thought for sure that nearly being shot and having his finger just about broken would make him furious. Instead, an opportunistic grin came over his face.

"Sure." He continued to cradle his hand. "My god, that was fast. I don't remember seeing your arm move."

"See Mikey, that's what I've been saying! These guys are the real deal!"

"You know what their friends look like?" Still cradling his hand, he looked over to Terry.

"Y-yeah, man!"

"Bring them to my office." His gaze met mine. "Let's have a chat, friend." Arc rolled his eyes, hearing the word friend, but I held up my hand to tell him to save it. As much as I would've liked to hear whatever insult he was about to make, I had a feeling we were finally taking a step in the right direction.

Chapter Twenty-Nine: Fight The Power

Mike led us down the hall and into a small door on the right, simply labeled "Management". Inside was an almost lavish-looking office. There was a bonafide leather couch off to the side, esoteric paintings on the wall, a desk made out of wood which had to be rare, and a whole assortment of knickknacks. He went to a large leather chair behind the desk and took a seat. He fished some pills from a drawer and popped them, grabbing a bottle of whiskey to wash it down. He took out some glasses, but I held up my hand.

"We're a waste of good booze, man. Can't get drunk even if I wanted to."

"I don't trust a man that doesn't drink."

"Fuck it, I'll have some, buzz." Arc took a seat at a metal chair sitting in front of the desk, and I took the chair next to it. He poured us each a small glass.

"So how is it we just went from you wanting us out to you feeding us drinks?" I asked the question and downed the glass in front of me. My expression never changed, barely noticing anything other than a nasty taste. Alcohol tasted better when it actually *did* something.

"A wise man can hear opportunity in the wind. I know someone I should talk to when I see one; besides, with an arm that fast, I assume I am lucky to even be alive right now." He was oddly articulate considering his appearance; never judge a book by its cover after all.

"He knows badasses when he sees 'em buzz." Arc put his hands behind his head.

"Your friend here is astute." Mikey gave a grin. Reya finally entered the room, and we exchanged glances realizing where this was going. The brothers followed and took positions next to the door, securing our exit. Terry found a corner to tuck himself into looking even more nervous than when we were hopping rooftops. "So, what exactly were you doing skulking in the back of my establishment?"

"Well? We're fugitives. I guess that's the quickest way to describe it." I studied his expression as he took in my answer. He seemed skeptical; about what I couldn't tell.

"Not many can successfully run from the Coalition, not these days."

"Not many get the chance to use their tools against them." I held up my hand to stop his response. "Look, I don't mean to be rude, but we aren't here to sight-see. We have business." I decided not to beat around the bush and grabbed my PCD from my pack. I flicked to an image I had taken on one of our many stops in the desert and then tossed the PCD face-up onto his desk. His head cocked to the side, and his eyes scanned the image before gently picking up the PCD as if it were an infant.

"Nice renditions." He seemed to shake off his shock and replaced it with skepticism. "Who's the artist?"

"Me if you're counting the art of photography. I took those images myself."

"You're pulling my leg. Who put you up to this?" Mikey started to get annoyed.

"Mikey!" Terry spoke up.

"We're doing business, kid!" Mikey's annoyance didn't go away.

"Listen to me! These guys can jump buildings, fight CORPS Elites, I saw all of this! I bet they've been outside the Habitat!" He was frantic, which

404

was understandable considering the day he was having.

"Is this true?" Mikey's gaze moved back to mine.

"Did you see my arm move?"

"So, it's true then."

"What's true?" Reya inquired, deciding to join the conversation. Mikey turned his eyes to her.

"The bald guys, seen any of them yet? They look like monks out of some ancient tale."

"They fight like them too, buzz." Arc grabbed the bottle from the desk and received no protest when he began drinking from it.

"Well, rumor has it that the Coalition had created some sort of new super-soldier. These soldiers are allegedly policing things, doing the dirtier jobs."

"You've heard correct." I took the conversation back over. "Weird flex, but I'm the first of 'em. The CORPS has been working on it for some time now, and we've been fighting their battles outside the Dome. Our turn here, man, why are you giving us the time of day?"

"Like I said, I know when I'm defeated. I enjoy breathing. Besides, I'm a businessman, and I have need of someone like you."

"John, this feels like a waste of time," Vern spoke up from the door.

"Well, it's not like reporting us is a big deal. We'd wreck your establishment on our way out. What do we get out of helping you with your business?" I kept questioning him. We needed a foothold in the city and information. Reya hadn't been a citizen for long, and I was a pseudo-immigrant.

"Information, places to lay low." Mikey leaned back in his chair, rubbing his chin as he thought. "You see, I'm a man who acquires things, things the Coalition seeks to control. Drugs, weapons, supplies, ancient relics, you name it."

"Things seem to have changed," I spoke idly.

"Hmm?" Mikey looked over at me.

"I grew up in the Undercities. Crime wasn't exactly common." Mikey let out a belly laugh.

"It was plenty common, still is. The Coalition is just really good at covering things up, putting a little icing on their cake. Not everyone does well in school, not everyone works well with others. Try as they might, there's a lot of misfits living here under everyone's noses. Y'know your little pad explains a few things."

"Such as?"

"Well, some of the contraband I can get a hold of doesn't have any production facilities here. Drugs, certain building materials, even bits of technology. I've always suspected it was coming from the outside." He stopped and put his hands on his desk, leaning against it. "So, what's your plan then? What exactly are you aiming for?"

"The CORPS needs to be exposed and we plan to do that. We have friends on the outside, the Tantillan Liberation Front, they'll have a lot more than some pictures as proof." He seemed astonished for a moment, considering my words.

"Lots of receptive ears these days. The Coalition has begun to crackdown in ways they never did before. Stifling thought, taking direct control over publications, even of the entertainment variety. Kids like Terrance here have begun to speak out when they're smart enough to have a hiding place to do it from. Which is exactly why you're kind of screwed." I quirked my eyebrow, giving him a slightly incredulous look.

"Why is that exactly?"

"A couple of months ago, the Coalition finished their new communications array. It's capable of tapping into, silencing, and even altering any signal imaginable. There's no way in hell anyone will be contacting anyone from here."

"Even if the TLF finishes their array, it will be blocked." Reya realized out loud.

"Then, we bring the relay down," I spoke as if it were as simple as pie. My companions agreed with the notion, but Mikey barked out a laugh.

"You're kidding, right? That place is swarming with Elites twenty-four hours a day. Hell, we've even spotted some of the monks loitering near the power stations. You have a fast hand, but you'll need more than that."

"Well, it's a good thing we have more than that, buzz." Arc gave him a wink and chugged the rest of the bottle down, calmly placing it back onto Mikey's desk. He seemed impressed by Arc's fortitude.

"Okay, so you're a lush. I don't see how that's going to help."

"Mikey, I'm fucking telling you, man! They jumped buildings, the lush threw an Elite. They dodged bullets!"

"Well, you seem to have the vote of the youth. How about this?" Mikey leaned forward in his chair and steepled his fingers in front of his mouth. "I can get you in touch with like-minded people, people who probably have some ideas on how to get in and out of certain places."

"In exchange?" I asked.

"You do a little job for me first. It'll serve as a way to prove you can actually pull this off. There's a facility not far from here, they do research on psychotropic drugs. Been a bit of a schtick for the Coalition these days, likely looking for better ways to control the populace."

"Mikey-"

"Enough Terrance, the adults are talking. These drugs, you see, are good for more than just research. They have recreational qualities for some people. You bring me something good from that lab, something I can barter better items and favors with, and I'll help your little insurrection." I glanced over at Terry and saw he was angry about something. I had the feeling Mikey was sending us on what would typically be a suicide mission. It was the perfect means to prove our mettle.

"Locating the relay isn't exactly worth as much as we're giving you." I met Mikey's eyes. Agreeing without a fuss would make us look desperate, and that was the last thing we needed in the presence of a shark.

"As I said, I'll also put you in touch with like-minded individuals. Trust me, you bring me back a box of goodies, and I will more than compensate you for your trouble. Seeing as we haven't seen each other until right now, there's minimal risk on my part." I looked around to my counterparts, whose expressions were a mixed bag of approval, indifference, and paranoia; honestly, I felt all of those things myself. I had come so far, it was time to finish it. We would need to learn about the real security of the place, find out how easily we could hit them and getaway. It was time to unleash the gorilla.

"Alright, how about this? Arc and I go, we get your contraband and even kindly bring it back to you. My buddies behind me stay here in your establishment, ensuring we have a place to come back to and also keep you company." I shot him a winning smile and raised my eyebrows a bit, awaiting his answer. He seemed suddenly uncomfortable with the reminder that he was not in control of the situation. He looked over my companions nervously, revealing his cards for the first time.

"They're just like you, huh?"

"I am offended. I'm clearly a unique specimen." Riley flexed his muscles like he was posing for some magazine and even gave his bicep a kiss.

"John, shouldn't you take all of us with you?" Reya seemed insistent, but more for my concern than her own. She could handle little old Mikey with her pinky-finger.

"Probably, but it might be better if we don't risk us all at once. Besides, two are less likely to get caught than five." She mulled it over in her mind a moment and then gave me a nod.

"You're nuts, Johnny, but so is Arc. I almost feel bad for the CORPS." Arc gave a hearty laugh at Reya's words and stood up, dusting off his shirt.

"Hey, John-boy." Vern approached me and put his hand on my shoulder as I stood. "Don't forget where you came from. You can't hurt any of those civilians, hell, even a lot of the scientists." I gave him a nod.

"Don't worry big guy, I'd rather be in and out quietly for now and Arc's more heart than he lets on."

"Watch your mouth, or I'll wash it out with soap." Arc pointed at me.

"I mean, I can eat soap? Alright, kids, we're off." I looked over to Mikey one more time, who suddenly looked overwhelmed. He had the look of a man who's suicide mission was about to be completed. We were talking about who we shouldn't kill as opposed to the inherent danger of the situation. It was likely what changed his attitude.

"Wait. Before you go." He reached into his desk and grabbed a couple of small round devices. They were silver and had little claw-like attachments on the edges. It beveled up slightly at the center and had a fair bit of circuitry on the flat side. He tossed one to each of us.

"What's this?" I quirked my eyebrow, inspecting the device.

"A little trick, some egghead buddies of mine cooked up. The Coalition has facial recognition sensors, among other things all over the city. You would get two blocks from the safety of my establishment and be discovered. Don't ask how it works; just stick it somewhere discrete, but not covered by clothing, and you'll look like an Average Joe to the sensor nets. Won't fool a good old-fashioned eyeball, of course." I gave him a look. Something told me he wasn't planning on giving us the stealth-tech at first. Something had given him a change of heart.

"Good to know," I stated simply, and he understood. Arc and I also exchanged looks. I looked back at Mikey. "Is this why you don't seem afraid the CORPS followed us here?"

"A man has to have his secrets. Let me have your PCD. I'll provide you with a basic layout of the city. The map will be a public version, so accuracy may vary, but it'll find you your target." I reached into my pack and handed him my PCD, which he hooked into a computer that attached to his desk. The top of the desk opened up, showing a touch screen he could work on. Clearly, the kid knew about the guy because a lot of people knew about the guy. We were bound to cross paths eventually. When finished, he handed it back. "I marked your destination for you."

"Geeze, what is this a fucking video game?" Arc barked out a chuckle and shook his head.

"Says the guy who's expected to fight armies. Alright, we're off kids, for real this time." We attached our sensor fooling devices to our shirts like badges. Our faces stood out more anyway. Fully prepared, we walked out the way we had entered. As casually as we could, we began to head to our destination. It only took a glance to have the map committed to memory, but I thought it best not to reveal all our cards, so I fiddled with the PCD a moment. I figured I would interface with it later and find out if he tampered with it.

Chapter Thirty: Drug Dealing Revolutionaries

"So, what's the plan? Loud and proud or slow and steady?" Arc walked with a purpose, excited to be out of the hole in the wall club.

"Depends on whether or not there are any of our cousins waiting for us there. Either way, we should probably cause as little trouble as possible."

"You're no fun." He smirked, and we kept walking. It was starting to get darker out as the simulation above us prepared for nighttime. The visible imperfections in the simulation was a stark reminder of still being trapped inside. It began to dawn on me what the purpose of the simulation was, and it put a chill down my spine. They were preparing to rebuild the surface, and they certainly wouldn't want raider bands and riffraff to get in the way of that. The people wouldn't see the CORPS clearing the continent for their return.

The streets near our destination were densely populated, and we decided to stick to crowds as much as possible. While it didn't seem like anyone was tailing us, it was doubtful that our faces weren't already a matter of study. We had just got there, so hopefully, we still had a silent advantage despite our somewhat glorious entrance.

Eventually, according to my own sense of direction and the map I saw, we neared our target. It was reasonably far away from where we had first entered the Dome, and I was banking on that being to our advantage. The area had fewer people roaming around and a lot more security forces. It seemed like the security was made up primarily of regular citizen servants. If there were any Elites, they had to be inside the buildings, and I couldn't sense any XRC sensor suites around the vicinity, though those sorts of senses were dulled without my CIHUD active.

Finally, we arrived at the building in question, a large block of white sitting prominently among the other structures. There was a garden just outside its entrance and two main roadways that went into it. One eventually led to a circle just in front of the main entrance while another moved to a fenced-off area in the back of the building. It wasn't touching the other structures; instead, it was given a comparatively wide berth by the others.

"Looks like shipments would go behind that fence," Arc commented, studying the building with me from in front of the entrance garden. It was imposing, and I felt an almost sense of nostalgia, remembering when the works of the CORPS filled me with wonder and awe. Now they also filled me with dread and hatred.

"Sounds good. It looks like there are guards everywhere, though." I looked over the fenced area and saw a concrete kiosk that served as a security checkpoint. I pointed over to it, and we began to approach, trying to keep ourselves out of sight from the guards at the front door and hoping to stay inconspicuous to everyone else. As soon as it appeared no one was watching, we walked up to the door. I half expected Arc to just rip it open, but instead, he knocked on it.

"Dude, what are you doing?" I whispered with my eyes wide. We weren't exactly hidden as the metal door had a window showing the cramped and dull-looking security kiosk. A middle-aged man stood from his chair and cocked his head queerly at our presence. He walked over and spoke through an intercom.

"Can I help you?"

"I saw some shifty-looking guy watching your kiosk. I think he's trying to case the place, buzz." Arc sounded calm but acted out the part of a concerned citizen well. He pointed at a random passer-by.

"Alright, thank you, citizen." Both Arc and I backed off the door, and the security officer first got on his radio. "We have suspicious activity outside the garden." He opened the door to get a closer look, and as soon as he did, Arc was on him. In the blink of an eye, he had his fingers around the now ajar door, ripped it further open, and pushed the guard inside. He gave the guard a right hook to the side of the head, and while it looked like he pulled his punch, he knocked the guy out cold. He was squirming a moment later, trying to come to, and Arc was already taking anything that seemed important, including a security card.

"Thanks, buzz." He calmly walked out of the kiosk and motioned for me to head to the gate, which was now opening. "Let's go, brotha."

"You are aware that concussions can be deadly, right?" I was a little frustrated by his seeming lack of compassion for the people we were essentially trying to save.

"He'll be fine, the CORPS have great doctors. Now c'mon, I give it another thirty seconds before someone knows something went wrong." There were times I found the man insufferable. We walked around the building and saw that it led to a garage door. As we approached, four normal-looking guards rushed out with sub-machine guns at the ready. As soon as the guards were clear, the door began to slowly close.

"Stay where you are!" Arc and I looked to one another and then forward as we both dashed towards the hail of gunfire. We separated, moving our way to opposite sides of the four gunmen. They weren't able to keep a bead on us or even lead us fast enough, so we effortlessly got our way around them. As soon as we did, we slid like a couple of sports stars, managing to get

414

behind the door before it closed.

"Don't think they were expecting that." Arc was wearing his ego as usual, but I pointed forward.

"Neither were they." We found ourselves in a warehouse, lots of space for vehicles to come in, unload, and take off again. There was yet another security checkpoint just inside. There was a large scanning device that the trucks would drive through when entering and waiting just beyond it were five more gunmen. Not waiting for their response, we began walking towards them calmly, both allowing our CIHUDS to extract from our foreheads.

"XRC Units!" One exclaimed. They all looked to each other, seemingly shat their collective pants, and began to run further into the building. A couple of them dropped their weapons so they could run faster. Arc continued walking, his grin only widening.

We decided to be as quick as possible, knowing our exit would not be as simple as our entrance. We had already done more than anything our jackass new ally could have mustered. We moved throughout the warehouse, and only seconds later, an alarm began to sound, signally an intruder alert.

"Fuck this shit," Arc exclaimed and walked over to the nearest shipping container he could find, tearing the doors open. There were boxes of items marked with serial numbers we didn't have the references to, but we did have scanners. The first box Arc came to was nearly a meter and a half tall and almost as wide. As soon as he tore it open, he got a disappointed look on his face.

"It's just plants." He took a whiff before analyzing it with his CIHUD. "Looks like cannabis."

"That's not surprising. It's a godsend of a plant when you can't exactly grow trees or mine fuel. It's also not contraband unless something's changed."

"Not our mark, gotcha." He grabbed another box and tore into it. The first thing we noticed was the small glass vial that fell to the floor and shattered. We both looked at it, then at each other, then at the box. We both grabbed another vial, the box being full of them, and took a moment to analyze their spectral signature and density. Soon our computers gave an answer.

"Hallucinogenic compound. Likely to cause you to be lazy, see shit, and hear shit." I had a smirk on my face seeing the information before me.

"Mine had bigger words. It also showed what I'm shit sure are Elites coming from inside the building." Arc began to bag up a bunch of the vials, and I did the same. It all seemed too easy. The bogies were closing, however, coming down a lift close-by.

"I bet they didn't expect us to come steal some drugs." I mused.

"Alright buzz, we can chat about it later." Arc slapped me on the back and pushed passed me to exit the container. We both began to run back the way we came and quickly arrived at the closed bay door. It opened upward like most shipping doors, and the mechanism didn't seem too strong from our inside view.

"Let's get 'er open, buzz!" Arc went to the left side of the door, and I made my way to the right. We got as much of a grip on the door as we could and, using our legs, lifted it. The machine creaked, snapped and whined in protest at our barbaric actions, but could not hold against the amount of force we were applying. With a loud snap, it flew open. Wasting no time, we rushed out of the building.

"Open fire!" Right on cue, we could see three Elites across the street, who had likely come from nearby patrols to intercept us. Luckily for us, our

CIHUDs had made us aware of their presence as the door opened. We quickly drew our sidearms and dropped the mutaphorm troopers while running. People passing by began to flee in a panic. Without hesitation, we started sprinting for our lives. Soon the entire city would be on us, and we had to be gone as quickly as possible.

Getting to the gate, we vaulted right over it, rolling when we hit the ground and taking off in different directions. We were attempting to confuse any attempts to find us but kept each other within our own sensor range. Arc and I were beginning to truly understand each other in battle, efficiently acting in sync.

Thanks to the device our friend gave us and the doc's enhancements, we were able to eventually get far enough away and blend in with the crowd. We spent nearly two hours running from street-to-street, rooftop-to-rooftop, and crowd-to-crowd. We had likely eluded our hunters long before we stopped running.

We decided not to meet up right away, instead opting to walk close enough to sense one another, but far enough not to be mistaken as a pair, taking a roundabout route back to the club. It was well into the Dome's simulated night when we finally made it back.

"You feel like that was too easy?" Arc asked as he finally caught up to me, and we made our way to the back entrance of the club.

"I don't even think a computer model could have predicted we were going to steal a bunch of drugs randomly. It does tell us something important, though."

"Yeah, they can't just muster an army on command and blow up whatever's in the way. We have the terrorist advantage." I hated the term

417

terrorist, but he was essentially right. We could strike anywhere, at any time, and they had no real way of preparing for it.

"Crazy to think about it." I opened the back door and walked through, still talking. "Here we are in what is basically *the* CORPS stronghold, and they're technically the disadvantaged one. We must be doing our job right."

Riley was standing just outside the office door, which told me our friend was being held captive in his own establishment until we got back. "Bless their hearts," I couldn't help but think with a comedic grin.

"Well, that took longer than I thought it would." Riley greeted us with feigned surprise.

"I'll bet anything he'll think it was quick," I commented with a smirk. Riley returned my grin and opened the door so we could all enter.

"He's moving when I have to take a p-" I heard Mikey talking as we walked through the door, and he stopped dead in his tracks as both Arc and I, unscathed, walked in.

"Did you even go? You've only been gone a few hours." He quickly regained his composure and attempted to assert some control over the situation. Both Arc and I set our packs down on the chairs in front of his desk, and each fished a vial out, offering them to him simultaneously. "What are you robots or something?" He took one of the vials and set the other on his desk.

"Close enough." I shrugged as he looked over our spoils.

"Got any proof this is worth a damn?"

"I know what I see." My voice had a finality to it, and somehow, he declined to doubt my word.

"I know what this is anyway. We've seen a few of these out in the wild. Where did you get this?" He toyed with the vial in his hand, looking up to me.

418

"The chemist down the street, where the fuck do you think we got it?" Arc sounded frustrated.

"You have to have known a guy; getting a couple of vials is nothing." It was at the moment that Arc and I looked at each other incredulously and then proceeded to pile his desk with the forty-two vials we had managed to grab before running. Stunned, Mikey stood from his desk. "Do you know how much this is?"

"Second box we found, buzz. We left plenty of witnesses of our escape."

"They know about us." I let my statement carry over to everyone.

"What do you mean?" Vern had been sitting on the couch off to the left and stood as he asked the question.

"The people, at least the mundane security forces. They even used the term XRC Unit." This got the proper attention from my companions.

"That would mean that they've been open about the project in some way. Why?" Reya was sitting on the couch still and stroked her chin in contemplation.

"I think it's because they openly send them to the surface to make it safe for the people. Plus, we have seen them openly displayed on their propaganda displays" I put my fingers up in air quotes with the word safe.

"Makes sense." Vern followed.

"They can't just open the doors, boom here ya go, everyone, let's go play outside. Nah, they need to ease it in." Arc smirked at his own comment.

"Look, I am sure this is all interesting, but can someone explain to me what XRC Unit means? Do you mean the monks?" And just like that, our bubbles were burst by Mikey's apparent ignorance.

"Wait, I've heard that term before!" Terry had been in the room with us, brooding in the corner, sipping a drink that had been brought to the office.

"Where?" I asked with seriousness in my voice.

"Well, my brother's a security officer in the Hub." His voice was trembling, and he was obviously afraid of us.

"What's the Hub?" Arc asked.

"It's somewhat the center of the city," Reya answered. "Many roads lead to it, and it is where much of the city's management is located," she motioned for Terry to continue.

"Right, well, my brother sometimes talks about shit he's not supposed to when he's drunk."

"Among other states of mind." Mikey's smirk could be heard in his voice.

"Yeah, whatever. Anyway, he said the last few weeks they've been getting training exercises about specific people they categorized as XRC Units. Said he didn't know what it stood for."

"Xavier Ronyn Cybernetics." I spat the name out. "It's what we are, kid."

"Xavier Ronyn." Mikey sounded thoughtful. "That name has come up recently. Can't put my finger on it."

"Anything important?" I inquired, looking to him.

"Nah, I think I heard it at the last Emergence Festival. They name off important CORPS scientists. It makes sense now that you mention it."

"Emergence Festival?" I was genuinely curious. I had missed so much in the last few years.

"Yes, we celebrate the day the Coalition ushered us up from the caves below. It's all getting a little religious if you ask me."

"Hey, fuck this history lesson, you made a deal, and we have a mission." Arc broke the discussion and kept us on track. "Quid pro quo mother fucker."

"Quite right." Mikey stood and began to pace like some sort of cliché master rogue revealing his plans. "Guys like me have been in high demand these days. I mean, you stood a pretty good chance of stumbling on any old schmo who could give you basic information."

"But you can do better?" I gave him an unimpressed look.

"No." He shook his head and met my gaze. "I won't stab you in the back." He walked back to his desk and placed his hands on it, leaning forward a bit. "I have no love of the Coalition, and I sure as heck have no love of being trapped in this city forever. I looked through your pictures, and I see opportunity and like I said, a good businessman can hear opportunity on the wind. Right now, there's a hurricane a-blowin'.'"

"I'm not in this to get rich," I said simply.

"Of course not. I believe that you're truly passionate about everything that you say, but as your friend here so elegantly put it: Quid pro quo, I help you, you help me, and the cycle continues in harmony. You see, as I said, a lot of people are demanding the services of people like me and these people I help are a lot like you and Terry here. Malcontents not prepared to use the system to their advantage; they would rather bring it down."

"You love your own voice, don't you?" Reya seemed to despise Mikey more than anyone else. I had come to learn that everyone in positions of power loved their own voice. It's usually how they got there in the first place.

"Actually, I do. Burning quips aside, these people believe what you seem to already know. There's a world beyond the Dome, and the Coalition is lying about it. They dream of meeting someone like you, and I dreamed of getting a free shipment like this. See where I'm going?"

"So, you plan to introduce us to these like-wise individuals then?" While he seemed to be trying to impress us, I didn't hate what he was saying.

"Exactly. Perhaps we'll need each other's services again soon."

"When are we meeting these people?" Riley finally broke his silence. He acted as our security man, and I definitely didn't hate that either.

"Not right away to be sure. They're a skittish bunch, for a good reason. Besides, it might be best if you lay low for a bit."

"You two sure you weren't tracked?" Riley pressed.

"Pretty sure. If Mikey's toys here worked, then we should have effectively lost them." My answer seemed to satisfy Riley.

"I have some rooms downstairs you can occupy for a few days while I arrange a meeting." Mikey offered. "I can't unload the merchandise right away anyway."

"Then, I guess we wait," Vern said rhetorically. We all agreed, having little choice at that moment. We could search the city for someone else, but there was no reason to look a gift horse in the mouth.

That night we were shown to the VIP guestroom, which inconveniently had only two beds and a couch for furniture. I plopped myself down on the couch, tired from the lack of rest over the last few days. I was at least ready to sit back.

"Can we trust him?" Riley asked, leaning up against the door frame.

"Nope. Not one bit." I gave a shrug.

"Then what, pray tell, are we fucking doing here then?" Riley was a bit frustrated. He reminded me of a more confident Ray.

"Working towards fomenting insurrection? I share your feelings about this situation, but we came in here blind, and I think we all knew we'd end up doing questionable things to achieve our goals."

"Sounds a bit like CORPS excuses, buzz." Arc took a seat on the couch with me.

"Well, I suppose you ain't exactly wrong about that. We can't just sit around and wait for an ethical way out of this situation."

"Preachin' to the choir, buzz. I think we've been too nice as it is."

"Of course you do." Reya rolled her eyes at Arc and then looked to me. "John, I speak for everyone here when I say that we trust you and are driven to succeed. Just don't let that need for revenge blind you."

"To be honest with you, with every passing day it becomes less and less about revenge. Someone has to do something about the CORPS; it might as well be us."

"As long as you keep that in mind, John-boy, I think we'll be on the same page," Vern replied.

The next two days went by a lot slower than I thought they would. All of us were a little paranoid about getting caught with our pants down, but after all we had been through, we took the time for a little R&R. The first night we did end up sleeping, finding our own little quiet places in the room, and just letting go.

Chapter Thirty-One: Introspection

"If only we had more time." Alonna's voice was soft and my body was numb. Everything was a gray haze, and I was unaware of my surroundings.

"This should have been done the right way." The world was rocking back and forth, like a ship lost at sea. "You're more important than you know." The only feeling that came through were soft lips on my forehead. As soon as they touched, I began floating, my eyes opening to see Dome City below me. The wind sailed around me, but I grew no closer to the ground.

"More important than you know." The voice echoed, and I saw the people below as a handful of them began to glow. Next to each, smaller lights appeared, splitting from the glow of the original. "Important." Her voice would not leave my mind. "More than you know."

I awoke in a cold sweat, the dream having disturbed me more than most. It felt like a cross between a fantasy and a memory buried deep and it left me with an uneasy feeling. Everyone was still resting, so I decided to get up and leave the room. We were in a club, after all, chilling in the crowd couldn't hurt anything.

The place was bumping with people dancing all around. It was built with the dance floor surrounding an island-style bar. Music blared from speakers above, and I could see people dancing on a second-floor catwalk. Folks were dressed in all manner of deviant clothing from black leather to sheer lace. People came to unleash their humanity the CORPS seemed to want to suppress. It was likely the last vestige of free thought left in a place choked of it. There, no one was judged.

I found myself a little table in the back corner, unoccupied, and away from the crowd. I never was one for large groups, and I felt more comfortable just observing, reminding myself of my goal. I couldn't let petty revenge blind me.

"This seat taken big boy?" I looked up and saw Reya standing at the table, a gentle grin on her face.

"Nah, man, have at it." I motioned for her to sit, and she obliged.

"Interesting place to hang out." She commented.

"Yeah, it's a nice change of pace considering. Funny because I avoided places like this in the old days."

"The old days makes it seem like a world away."

"Sometimes, it feels like it is. So, what brings you down here?"

"Likely the same reasons. No point in sleeping, so I got curious as to where you wandered off to." She gave a dull sigh. "Do you ever wish you could go back to that life? A simple existence without conspiracies and endless wars?"

"Nah," I spoke definitively. "Not at all." She turned and gave me a curious look. "Back then, we were ignorant sheep."

"They say ignorance is bliss."

"Just because you can't see something doesn't mean it's not there. I'd rather see the evil in front of me than miss the lies behind me."

"You know, John, for as simple as you try to put yourself out as you're a lot smarter than you let on."

"Yeah." I chuckled lightly. "Pain will do that to a man. I used to be a pretty simple dude. Lys used to say I could entertain myself with a rock if I had something to throw it at."

"You've mentioned her a lot. Who's Lys? I don't mean what happened
425

to her, I mean, who was she to you? You sound like you were in love with her." With that comment, I gave out a hearty laugh, which seemed to confuse Reya.

"Oh man, if Lys could hear you ask that. Nah bub, we weren't lovers or anything. She was my sister from another mister, my bro with breasts, the dudette of the year." Reya snorted out a laugh, and for the first time in a while, I genuinely smiled while thinking about Lys. "We always joked that whoever we ended up dating had worse than a parent to worry about."

"You weren't attracted to each other?" I almost got frustrated at the line of questioning, and that too was nostalgic. I had answered that one a million times before, seemingly a million years ago.

"If you mean sexually, sure, she was a catch for any man, and I like to think I ain't so bad looking myself, but nah, was never about that. Would've felt like kissing my sister, hot or not. Lys had a rough life before the mutaphorm attacks. Deadbeat dad, a mother who drowned her sorrows and so she spent a lot of time with my family. We got really close, and the rest is history."

"Soul mates, then." She held her hand up before I could protest. "Nothing romantic about it. Just best friends. This actually explains a lot, really."

"Analyzing me now, are you?"

"Well, it is a good idea to get to know the people you are with."

"What about you? Any best buds or significant others?" Reya smiled gently and shook her head.

"Nothing more than I already told you. I dated some guys, was even going to marry one of them. I definitely loved him, but it felt more like what I

426

was supposed to get married and start a family than an actual choice. I had some friends, but, well." She looked down at her hands, fidgeting her thumbs. She looked back up. "Amazingly, when I was captured I ended up meeting someone truly special, but it wasn't peaches and cream."

"Met someone? While under CORPS employ?" She gave a nod.

"Well, it was my handler, Dr. Langstan." The name felt like being punched in the gut. While I was in no way responsible for his death, it wasn't something I was prepared for. "He was, I don't know, adorable. Soft-spoken, very sweet and kind. Apparently, there was some sort of mix up with another unit's mission. He was sent out and never came back." A sad look washed over her face, and I suddenly felt like I knew more about my friend than I had before. "Are you okay?" She looked into my eyes, seeing the distress I felt over the memory.

"I knew Langstan. He was there the day the TLF attacked our convoy. Some convoluted plan of Alonna's to break me free." Reya looked down, and there was a slight twinge of anger, but she pushed it back.

"I suppose I should thank her. You eventually led the TLF to break me out too." I reached out and grabbed Reya's hand reassuringly. She smiled at the gesture.

"No one should thank her. She has a lot of sins to atone for." Reya pulled her hand back quietly and met my gaze again.

"Why do you hate her so much?" The question caught me by surprise. I always thought such things were obvious, but when I tried to actually put it into words, I found myself at a loss. Considering my state of being, that was impressive.

"I-uh, well." I took a deep breath. "It's like this: Alonna's on Ronyn's

427

level. Not just any scientist, not just easily replaceable. She was part of what destroyed Lys's life, that ended my friend Ray, that's ruling the people around us with a clenched fist, that's blowing the TLF to kingdom come on their own soil. She represents everything I hate in this world."

"Except you don't actually hate her." Reya was smirking again, like a hunter who just snared their quarry. I had to take in another breath and then just let it out, staring off for a moment.

"I guess you're right." I looked to Reya again.

"You care about her deeply." Her face became solemn-looking, and now she was searching my eyes for evidence.

"What the fuck makes you say something like that?"

"Literally everything. It makes sense, John, it's why I fell for Langstan. She's sweet to you, at least as much as she can be, cares for you physically, perhaps even mentally when she can, and she orchestrated your escape. Easily replaceable or not, not every handler would have done that. You're also attracted to her. Men are terrible at hiding when they sneak a peek."

"Hey, I'm still mostly human, after all." I crossed my arms over my chest, almost pouting at Reya's comments. She was right, though. "Call it a love-hate relationship. She shouldn't get a reprieve for her sins, but y'know, sometimes I wonder what she could have accomplished in different hands. The lives she'd save, suffering she could ease. Instead, she's a puppet, like we were. As fucked up as it sounds, she was a victim as much as I was. I guess it's why I feel pity more than hate."

"Now, you're being honest. Not all handlers are good people. Before you attacked the labs, my replacement got a little grabby." She seemed to shudder a little remembering the situation.

428

"Grabby?" My interest was piqued by this.

"Yeah. He walked straight into my cell with an armed escort. Ordered me to undress, said there was no time. There isn't much to the story. By then, Vern and Riley had managed to escape their cells and were looking for anyone else ready to run."

"It's not like they could've stood a chance against you anyway."

"Even I can't dodge bullets from that close."

"Maybe not." I stopped to think. "That's weird."

"What?" She cocked her head to the side.

"Well, I don't know. Our brain-meat machines are always trying to add stuff up that doesn't seem directly related, but it just seems weird to me that every handler I have come across had some sort of infatuation with their unit or even vice versa. When Arc and I wrecked that bitch in Libsal, Mickey reacted like I killed his wife. Alonna taught me firsthand what you women go through when you're around someone who wants you, but you don't want them back. You fell in love with Langstan. I dunno, whenever a bunch of coincidences occur with the CORPS, I get suspicious."

"Hmm, come to think of it, Vern mentioned that Riley hasn't been himself since his handler was killed before our escape from the labs and Vern has no idea what happened to his. What about Arc?" She donned an investigative look.

"That man's a total mystery, but y'know, I wouldn't doubt it if something ridiculous happened to his handler. Wait, time out, were Vern and Riley's handlers women?" The thought had finally donned on me. Reya seemed to be struck by the question as well, as if such a thing should have been more obvious.

"Yes, yes, they both were."

"The one from Libsal had a man. In fact, Doc was replaced with a man, and when Langstan was with me, they made sure to stress it was specifically temporary, just a fill-in while she was away." I thought about my dream again, and a shudder ran down my spine. Just how far were the violations going to go? "We need to find that array and get a hold of the TLF sooner than later, I think."

"Eye on the prize John? Come on, enough of this, let's go relax with the boys." I gave her a nod, and we both stood, leading one another out of the noisy club and back to the confines of our friends. Before we walked into the room, I stopped Reya and gave her my best grin.

"I think Lys would've liked hanging out with you." She gave the grin back to me, realizing the level of compliment it was. Reya reminded me of a sort of Lys-stand-in, another sister to help keep me in line.

Chapter Thirty-Two: Uncomfortable Allies

We all spent the remainder of our time relaxing, but eventually, Mikey came through with his promise. It was sometime in the very early morning that Terry came bursting into our room. At first, we all stood, expecting some sort of trouble, but it quickly became apparent he was more concerned about being on time than worried about some threat.

"Hey! Oh, uh, sorry, guys. Mikey said to come to his office, time to meet some friends or something." We all took a moment to look at each other, all resisting the urge to place our faces in our palms. I gave a bit of a shrug and decided to grab my gear.

"Well, kids, you heard the man, time to go. He either delivers or we find another way."

"Sounds good to me, buzz." With that, everyone grabbed their stuff and headed up to Mikey's office. Surprisingly, he was the only one there when we entered.

"So, where's your buddy?" I asked as soon as I assessed the room.

"You'll have to meet him. He's an extremely paranoid person. I will say this: He is convinced you're not what you say you are."

"Then we'll have to prove it to him," Vern spoke up.

"My thoughts exactly. I'll be bringing you to a place to meet."

"I wonder what he's so paranoid about?" Reya wondered.

"Sounds like a healthy reaction to CORPS bullshit to me," I spoke candidly. I would be more concerned if he wasn't paranoid.

"Well, he doesn't like tardiness. Makes him skittish. Follow me. Let's go, Terrance."

"W-wait, me? Why do I need to go?" I was just as surprised as Terry.

"Because we need to prove you're still alive." Mikey held his hand up to stop any incoming replies. "Trust me, it'll be easier to just go with the flow." I took in a deep breath and decided to do just that. Mikey led all of us out of his office and out the backdoor of the club. Waiting for us outside was a large white vehicle. It looked like the smaller personal cars that populated the streets, but was a bit taller with more seats. We all piled in, and Mikey himself got in the driver's seat, bypassing what seemed to be an autopilot system.

We drove through the city within the relative safety of what Mikey called a van. Being in a vehicle allowed us to blend in with the rest of traffic, and as far as we could tell, no one seemed to be following us. Mikey drove to what looked to be an industrial district. The streets were lined with large warehouse-style buildings, many of which had extensive pipe systems running from roof to ground. Likely, the pipes served as some sort of exhaust system to prevent pollutants from filling the dome.

Finally, we drove to what could only be described as the most average building on the block. It was a warehouse surrounded by others like it, and very little activity went on around it. We entered the building through a large bay door that opened as soon as we pulled up. Everything was a bit ominous, and Mikey didn't do much explaining on the way there. We didn't exactly ask many questions either. Our paranoia of the CORPS's all-seeing eye made us clam up in most situations.

We parked in a void of a storage bay. No boxes lined the loading areas, and no other vehicles were in sight. The whole place stank of a trap.

"Just for the record." Arc looked over to Mikey, sitting in front with him. "If this is a trap, I kill you first." Surprisingly Mikey gave a chuckle in reply.

"I wouldn't dream of betraying people like you. I enjoy breathing."

"Smart man." He gave Mikey a hearty pat on the shoulder.

"Alright, boys, let's dispense with the measuring and get this over with." Reya interrupted.

"Quite right. Let's go Terrance, time to prove your new friends' innocence."

"Wait, innocence, what the fuck is going on, Mikey?" Terry was looking to us and then back to him. I was beginning to piece things together. The CORPS likely said we killed the kid as some cover story, but why it was necessary to disprove that was beyond me.

Mikey led us deeper into the building, eventually leading us to an elevator that brought us to the top floor. When the doors opened, we were greeted with a dusty office-style hallway. Obviously, it hadn't been occupied for quite some time, if at all. I imagined that Dome City was a lot like the Undercities, built with room to grow. Eventually, we were led to a door at the end of the hall, and Mikey opened it, motioning for us to enter.

I was the first to walk in confidently. The room itself was much cleaner than the rest of the place, containing a desk, a couch, some chairs, and even paintings on the wall of places I didn't recognize. Judging by their look and apparent age, they were paintings Underdwellers had managed to save before being ushered into their new home. At the desk sat a man that looked to be no more than twenty-five. He was handsome in his blemish-free features, darker skin, and short, well-kempt hair. He was wearing basic gray fatigues, a getup a lot like our own. His face was calm, studying all of us as we entered, sitting there with steepled fingers. Whether for dramatic effect or part of the

433

plan, Mikey made sure that Terry entered last.

"So, you weren't full of shit this time Michael." He analyzed the kid carefully before looking over to the rest of us. "Which one of you is the leader of your little band?"

"We don't do the leader thing, but I do have the biggest mouth," I spoke up to which Arc belched out a laugh.

"Second biggest, buzz."

"Well, mine's smarter."

"Not gonna argue that."

"Great, this is what you send me, Michael?" The man looked annoyed, though he seemed very interested in Terry's presence. "At least they're not the killers the Coalition is working hard to make them out to be."

"Maybe you should start from the top." I offered.

"Not yet. I was told by Michael that you are XRC Units. I highly doubt this claim, but I did see the footage of your little kidnapping escapade."

"No one kidnapped me! They saved me from the security forces." Mikey put his hand on Terry's shoulder to indicate it was time to remain calm.

"Fair enough." The man before us said before addressing me again. "Do you have evidence that you're an XRC unit?" He raised his right brow, waiting for my answer. I gave a simple shrug and let my CIHUD pop out of my forehead. "Well, that is a dead giveaway, isn't it?"

"Alright, I've had just about enough of this. Who the hell are you, and why do we care to meet you?" I decided to channel my inner Arc, losing my patience with the man's arrogance.

"Me? I am XR184, otherwise known as Cole. Now, I get your impatience, but you of all people are aware of the dangers a renegade of our pedigree faces. That leads me to my next question. How were you able to bypass the Fail-Safe?" His emotions began to betray him. He seemed most eager about that answer than any other.

"Well." I looked to my companions and got what I could see as looks of approval before looking to our new acquaintance. "My handler was none other than Dr. Alonna Lyrul, the inventor of our little swimmers."

"Our what?"

"Nanomachines. Anyway, she's how I escaped and how my companions here were able to join the good fight."

"Do you mean to tell me that she neutralized your fail-safe?" His eyes widened, and he seemed astonished.

"Yeah, that's exactly what I mean, bub. She defected for lack of a better term, though I haven't exactly figured out to who's side. She's definitely stranger than your average CORPS egghead." Cole stood and began pacing behind his desk, thinking about his situation. Clearly, he didn't expect Mikey to actually come through. "Wait, have you not?" I finally asked, putting two and two together. Cole looked at me and shook his head.

"No. Conveniently, I learned about how the fail-safe works prior to my rather quiet escape. Their communication arrays send out a signal, and our nanomachines receive that signal. They can change it to include data, so at any point, they can make the signal say something like, kill your host."

"So how the fuck are you alive?" Arc interjected.

"Learning how the signal worked allowed me to find a way to block it before I escaped. These empty warehouses are designated for eventual housing of sensitive materials and data. As such, they are heavily shielded, even from the array itself. They have internal ways of keeping tabs on such places."

"So, you're hiding out." Vern deduced.

"In a sense."

"You're a dead man walkin'," Arc stated logically.

"To put it bluntly, yes. So here we are. Before me is five escaped XRC units who have clearly foiled the fail-safe and are not random murderers of teenagers. Well, Mikey, you definitely came through."

"About my payment?" Mikey inquired. I was curious as to what sort of payment, considering the lack of currency.

"Don't worry, there won't be a security sentry in sight when your boys make the trade. You'll have your toys." Cole gave Mikey a winning smile who returned it with a nod of his own.

"Well then, I'll get everything set up. C'mon Terrance, we're done here." Terry looked disappointed and was about to protest when Cole stopped them both.

"The kid has to stay." His calm demeanor was somewhat disconcerting. It was apparent he had a flush and wanted to make sure everyone at the table knew it.

"Excuse me?" Mikey didn't seem to be pleased. He was oddly protective of the kid. "Why exactly is he staying?"

"Mikey, how will tonight's demonstration work if we don't have the proof of Coalition lies?" He raised his eyebrows, his face exuding diplomacy. I was beginning to warm up to the guy.

"C'mon Mikey, I'm officially an adult, I want to help them!" Terry's eyes were pleading with the man.

"Fine. But if something happens to the kid, I'll make sure everyone knows it." His gaze was deadly serious, locking eyes with Cole, who simply nodded.

"I give you my word; we will keep the boy safe." Mikey took a long moment to look over Terry before walking away to leave the building.

"You trust him?" I asked, looking back over to Cole.

"No more than he trusts me. We have reasons to stay aligned, and apparently, as long as we keep this young man safe, we'll stay that way."

"Alright, not gonna lie, I'm done with the act bub. What do you want from us, why do I want to be in this room?" I crossed my arms over my chest, giving him an agitated look.

Pouring on the cliché, Cole stood, put his hands behind his lower back comfortably, and turned away looking at the wall. "I have been working on a plan for months. The move up here shocked the populace a little more than the Coalition expected." He began to pace back and forth behind his desk, occasionally stopping to look at his audience. "They told us that they had been developing technology to clean the atmosphere and to build Habitats like this one, but smaller. The very existence of this place means that they do have the technology, but people began to doubt the world is actually dead."

"Makes sense. Seems too planned." Vern commented.

"Exactly the issue. Then we began to manufacture weapons and vehicles, and food production rose by nearly one-hundred and fifty percent above necessary levels." We began to look among one another, realizing the implications. "According to the Coalition, the increased production was to combat any holdovers from the war, such as other unknown shelters or beings that had adapted to the environment. That alone began to stir questions. Around that time, just a year or so after coming up here, the general media was shut down."

"Shut down? They've never done anything like that before." I began to stroke my chin, pondering the consequences.

"Indeed. There was no announcement other than to say the resources needed to be reallocated to other essential projects. See, another claim they made was that the Undercities were falling apart. We were one solid quake away from being crushed. Now, I honestly don't doubt that one, but it was convenient none the less. Fast forward, and you have an overworked population that has been gently silenced. It's a pressure cooker ready to blow."

"Where are you going with all of this?" I was getting impatient again.

"Before I escaped, I made contact with likeminded individuals throughout the Habitat. The mindset was that the Coalition has been lying, and we have to retake control of our people. I saw firsthand how many Elites exist now. Do you know how they make those?"

"Actually, I have always wondered," Reya spoke for all of us.

"Some of them come from the Pit." Arc reminded us, though Cole either ignored it or gracefully carried on despite it.

"People who would have otherwise died from something they can prevent or heal but can easily pass off as too severe to treat, are taken. They receive some sort of chemical and gene-therapy procedure that alters their minds and bodies. They are singularly loyal and long-lived. They've been doing it for years."

I, for one, was shocked by the news. We were basically fighting our dead family and friends whenever we went up against the CORPS's monstrous troopers.

"How did you find all of this out?" Reya inquired.

"I witnessed a kid, not much younger than Terrance here-"

"Dude, c'mon, I hate that name."

"Terry." Cole corrected himself respectfully. "Well, this kid was involved in a transit accident and had broken his spine. That's easy as pie for the Coalition these days. They've been bringing in technology that was otherwise unknown until recently. Very powerful biotech."

"The TLF." I came to a sudden realization. "The Tantillan Republic were renowned for their biotechnology. It's supposedly what started the war. I have witnessed firsthand that at least some of that knowledge survived."

"You mean the Coalition stole technology?" Cole put both hands onto his desk and leaned forward.

"Probably? There's a whole war going on outside of this Dome of yours. The world was bombed in some places, sure, but a lot of it survived, and some of it has begun to thrive again. Hell, we know why they've been building up their forces. They plan to wipe out what's left out there to make it nice and cozy for the people in here." I explained the situation in simple terms, but it elicited an alarmed reaction from Cole. He began to pace again.

"That? That makes entirely too much sense. It would explain everything up to this point, but why? What the hell is the point?"

"Science, buzz," Arc remarked.

"It has to be more than that."

"Honestly, I wish it were, but it ain't." I offered my insight. "They're rebuilding our species from the ground up, and it involves tossing out the trash." My tone never changed. This was old news to us, and I wanted to convey sheer honesty.

"How have you come to all of these conclusions? How have you managed to get so far, to begin with?" Cole finally retook his seat, the information taking a lot out of him.

"Well, to put it simply, when I escaped, right after the fail-safe nearly put me down, I got into contact with the TLF forces still left. They had taken in Alonna, and with her help, the fail-safe was neutralized. Later I found Arc here." I motioned to each person as I got to them. "Then, through a series of lucky breaks and a little planned chaos, we ended up coming across the XRC Labs. We wrecked the fucking place and found our three remaining buddies here. After that? We came here." I tried my best not to look away from Cole as I spoke, projecting as much honesty as I could.

"That's quite some story." He looked down at his hands. "Tell me." He looked up again. "What brings you here? What's the point?"

"We all came from the same roots. We're all Underdwellers of a kind, and none of us asked for the situation we're in now. When we found enough evidence to take some mass genocide claim seriously, we decided that we couldn't just let it happen. Cole, we have TLF forces on stand-by and an uncouth number of surface raiders just itching for a fight, all capable of providing assistance if we can contact them. We're here to bring down or otherwise take control of the Communications Array." Cole was mulling everything over in his head.

"Okay." He seemed to become more confident as a plan came to mind. "Tonight, as I said, there's a demonstration. We're going to expose the lie about Terry here during our peaceful protest. It won't be enough, though, we would need more demonstrations, and the array could be our ticket; the ultimate demonstration. Please tell me you brought some sort of proof of the outside world."

"Well, John has photos, and we have memories. Just the idea should be enough." Reya interjected and provided needed insight to Cole. She was right; the seed was all that needed to be planted.

"If we take control of that array, we can find a way to get enough TLF troops in here to turn the population against the CORPS. It would be a bonafide revolution." I spoke now with more hope in my words than I had before. The plan seemed somehow viable, but then I realized there was an element I forgot about. "How does Mikey play into all of this?" It was an honest question.

"Good old Mikey is of course making trades and gathering influence among groups I generally keep at a distance. It's interesting what effects civil unrest can have. Either way, our demonstration needs to be loud and proud enough to distract security forces long enough for their little trade to go down. Terry here should ensure that. I have a feeling the Security troops will get violent sooner than later."

"Look, man, we have no intention of killing anyone. If we're gonna win hearts and minds, we need to not be assholes about it." As I said this, Cole gave me a grin that was a little disconcerting, to say the least.

"You're an XRC unit, John. I'm sure you can find a non-lethal alternative that normal thugs couldn't hope to achieve."

"This all seems a little too convenient." Riley finally made himself known. He was the paranoid voice, always making us ask questions. "Mikey and you? Terry led us directly to where we needed to be?"

"That does seem very convenient." Cole looked to Riley and held up his hands disarmingly. "Inevitably, to quietly communicate among like-minded individuals required dealing with unsavory ones. I was able to accomplish a lot before the fail-safe became a problem. You would have been led here by any

441

old thug. The only lucky thing is that you were brought in by an Old School type. Honor, integrity, that sort of thug I can work with."

"We never stop watching our backs." Riley was firm.

"Alright, bro, we hear ya." Vern looked to his brother, and they gave each other a nod. "What's this demonstration? What are we talking about dealing with here?"

"That's simple enough to explain. We have a permit for one-hundred individuals to gather and peacefully demonstrate. We will have closer to one-thousand."

"Prompting a response from the security forces," I added.

"Exactly. I was worried that this demonstration was going to include a random XRC unit dropping dead from a fail-safe. What has fallen into my lap instead is much more potent. You five can keep the demonstration alive, embolden the people." I thought about his words and precisely what they could mean. We couldn't be seen as monsters.

"So, we show them that Terry's still breathing," I started. "And then we keep the demonstration safe, non-lethally." I gave Arc a bit of a glare, to which he shrugged, looking incredulous.

"What?"

"Anyway." I looked back to Cole. "I see the logic in this, but what about the Array? We have to find out where the controls are located and whether or not it needs to come down or if we can actually control it."

"That I can answer, and I will do so for free. The Array has two large satellites to amplify their abilities, that much is true, but the Array itself is controlled through the CORPS Administration Building at the heart of the city. It's heavily fortified and prepared for an assault. Many security barracks,

442

for instance, are based near there."

"Then how do we plan to enter?" Reya inquired.

"Tonight's demonstration must have real impact. People have to talk about it for a long time after. We need to stir the pot and plan a bigger one, a bigger one at the Administration Building." Cole stood again and began to pace once more. It felt like some warlord planning their coup.

"Could be dangerous for a lot of regular folk. A lot of people could get hurt." My conscience wouldn't allow me to divorce myself from the random lives that would be lost.

"And what's the alternative? According to you, the Coalition is planning some sort of genocide. Time is running out. A few lives to save many more has to be considered." He held up a fist to accentuate his words, and I wasn't sure I liked his attitude. His heart was in the right place, though, and we weren't exactly swimming in allies.

"We'll try this plan. We have to try to minimize casualties, though. We can't forget our roots." My friends, Arc included, looked to me, and nodded in agreement. No matter the differences we had, the CORPS had failed at turning us into machines. Although augmented, we were still people.

"Sounds like a disarmin' contest to me, buzz." Arc got a grin. He knew there would be plenty of action. These days, it was difficult to challenge us. Keeping hundreds of ordinary people safe was a challenge.

"Tonight, the people will march, and when they do, you will be there to protect them. I will make the necessary arrangements. The offices up here have basic furniture. Some areas had been worked on. Feel free to take some time to rest. I will get you when it's time." He offered his hand across his desk, and we all took a moment and shook it. A plan had been formed, and we had

443

to trust each other to make it happen.

Chapter Thirty-Three: Not So Peaceful

Many times throughout my journey, I had stopped to imagine how I had come to the point I was at. I escaped the Undercities, lost my friends in the process, and became some sort of cybernetic monster. I had a significant impact on the social workings of the surface world by becoming a raider band's walking demi-god and made contact with a once thought dead society in the form of their resistance faction. I traveled the continent seeing new cultures and new places to fight and kill people in. I wrecked the facility making the cyborgs and made it all the way back home just to find they moved into a dome. To top it all off, I was supposed to foment some sort of revolution within said dome. The world wasn't crazy, it had gone completely wrong.

There were enough spare rooms for us to find privacy in. While we did spend time discussing strategy and plans, we also spent a lot of time in quiet contemplation. It hadn't been easy for any of us to get a quiet moment that we felt like we chose to have. Everything was happening so fast, and it looked like there was no other course but onward.

Ironically enough, I was having a hard time finding peace in an empty room. While I had lived alone in the Undercities for several years, I had grown used to having someone with me at all times. I was usually assigned to babysit Alonna, and part of me missed the conversations we sometimes had. Thinking back to the fight in Libsal, how she dragged the bisected commander to safety, I was still impressed. I had never met an egghead that could also be described as a bit of a badass.

It was a pity really; in another world, she would've grown on me pretty quick. Maybe I was unfair to her, but I still saw Lys's face when I closed my eyes, and I could never let it go. Just following orders can't be used as an excuse, lest we damn ourselves.

After several hours, we were assembled back into Cole's office. The plan was simple, if a little misguided. We were going to an area near one of the satellites that made up the CORPS's communication array. It was a business district with a lot of office buildings and basic municipal access. People were going to walk out of their jobs all over the city and make their way to the demonstration. Terry would reveal he's still alive to the crowd, and we'd try and keep the peace. It all sounded a little crazy to me, but at that point, we needed the people's approval and couldn't exactly have them thinking we were murderers.

Cole would provide any equipment we didn't already have and a vehicle to get to the festivities. He wasn't kidding with his resources; apparently, he had made more than just a few friends when he escaped CORPS custody. It felt weird being a bouncer at some hippy protest, but that was our reality. We needed more than just some ruffled citizens. It was time to up the ante.

"Arc, I have a plan," I spoke as soon as he got in the passenger seat of the simple black car we were provided.

"Why do I have a feeling I'm only gonna half-like this?" He crossed his arms and waited for my reply with a stern look.

"Well, we're gonna need more than a few uppity civilians after tonight. You reckon that Sons camp is still outside the Undercity entrance?"

"I would be shocked if it wasn't."

"Judging by what Cole was saying, after tonight, we might be stuck in this dome for a few weeks. Maybe even a month or two before we can say

446

mission accomplished. Get me?"

"Yeah, I get you. You want backup." He grinned. "I three-quarters like this plan."

"Good 'nuff. I don't think you should go alone, though." I looked to the backseat at Reya. "He's gonna need a tech-head."

"I had a feeling you'd say that." She looked over to Arc and gave him a grin before looking back to me. "I'll babysit him for you."

"Oh, fuck you both. So, let's get this straight, I'm going to go get the Sons and then do what? Bring them here?"

"Yeah, as many as they can muster as quickly as they can. You and Reya can find out how the stalkers get into the sewers and use it as a secret entrance."

"There were access hatches we never explored." Reya mused.

"If we can get the people riled up and then take the array literally right out from under them, we'll have them by the balls."

"The array!" Vern exclaimed, a lightbulb clicking on in his mind. "If we take control of it instead of destroying it, we could do more than just open up communications to the TLF and others-"

"-We could shut the Coalition's communications down completely." Riley finished his brother's sentence.

"So, it's a plan then." I finished the thought off. "You'll need to contact the TLF when you get out so we can set up a flank. Then we'll use the Sons and send the CORPS back to smoke signals. If Cole's fool-ass plan actually works, we'll have a third group for them to contend with at the same time."

"Alright buzz drop us off then. We'll take whatever shit we need and get back at ya." He held his hand out, and I took it firmly, shaking it as one would a brother-in-arms. I turned and gave Reya the same respect. Turning back to the wheel, I drove us out and through the city.

"Uhm." Terry, who had been silently eyeballing us the entire time, finally broke his silence. "W-who are the Sons?" Arc and I looked to each other with a smirk.

"Well, kid." I looked at Terry through the rear-view mirror. "The Sons of Rellen are a group of maniacs that do just about anything we tell them to."

"Live on the surface, pillagin' and shit," Arc added.

"Yep. You're in the big game now, kid."

I wasn't sure what trickery Cole had managed to make the authorities overlook our presence, but so far, it seemed to be working. Apparently, no system was immune to efforts to subvert them. If there's a will, there's a way. As soon as we got to an area close enough for Arc and Reya to try and find their way back to the tunnels, we let them out. I hoped silently that it wouldn't be the last time I saw them.

"Think Cole is gonna be mad?" Vern asked, honestly.

"Fuck Cole," I spoke simply and drove to our destination. "If they aren't successful, he won't be successful." I felt Riley's meaty hand pat my shoulder from the backseat.

"Don't worry, John-boy, all we have to do is play bouncer. They get to have all the fun." I laughed at the sentiment. While I trusted Arc and especially Reya, I knew they would need the firepower more. Unleash the beast as it were.

Finally, we made it to the parking garage a kilometer from the actual protest site. Apparently, one of Cole's friends would be taking the van, and we would find our own way back. Cheeky, but probably smarter to leave fewer strings attached.

We left the van and walked out of the multi-storied garage onto the city block. We soon heard a commotion well before reaching the location and began jogging towards it. In no time, it became apparent that the one-thousand-person figure was horrendously underestimated. When we arrived at the designated area, we turned the corner towards where the people would be protesting, and we were immediately met with a wall of angry bodies. The street was packed with thousands of people. Apparently, word spread faster than Cole thought.

The crowd was made of an incredibly mixed bunch. I realized that the offices they were protesting at belonged to various administrators and to put it basically, the people that signed their day off requests and privilege bumps. The signs themselves ran the gamut, with many people chanting their contents, some boosting the signal with megaphones.

"No Rest Days, No work!"

"Entertainment Is a Right, Not a Privilege!"

"No Press, No Work!"

"How are we getting through this mess?" I put my hands to my hips, coming to a stop, surveying the area. Riley got the bright idea to hoist Terry up onto his shoulders.

"What the-"

"Easy kid. You're the star, remember?" I gave Riley a look of approval, and we began pushing through the crowd, loudly and proudly. Eventually, some in the crowd began to notice who was hoisted above us. For a moment, some of the chanting turned into murmuring.

"What now, John-boy?" Vern inquired. My CIHUD popped out, and it suddenly struck me with an idea. I pushed my way through the crowd, snatching a megaphone out of the hands of one of the protesters and approached a lamp post. Quickly, I climbed up the post, planting my feet onto it. I held myself up with one hand gripping the post while my other hand used the megaphone. From there, I was able to see the gathering security forces, including accompanying CORPS Elites, dressed for riot control.

"Go ahead and take a look! Good ol' Terrance is alive, and that's not the only lie the CORPS has been telling you!" The murmuring quickly turned into confused banter and shouting, but I persisted. "I've come from the outside to tell you more of their lies! The world is alive, and they'll kill anyone to-" I wasn't able to finish my sentence as the sudden glare of a distant scope caught my attention and I let go of the lamp post, dropping down. The ricochet of a bullet could be heard from the post as my feet touched the ground.

What happened next was hard to follow, even for people like me. As soon as the shot had been fired, the crowd began to panic. Protecting them would be next to impossible, even if we had all five of us. Someone was going to get hurt, or worse.

"Riley, get Terry out of here! We'll meet up soon!" I didn't get a reply, but saw Terry quickly disappear into the crowd. That was all I needed. Vern could handle himself and knew the plan. It was time to truly test what we were capable of.

As soon as I found a break in the crowd large enough, I leaped into the air and landed at the front of the protesters nearly twenty meters away. The force of my landing pushed a few people off their feet but it wasn't anything lethal. I found myself in front of the security forces and the Elites who were fixing to take aim at me. From the quick readings, I was able to get, I couldn't find who had the sniper rifle. Everyone in front of me seemed armed with beanbags and electric batons.

"Gotta find the gun." I thought to myself and waded into the group in front of me, hoping to wedge an opening for people to getaway. The first few who came at me were regular security forces. I opted to disarm them as they came forward, almost leisurely taking weapons from hands, tossing them towards the crowd or outright breaking them as fast as they could swing. I was surrounded and yet untouchable.

"John!" My enhanced hearing picked out Vern's voice from the crowd. I glanced and saw him amid the chaos, trying to herd the flock away from the fight. His arm shot up and pointed at a window on the far-right end of the street. A baton came towards me, interrupting my focus. I grabbed the officer's baton wielding wrist and pulled him into an Elite nearby, the first of several to approach, jamming the business end of his baton into the trooper's spine.

Looking back up at where Vern had pointed, I could see the glint of a scope and knew they were taking aim once more. Acting quickly, trying to minimize casualties, I made two moves. First, I maneuvered over to one of the security officers, quickly dodging a bean-bag round from another at my side. I one-punched my target and pulled out the special smoke grenade I got from the TLF, the only one I had felt was safe to bring. Instead of tossing it down and blocking the gunman's sight, potentially triggering panic fire, I instead went for a bold move. Tossing the grenade with all of my strength, it sailed down the street, flying through the window and landing in the sniper's nest.

Within moments, smoke puffed out from the window, giving us time. The entire situation had gotten out of hand fast, and I could only hope that Riley was successful in getting Terry out. I was still busy dealing with the security forces in front of me. Much of the ordinary officers had been taken down, and the Elites were advancing fast.

I ducked under one baton, side-stepped another, stepping both feet over a sweeping third. Using the motion to gain momentum, I kicked one of the Elites into another behind him. I twisted again, back handing another soldier. It seemed like an endless stream of enemies. I didn't think the situation could get any worse until suddenly it did.

I sensed them before I saw them, three CIHUD signatures advancing from the security group directly towards me. The security forces were busted, the people would likely get away without much of a fight. I had to get the bald bastards off me and fast. I began to sprint through the crowd of people and fallen foes, making my way to the nearest building. I scaled it, using my hands and legs to jump from windowsill to windowsill. This entire spectacle was way more public than the CORPS had hoped for, so I decided that being a bit over the top was necessary.

To my frustration, only two of the signatures continued to advance. Eventually, two of the monk looking XRC soldiers became visible, making their way up in the same fashion I did. The other must-have been hunting for Vern and Riley. Two out of three ain't bad, so I counted my blessings.

I wasn't about to fight both head-on, so I continued to sprint, running from rooftop-to-rooftop. I knew they could follow me, but they weren't near the crowd. Once I was far enough to feel safe, but close enough to still see the riot, I turned to face my foes. They landed directly in front of me, just ten meters away on the other end of the roof. It was time to test a theory.

"Two against one is a little unfair, don't you think?"

"Surrender XR001."

"Turned you into robots, I see. Free-will wasn't good enough?" I slowly drew my sidearm and began twirling it in my hand. "Not the life for me, pal." They watched me intently, trying to gain insight into my moves. With a quick flick of my wrist, I tossed the weapon into the air and caught it with my other hand. I immediately fired the gun twice, aiming low, where it would be more challenging to dodge. The assailant on the right got hit in the side as they dove away, though the hit didn't look lethal. The other having a fraction more time to react came out clean. I used the distraction to turn and leap off of the roof, landing in an alleyway below. It would seem the CORPS's pets couldn't handle chaos very well.

Looking to my left, I could see that the crowd was still scattering, creating a lot of noise and hubbub. The demonstration had quickly devolved into a full-scale riot. While it was less about looting and more about getting away from the armed CORPS lackies, there was still an apparent urge to wreck anything in sight. I had no time to contemplate the scene, instead finding a door into the building in front of me.

The door wouldn't open when I approached it. I tried to grip the side of the door, pulling in the direction it slid open. With a few grunts and the snap of the locking mechanism breaking, the door came loose. I didn't enter it though, first checking to make sure they hadn't spotted me yet. With the coast clear, I quickly yet quietly, made my way back into the rampaging crowd. I knew they had heard the door open and hoped the fact that I appeared normal to their CIHUDs would complete the ruse.

Making my way into the crowd, I could see that the area surrounding the protest site had been turned almost literally upside down. Cars had been flipped onto their tops, glass displays were shattered, and small fires had popped up from the scuffle with the law. Apparently, the situation in the city was worse than I had realized because the people reacted like a pressure cooker finally bursting.

I began to frantically look for Vern and Riley. They were big boys, and to be honest, I was more worried about my hide being tag teamed. So far, my pursuers hadn't figured out where I had gone yet. I spotted Vern first, further down the street and closer to where the protest had begun. He had probably been looking for Riley and Terry, though he noticed when I waved to get his attention.

"I've had about enough of you Divisives." I heard the phrase like seeing a piercing light through the fog. I turned and saw three Elites surrounding a couple of young protesters. One was a somewhat scrawny, punkish looking guy, and his partner was an equally small man, dressed a little more conservatively. The one in the leather and spikes was standing protectively in front of the other, and a security officer was approaching both of them with a baton in hand. The other scenes, though similar, were different, and I began to realize that some of the other scuffles going on around me actually appeared more personal than the situation called for. Some citizens had even started to assist the security forces, and others looked like they came looking for a fight to begin with.

"Hey!" I was closer to the two men and decided to intervene, hoping I could get some sort of answer out of them. The Elites immediately turned and pointed their now very lethal weapons towards me. Before they could complete their turn, I pounced forward, my fist connecting to the face of the middle one while my other arm reached out to grab the weapon of the right Elite, prying it from his hands with relative ease, and tossing it like a brick at the final one. Grabbing ahold of the Elite I had disarmed, I yanked his arm

454

behind his back, lifted up harshly to break it, effectively neutralizing him. The third had been efficiently knocked out cold from the impact of the gun.

"You." I pointed at and advanced towards the security officer. Grabbing the front of the officer's shirt, I lifted him into the air like he was a mere bag of feathers. "What's a Divisive?"

"T-th-they go against the Unity! They speak against the Coalition!" I really should have thought my plan through a little better or at all really because the warning my senses gave me was a millisecond too late. I still had my CIHUD out and realized that my two bald friends had found me, and one was taking aim. I threw the officer to the side and dove but took the round they had fired into my upper torso. The bullet tore through my back, creating a vicious exit wound. The impact spun my body, and I hit the ground hard.

The implants provide an unbreakable endurance, and I was on my feet almost as quickly as I had fallen, although my breathing was labored, and I couldn't move my right arm effectively. I began to dash when they fired more rounds, just managing to escape the shots. Blood was pouring from my wound, and though the nanomachines were doing their job, I was quickly losing my strength. I scrambled for an alley on my side of the street.

Several more shots whizzed past me, and one finally found purchase, sideswiping me on the left and nearly sending me down again. Making it to the back of the alley, I scrambled to the left, putting my back against the building. I slowly slid down until I was sitting, leaving a blood smear on the wall behind me. Everything began to get blurry, and my sight was starting to fade. I closed my eyes tight, shook my head, and then reopened them, trying to clear my thoughts. I drew my sidearm, waiting for the inevitable execution.

A solid minute passed by, and I saw no one come looking for their

Part Three: Home Again

fallen prey. Something was happening, and I was unable to do anything about it. People rushed and ran around me, the security forces seeming to finally win the day and slowly regain some semblance of control over the situation. The sounds began to echo in my mind, and one minute turned to two, which then became three. I would've made it to four, but either from my wounds or the nanomachines trying to keep me alive, my eyes closed, and I lost consciousness.

Chapter Thirty-Four: Breaking Point

"It never ends son." My father was a large and somewhat burly man. I looked up to him in more ways than one. A graying goatee adorned his warm expression. *"War, hatred, greed; it's why we're down here and why we'll be back again. Don't lose your humanity boy, it's all we have left."*

We were not in any kind of room, and my father slowly faded into the darkness that permeated everything. While I felt small, even child-like, everything appeared as an endless abyss around me. Before my eyes, scenes began to play out, like watching some sort of screen. People fighting, uprisings, genocide, hatred, and perverted love.

"There will come a time son when you realize that all the reasons we hate each other are figments of our imagination. Made up excuses of self-appointed righteousness." I heard his voice and longed to see his face again.

"Oh Johnny, controlling your anger doesn't mean letting people walk all over you!" My mother's soothing voice made the bloody nose from my youth feel better. Fight, don't fight, I could never figure out what she wanted.

"Don't let your heart grow cold John, there's nothing left after that." Lys's voice was saying words I never remembered her speaking. Was it really her or just me in disguise?

"Sorry, John-boy, no martyrdom for you today." *Vern's voice was an echo, somewhere far off in the distance and yet right next to me at the same time. I felt like I was floating in the ocean, being tossed violently about by the waves. I flailed helplessly, being taken to whatever hell likely awaited me.*

"Holy shit, is he going to make it?" *Other voices spoke around me, calling out to me, like Vern's they seemed close yet also very far away.*

"First in, last out." Alonna's voice spoke in my ear, seeming sensual and sultry. *"This doesn't end with you, John, it begins."*

"Wakey wakey, eggs and bakey!" My eyes were fluttering open, and my head was pounding. When I suddenly realized I had made my way back to reality, I sat up quickly with a gasp. My hand immediately went to my chest wound, but there wasn't much there anymore. I felt a hand press onto my chest and push me down onto the bed gently.

"Whoa, whoa John-boy, relax." It was Riley who was sitting next to me. "Well looks like I'm the winner."

"Winner?" I looked to Riley, confused. We were in one of the offices of Cole's hideout. I was laid out on a couch, no shirt, though otherwise clothed, which was a change from the last time I woke up that way.

"Yep, the one who gets the privilege of getting the wake-up shift." I suddenly realized there was an IV stand next to me, and I was hooked up to what appeared to be saline and a nutrient bag as well. "You can probably pull those out now."

"How long have I been sleeping?" I felt like I was suffering the worst hangover in the world, though the feeling was beginning to subside. I absently removed the needles from my arm.

"About two weeks, give or take a day." I looked to Riley with shock on my face.

"Two fucking weeks?" I moved to sit up again, this time being allowed to, though he stopped me from getting up.

"Whoa there tiger, relax. The good guys mostly won. Nothing to worry about for the moment, well kind of sort of anyway."

"What the fuck happened?"

"You got shot ya big dummy." I gave Riley an agitated look.

"I mean after that, dipshit." He chuckled at the insult.

458

"Right, right. Well, Vern and I were making our way towards you in the crowd when we got into a scuffle with who I assume shot your ass. They didn't live to tell the tale."

"Well, that's good to hear. What about the kid?"

"Safe and sound back at Mikey's club." I was happy to hear our charge was safe.

"Hey Riley, have you ever heard the term Divisive before, as a way to describe someone?"

"What like a contrarian or something?" He raised a brow and stroked his chin in thought.

"No man, not like a contrarian. Like it was a proper category of some kind. Like giving a name to a deviant."

"I think I remember the Arbiter using the word when we first got here, but I dunno homeboy. It would probably be best to ask Cole about that sort of thing. Well, you're up, I'm getting dinner. Just relax, I'll have everyone meet in here." Riley stood up and gave a stretch. "We were worried about you for a minute there. A normal man would be pretty dead right about now."

"Yeah, well, good thing we aren't normal."

"A very good thing." He gave a wink and walked out of the room. I laid back for a minute and stared at the ceiling, contemplating everything that had happened. As weird as it was, I was missing Alonna even more. Her insight would have been invaluable at that point. It was quickly becoming apparent that in the five years I had been gone, my people had experienced a great deal of civil unrest. The transition to the surface probably wasn't as smooth as the CORPS had initially planned. With the war about to be kicked into high gear, concessions were obviously being made. Of course, I could've been dead wrong; the CORPS very well may want a healthy amount of civil disobedience, and that was the insight we needed.

After only a few minutes, Cole, Riley, and Vern entered the room. The brothers found a seat and got comfortable while Cole infuriatingly began to pace.

"Glad to see you're okay," Cole commented, giving me a quick glance.

"Honestly, it's not even the most shocking thing I've survived."

"No doubt. Look, I'm going to be frank here: we're in trouble." I gave Riley some side-eye who merely answered with a shrug. "The incident two weeks ago stirred a hornet's nest the likes of which I am unsure we can handle."

"You underestimate us." Came Vern's simple response.

"You underestimate the Coalition." Cole retorted. "Right now, things are pretty messy out there. The Coalition have all but declared martial law. There's a very strict curfew in effect, and they've begun searching the city."

"For?" I asked rhetorically, knowing damn well what they were looking for.

"Us."

"Well, you said yourself they won't find this place."

"I said they wouldn't suspect this place, but at this point, they're randomly searching districts each day."

"We're the most wanted, John-boy." Riley gave a grin.

"Yeah, and you're dead." His brother added.

"Really?" I couldn't help but chuckle a little at the thought. "Don't get my hopes up like that."

"Poor taste jokes aside, your friends are right, they're wanted and worst yet they've managed to bypass our sneaking device. Every sensor array, every

460

camera will be able to pinpoint you with accuracy."

"So, we're trapped here with you then?" I didn't like the prospect.

"In a manner of speaking, yes. When we leave here next, we had better have a plan for the end game."

"Well, then you're sort of fucked, aren't you?" I cocked my head to the side, studying Cole's reaction, who merely grinned.

"I have some aces up my sleeve. There's a couple of vehicles in the building that are coated with the same signal blocking material as this office block. While we'll easily be spotted, I'll have a fighting chance."

"Better than nothin-" I was interrupted by a somewhat quiet alarm, sounding from Cole's pants pocket. He reached in, producing a mini PCD that he used to work the security systems of the building.

"We have an intruder." His voice dripped with dread at being caught off guard. Then his expression changed to frustration. "It's that Arc friend of yours."

"Arc? Well fuck yeah, he must've succeeded. Is Reya with him?" I was curious and a little worried at the same time.

"He's alone, but the enemy knows of him too. He might have just led the Coalition right to us."

"We ain't staying here much longer anyway. Fuck, I hope Reya's okay."

"Sames." Vern agreed. Cole opened up the lower level security doors using his PCD, and Vern walked out to meet him.

"Before you get all pissy Cole, he's probably under the impression that your devices still work. Either way, it's the kick in the ass we need to start making a plan." I honestly didn't want to hear whatever he had to say about it.

"Forgive me if I like time to plan."

"Well, you best learn to fly by the seat of your pants homeboy. It's how we get shit done around here." Riley spoke and gave him a smirk. It wasn't long before Arc made his presence known. The door slid open, and in he marched.

"Just relax, man, we're not going anywhere for a minute." Vern was behind Arc, apparently trying to calm him down.

"We need to talk, buzz." Arc looked squarely at me, and I looked to the others before meeting his eyes.

"Uh, so talk?"

"You'd probably prefer it to be man-to-man." His eyes were serious, and he seemed somewhat worried, which was disturbing in and of itself.

"Before you go any further, where's Reya?" Riley interjected.

"She's fine, got her chillin' with the Sons. We managed to find our way into the sewer system, but fuck that shit, man, we really need to talk alone."

"I appreciate you respecting my privacy, but I'm not in the business of keeping secrets."

"Fine, y'know that's the whole fuckin' point anyway. Reya said I should leave it alone, but buzz, you've been lied to enough, and I ain't gonna keep it going through omission."

"Just spit it out, man." I was getting aggravated by the suspense.

"Alonna's dead." As soon as the words came out of his mouth, the wind escaped my lungs. My mouth was agape, though I hadn't noticed. My mind was reeling, the implants battling emotions it hadn't had to contend with yet.

"What the fuck happened?" My words came out as a whisper. I didn't notice that I had stood, my eyes not leaving Arc's.

"You're really gonna make me say this in front of everyone, aren't you?"

"Alonna? Wait, do you mean Doctor Alonna Lyrul?" Vern gave Cole a nod in confirmation, and then a look that said shut your trap.

"Just tell me."

"Nah, you have to tell me something first, and you're gonna be fuckin' honest about it. Did you two, y'know, fuck?" His question wasn't helping the deluge of emotions; I sure as shit didn't need him adding confusion to the mix.

"No, Arc, we didn't fuck, alright." My lips had become pursed as anger began to drown everything out.

"Well then buzz, she either extracted your sperm or fucking raped you when you were passed out." The shock of the statement hit me with enough force that I had to sit back down.

"Arc, you need to start making sense, now."

"John-boy, he's right, we're gonna give you a minute." Vern motioned for his brother to join him. Cole showed no intention of leaving, but Riley grabbed his shoulder and escorted him out of the room.

"Look, you know we're brothers, me and you. You know I wouldn't fuck with you, but I can't just abide by what the TLF wants or what Reya thinks is best about you not getting distracted." He took a deep breath, he obviously had a lot to say without any idea on how to say it. "When we got out, we contacted the TLF to let them know the plan, have them try and set up some sort of perimeter near the dome. We also got more than just the Sons camping out-"

"Arc!" I growled out.

"Alright, alright, man. According to Delantil, Alonna got real sick a few weeks ago. She was refusing treatment up until she couldn't refuse it anymore. She was pregnant, John." My eyes widened in shock.

"Pregnant?"

"Yeah man, and the TLF used a sample of your DNA they picked up when they first took you in, and well, the baby is yours."

"Was mine," I spoke with a deep sadness thinking about the entire thing.

"Well, no, is yours, just let me finish. She wouldn't let the doctors save her through an abortion; she had her reasons, I guess, but she opted to have the kid saved using an artificial womb. Real simple as far as the TLF is concerned, but it gets more fucked up. The baby killed her."

"Wait, how?"

"Dude, I dunno how to say this, so I'll be blunt. The baby is like us. Alonna's body was swimming with nanomachines, your nanomachines. Her body was rejecting them. Look, here." He reached into one of his leg pockets and produced a data-stick for PCDs. "She recorded a confession for you." I stared at the data stick for what felt like an eternity before taking it from Arc. "I'm gonna give you a minute to let this sink in." Arc turned towards the door and quietly walked out.

I was staring down at the data-stick in my hand, unsure whether I actually wanted to hear Alonna's message or not. I couldn't explain the flood of emotions inside of me. Grief, sadness, rage, violation, fear, guilt, hatred, and even longing all coalesced into a torrent of feelings that even the CORPS's magic couldn't quite handle. I didn't love Alonna, but she had become a friend, and I was tired of losing friends.

Finally, I steeled myself, grabbed my PCD from my bag and plugged in the data-stick. Interestingly enough, it contained a lot more than just a confession. Several files had been saved onto the stick, and they had some interesting labels such as *Coalition Biometric Scanners* and *Killswitch*. The first file I opened, however, was labeled *I'm Sorry*.

Alonna's face came on the screen, and although her eyes were sunken and expression exhausted, my eyes discerned the strength and beauty she had always possessed, that I often took for granted.

"Hello, John. I'm not sure what I'm doing right now." She wiped a tear from her eye, sniffling. "For me, that is very hard to admit." She sighed deeply. "So, I guess I will start with simply saying, I'm sorry. I'm sorry for everything that has ever happened to you, for your friend Lys and the others, and for being a direct player in taking your life away. Goodness." She let out a light chuckle, wiping away another tear. "I do not think I have truly cried in years. I guess I can thank you for that, for reminding me that I still have a heart." Part of me couldn't help but smile at her comment. She was right, I always took every opportunity to remind her that she didn't have to be a cold-blooded CORPS scientist.

"For a moment, I will frustrate you as I always had and be the scientist. There is no way to explain it that does not sound-" she paused, looking for the word, "-heartless. Not that it was the first time, but I lied to you when you asked me about Project Perfect Conception. I knew exactly what it was." She looked down and away from the camera for a moment. It seemed like she was fighting more than just her emotions. Finally, she looked up again. "Remember the talks we have had about the intentions of the Coalition? I never lied to you about that. They do desire to expedite our evolution, to create an intelligent being that can survive anything. You were a step in that direction, but it was

465

less about your enhanced abilities and more about whether or not you could impart them."

"We knew there would be risks involved, that baseline mothers would possibly be susceptible to rejection syndrome." She gave a light laugh and held out her arms. "Here is that theory in action." She shook her head, putting her arms back down. She had to take a moment to calm herself. "In all honesty, I probably deserve this, but this is not about me. This is about you, John, because I did it again. I manipulated you one last time." Her breath caught, and she wiped her cheeks again. "No matter what you have been through, no matter the trials, you still try to do the right thing, to be a good man. You slip, but you try. Xavier could not break you, and I saw that strength. You are a man of your word and of responsibility. I knew this, and because of that knowledge, I know you will take are of our daughter when you're through." She smiled weakly. "She will have a father."

"I took advantage of your body while you were unconscious, and I completed my ultimate goal. I did so not only knowing the ethics of the action, but knowing you would take responsibility for my crime."

I stared coldly at the screen, the cursed machines coursing through my body robbed me of my own ability to cry. The emotions were there, but as always, I was in control, and at that moment, I didn't want to be. I felt violated and yet sad at the same time. "There is something you must know." She became gravely serious. "The Coalition is not omniscient, no matter how much they pretend to be. They cannot plan for every contingency, there is not a master plan for all events, and the thing they cannot handle the most is unbridled chaos. You, John, are unbridled chaos. You are the wrench in the gears, and though I can never make up for what I have done to you, I can still

466

help you. On this data-stick, I left a few more personal messages about our daughter and her future, but those must wait. Instead, I have provided you with much more."

Suddenly, looking into her eyes through the screen, I felt like we finally saw eye-to-eye in a profound way. Her sickly features and weak voice could not mask the same vengeance fueled rage that now consumed me. Finally, after her death, we were on the same page.

"You will find files, information about Coalition security systems. Do not expect miracles from me, that will be for you to perform. The thing you really must remember is that Xavier Ronyn is in the Habitat with you. His promotion will be integral to taking over the communications array. The data-stick you hold is the key, and he must turn that key himself." She took a breath and closed her eyes before looking to the camera again. Our eyes met, and the finality of it all struck me. "I-I." she gritted her teeth and shook her head. "Take care of our daughter, let her be like you. Goodbye, John." She reached over, and the video clip ended.

For a long hard moment, I stared at the PCD, my face expressionless, my mind for the first time since everything had started was quiet. As if in auto-pilot mode, I stood and walked over to my clothes and equipment Riley had left out for me in the room. With a frightening calm, I donned my outfit for what felt like the last time.

Ever since the day I awoke in my cell at the XRC labs, my mind had been a bastion of control. Every thought was meticulously laid out, every plan methodical even if it didn't seem like it to observers. I could feel rage, but rage could not consume me. Then my mind snapped back to the moment I first met Alonna when she came into my room, and I nearly scared her half to

467

death. The memory wasn't about her or my actions, but my feelings. Rage couldn't control me, but I could control Rage; I could become it, and suddenly, that's exactly what happened.

"Ahhh!" I screamed out in an ear-splitting battle cry. I flipped the coffee table in front of the couch I had been laying on, sending it flying across the room. I let the adrenaline pump through me and knew it was time to finish the mission. One way or another, Xavier Ronyn would lie dead at my feet.

My friends rushed into the room immediately, Arc first, followed by the brothers, and then Cole, who was about to speak about the state of the room. "Don't." My word came out like a weapon, my finger pointed at him. I looked to Arc and then the others, my eyes a burning fire, but my body was utterly calm. "It's time. I'm done. This is his last day on this world."

"John, we need a pl-" Cole tried to speak.

"We have a plan! Arc." I snapped my vision to him. "Can you get the Sons into the city?"

"You bet your ass I can. Like I said, Reya found the way the mutaphorms got into the sewers. I could have them marching in the city in an hour."

"How many?" At this point, Arc's grin widened.

"Those kids are a loyal bunch buzz, but they don't follow every order. They called in reinforcements to the camp we left behind. We have hundreds waiting in the tunnels. We can get them in, but once they're in, there ain't no being quiet."

"You're fucking-a-right there's no being quiet! I'm done with all of this."

"Wait, you're bringing the Sons in here, now?" Vern suddenly looked startled by the very idea. "What happened to preventing collateral damage?"

"Collateral damage? What the fuck do you call two weeks ago? You think I want people to die? We're stopping a genocide."

"And getting revenge," Riley spoke lowly, glaring at me.

"No, it's not about revenge anymore. Ronyn needs to die before he can ruin any more lives. Will that make me happy? Fuck yeah it will, but that doesn't change how necessary it is."

"This is about her, isn't it?" Arc asked, crossing his arms over his chest.

"What of it?" I already knew I wasn't going to enjoy what he was about to say.

"What do you mean, what of it? She fucking raped you buzz! She went to town while you were out, and now you wanna smash shit up for her?" It was at that point I found myself right in Arc's face, who had put his arms at his side and glared right back at me.

"She was raped too, rape of the mind. Don't you fucking see that? The whole world got fucked if ya hadn't noticed. She ain't the reason, just the breaking point. I was starting to care about her, and there's nothing fucking wrong with that!" Our friends watched us closely, ready to break up a fight, but Arc cut the tension with his aggravatingly cocky grin.

"Now you're being honest. I ain't going to war with a man who can't be straight with us." He took the first step back and looked to Vern. "Vengeance should be what we all want right now. Someone has to set this shit right."

"I don't get how we are suddenly capable of doing that," Cole spoke up. "The Coalition still outnumber us ten to one, they still hold all of the cards."

"No, not quite." Riley put it plainly. "Y'see, our buddies on the outside have an array of their own, based off of the Coalition's designs."

"Once we were outta the Dome's influence," Arc explained, "we managed to contact and rendezvous with the TLF stationed nearby. That's how I have the data-stick. They're arming up and getting ready for our word, buzz."

"We have a lot of defectors in our circle," Vern added.

"What difference does that make?" Cole was getting more and more frustrated.

"The difference should be clear." Riley showed his patience. "If we shut down the array on this end or even take it over outright, we'll be able to prevent even basic communication among the Coalition forces. We can send them back to smoke signals."

"We can also prove our point to the people," I spoke assuredly. "We can send a message to all those TV screens. We can wake them up."

"But how do you plan to accomplish this? Even if we get into the Administration Building, we have no idea how to take over the array, let alone destroy it without taking out a city block at the same time."

"Xavier Ronyn." The name dripped from my mouth like venom. "Alonna said he's our key."

"So, he *is* here then," Arc spoke lowly, knowing what it meant for me.

"Of course!" Cole finally lightened up. "The biometric security measures of the Coalition are unhackable and cannot be overridden. He would have to be alive, though, in order to provide us access." He was quickly onboard.

"Then it's settled." As I spoke, a chime began to sound from Cole's pocket. He produced his PCD and gave a big sigh looking at it.

"Not a moment too soon, either. We have to leave, now." He showed us the screen, and we could see security footage of the street. Elites and security officers were roaming around, likely looking for Arc.

"Convenient timing," Arc muttered.

"Inconvenient. The device I gave you was compromised before your return. They likely know exactly where to look."

"Great, we'll have to fight our way out." Vern shook his head.

"I have one last ace up my sleeve. There's sewer access at the bottom level. We should be able to get out from there before they storm the building."

"Wouldn't they know about that?" I inquired logically.

"It's a risk, but you'll have to take it."

"Wait, what about you, buzz?" Arc quirked a brow.

"I'll cover your escape. You're right, this plan is a one-shot deal. If you guys don't make it, there won't be other chances. I planned to die for this cause, one way or the other. Just promise me something." Cole walked over to me and put his hand on my shoulder, giving it a light shake. "Liberate them, John. They can't be slaves to the Coalition any longer, no matter how good life may be in here."

"I'm gonna show them the sky." We met eye-to-eye for what I knew would be the last time. He took my arm, and I took his in a warrior's handshake. We patted each other on the shoulder, and then I looked to the others. "Time to go, boys."

"Take this." Cole handed me his mini PCD. "There's a map of the sewer systems I kept for my own escape. You should be able to use it to get under the Administration Building."

Part Three: Home Again

"Time's up, boys." Vern interrupted. With that simple statement, we all moved to gather our things and prepare for our last stand.

Chapter Thirty-Five: Unbridled Chaos

The plan itself was insane. There were possibly hundreds of thousands of soldiers tucked away into hidden areas of the Dome. Would the CORPS sick them on the populace? We may have been potentially endangering everyone, but we had to do something. My gut instinct said that if we succeeded, the CORPS would be crippled, and it would be the only way to save millions of lives. We would bring Unbridled Chaos to the epitome of control.

We managed to make it out of the building before it was stormed. Cole had remained in his office, waiting for the final confrontation. I had misjudged him severely; he was braver than most of us. Part of me still wondered if he would betray our plan to the CORPS, but that was the logical machine talking; my instincts said otherwise, and they had never steered me wrong.

The sewer access was located in a maintenance closet attached to the garage. We opened the hermetically sealed hatch and descended the ladder into the literal bowels of the city. It was probably a bit of a misnomer to call it a sewer. Much of the waste was being processed through vast pipe systems to what I assumed were reclamation centers. At least we didn't have to slog through floaters. It was more like walking through concrete tunnels than a sewer proper.

"So, what direction?" I asked Arc, handing him the PCD.

"Well, let's see here. We're a few kilometers away from our entry point. The tunnel we found ran to a run-off area, probably where they dump anything they can't recycle." Arc started us off.

"Makes sense," Vern offered. "The Undercities were basically a giant hole in the ground. They could probably dump waste down there for centuries, and you'd never notice." Vern's analysis seemed accurate enough.

"This place is entirely too big not to have sewer access just about everywhere." Riley finished off the point. The sewers themselves traveled like a maze created by the biggest jerk ever to construct labyrinths. Only by virtue of our enhancements were we able to navigate the city from its underbelly.

"I'm a little concerned here, buzz." Arc suddenly spoke up as we walked. "Doesn't it seem weird that they can't just, I dunno, use some mumbo-jumbo sensor grid to detect the eager dogs we brought with us?"

"They're distracted," Vern answered. "It makes sense when you think about it. There's been demonstrations and police versus civilian confrontations ever since the riot broke out. All hands are dedicated to keeping the streets safe. Plus, I think we're naive to treat the Coalition as perfect."

"They're not omniscient." I meant to think it, but instead stated it as pure fact. "They make mistakes, so ya ask me, it's a little bit of both."

We pressed onward towards our destination. We didn't meet any opposition along the way. The CORPS must have detected the TLF forces that were waiting a safe distance away from the city. If they had discovered the Sons in the sewers, they would be preparing for that as well. Pouring troops down manholes would be even more suspicious than everything the CORPS had done up to that point. Their lies would be our advantage.

The shaft eventually came to a dead-end, the pipes feeding into the wall and continuing on elsewhere. At the center of the wall was a hefty looking security door that had been welded shut.

"Well, that puts a damper on things," Riley commented.

"Fuck, man, they should be right behind this door." Arc's voice reflected his frustration. Then he looked up with a classic light-bulb moment. He walked up to the door and pounded on it, like a cop that just wanted to talk it out. Sure enough, a banging sound was heard from the other side and then very faintly a voice. I don't think a normal person could have picked it up, but it was Reya.

"Anyone catch that?" I couldn't quite make out what she was saying.

"Nah, man, why don't we just blow the damn thing? We should still have explosives from when we first showed up. We never used 'em!" Arc was reaching for the duffle bag I was carrying.

"Look at the door dip-shit, it swings open on our side. We ain't getting it open that way." I answered, pulling the bag away.

"Well, what else are we going to do?" Arc was barely able to finish his sentence. We were immediately blown off of our feet by the shockwave of an explosion from the other side of the door. Luckily no one was struck when the door flew a few meters forward, landing with a thwump on the floor.

"Are you crazy?" I heard Reya's incredulous voice cry out as soon as the ringing in my ears had cleared up. We all stood and saw an incredible sight on the other side of the door. It was the tunnels that led to the massive tram system we had originally came through. Cramming it were hundreds of uniquely dressed, armed, and chomping at the bit Sons of Rellen. Reya was chastising one young woman who had a bald head and a face full of markings arranged in a complex set of patterns, like someone had drawn on her face with their fingers. She held a detonator in her hand.

"Damnit, they probably know we're here now." Reya's voice was exasperated. "These people are lunatics! What were we thinking?"

"We were thinking exactly the way we needed to," I spoke with a somewhat cold tone. "We'll fight order with chaos. Good to see you're still in one piece."

"Likewise. What the hell are we doing?"

"We're finally doing shit my way and wrecking stuff!" Arc proclaimed proudly. Reya cocked her head, exasperation becoming full-on flabbergast.

"What is he going on about?" She looked to me as if she was about to get some semblance of sanity, but certainly found none.

"We have a one-shot deal. We're taking the array, and we're using Ronyn to do it. The city's under martial-law now, curfews, marching soldiers everywhere, the works."

"I'm away for two weeks, and you guys turned the place upside down?"

"It was a pressure cooker, you knew that." Riley spoke up for our plan.

"So, what the hell is the plan then?" Reya put her hands to her hips and gave me a look that said I had better start talking fast.

"We're taking the Sons and storming into the city directly below the Administration Building. We'll take the building and find Ronyn." I explained.

"How did you confirm he's here?"

"A few last gifts from Alonna." I took a moment to look over Reya's shoulder at the scene before me. The Sons always had a knack for being the most interestingly dressed bunch. I realized the horror people will feel when they come pouring out. We had to make sure the Sons understood who the real enemy was. No matter how much rage I was riding, I couldn't forget myself. "Excuse me." I politely moved passed Reya and towards the crowd.

"The First." I heard someone yell out as the crowd slowly meandered its way into silence. I continued to walk, the Sons parting way for me, eventually closing the gap and leaving me at the center. My story had obviously spread to all of them, along with whatever conditioning Arc had administered on his own. It still felt a little wrong, but at least we never lied to them.

I pointed at a wirey looking fellow, his clothes hanging off like rags over a larger jumpsuit. On his back was a speaker attached to what looked to be an antique radio with speakers. I crooked my finger, and he came scuttling towards me, a mix of fear and awe in his eyes. He was smart enough to know what I wanted and handed me the mic, which was frustratingly attached to a wire.

"This is the moment you have all waited for. A true test of your Strength." My voice boomed from the speaker on his back. "Up until now, you have fought the mewling farmers and cowering townsfolk. It was all training for this moment where your Strength is truly needed." I pointed towards the ceiling. "Above us now rests a city the likes of which you have never seen. In it are people who need your Strength; Strength to fight the mightiest foe you have ever faced. This is your true test of Strength, for you cannot be wanton! You must protect those who cannot protect themselves. That takes true Strength, real Strength."

There was murmuring, unsure whispers, and so I decided to ride the rage. "Any of you that wants to challenge my judgment, you're more than welcomed to try." I look throughout the crowd, and slowly the murmuring began to fade. They knew where they belonged. "Any who offer their aid shall fight by your side! Give them a weapon! To the CORPS Elites, show no mercy!" As soon as I uttered this phrase, there was an eruption of cheering and war cries. I swung my arm to the side to silence them, and obediently they quieted down, starting with the front and ending with the back. "This is the moment of your lives that will prove your true worth. The CORPS is the enemy, the people above our charges. We move soon to take the CORPS Administration Building. As soon as we have it under our control, you will make a perimeter. Show me your Strength!" The cheering that erupted held more confidence. The Sons were riled up.

I was never much of a speechwriter. While I had always been a social sort of guy, it was the implants that were giving me the presence of mind and a sharp tongue. The confidence flowed through me, and I channeled my rage through the Sons. They would be my instrument of Unbridled Chaos. They surrounded me, and I was quickly hoisted onto the shoulders of two burly men beside me, the others reaching over to idolize their First. Once upon a time, I would've balked at this, but now it was time to fight fire with fire. I raised my fist into the air, and so did they. After a long moment, I was set down and found my way back to my companions.

"Do you really think this is wise?" Reya asked, tilting her head.

"Nah, I don't, but what else can we do? Y'know these mother fuckers have been at it for centuries. If we don't finish it, who will? Delantil? F'Rytal, if it even still exists? Nah, we have to make our stand." She nodded her head and took a few steps forward, putting her hand on my shoulder.

"I hope you're right." I put my hand onto hers and gave her a nod as well.

"I know I am."

"Alright, kids, if playtime is over, we have a whole lotta bodies to move through cramped quarters." Arc waved his arm out to refer to the Sons all around us. He handed me Cole's PCD, and I began to look at the sewer schematic superimposed on a basic map of the city. I waved over a couple of Sons lieutenants to listen in on the strategy.

478

"They simulate an atmosphere in here to help keep crops regular and probably to prepare the people for eventual transition out. They have drainage access in most of the major streets as a result. The problem is, they're bottlenecks. We'd have to come out single-file, and as soon as that happens, they'll likely lock down the Administration Building, and we'd never get in." My friends stood around me, forming a war room style huddle. We were deciding the fate of millions.

"Well, dumb-dumb, if they'll lock it down, what do you expect to accomplish?" Reya was still the most doubtful of our group, likely fearing the collateral damage the Sons would cause. I answered her with a grin.

"We're going into the building from below. Chances are, whatever maps we have won't show any actual access point into the building. So, we'll make our own. We can still extrapolate where the building is and blow a big old hole right under it."

"Lovin' the plan, buzz!"

"Okay, so we're just going to blow up the bottom of the building?" Reya was back to incredulous.

"Nah, just blow a hole under it big enough for us to get in. Once we're in, the Sons will come out of every access point within half a kilometer and make a perimeter around it. I'm hoping anyone who's ever been called a Divisive sees this and takes the opportunity. Riley and Vern, you're going to stay outside with the Sons and make sure they stay in line."

The two brothers looked to one another and gave a nod before looking back to me. "Sounds reasonable."

"Arc, Reya, and I will take the building. We'll bring in some Sons with us to secure the exits from the inside as well. We have one shot at this. We

479

find Xavier Ronyn and use him to gain access to their central computer system so we can take the array." I looked to the two lieutenants I had motioned over. "Get some explosives ready. I want ten of your best men to accompany me."

"Your will shall be done, First!" They gave reverent bows and moved into the crowd, beginning to spread the order throughout the troops. I took a moment to play the file about biometric security. Once again, Alonna's face appeared before my PCD. Her voice came out raspy and weak.

"I was hoping to be finished this before you left. All you have to do is have Dr. Ronyn place this data-stick in any terminal connected to their main computer systems. That's the only way you can take control." She had to stop a moment to hack and cough. The sight brought a foreign mixture of guilt, violation, and rage. "Xavier must be the one to place the data-stick in the system. It's the only way passed the biometric security. If you plan to disable the array or even their security systems, you will need someone with his access." I stopped the video and looked to my compatriots. Riley gave my shoulder a pat, and Arc gave me a nod. It was time.

As soon as everyone was ready, we began to move to our destination at a snail's pace. With how cramped the sewer tunnels were and how many Sons had shown up for the party, we were in a tight spot.

As we moved our way through, I began to hear what I would eventually come to know as war rhythms coming from the Sons behind us. They sang in near unison, mostly guttural grunts and rising cries in harmony. It was like beating drums with their throat, the sounds of their intentions reverberating throughout the underground. I was beginning to find it hard to believe that none above could hear it. If they couldn't, they soon would.

Finally reaching our destination, in a startling sort of unity, the Sons began to find their way throughout the surrounding tunnels, making their ways to the ladders of manholes and other various access points. They waited patiently for the signal to rise up. We were stopped short of getting too far directly under the Administration Building.

When we got close to the actual target, we were suddenly met with a wall that seemed to go further underground. Unlike the bunker-like architecture that made up the sewers, it was a metallic barrier that actually seemed to cut off some of the access to the pipe system. The pipes hit the wall and then continued through it. The nanomachines were unable to identify the material due to a large amount of electrical interference emanating from it.

"This has to be the array or access to it anyway." I put my hand to the metal, but immediately snapped it back when it was shocked by the surrounding energy field.

"Think we can blow it?" Arc inquired.

"Doubt it. We won't be getting through this way, but we should be under part of the building where we stand. It's not exactly the heart of it, but we'll be inside. Alright, brothers, you're up." I looked over to Vern and Riley, who gave me a nod each before Riley let his booming voice echo through the tunnels.

"Demo team to the First, the rest move up now!" He called out, and the loyal raiders began echoing the order back to the others. It wasn't long before they began scrambling up and out of their various access points, spreading onto the city streets above.

Ten Sons approached the three of us that were left, one carrying a bag of what I assumed were explosives. They were a mixed bunch of somewhat gender fluidity. They each carried on their persons trophies of their exploits.

481

Rank insignia from unknown surface forces, claws from mutated horrors, battle scars surrounded by tattoos to make them more prominent, and the brightly colored red, mixed with sullen black that seemed to be traditional Sons colors. One approached, their hair a bright red, long, set straight down one side and shaven on the other.

"We are honored to go into battle with the First."

"Glad to hear it, now blow the ceiling." They looked to each other with sadistic grins and began pulling explosive packs from their bag. Whatever it was, included some sort of tough adhesive as they were able to easily stick the blocks to the ceilings. They placed electrodes, all apparently set to the same detonator. Once they were all set up, we moved as far back as we could, turning a couple of corners to shield ourselves from the concussive force. We also waited for the rest of the Sons to clear out, the sounds of battle above already apparent.

The same member of the Sons approached me and handed me the detonator, which I wasted no time in smashing its button. The walls shook, the blast and debris announcing our arrival. The ground quaked, and dutifully, the ceiling collapsed, exposing the interior of the CORPS Administration Building to our tender, loving ministrations.

"Move in!" I cried out, and we all ran for the debris. Unfortunately, the explosion did its job too well. Arc, Reya, and I were forced to begin clearing the way. It wasn't difficult to expose the hole in a matter of seconds, and we were up and into the building.

The hole we made had broken into some sort of common area. It ended with two hallways on either side, likely leading to various conference rooms or public meeting spaces. The off-white walls were adorned with

482

paintings and effigies on display, likely of prominent CORPS members new and old. There was a beautiful red runner moving in both directions. A sizable chunk had been blasted apart by our glorious entrance.

My CIHUD immediately picked up on the Elites standing at the far end of the room we had entered, four of them, waiting for their chance to pick off whoever dared pop out. They never stood a chance. My friends and I marched out of the hole and accurately fired enough rounds to near-simultaneously neutralize the enemies. Our ten allies piled out of the hole and skillfully took up defensive positions at either end of the hallway. We began to walk by several paintings before Arc and I had to step back, double taking at one of them.

The art depicted a man with a jarhead style crewcut, his lab coat seeming more like a uniform and actually sported some medals. It was the name that caught our eye. "Dr. Emmanuel Rellen: Social Engineer." Arc and I looked to one another in bewilderment.

"Drah Rellen." We spoke in stereo.

"What?" Reya asked, stepping behind and between us. As soon as the question came out, the lights dimmed, and an alarm began to sound all around us.

"Lockdown Procedures Initiated. All non-essential personnel report to your designated shelters. This is not a drill." The voice came from all around and honestly came much later than I had expected. It stood to reason that they weren't expecting to have to defend the hall we were in, and thus it afforded us the few seconds we got.

"C'mon, we have to find the Control Room." Reya waved us along, and I looked a little confused.

"We have to find Ronyn, that's our priority," I spoke matter of fact like.

"Then he'll be there, it's gotta be the most well-defended room in the building." I was about to ask how she knew all of that, but she preemptively answered. "They used to give tours."

We didn't have much time to discuss anything else further as two of our new friends dropped suddenly. From the hall came two XRC soldiers dressed for world war. Arc, Reya, and I moved for cover, getting ready for the fight of our lives when suddenly, an extraordinary thing occurred. From their corners, four of the Sons moved from their cover. Unfortunately, two more were immediately cut down, but not before all of them managed to fire off the weapons they carried. They looked like some sort of ancient blunderbuss sporting a large drum attached to it for the ammunition. What came out of the weapon was astonishing. At first, I assumed that the EM fields the XRC soldiers wore would easily deflect scatter-shot rounds. Instead, the room was filled with a barrage of pellets wide enough that neither of the soldiers were able to escape their wrath. Most of the projectiles were made out of non-magnetic metals.

As soon as we realized they had been hit, we opened fire on the wounded and disoriented soldiers, finishing them off quickly. One of our remaining friends tossed me their strange-looking weapon.

"We learn from our battles." They gave a toothy grin and we all marched out of the hallway. From our CIHUDs we could already see that dozens of bogies were closing in on our position. We decided not to stay in more than one place for too long.

Eventually, the hall spilled out into a massive foyer, with an ornate set of stairs going up to a second floor. There were massive, marble pillars that looked more like decorations than actual supports. The center was a circular desk with now vacant chairs in front of computer terminals. This was likely where the public came in to greet their taskmasters.

The seats of the desks may have been empty, but the lobby itself was not. Standing by the entrance doors that were now sealed by a bulkhead, were several Elite guards, and we could already sense others coming from the floor above. The stairs led to walkways and more doors, which soon opened, revealing yet more enemies.

I was the first to enter, followed by Arc, and a couple of the Sons that were left. My reflexes had not dulled from my last encounter, and I acted swiftly, dropping my new yet awkward weapon. My hand reached down to swipe a spike grenade from the belt of the Son next to me, tossing it towards the group in front of the main doors. As the grenade soared through the air, I dove behind a pillar holding up the second-floor walkway. In the blink of an eye, I shot the explosive when it was right in front of the enemies guarding the front entrance, sending shrapnel all around and through them.

There was very little time to celebrate. The floor in the center of the room sporting the CORPS's sword and shield symbol spun for a moment before rising up, revealing a twin-gunned turret. It turned menacingly towards the door we had entered. From behind me, Arc and Reya both pointed their sidearms towards the turret as it made an ominous roaring sound, preparing to fire off its payload. My friends weren't aiming for some weakness, instead sending their bullets sailing into each barrel of the turret. When it tried to fire, the impact of the shots caused a jam in the barrel, creating a series of backfires within the dread-machine. It sputtered and smoked, and was quickly rendered useless.

The CORPS was having none of our little party, and quickly, reinforcements were on us. By now, the remaining six Sons had piled into the room and took up defensive positions around the center desk. From the top floor, several Elites jumped down, attempting to overwhelm us. They were cut down as soon as they landed, but more began piling in from the doors above. I ran for the fallen soldiers in front of the door, rolling and grabbing one of their rifles. I began to fire at enemies as quickly as they appeared.

Elites were called such because of their combat prowess and tactics. When another couple of soldiers jumped from the railings above, one dropped a flash grenade down with them. They seemed wholly unaffected as the blinding light, and deafening bang rang out. It didn't hinder cyborgs either, but two more of our Sons troopers were felled in the confusion.

Reya quickly dropped the Elites that hit the ground, and then Arc swept a group up top with one of the fallen Son's rifles. I slowly advanced towards the desk, firing fast and deadly bursts as I moved, cutting down the remaining fighters above us.

Everything seemed to quiet down until the main doors at the head of the stairs above opened. From it, two men with basic crew cuts and the seemingly signature clothing of XRC units walked through. Between them was an unwelcome sight. She sported the same sort of crazy energy weapon she carried back in Libsal, only this time, it was smaller and didn't contain a cumbersome pack. We held our fire, waiting for the right moment to strike. She watched us, and the two beside her slid down the railings of the stairs. As they landed, they trained their sidearms on us, slowly advancing.

"Wait." I held my hand up, signaling the Sons to be patient, knowing full well their special weapons were useless in an open room. We needed to wait for an opening.

"Where's Dr. Lyrul?" I was taken aback by the question our old nemesis had asked, unsure why she didn't just get on with it.

"She's dead." My voice was cold and somewhat heartless. She seemed struck by the answer, contemplating her next move.

What happened next, I could have never predicted. The weapon that our foe from Libsal brought made its usual whine, powering up. My CIHUD gave no immediate warnings when she cleaning fired twice, hitting the two unsuspecting allies she had walked in with. They both suddenly sported two holes that ran clean through their centers and dropped to the floor. Somehow, she had managed to fool their defenses long enough to get the shots in.

Casually, as if nothing happened, the woman began walking down the stairs towards us. No other enemies seemed to be entering the lobby as she advanced with an odd sort of grace. When she got to the last step, she made eye contact with me.

"So, we're even then." At first, I was confused until my mind went to Mick, and then it connected to Alonna. I rested the rifle on my shoulder and boldly I walked towards her.

"I guess you could say that."

"Are you here to kill Ronyn?" Her voice was grave.

"When we're done with him. This is his last day on this world." My voice reflected her confidence.

"Good." She began to walk around the desk as if we weren't standing there while contemplating the easiest way to end her life. She made no comment for a moment, positioning herself in front of the barricaded entrance. The weapon powered up again, and she directed the invisible stream of energy towards the blocked entrance, essentially cutting a massive opening in the metal bulkhead. With a loud groan and creak, the metal she cut out dropped to the ground. It wasn't long before Sons from the outside began piling in. Gracefully, our unusual ally walked out of the building, taking a moment to set her bulky weapon down while placing her free hand onto her stomach.

"What the fuck just happened?" Arc asked, looking to me, and I could only give a shrug as my answer.

"It won't be long before they scramble more soldiers our way. We need to find that Control Room." I spoke and walked over to the weapon that our frienemy had left behind. If it cut through that door, it would likely get through others.

I took a moment to take a peek outside as more Sons troops began to pile in. The streets were a mess, but not in the way I had initially expected. There were scores of bodies littering the ground, a larger than expected number of which were CORPS Elites and security officers. Many Sons laid dead on the ground, and it looked as if we had lost nearly half of our number already. The battle in the streets had been devastating in a short amount of time. What truly struck me, though, were the civilian corpses. There were dozens of them, all with some sort of small-arm or makeshift weapon nearby. The game suddenly had three players.

"John!" Riley called out as he and his brother scrambled to get inside. Vehicles were approaching from all sides, and it seemed whatever dent we had made in the forces within the building, mattered little in comparison to what was on their way. "You guys managed to get through the bulkheads!"

"Not us, but no time. Get everyone inside, we can secure the building better from within."

"That's a lot of people, man," Vern interjected. "Your Divisives decided they wanted a piece of the action. We'd probably be dead if it wasn't for them."

"Dude, I don't give a fuck if twinkle-toed elves wants in on the action, if they're on our side, get them inside." With a nod, the brothers turned and began ushering in as many as they could while remaining in cover. I could already hear the return fire from the outside and realized whoever came in during those next few seconds were all we had left. Considering it nearly filled the vast lobby to capacity, I was more than happy with it. We had dozens of regular people, including men, women, and teenagers who had apparently been preparing for such an event. It suddenly became clear to me how a man like Mikey could have black market business in a place like Dome City.

With expert grace, the Sons managed to barricade the hole in the front bulkhead. While it wouldn't last long, the CORPS would be dealing with one hell of a bottleneck. All available hands began clearing the floor we were on. It seemed like if there were any more soldiers left inside, they were taking up defensive positions.

"Alright, you two, you think you can man the fort down here?" Vern and Riley gave me their warm as ever smiles.

"Got get 'em John-boy." Vern nodded.

"Put an end to this shit, huh?" Riley gave a smirk. I patted them both on the shoulder and turned to address the rest of our ragtag team.

"Keep this floor secure. We're heading for the Control Room." While I had been talking, I noticed Reya was at one of the less mangled civilian information kiosks. I meandered over, handing the large energy rifle to a Sons trooper. "Weird what ends up becoming a security risk, huh?"

"Something like that. C'mon boys, we're going up." Reya grabbed her equipment and crooked her finger at Arc, who dutifully met up with us. Quickly, the four remaining Sons troopers we had brought in with us gathered, and we welcomed the company. Together we began to march up the stairs.

The CORPS Administration Building was a relatively straight-forward sort of place. Offices made up a large portion of the interior, many of which had been locked down like dozens of little panic rooms. Likely, our sudden entrance meant a lot of civilians got stuck in their offices and cubicle hubs. The place also included conference halls, presentation rooms, and all manner of bureaucratic niceties.

We thought we would have a hard time finding what insanely defended room was the Control Room, but the level of security we encountered was a dead give-away. We turned down a very meticulously detailed and open room. The ceilings were tall, the room lined with two rows of what appeared to be marble columns. The floor had a beautiful dark sheen to it, accenting the dark blue hues of the rest of the chamber. At one end was another massive metallic security bulkhead. It looked as robust as the one on the first floor and just as well protected.

When we approached, ten Elites came rushing out from the cover of the pillars and artistic displays. Their weapons fire filled the chamber and forced us to seek cover in the adjacent hallways. It wasn't just the Elites, but turrets had emerged from the floor and ceiling, four in total.

"EMPs?" Arc asked from the hall across from mine. We were both against the wall adjacent to what had to be the entrance to the Control Room.

490

I gave him a nod, and we each grabbed the lone EMP grenade from our belts. We each pulled the safeties and bounced them into the entrance hall. The EMPs went off, sending sparks flying from the electronics in all directions and sending the turrets off-line.

With the turrets out of the way, Arc and I reloaded our sidearms and began blind firing into the entrance room. We only needed to stick the barrels out slightly, and using our CIHUDs, were able to easily cut down the Elites that weren't in cover. As soon as the rest were behind the pillars, Arc and I stepped out from hiding, Reya and the others followed suit, introducing a barrage of weapons fire. The mutant soldiers didn't stand a chance.

When I moved into the entrance hall, I was immediately tackled up against a wall by a youngish looking male XRC soldier. They had been hiding just around the corner and somehow had managed to elude our sensors, likely due to the EMP grenades we had used earlier. The force of being slammed into the wall knocked the wind out of me, and I felt my back crack in decidedly unhealthy ways.

My attacker's victory was short-lived. Reya immediately grabbed onto their shoulders before their fist could deliver a deathblow. She yanked him off of me, and then hooked his leg with her foot tripping him in two quick motions. Arc, without hesitation, aimed his weapon and domed the enemy before they could react.

The smoke settled, and the room quieted down again. We found ourselves once more surrounded by our fallen foes and wreckage. We were on a roll. I held my hand out expectantly, and soon one of the Sons sauntered over with the energy weapon I had given them. I pulled the gun close and aimed at the metallic bulkhead, firing a steady stream of invisible energy. A convenient read-out on the weapon indicated it was already low on power, so I kept the entry small.

When the laser had nearly finished making a man-sized cutout, weapons fire from the other side interrupted the fun. The cut metal chunk flew off, and bullets came screaming through it. I dropped the weapon and dove to the side, getting clipped in my shoulder, causing me to spin before slamming to the ground. I quickly scrambled for cover.

"Same fucking shoulder! Every time!" I grimaced in pain and frustration. The gunfire from the Control Room stopped, and we were suddenly in a stalemate.

"Arc, you got that shield belt still?" In the heat of the moment, Arc looked confused, but gave a grunt and a nod. "Give it to me."

"What?"

"Just do it!" I noticed he was wearing it, though he hadn't activated it yet. He unhooked the belt and tossed it over, which actually caused a torrent of gunfire to stream from the hole. I took the belt and strapped it to my body, now wearing both shield generators. I looked to the Sons who were taking cover by my side. "Give me two of those grenades." They obliged without question, and I moved as close to the entry hole as I could.

"John, what the fuck are you doing?" I heard the question, but ignored it, hitting the button on one of the shield belts. My CIHUD went a little crazy as a hazy outline enveloped my body, causing my hair to stand on end. I took a deep breath and stormed forward into the Control Room.

Several scientists were cowering in the corner, one banging on a wicked-looking security door with a betrayed look in their eyes. There was no sign of Ronyn, but plenty of his work. Four XRC soldiers were taking aim with powerful rifles as well as a dozen Elite security troopers. The world seemingly fell silent and somewhat still as I pushed through. Bullets that weren't crushed by the energy field ricocheted harmlessly away, but the shield was already nearly depleted barely half a second later.

The room was littered with long rows of desks and terminals; massive holo-screens lined both sides of the wall showing various security footage and data readouts. Everything in the room was bathed in a soft, blue light. I chose to dive behind one of the terminals, hurling one of the two grenades into the trajectory of an oncoming shooter. The shield failed without much fanfare, and I hit the second shield belt button as soon as it did.

The grenade went off, the concussive force causing all of the enemies to dive away to various safe spots. As soon as they did, I tossed the other grenade into the air and towards the back. I ducked my head between my knees and curled up to protect myself. The final explosion sounded off like a crescendo, a sort of final note to the roughest battle I had ever fought. My ears were ringing and would take a few minutes to recover. Dust trickled down from every direction, but there were no other movements.

I didn't hear any yelling or screaming, instead seeing Arc, Reya, and finally, the Sons streaming in from the hole we had made. I pulled myself up from my position and hoisted myself on top of the terminal I was hiding behind. I could see the destruction and couldn't detect anyone alive enough to pose a threat. Any that remained were quickly cut down by my posse as they rushed in. I felt hands on my shoulder turn me around, and it was Reya, yelling at me. The ringing in my ears was slowly fading.

"- you okay?" I gave her a nod and shook my head to get ahold of myself. Regaining my composure, I gently pushed passed Reya and walked to the Sons that had been carrying the energy weapon, taking it from him. I walked over to the security door and placed my hand on it, closing my eyes to concentrate on my sense of touch.

"There's someone in there." Arc and Reya took positions behind me, and I used what was left of the weapon's power, carving open the panic room door like a holiday bird. With the hinges and sides of the door cut open, Reya and Arc moved over and carefully pried it away. The room was essentially a walk-in closet made of apocalypse preventing metal. There was a terminal attached to the wall and what looked to be compartments for food and water. What interested me was Ronyn, cowering in the corner. Seeing me, he stood, attempting to seem dignified.

"Your revenge will accomplish nothing, and I will not assist you." No words came from my mouth. I advanced forward, grabbing Ronyn by the throat and dragged him out of the room. Whatever defense screen he had been using before was likely unable to detect my nanomachines and thus never went off. I found a terminal that hadn't been completely wrecked by the explosion. Releasing his throat, I bodily tossed him at it. He sputtered and coughed, about to say something else, but was stopped when I grabbed his hand. I pried it open and forced him to take the data-stick I had been carrying, breaking a couple of fingers along the way. He screamed out in pain, but I had no care for that in the world.

"You are still the brash fool. This system will not work for you." I ignored him, taking his wrist in one hand, and keeping Ronyn's fingers on the data-stick with the other, I forced him to insert it into the terminal. I let him go, causing him to crumple to the ground, cradling his mangled hand. He looked up to me pitifully. "If you think I will help you do anything with this

494

system, then you truly are delusional."

"Biometric data accepted." Alonna's voice suddenly chimed over the comm system within the Control Room. The CORPS weren't into voice commands and talkative computers; this was a statement. "New super user recognized. Welcome, John." At no point in my life had Alonna's voice actually been so soothing. The confused look on Ronyn's face when her voice came on the comm was the most priceless gift I had ever been given.

"So, is this where you have your fun, proving the animal that you are?" Ronyn virtually spat at my feet, the fear evident in his eyes.

"No." I simply gave Ronyn one solid hook to the chin, putting as much power into it as I could. His body spun, sailing a few meters before slamming brutally onto the ground. The force was more than enough to snap his neck and mangle his face nearly beyond recognition. "You'll go out the way all my friends did. Quickly, needlessly, and violently."

"John, you'd better hope she didn't need him still breathing," Arc spoke uncharacteristically nervous. I shrugged it off and used my good arm to operate the touch panel of the terminal. I reached into my pocket and pulled out my data-cable, hooking myself into the system.

Alonna's hacking wizardry had worked wonders, I had total access. Her software had somehow used Ronyn's biometric access codes to designate a new head of the computer household. I wasn't hacking into their security, security was letting me right on through.

The system was oppressively large, controlling many aspects of the city itself right from the Control Room. I decided to just go for sweeping changes. The terminal I was equipped with had a camera, so I made use of it and went right for the city-wide PSA system. While I did the computer work, Arc and

Part Three: Home Again

Reya barricaded off the exit of the Control Room. Soon, on every monitor, even the security feeds of the room we were in, my handsome mug appeared.

"People of the Habitat. I speak to you now as a friend and former resident. Some of you may even know me from when I lived in the Undercities. I know life has been crazy the last couple of months, but it's about to get stranger. I'm not here to provide comfort. Five years ago, I left the Undercities to find the surface, and I did. I tell you now that the CORPS has lied to you. I've come from the surface, and the rumors that are likely spreading of the strange people running around main street are true. We've brought the outside world with us." I took a deep breath and just kept on talking. I had rehearsed what I would say so many times, and yet my mind was throwing it all away for something different.

"Right now, the CORPS are using you to endlessly fight a war that did not end two-hundred years ago. People still live and die to protect their homes, and you have been unwittingly used to deprive them of their lives and liberty. We've come to liberate you, to give you the destiny that's been deprived of us all. To let you see the sky. I have, and it's beautiful, its air breathable, and everyone under it deserving of life. The CORPS would deprive you of all of these things. They murdered our families when they allowed the mutaphorms to attack our people, they used their bodies to create the Elites that haunt your streets. You break your backs laboring to make it all possible. No more." I set the recording to loop everything I had said. I grabbed my PCD and uploaded some of the images of the outside world I had taken, allowing them to loop with the video.

"Hey kids, I'm gonna need your help if we're gonna survive this," I stated. We still had the issue of the multitude of soldiers at the front doors,

496

waiting to come in and end our little insurrection. Reya and Arc moved towards terminals of their own and jacked themselves into the system with me. I used my access to let them into the system

Together we began to work fast. The first thing we did was shut down the communication network. Instead of trying to find the CORPS communication signals, we blocked everything that wasn't on a very specific frequency and code. We sent that information to the TLF as quickly as we created it, crippling the CORPS's ability to fight them in one fell swoop. We had only been hooked into the system for a few minutes.

From there, we shut out the military section of the Habitat, no longer allowing them to send in reinforcements to the city, trapping them to eventually contend with the forces on the outside of the Dome. Every piece of security attached to the city's mainframe came under our control and was used against their makers. Their own drones were released from the military sections and used to clean out enemy forces within the streets, attacking them with surgical precision.

Whatever Alonna's application had pulled had the side-effect of neutralizing every administrator the system had. Only I and those I deemed worthy had access to literally the city itself. The mission was successful. Ronyn laid dead at my feet, the CORPS communication network was knocked out, and their security systems were fighting against them. The city would actually become ours.

After we had secured our position, Reya, Arc, and I took a moment to rest. Arc approached me first, giving me a hearty pat on the back before spitting on the body of Ronyn.

"Took ya long enough."

"Yeah, I guess it did." I was staring down at Ronyn. I knew his death wouldn't make me feel any better, and maybe that was necessary. It wasn't about payback; it was about protecting his future victims.

"Are you going to be okay, John?" Reya asked, gently prodding the gunshot wound I was still sporting. Slowly I looked away from Ronyn's corpse and gave her my winning smile.

"Me? I'm livin' the dream over here. I'll be just fine."

An entire day passed before we were safely able to leave the building. Surprisingly, our exit was met with fanfare. The surviving Sons cheered in reverence, referring to us as *The Five* and the Divisives that had joined our cause were eager to show their gratitude. Not everyone, however, was entirely thrilled with their sudden freedom. Our message had reached every man, woman, and child within the city, and the reaction was not completely positive. Riots would begin breaking out during the next couple of days, further splitting the remaining loyal forces. It would be weeks before order was restored, and the CORPS properly beaten back. We took stock in our victory and knew that the troubles of the people of Dome City had only just begun.

Epilogue

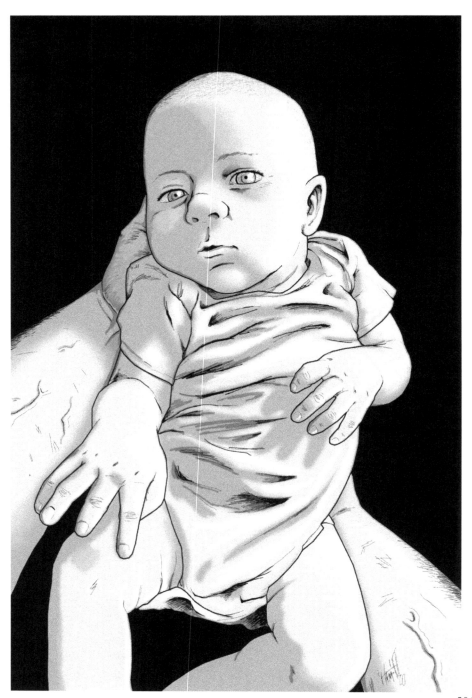

Responsibilities

Everything in my life had led up to that one monumental moment. My family's death, Lys being ripped away, the augmentations, and Alonna's defection. I was victorious, but in the end, I had lost so much that I wasn't quite sure what I had won. I spent the first few nights awake, thinking about such things. It would be days before I watched any more of Alonna's videos, letting everything sink in. Eventually, I decided it was time to settle down, and I began to read the gifts she left behind, starting with *Our Daughter*.

Days turned into weeks, and still, no reckoning came. During the first six months since storming the Administration Building, nearly twelve-thousand people in all had died in the struggle, and that was just inside the city. The battle had raged outside the dome for some time, but the CORPS being unable to communicate in even the most basic fashion had been rendered impotent. Most of the CORPS loyalists eventually surrendered to the combined forces of the TLF, Sons of Rellen, and their Divisive neighbors.

The TLF had managed to breach the outer entrance of the Habitat after days of fighting, but instead of finding a monumental army waiting for them, what they found were empty barracks. The running theory was that the majority of the remaining CORPS forces decided to abandon the city and leave through the tram system. There were other tunnels, but where they ended up, no one could really say. The computer databanks had no answers, and whatever escape route they used was separate from everything else. With time and effort, the CORPS might have been able to retake the city, so it was a mystery as to why they would leave it behind. None had seen them come out of the old Undercity entrance either. They had simply vanished, retreating into obscurity.

I looked outside at the city below, relaxing in a lovely top floor apartment, usually reserved for city officials. I was among the closest they had to that sort of thing after the turnover. A lot of their most sensitive information had either been wiped previously or immediately due to some last-minute fail-safes, and the CORPS's disappearance would likely remain a mystery. It didn't matter to me anymore; whatever struggles society had in store were no longer my concern. My concern cooed softly in my arms, wrapped in a bundle of brightly colored blankets, sporting a small tuft of dark hair.

Never in my life had I imagined myself as a father. Lys would have laughed at the very notion and then probably reminded me why I would've made a good one. I had also never been so smitten by something so tiny. Even the machines inside my mind couldn't counteract the feelings I had, and somehow, I imagined they weren't meant to. Fatherhood, in more ways than one, had been my ultimate purpose.

The door to my flat slid open and in walked Arc, fresh from some expedition to look for CORPS remnants in the city. Some were still loyal, and it seemed the war was far from over.

"Ah, there ya are, being all cute and shit." He had a duffel bag with him that I figured contained his clothes and other essential items. He plopped them down on a gray sofa in my living area before sitting down to get comfortable.

"Planning on staying for a bit, are we?"

"You know me too well. I figured we can bunk for a few weeks before I head off on some adventure." I took a seat in a chair that sat in front of the sofa. It was a nice little meeting spot for friends.

"Going anywhere fun?" I gently bounced the baby in my arms.

"Probably not. We're trying to figure out where the CORPS ran to, and we've also been tryin' to integrate the Sons with society here."

"How's that working out?"

"It's not, so they're leaving. Peacefully. The city life isn't their cup of tea." Arc put his feet up.

"Probably for the best." There was a quick knock on my door before it slid open again, revealing Reya, Vern, and Riley. I stood to greet them, walking over and carefully giving each a hug.

"Oh, my goodness, she's so cute." Reya barely spaced out her words as she reached over and all but snatched my child out of my arms. "Have you thought of a name yet?"

"Yeah, actually, I did. Her name is Lyssa." Reya smiled warmly at me, seeming to understand the importance. "So, what are you chuckle heads up to?" I got some hearty laughs.

"Well." Riley started. "We're going to be heading up the new security forces here in the city. There are actually a few other cyborgs that joined our cause, which probably isn't entirely surprising. We're gonna be working on the transition, getting everyone to work together."

"We'll also be transitioning people into and out of the city. Not that it's a big shocker, but a lot of people want to see the outside world." Vern finished.

"Well, aren't we just a bunch of busy beavers." I took my kid back from Reya and made my way over to my chair in the living area. Of course, my doorbell chimed right as I got comfortable. Riley was on it however and opened the door revealing General Delantil and what was likely a couple of

504

bodyguards behind him, though only he walked through the door.

"Well, it looks like you've settled in nicely."

"What do I owe the pleasure?" The General gave a warm smile and pointed at the bundle in my arms.

"Interested in probably the most fascinating child to ever grace our hospitals. There's a lot of people back home eager to hear about her progress."

"Well, she's doing great, growing very fast like your doctors said she would. She doesn't eat a whole lot. Pediatricians just said to feed her when she's hungry."

"How often is that?" Arc asked curiously.

"Once every other day so far. I mean, she's only been with me for a couple of weeks."

"Remarkable. When we learned she was ready for full-term delivery after only six months of gestation, it caused a big stir among the medical staff. Well, I wanted to extend an offer to you and your new family here to dinner. A little bit of hobnobbing with the new politicians."

"Sounds horrible, we'll come and keep you company," I gave Delantil a smirk, getting a laugh out of him. "Is R'yalax gonna be there?"

"I tend not to leave home without her if I can help it. She's indispensably useful as always."

"Well, I'll see you there then." He gave a polite bow to everyone in the room before making his way out.

There we sat, newly found friends, brothers and sister at arms. I had lost many loved ones on my journey but made others. It felt a little sad knowing they would all be off on their separate journeys, making a difference in the world while I sat behind, being a dad. In my mind, I could hear Lys giggling

Epilogue

behind me, smell Ray cooking up something in the kitchen, and even witness Alonna watching over her little girl. It was an almost spiritual sensation and it was all I had left. My past was somehow at peace, and sleeping in my arms, my future awaited me.

On The Author, By The Author

I started writing very early in life, weaving short stories, and creating a virtual army of signature characters. If there was one particular activity that contributed the most to my writing and desire to become a weaver of tales, it would have to be good old-fashioned Dungeons and Dragons. I spent a large portion of my adolescence crafting collaborative stories with my friends and family, often finding myself in the Game Master's chair. It cannot be overstated how essential the skills I learned while Role-Playing are to my author's journey.

The first ideas for A World Gone Wrong surfaced over twenty years ago when I was starting High School. For years I developed the story in my spare time, creating a world, its villain, and its various heroes. At first, it was a fantasy but slowly meandered its way into the Sci-Fi Epic that it is today. Despite the changes, there was always a protagonist named John, an antagonist called Xavier Ronyn, and an Illuminati style organization known as the CORPS. Eventually, the story found some coherency, and I began to build a world. The World Gone Wrong itself is truly massive, with a large amount of fleshed out details that will produce stories for years to come.

Unfortunately for all of us, life can make achieving our dreams difficult. I became a father of a beautiful girl and a handsome boy. Like most blue-collar Americans, much of my time was spent working, being a dad, and generally not writing. Unfortunately, in March 2017, my ability to work would come screeching to a halt when a construction-site accident left me physically mangled; nine months later, I would lose my lower-right leg. Suddenly faced with a large amount of free time spent relegated to a bed or chair, I began to write again. Within a year, the first draft of A World Gone Wrong was nearly complete, and I was suddenly faced with the realization of a dream: to become a published author.

Now I study computer science and continue to work on the series. There are plans for novels, novellas, collections of short stories, and even my very own Pen and Paper RPG. The future is bright, and I hope to have you, dear reader, along for the journey.

Lightning Source UK Ltd.
Milton Keynes UK
UKHW021112170520
363416UK00011B/333/J